DUNCAN

DENNIS MCCORT

gatekeeper press

Columbus, Ohio

Duncan

Published by Gatekeeper Press
2167 Stringtown Rd, Suite 109
Columbus, OH 43123-2989
www.GatekeeperPress.com

ISBN (paperback): 9781642373714
eISBN: 9781642373592

Printed in the United States of America

To my wonderful wife Dorothy, who is truly a co-creator of this book.

It was the best cut at the ball little Joey Simmons had ever taken, but he fouled it back over the chain-link fence. As catcher, Zach Moss had the job of retrieving it. He slipped down through the hollowed-out area under the fence, looked both ways before crossing the empty street lined with warehouses and loading docks, and darted across to where the ball lay nestled against the curb—just a few feet in front of the charcoal van. It was Sunday afternoon and the area was deserted. As Zach reached down, out of the corner of his eye he spotted the tall man in the black polo shirt leaning casually against the van's open sliding door, kicking a crushed paper cup to the curb.

"Whatcha got there, pal?"

"A baseball," Zach answered shyly, noticing the van was empty.

"Wow, that looks like a Phillies ball. I'll bet you caught it off the bat of Ryan Howard or some big slugger like that, huh? Could I have a look?"

Zach hesitated, torn between advancing and retreating, politeness and caution. That hesitation sealed the boy's doom. The man made as if to reach for the ball, but grabbed the little wrist holding it instead. It was a deft move, a practiced move, and lightning fast, carried out with the larcenous dexterity of a seasoned pickpocket. The boy was so stunned that he forgot to scream.

The sliding door slammed shut and the man was behind the wheel pressing the accelerator before the boys on the ball field knew what was happening. He had kept himself on the sidewalk side of the van during the entire abduction, carefully hidden from their view. Zach knew he'd done something very wrong, even though he hadn't meant to. All those endlessly repeated parental warnings raced across his mind, all the "Don't ever listen's" and "Always avoid's" and "Run screaming from's." Could he have another chance? Please! He'd do it right this time. He splayed his fingers against the window, crying out— too late—to his friends as the van pulled away. He hadn't noticed that its windows were dark-tinted, transparent only from the inside.

Passing through the industrial outskirts of the city, the van headed up Old York Road into the northern suburbs. It neither sped nor lagged and it obeyed all traffic laws. The man at the wheel enjoyed a supreme confidence in his trapping skills. It was a craft, an art even, and he had mastered it. Soon there was more wilderness than houses, until at some point the van turned left off the main road onto a poorly marked crossroad that, in short order, forked at a dirt road. The van took the dirt road across a tiny rustic bridge spanning a creek, continuing then across a cleared, open field on the right, at the end of which stood a modest white colonial house atop a gently sloping lawn. Potted plants overhung the small porch with its two rockers diagonally facing each other on either side of the front door. The place stood in the open, yet was well hidden by hilly wilderness beyond property boundaries. The dirt road saw little traffic.

The van pulled off the road and circled around to the rear of the house, stopping next to the angled steel cellar doors. The man got out, looked around and inhaled deeply, basking in the mellow sunlight of late afternoon. He was alone, the only sound that of the gently rustling trees. He slid open the van's side door and leaned in, hands braced against the roof, ogling his prey with satisfaction. And lust.

Terror widened the boy's eyes, making them—and him—all the more alluring to his captor. He cowered, pressed against the corner of his seat, his body balled up in futile self-protection.

"What do you want, mister? Why am I here?" he asked tentatively, knowing full well the man knew he knew why he was there.

"All in good time, Zach, all in good time," the man chuckled. He'd heard the other kids call the boy by name weeks ago when he first began scouting him. He always made sure, if at all possible, to get a kid's name before taking him. The process went much smoother that way. Strategic use of a boy's name soothed the boy with the delusion that, despite appearances, his captor was well disposed towards him. A tactic that would make an adult instantly wary tended to pacify an eight-year-old. He'd learned that the hard way many years ago from the debacle in Austin when the words, "Whaddaya say, kid, let's hang out," triggered a shrieking that forced him to start, rather than end, the process with lethal violence. After that, from Atlanta through Nashville and Blacksburg and on up the east coast—it was his first "tour"—he made sure to get the name up front and learned to soften his diction. It was part of his evolution from a seat-of-the-pants amateur predator to a serial pedophile of deadly proficiency.

"Why don't you climb out of there and come in for a cold drink, Zach? You must be thirsty. Catchers eat a lot of dust. They need to rehydrate all the time."

"No! I don't want to! I wanna go home!"

"I'd like you to think you *are* home—for now."

"No, I'm *not!*" the boy cried with mounting panic. He began to whimper.

"Come on now," the man said, mildly irritated. He extended his powerful right arm inside, like reaching for a prize in a grab bag, and gently but firmly pulled Zach out of the van. Then, bending over slightly while holding onto the boy, he pulled open the already unlocked cellar doors with his free arm.

Instinctively, Zach began to buck. He tried to pull away and squirmed furiously—to no avail. He had never felt such physical strength before. It was like trying to jerk a piece of wood loose from the vice in his father's basement tool shop. Even when, not so long ago, his father would playfully toss him up in the air and catch him coming down like a medicine ball, it was nothing like the sheer physical resistance, the total control by another, he was feeling now.

The man carried the boy down the steps, bracing him on his hip like a surfboard. They entered a finished basement, though one that had the same dank, musty air all basements have, with or without dehumidifiers. The smell of the air caused a new spike in the boy's panic, suggesting as it did the mold of the grave. Even at eight Zach was aware of the connotations of mold. The man cuffed him, as if scolding a pet, and got off on it. It was all part of the one-way foreplay.

The man carried him to the far end of the dark basement, which was largely uncluttered by the usual piles of stored junk, as if the house hadn't been occupied long enough to accumulate much to store. There, well behind the furnace and hot-water heater, was a small, inconspicuous room, walled off from the rest, no doubt originally intended as a study or office. But the man had converted it to a kind of private pleasure cave. Richly paneled and lushly carpeted, hung with lurid pornographic images, both paintings and photographs, of naked children, many interacting with "erect" naked men, the windowless room was the sick expression of what had become the man's sole reason for being. He had left the door unlocked and ajar for quick and easy sequestering of his latest prey. Lowering the boy onto the quilt-covered king-size bed that occupied more than half the room's space, he raised an index finger to his smiling lips to shush the signs of panic contorting the boy's face and body language. Then he leaned forward and switched on the portable CD-player on the night-stand. The soft strains of "So What" filled the room, the opening track of Miles Davis's cool-jazz masterpiece, *Kind of Blue*, with the insouciant opening base sequence introducing Davis's smokey trumpet. It was always the same music, always "So What," setting the same naughty jazzy mood— anything else would have been unthinkable to him.

As the man pulled his shirt over his head and began unbuckling his jeans, the boy's whimpering swelled into alternating sobs and shrieks. He had no idea he was playing right into his predator's game plan, for the man's lust was spiked above all else by another creature's helplessness. He wanted the boy to beg for his innocence, his bodily integrity—his life. He craved the dark bliss of godlike power over the destiny of another, especially when that other was fully aware of his own utter dependency. This was his drug, his elixir, immeasurably more potent than the heroin he had tried so many times, which, while bestowing bliss, had also dulled his senses, and he lived for the sharpening of his senses. This got him out of bed in the morning.

"Zach, Zach. It's all right. We're just gonna cuddle for a while. Okay? Just lie together and hold each other and make each other feel good, you know?"

"I wanna go *home!*" the boy bawled in tearful protest, apparently shocked by the urgency of his own voice, for his sobbing escalated, opening up to a pathetic wail fueled by panic.

Its only effect was a quickening of the man's desire. Stimulus ... response. No one could hear them there, and it was all just becoming so delicious. As the man slipped out of his jeans, Zach's eyes were riveted on the bulge in the crotch of his briefs. At eight, he had just enough sexual awareness to know what that bulge meant. Still, it was his dim but nightmarish sense of what might come afterward that intensified the stabs of panic.

The man lay down on the bed and snuggled up to his prey, whose flinching reflex merely spiked his lust once again. The man was lost within the dark caverns of his desire, the boy trapped within those same caverns.

"This is so nice," the man breathed dreamily, reaching down deftly to their mutual nether regions while pressing the sobbing boy to him with unnatural strength ...

The sun was down and a purplish twilight graced the overgrown area behind the house as a dark figure strode purposefully from the cellar doors in the rear into a little copse of oak and cedar about a stone's throw away. He was carrying a base fiddle case. But his firm grip and taut right arm left no doubt that the case's contents were heavier than any fiddle.

After a while, the only sound to pierce the darkening stillness was the rhythmic thrusting of the spade into the soft earth. Far from being drained by the effort of the cleanup, the man felt juiced, energized, expansive, and, at the same time, utterly relaxed. He reveled in the digging, each thrust of the shovel a little aftershock of that explosion of pleasure for which he lived. Finally, dropping the shovel behind him, he sank to his knees, opened the case and stared for a while at the olive-hued double-strength trash bag that served as a shroud for the lifeless body. Gently lifting the body from the case, he lowered it into its shallow grave, again staring and carefully straightening out both the bag and the body it contained, though without attempting to pose the body in any way. No tableaus, no "necro-symbolism" to titillate the profilers. Just putting it where it belonged.

2

As it did every school morning at 104 Wildwood Drive in DeWitt, an upscale suburb of Syracuse, the yellow bus pulled up at 7:25 sharp, its brakes squealing. Nate Driscoll bolted from the breakfast table and ran into the family room where his young mother sat propped up in her custom-fitted, motorized wheelchair. Hattie, her black Haitian caretaker, was spoon-feeding her oatmeal.

Normally, Julie Driscoll would be in the kitchen eating with her son, but she'd caught another cold and didn't want to infect the boy. It had been just one cold after another since the accident. Nate hugged her anyway as she cautioned, "Careful, sweetie, I don't want to give you this bug." But the boy had already deposited "Duncan," his pet toy animal, on her lap and was halfway out the door. Hattie ran after him, calling out, "Hold on a minute, Nathaniel! Don't forget your lunch!"

"Here," she smiled, handing him his Spiderman lunchbox in the doorway and tousling his hair. "Gotta go," he said, then made a beeline down the driveway for the bus, leaping onto the high step and disappearing among a sea of little bobbing heads. Hattie watched as the bus pulled away, only to stop again four houses down the lane.

"That boy would forget his head if it wasn't screwed on," Hattie laughed as she resumed her feeding duty. She said it in her lilting, ever so slight French-Caribbean accent, as if she'd just made up the expression on the spot. Julie Driscoll laughed, more at the woman's presumption than the remark itself.

Over the long months of her slow and torturous convalescence, Julie had come to love this sassy, forty-ish immigrant from Port-au-Prince, more as an extension of her maternal self than as her caretaker. Hattie had been working for Home Helpers of Central New York in Syracuse when she met Julie and her husband Mark for an interview at St. Joseph's Hospital a few days before Julie's discharge. She had been in the States for less than a year, after emigrating in the wake of the Haitian earthquake of 2010, and had already been awarded her agency's highest rating. When Julie finally left St. Joe's on a dreary morning in June that saw a snowflake or two in the chill Syracuse air, Hattie was there to push her wheelchair. She accompanied her and Mark to the Driscoll home and never left.

Julie and Mark thanked heaven for such a gift of devoted care. By her job description, to be sure, Hattie was there to tend only to Julie, but she considered close attention to Nate's needs to be an essential part of that care. For her there could be no boundaries of any substance between mother and son. This refusal to restrict or categorize her caretaking duties was part of her strong familial temperament, but also a product of the Christian-Voodoo beliefs with which she had been raised in her homeland.

Still, Hattie was no hardliner. A literate woman who enjoyed reading, she carried her superstitions lightly, more amused by them than concerned with their truth-value. And she had no qualms about letting them slip over a bit into her caretaking practices if she thought it could be "therapeutic." So it was that she applauded Nate's decision to leave the aforementioned Duncan with his mother every morning as her "guardian" during his hours away at school. This guaranteed that Mom would not "leave him" while he was away; it also dove-tailed nicely with the old-world image of Duncan Hattie entertained as a sort of totemic animal protector of the family. Such animal spirits were a particularly strong element of the neighborhood voodoo culture in which she had grown up. True, Haitians were usually drawn to effigies of their own native animal life for their totems, such as caiman crocodiles or wild boars or even the brilliant pink flamingos, and Duncan was only a cute stuffed gorilla, about eighteen inches long. But Hattie, nothing if not practical, believed you used what was at hand. Thus Duncan the Protector.

The little guy had been in the family from the instant Nate spotted him in the display window of the gift shop at Hancock Airport in Syracuse. It was instant bonding, the signal event of young Nate's life, and, even now at nine, he'd occasionally come running into the house after school, drop his books on the kitchen table and find his mom for their "quality time" chat, the subject of which would be, as often as not, the great day on which he found Duncan. And she would begin the ritual, in which they both took such delight, of recounting the by-now family myth of the origin of the noble stuffed beast: "Well, it was a cold autumn day, the Tuesday before Thanksgiving," she would begin in her best storytelling voice, though her words were slow and labored, a consequence of the accident. "I'd taken you with me to the airport to pick up your Aunt Liz who was coming to visit for the holiday. You were only five years old so you couldn't drive."

An explosion of guffaws.

"The flight was delayed so all we could do was sit around and wait. Well, that didn't exactly suit you!"

More guffaws. Always in the same spots.

"So we walked around the lobby for a while. At a certain point, I suddenly realized you were no longer walking with me. Panicking, I looked around for you and felt instant relief when I spotted you standing transfixed in front of the gift shop window, about a stone's throw behind me.

"'Nathaniel!'" I called out to you. And you made a mad dash, but not towards me – oh no, you had other ideas. You ran into the shop and, even before I could get to the entrance, you came running out of it like a shot, shouting, 'Mom! Mom! Look what I found! I have to have him! I just *have* to! Pu*leease*?' You were jumping up and down, waving this stuffed toy back and forth. I couldn't even make out what it was. Just something dark and furry with long arms."

By now, whenever Julie told him the "legend of Duncan," Nate would be holding his head in his palms and leaning on the tray of her chair, totally lost in his mother's animated face and in this story which he intuitively felt to be the story of his own beginnings.

"'Sweetheart,'" I said to you, "'you can't just run out of a store with the merchandise … '"

"'What's merch-,' I asked you, right, Mom? – I remember."

"Yes. 'That's all the things the store sells,' I explained to you. 'You have to *pay* for something before you can take it with you. Otherwise you're stealing and we don't steal. You don't want the policeman to come and arrest you.'"

"'Arrets?'"

"'Ar*rest*. You know, take you to the police station and put you in jail.'"

In telling the tale, Julie no longer hesitated to mention "jail" to her nine-year-old son. When she first began telling it a few years earlier, it was euphemisms like "keeps you there until Mommy and Daddy come and get you." She always tried to be sensitive to her son's need for a gradual exposure to the world outside the bosom of the family, aiming for a middle path between protection and risk. Some might say she was oversensitive, especially since the accident and her anguished struggle to come to terms with her own helplessness.

"Get to the part about his name, Mom. That's my favorite."

"Okay, okay, don't rush me now," she would say in faux irritation. "Anyway, you just kept jumping and jumping and finally blurted out—"

"—I know. I know. 'You have to let me keep him, Mom,' I said, 'because I already know his name! That makes us friends. I think me and Duncan may already be *best* friends!'"

"'Nathaniel,' I said to you, 'best friends with some-one you've just met? . . . What is it anyway – ah, yes, a gorilla.'

"'Don't worry about it, Mom. Me and Duncan will figure that out!' you answered. I couldn't believe how insistent you were; the matter was non-negotiable. Usually you're willing to wait for a toy you want, till your birthday or till you save up enough allowance.

"'Duncan, is it?' I said. 'And how do you know his name is Duncan?'

"'That's easy. He carries it with him, just like me on my good jacket and my lunchbox,' you answered and smiled so proudly, as you held him up and showed me the little label sewn into his side. It read 'Dakin,' which is the toy company that made Duncan. I didn't have the heart to correct your tiny misreading, especially since, so far as I knew anyway, it was your first attempt to 'read the world'—you know, to apply the letters you'd been studying so hard with Daddy and me and in day-care to a real-world situation. Of course, it also clinched the deal. If you could read—or almost read—Duncan's name, he had to be yours."

And on it would go for a while as they kibitzed and recalled this and that from the "old days" (Good God, already there were "old days"!). After a while, Nate would ask to go practice his drums in the garage or go out and play, and, if he didn't, Julie would bring it up herself and

22

insist he go out and find his friends. She didn't want him becoming emotionally housebound.

But those after-school chats were good times for her, even necessary times considering the circumstances. Private moments with her little boy were about as good as it got for Julie Driscoll these days, what with all the major parts of her life so brutally severed by the accident, perhaps forever. Work, married life, ordinary mothering, social ties—all ripped away, or at least badly torn, by a "pillar of the community," who should have been tackled when he drunkenly reached for his car keys that star-crossed evening. Again and again, like moths to a flame, Julie's thoughts would be drawn back to the moment of that horrific collision. It happened at the intersection of Jamesville and Nottingham, as she drove home after working late at the university library on a blustery March evening of the previous year. She saw him coming from her left like a flash a split second before he hit – two blinding headlights, brights, followed by a shattering explosion of sound. Then darkness. Between then and coming to in the emergency room, she remembers being totally engulfed by that darkness, thinking, almost chanting, over and over like a guiding mantra: *I stopped; he didn't. I stopped; he didn't. I stopped; he didn't …*

She hated reviewing memories of the accident, mainly because, so far as she could tell, it didn't do any good. She didn't feel she was "processing" the trauma, which the psychologist said was essential. The memories, all grisly, were the fuel of nightmares, and seemed like so many facets of a toxic obsession, an obsession just as strong now, she felt, as it had been in the hospital's critical care unit where it began, if not stronger. Usually she would try to turn her thoughts to the more distant past, to happier times "B.A." (before the accident), when life was rich and vibrant and so full of promise. She would think back to the spring when she had just completed work for her Ph.D., successfully defending her dissertation on the German philosopher Friedrich Wilhelm Joseph von Schelling. How sweet those days were, the last she and Mark were to spend on the Homewood campus at Johns Hopkins. They were going to be one of those rare "academic couples" that actually had a successful marriage, that is, two tenure-track professors living at the same address and working for the same university. No quarterly transcontinental flights for them! They would have parallel but intertwined careers in the hallowed groves of academe, she teaching and doing research in the German idealist philosophers, he in the English Romantic poets.

That's the way they had laid it all out mere weeks after falling in love at first sight in the hermeneutics seminar of the Hopkins graduate school. And when, a few years later, they bought the house in DeWitt just before

Nate was born, it was going to be "circa 1800 intellectual fireworks" between the Germans and the Brits at 104 Wildwood Drive: Schelling, Hegel, Fichte and Kant versus Blake, Coleridge, Keats and Shelley. It would be a sassy and sexy marriage made in academic heaven, a marriage of literature and philosophy, with plenty of synergistic ideas and history and fierce but friendly competition. All at the "salon Driscoll," a watering hole for scholars, thinkers and writers from all over the Central New York area and beyond.

That had been the dream anyway. Now, sitting there in her chair that morning while Hattie cleaned up after breakfast, she worried that she was too given to such sentimental reminiscing. It couldn't be healthy to be so attached to the past, especially at her age and in her circumstances. Even the fondest memories would wear out if you mentally fondled them too much; they needed to be leavened, offset, by present-time experience, just the thing she was low on, and with bleak prospects for improvement.

Of course, no sooner would she caution herself in this way than her mind would drift yet again, as if by a separate, alien will, back to happier days. (In its own way the pull to the happy past could feel as oppressive as that to the recent.) On this morning she was borne back again to that Thanksgiving break that had brought them Duncan, and to the several other Thanksgivings before and after it, when the larger clan would gather together at the Driscolls to celebrate the holiday in the brisk upstate autumn season, always on the cusp of another punishing winter. Huge buffet tables of food and drink would be set up in the dining room of the old colonial house on Wednesday evening. There was an unceasing stream of chatter and badinage and benign teasing that animated this group of still young adults who richly enjoyed each other's company, all the more because they didn't see each other very often. There was, of course, Aunt Liz, Julie's sister, who was there solo, the ex-wife of an alcoholic idler who had soured her on men. Then there was David Driscoll, Mark's older brother, a mechanical engineer who always came with his three kids, his annoying terrier with the extremely annoying name "Sparky" and his sharp-tongued wife Moira, who knew just how to send Aunt Liz into hysterics with her sardonic comments on the faults and foibles of the others. Several other relatives, most of them on Mark's side, were also regulars. And there were usually a few friends, maybe a university colleague or two in philosophy or English who lived in the Dewitt area, or "academic ghetto," as they affectionately called it. And always there was Pete Gutierrez, the social worker who lived across the street with his wife Carmella and a houseful of kids, some their own, the rest "on rental" from the agency Pete worked for. They usually had the charity to show up with no more than half of them, even when Mark and Julie chided them, every year, for leaving the others at home.

But whatever the cast of characters, Julie thought as she smiled to herself, it always coalesced into a lively mix of stellar wit and conversation, almost like an old Preston Sturges comedy, because she and Mark had the social gift of making people feel welcome—indeed indispensible—in their home. And they were equally adept at hosting sparkling parties and serious living-room seminars. But it was especially at Thanksgiving that they brought out the best in everyone there, with all the conviviality peaking on Thursday afternoon at the grand sit-down dinner of turkey—twenty pounds minimum— "with all the fixin's." And no matter how animated the table talk, how raucous the laughter, Mark would always stand up near the end of the first helping, his six-foot-three-inch svelte, bespectacled figure drawing all eyes to itself. And even though he already had their attention, he would raise his wine glass, tap it three times with a spoon and utter some words of thanks, before going around the table "officially" welcoming each guest. And of course he would always end with the same joke, revealing Wild Turkey as the only fowl he truly cared for. Unfailingly, everyone would groan or scowl, which was his cue to hold up his drumstick, tap *it* a few times with his index finger and ask stupidly, "Is this on?" And at *that* everyone would roar – a joke so lame it was actually hilarious.

What would become of all that now, she worried. Would there ever be a "salon Driscoll" again? Hattie came by and brushed a strand of her blond hair back from her dainty brow.

"Would you care for another sip of coffee, Miz Julie?"

"No thanks, Hattie, I think I'll just stroll out onto the deck for a bit of sunshine." And with that she leaned her head slightly forward, activating the tiny mercury switch pinned to her hair that powered the wheelchair. She rolled down the little ramp Mark had cobbled together for her and out to the middle of the spacious deck, closed her eyes and just let the brilliant morning sun caress her face as it rose above the swaying silver oaks, all resplendent in their finest Fall foliage. She couldn't feel her noble little sentry sitting on her lap, but Duncan was there all the same, as always.

It was a splendid morning, but her mind neverthe-less moved, again on its own, into dark territory. What about her marriage? What sort of shape was it in at this point? And if it was in less than ideal shape, what could *she* do about it anyway? By what definition could she even consider herself a wife? After all, beyond watch-ing, she could no longer even take care of her husband's simplest sexual needs, and she didn't know whether she would ever be able to again. She had just about given up hope of ever getting any real help from the doctors, whose uneasiness she could sense whenever she tried to discuss the subject in any depth. Even the psychologist could do little more than recommend a wait-and-see attitude. *Wait for what!* she asked herself, the tears welling up. And how long would *Mark* wait? How long *could* he? She didn't know. It was only on rare occasions that they had even aired these anxieties between themselves at any length, what with the massive adjustment to the traumatic change of lifestyle they'd been going through.

Julie felt the stinging heat of shame and inadequacy course through her immobile body, even though she was perfectly aware on a rational level that she bore no blame. It didn't seem to matter. The roles of wife and mother were so deeply ingrained that, even with all her critical philosophical consciousness, she still felt bound by their exigencies. It was as if these identities retained some inscrutable archaic hold over her 21st-century mind. She felt bad for Nate too, that she was no longer able to hug or hold him, to initiate any physical contact with him, or even just enforce the rules about home-work, hygiene, his room and a thousand other things with the implied threat of a strong, agile body. She was a mother who couldn't do maternal deeds, and that was no mother at all.

Still, she felt that, on balance, Nate was holding his own. He was strong and resilient, with a steady, unruffled outlook on life. "An old soul," as his father liked to say. She didn't need to worry about him too much. But Mark was another matter. He wasn't so steady as his son, hadn't been even before the accident. He had his insecurities, which occasionally leaked out in lingering resentments and petty jealousies. He mostly kept this darker side to himself, the more so now, but Julie knew it was there and she knew when it was likely to show up. She was especially wary of his tendency to tease her or make light of her academic successes, of which she had had more than he due to her greater scholarly productivity ("You know, you don't have to go running right to the publisher with everything you happen to scribble!") Of course, that particular bugaboo was on hold for the time being. Who knew what, if anything, lay ahead for her professionally? Drastic way to resolve an envy issue, she smiled to herself cynically.

Needless to say, Mark had been the perfectly attentive husband since the accident, tripping over himself to tend to her every need. At times Julie thought she even caught him scowling at an aide just for doing his job since that left less for *him* to do. She knew that some, though certainly not all, or even most, of Mark's solicitude was being driven by guilt, and that to that extent it wouldn't last, couldn't last. Would the marriage survive

Mark's inevitable awakening to sober reality? Could he come to terms with things as they really were and would probably remain? She liked to think so—still, she fretted over the uncertainty of it. She dreaded suffering the same unhappy fate as her own parents back in Cedar Rapids, who got divorced as soon as she moved to Baltimore for graduate school, and who had raised her and her two sisters living separated from each other most of the time.

She looked down and saw Duncan nestled there in the nook between her left arm and her side. She liked having him there: he reminded her of Nate. It was like keeping a little piece of her boy with her while he was off at school, and, in this moment, the presence of the nappy toy gorilla brightened her darkening mood and reminded her it was time for her morning meditation.

Still facing the sun, she held her head erect, closed her eyes and inhaled deeply. As she slowly let her breath out, she thought with gratitude of her friend Maxine in the anthropology department, who had encouraged her to take up the practice of counting the breath, Zen style. It took little persuasion; trapped in this now alien body as she was, she quickly saw the wisdom of using the power of her mind to gain whatever freedom might be possible from her corporeal prison. One … two… in and out … in and out. Slowly. Smoothly. Up to ten and start again. Gently focusing the mind only on the breath, becoming one with it. Only breath. Nothing but breath. Breath. Noticing even the tiny transition points between in and out, the cusp, where there was no breath, neither in nor out, just ... nothing ...

Lunch **period at** W. H. Smythe Elementary was almost over and a handful of kids who had skipped out of the cafeteria for a decent burger at a nearby eatery were sneaking back to afternoon classes.

"What's your deal, Driscoll?" Jake Rensky barked.

"I told you, I don't have any deal." Snickers and laughs all around.

Rensky snorted and rested his massive *World Geography* book on Nate's head as the latter was about to get up after fishing around on the floor of his locker for his gym sneakers. Then the young tough leaned his fleshy elbow down on the book and crossed his legs, affecting a pose of casual relaxation. Rensky's lackeys found this hilarious, of course, laughing and shrieking like banshees and drawing the interest of other students passing by.

But today Nate was having none of it. Fed up to here with the non-stop teasing and bullying, he ripped himself out from under the textbook in one swift, deft movement, leaving Rensky to collapse onto the floor like a sack of potatoes, his own head now lying on top of the thick tome. This confused the bystanding gang, one or two of them hooting in grudging admiration of Nate's lightning agility, while the others either snickered timidly or shouted obscenities at this "little prick" of an upstart who dared humiliate their leader.

It was these high-pitched obscenities that actually saved Nate from dire reprisals from the mortified Rensky, who was just getting up and starting to cock his thickish right arm. Mr. Spencer, a sixth-grade teacher with the physique of a middleweight on fight night, who was subbing for the absentee hall monitor that day, heard the hubbub and came running over: "Hey, hey, what's with the foul language, you guys? You know better than that! . . . What's going on here? Fighting in the hall? Rensky—you again? Why don't you pick on somebody your own size for a change? Driscoll, get outta here. Get your ... *self* to class. Rensky, you come with me. Let's you and me have a little talk."

"This ain't over, Driscoll," Rensky scowled as he and Mr. Spencer headed down the hall toward a little conference room off the teachers' lounge.

"Hey, hey, we'll have none of that," Mr. Spencer scolded, putting his arm around the budding bully's shoulder. For in truth, Mr. Spencer secretly loved it when his boys "got into it" every now and then. He was a pugnacious gym rat himself and barely mature enough not to take a rooting interest in hall fights. He liked the short-fused, tough-guy Rensky, a kid after his own thuggish heart. As for Nate, he had never taken much interest in this small, quiet kid who seemed to keep a low profile. The teacher had no particular feeling for him one way or the other. He was, however, aware of his mother's dire condition and instinctively acted so as to protect the boy from any disciplinary consequences stemming from the scuffle.

Nate was just glad to get out of there and headed off to his twelve-thirty gym class down the hall. He wasn't worried about Rensky, whom he regarded more as an annoyance to be avoided than a threat to be feared. He had other things on his mind, chief among them spending the next period playing in a fast-paced basketball scrimmage, which meant escaping the boring calisthenics that fell to boys who came late to phys. ed. or who belonged to the species of nerd that abhorred anything athletic. Hoisting his backpack onto his slender left shoulder, he leaned his right palm against the heavy fiberglass door to the boys' locker room, struggling to push it open. It resisted but finally gave way to a second effort.

He was immediately spotted by his best friend, Jamie Poindexter, who waved and shouted to him while in the midst of pulling up his elastic protector, in his excitement almost toppling over the bench bolted to the floor in front of his locker.

"Whoa, Dex, don't go busting your balls or you'll have to do calisthenics."

Jamie laughed, gingerly moving the strap into place. "Where'd you go? You left the cafeteria early."

"I had to pick up my sneakers and had a little run-in with that dickhead Rensky."

"Him again? What's he got against you anyway?" Jamie asked as he pulled a pair of gray gym shorts with red side stripes halfway up over the beginnings of a pot belly.

"Who knows? He's a jerk. But I got him good today. I was crouched down at my locker and he came over and was leaning on me with this humongous book and I pulled out from under him real fast and he went down like a ton of bricks."

"Oh my God!" Jamie shrieked. "Are you serious? Rensky went *down*?"

"Yeah. He was just lying there, on the floor, you know, with the book under his head like a pillow."

Jamie gave three hard slaps to a locker, giving way to a fit of hysteria, which ended in a fit of coughing and a flushed crimson face. "Shit, man, I wish I could've been there!" The reaction caused several boys dressing along the aisle to look over.

The two friends finished changing and rushed into the gym where Coach Peruzzi was almost finished assigning boys to teams for the game on center court. They had gotten there just in time. Coach P., himself an old jock of a defensive lineman who was now almost double his playing weight, snarled, "Poindexter! Shirts! Driscoll! Skins! Now let's get it on!"

Though he would never say so, Coach P. was pleased that Nate and Jamie had showed up on time, since he enjoyed watching these games, enjoyed spotting young boys' nascent physical prowess, whatever the sport, and he had already made up his mind that Poindexter and Driscoll were among the most athletically gifted of their class.

And in truth they were, though you'd never know it by their physiques. Jamie was taller than the average nine-year-old, but also a carboholic with a killer sweet tooth and an addiction to strawberry Pop Tarts. His dozen or so extra pounds and shuffling gait reflected this. Nate, on the other hand, had his mother's diminutive stature: at nine he was a seventy-pound runt soaking wet, his blond head still slightly too big for his sheet-white, boney frame. He had definitely inherited his mother's pretty, corn-fed, mid-western face. But as a skin player in the scrimmage, he looked every bit the "plucked chicken" his dad affectionately accused him of being. Mark enjoyed telling people that, whenever he watched Nate pounding on his drums in the garage, between the white sticks, the white drum skin and his white son, the whole affair looked like a tempest in a milk bottle. He also liked to quip that he never had a problem locating his son in the crowded surf at Cape Cod where the family often vacationed. All he had to do was quickly scan the crowd of swimmers until his eye was stopped by a blinding patch of brilliant white. That was Nate.

On the court, however, the two friends transcended their physical limitations. Despite the overweight, Jamie was far from slow. He was, in fact, a strong sprinter with good agility, including deft dribbling skills and quick fake-out moves to the basket. Also, in some ways his slight heaviness was probably an advantage: it seemed to steady his shooting stroke, making it more accurate. As a point guard Nate was his natural complement, and in their driveway and playground games he could almost close his eyes and lob passes in to Jamie for easy buckets. That day, however, they were on opposite teams.

Nate himself was easily the fastest player in the scrimmage, and Rensky, if attacked by a fit of honesty, could now speak for his quickness from bitter experience. Though he looked more like a six than a nine-year-old, Nate's speed was marked by an unusually mature level of physical coordination. He ran with a tight gait, straight and true and with purpose, showing none of the awkward flopping around and wasted motion typical of boys that age. Again and again in the scrimmage he made crisp and sure passes inside to his "big men," occasionally even of the no-look variety. He didn't shoot often, instinctively aware that he needed another year or so to develop his shot, but on those occasions when he did shoot, the ball went in as often as not. Though small for his age, Nate was a strong boy, but his strength was wiry, not brute.

The game was now in full swing, the ten players on court moving at peak energy. Occasionally, without bothering to call time out, Coach P. would make a substitution or two to involve more kids and keep the pace up: "Hawley! In for Gerber … O'Brien! In for Mackey! On the double! Let's go. Let's go!" he'd bark, clapping his hands with a force that bounced the sound off all the gym's hard surfaces, snapping the nerdy kids to from their desultory chin-ups and sprints along the sidelines.

Since Coach P. loved watching them, Nate and Jamie were rarely taken out of the game, which may or may not account for what happened.

It was late in the scrimmage, with the kids beginning to breathe heavily and stand around bent over with their hands on their knees. Coach P. had worked them pretty hard, calling almost no fouls, which would have stopped the action and given them a breather.

"Come on, shirts!" he bellowed. "Time's running out and you're four behind! Get the lead out, Poindexter! You're running like my grandmother today, and she's in a wheelchair!" He spit the words out with mock contempt that was actually only half mocking, for, although he liked Jamie and admired his skills, he also secretly resented the boy's flabbiness and slovenly attitude towards conditioning, these being an unconscious reminder of his own poor work ethic, which had long ago sabotaged his hopes for a pro career.

Frantic to catch up before Coach P.'s deafening whistle signaled the end of the game—and the class—, the shirts rushed the ball up-court at almost fast-break speed. Little Tim Klinger, Nate's opposite number as the shirts' point guard, heaved the ball forward towards Jamie, who, however, was still running and not yet in position to take a pass near the basket. Instinctively, though, he knew the ball was on its way to him and turned to grab it while still in full gallop, and the next thing he knew, he was laid out on the floor under the basket, looking up at the net with an Oriental gong ringing in his head.

In turning his eye back towards the ball, Jamie had not seen his defender slide in in front of him to take the charge. He hit the kid full force, all hundred-ten pounds of him, and the two of them went careening down, slamming into none other than Coach. P. himself, who was standing just out of bounds behind the basket with clipboard in hand and whistle poised to blow. The fact is, the coach took a pretty good hit, though he held his ground and remained upright, even acting out a little pretense of a mortal danger barely evaded. "Whoa, whoa there! I don't think my Blue Cross covers this."

The kids, however – and not just the skins either – took this opportunity to rag on Jamie for his clumsiness. Like Nate, Jamie too was a favorite target of the school bullies and teasers, he for being big and fat, his friend for being small and skinny. Their common victimhood was the negative side of the bond that formed their friendship. Nate, of course, was the first to rush over and help Jamie up, so that the two of them were just standing there under the basket looking at each other sheepishly. Most of the other kids there knew they were close and, perhaps resenting the exclusivity of their friendship, a few immediately seized the opportunity to do a number on both of them. "Hey, look! It's Frick and Frack!"

"Yeah! Shrek and Mighty Mouse! What a pair!"

"The dynamic duo!"

"Watch out, Driscoll! If he falls on you, you're roadkill!"

And on it went, becoming infectious as such thoughtless cruelty so often does among tweens. Others laughed and hooted, inspiring more of what passes for wit at that age, all of it culminating in that singsong juvenile quatrain that must be almost as old as childhood itself. One of the players standing nearby turned to the others and chanted at top speed, stomping with his right foot to keep time:

> Fat and skinny had a race
> All around the pillowcase.
> Fat fell down and broke his face
> And skinny won the race.

It was a laugh riot, abruptly ended only when Coach P.'s ungodly whistle paralyzed everybody's nervous system and sent the whole class scrambling off to the shower room.

Nate Driscoll had the misfortune of possessing certain physical and psychological characteristics that made him inviting prey for the bullies, the badgerers and the needlers at school. For one thing, he was small, but without the finely honed defenses that usually enable smaller boys to fit in, like a glib tongue and a ready sense of humor. Not that Nate was deficient in these – quite the contrary – it was just that he was a bit introverted and tended to display his sense of the absurd mainly to family members, his friend Jamie and one or two other students to whom he was drawn. He liked to keep his own company and was by temperament pensive, at times to the point of brooding, a tendency that had certainly been exacerbated by recent events.

Then too, Nate was the child of academics, of professors, and shared his parents' habit of quiet reflection, of mulling an issue over, even doing his own child's brand of Wiki "research" on it, sometimes for weeks or even months, before venturing an opinion. One day, about a year after Duncan entered his life, Julie, who was then still ambulatory, asked him what he wanted for his sixth birthday. They were having an after-school catch in their spacious back yard. Nate, having just caught his mom's throw and question simultaneously, just stood there thinking. Looking down at the pink rubber ball as he turned it over in his hands, his brow fiercely knitted, it seems he entirely forgot he was in a game of catch, until Julie, becoming impatient, shouted, "Earth to Nate! Earth to Nate!" Coming to, he laughed and returned her throw, but still not an answer to her question. It was weeks before she was able to pry anything out of him on the birthday issue. The question of a gift had engaged Nate's mind that afternoon as a matter of the utmost importance, deserving of the most careful deliberation. He realized he had felt this way ever since receiving the gift of Duncan the previous year, as if the "little monkey" had awakened him to the profound impact a gift can have on a life. Birthday gifts were not to be taken lightly.

So Nate usually thought before he spoke. And when he spoke, he used words concisely and economically, rarely exaggerating and seldom even amplifying his remarks, unless prodded. This laconic style of his was often mistakenly viewed by others as aloofness, as if he considered himself their superior and couldn't be bothered "kicking back" with them. This misreading, in turn, tended to inspire in them an odd kind of respect, which, because it was resentful, incited teasing and bullying. When teased, Nate was not one to hurl back a swift retort, which, of course, only encouraged the teasers to up the ante.

Nate, for his part, was not unduly concerned with issues of "socialization" at school. He was a top student and took the social side of school mostly in stride, enjoying his few, select friendships and largely ignoring whatever slings and arrows came his way from others. He had an independent streak in him, did not crave popularity among his peers and, at nine, was self-aware enough to understand, in a rudimentary way, why this was so. It was because of Duncan. Duncan was his protector, his guardian, his spirit of self-affirmation, and had been so from the very first, long before Nate was mature enough to formulate such ideas. In the beginning Duncan was simply there as part of him, wrapped in his left arm and accompanying the boy everywhere, unless there was some compelling reason from mom against it. When

Nate started school, Duncan did too, stowed in the bottom of his backpack beneath his lunchbox.

This arrangement probably would have continued to the present day but for two intervening factors. One was that Nate gradually grew uneasy over the possibility of some kid ransacking his backpack and finding Duncan in it. While the ribbing would not have devastated him, he wasn't fool enough to invite it either and thought it might be time to start leaving his alter ego at home. The other was Hattie's suggestion that he did indeed have a very good reason to leave Duncan at home on schooldays: as protection for his mom. He did not consider at the time that Hattie might have had the ulterior motive of weaning him off the little guy. This only occurred to him when, shortly thereafter, his father began subtly suggesting to him that maybe he was getting a little old to be carrying around a stuffed toy, even if it was well hidden in his backpack. That sort of thing was all right for girls; they were allowed to bring all manner of baby things to school—dolls, Pretty Ponies, pop-up books—without fear of reprisal. But boys needed to put all infantile things away, ready or not, and get on with it.

So it was that Nate let go of Duncan, or at least the corporeal part of him, early in the Fall term of fourth grade. It took no more than a day or two for him to get over any sense at all of deprivation. He sensed that Duncan was somehow not bound by his physical form, which was, in any case, nothing organic but mere cloth, plastic and stuffing. In fact, after turning the little ape over to his mom, he felt its presence, its aura, somehow even reinforced in and around himself, wherever he happened to be. He could not have put it in these terms, but he was learning a profound spiritual lesson having to do with energy and the fluidity of identity. It was a largely unconscious process of education, taking place parallel to, but not yet intersecting, the conscious, deliberate sort provided by school.

4

The noonday sun was bearing down, so Julie steered herself back into the family room, tossing her head back a bit as if to search her mind. After an uneasy meditation, she had just sat there on the deck, stuck on the treadmill of squirrel-cage thinking. She had read that you're not supposed to judge the quality of a particular meditation session, that they're all "good," even the ones where you can't hold focus for more than three seconds at a time.

Fair enough, she thought, *but what just happened to me out there has got to be something else. I can't remember ever having had such an intense anxiety attack in my life, not even that time way back in girl-scout days when I wandered off on a hike and got lost in the Sawtooth Mountains. Maybe I've cracked open some weird access to my unconscious and now I'm stuck with a raging Pandora's box, a psychotic break. I've read that meditation can do that to you, especially if it's prolonged, like one of those week-long Zen retreats … Great, that's all I need at this point – the dual imprisonment of body and mind. I'll be the first schizophrenic quadriplegic in medical history. The first schizo quad!*

The absurd expression made her laugh, relaxing her and allowing a measure of reason and logic to intervene, along with a dash of intuition, to temper the runaway emotions. *Wait a minute. Come on, Julie! You don't meditate that much, certainly not enough to mess with your head. And whatever this anxiety may be about, it's definitely not about* you! *It's about something or somebody else. I don't know how I know this, I just do. I'm sure of it. But then, what? Or who?*

Both vexed and pensive, she sat there absently watching Hattie, who was busily coming and going, performing a variety of small tasks including changing the sheets on Julie's hospital bed, doing a load or two of wash and dusting and vacuuming around Julie's preferred locations to minimize the chances of infection or allergic reactions. They had moved the flat-screen TV to the living room and turned the family room into a makeshift bedroom, setting up Julie's bed therein and a Japanese Shoji screen at the entrance for privacy. This gave Julie direct access to the deck. At some point they did intend to convert the room to a permanent bedroom, but right now all structural renovations were a low priority.

"Hattie?" Julie asked, in an oddly quizzical tone that immediately caught the aide's attention.

"Yes, Miz Julie," she responded eagerly, folding her chemically treated dust cloth swiftly and with finality, then slipping it into the right-hand pocket of her crisp blue smock, as if to show Julie that she had her full attention.

"Would you mind getting me a Xanax?"

"Certainly, ma'am. The bottle is in the kitchen, together with the aspirin and the cold medicine. I'll go get it right away … Is anything the matter?"

Julie loved listening to Hattie's soft, deep, womanly voice, with its barest trace of a Creole accent, noticeable now mainly in its tendency to use "d" or "t" for the difficult "th" sound, as in "togedder wit dee aspirin." In fact, it was precisely this "flaw" in Hattie's otherwise impeccable English that Julie loved the most; its childlike quality delighted and soothed her.

French Creole was Hattie Dalembert's native tongue, but she made it her business to learn English in the aftermath of the earthquake, once she had made the critical decision to seek a new life in America. She threw herself into linguistic interaction with the American medical and humanitarian groups that swarmed into Port-au-Prince in the massive rescue effort. She learned to count in English by sorting bodies. She absorbed medical terms in the field almost osmotically from sheer repetition over a period of months ... *penicillin ... bacterial infection ... amputate immediately ... hook up that IV line ... set up a temporary morgue.*

It helped enormously that so much of the vocabulary was already familiar to her from her Latin-based Creole French and that she had grown up listening to the pidgin English of her cousins on frequent visits to nearby Carrefour, a hodgepodge they had assimilated from too much American TV. All she needed was fifty or sixty essential verbs to connect the nouns. By the time she landed at JFK on a steamy August evening in 2010, she was fluent enough to find her way around the vertiginous borough of Queens, order a meal in a fast-food restaurant and check into a Ramada Inn. The very next day she was on a Trailways bus headed upstate to Syracuse, this on the advice of an American emergency physician she had worked with in the capital city who told her that "the 'Cuse" was "a good ed-med city. Great schools, great hospitals, though the rest of the economy has been in the toilet for decades. Plenty of jobs for aides."

"No, not really," Julie answered indecisively, smiling wanly at the elaborate red and beige floral patterns in the rug. "I just didn't sleep very well last night. I don't think that new Tempur-Pedic pillow agrees with me." She raised her arresting blue eyes, their loveliness now softened by sadness, to Hattie's, making a futile effort to brighten her smile.

Hattie sat down on the edge of the tan leather sofa and put her palms together between her kneecaps, a gesture betraying her ambivalent feelings over what she was about to suggest. Julie turned her head slightly to the left, rotating her chair so as to face the aide squarely. She could tell the woman was ill at ease, a mild frown coming over her smooth ebony face with its intelligent eyes and full, expressive mouth.

"Miz Julie," Hattie began, "I know I'm only an aide in this house and I don't want to overstep my bounds, but … I would like you to feel free to talk to me about anything … at any time. I mean, not just health issues, but … the inner concerns as well. You know, especially with a condition like yours, there's no separating the outer from the inner, body from mind. And you're alone so much of the time—right now anyway. That can be difficult for a woman like yourself, so accomplished, who's used to being involved with people, with students, teaching, doing serious work. So … if you ever need an ear for any reason—"

"—Hattie, I think I just had some kind of panic attack out on the deck."

The aide's eyes widened. "Oh! I'm so sorry, Miz Julie. Are you sure? Let me go and get that Xanax for you right away." She rushed out to the kitchen and came back with a glass of water in one hand and the tiny white pill in the other. As Julie swallowed, Hattie caught the fragrance of her freshly shampooed hair—shampoo applied by her—and felt a pang of affection for her helpless charge, sitting there in, of all clothing, a jogging outfit. Sitting back down, she straightened up Duncan, who had tipped over on Julie's lap.

"Do you have any idea what might have brought it on?"

"Not a clue."

"Well, it's not as if you don't have good reason, Miz. God knows …"

"At first I thought it might be the meditation, that I might be doing it wrong or something. But I dismissed that after a moment, especially when it dawned on me that the anxiety wasn't … how to put this … wasn't self-directed. It wasn't about me."

"How do you mean, Miz?"

"It was about something else, some other thing, or situation, or person … Oh, I don't know. It's all so confusing, … and upsetting."

"Yes, Miz Julie, I'm sure it is. But, if you'll allow me to say this, we'll deal with it together—that is, if you're of a mind to. Two heads are better than one, especially with something as troubling and mysterious as anxiety. I know this very well from my rescue work after the earthquake. Fear and panic among the people did at least as much harm as the maiming itself. There just wasn't enough time, and enough available ears, to listen to the wounded, to help them get out their crushing fears. The numbers don't show it, but I'm sure many died from the emotional stress ... But in your case, Miz, we are not even going to give fear an opening, okay?"

"Thank you so much, Hattie. I know it's a cliché, but I really don't know what I'd do without you."

"Cliché or not, it's nice to hear," Hattie cackled in her deep, throaty way, getting up to leave.

"Oh, and Hattie, one more thing, please," Julie said smiling as the aide walked off. "Please call me Julie. No more titles between us, okay?"

"Okay, Miz ... uh, Julie," and she left the room, cackling again.

5

Under the boardwalk—boardwalk! *Watch them sand snakes. They'll get you every time. That sumbitch is eyin' me, rockin' back and forth like that. Keep him away from me, Ma! Keep him away! I could play him like a flute or a clarinet. If he bites me, I bite him right back. Sammy, put Miles on and get me my Pappy's, will ya? … What? We're out? Fuck me! Why didn't ya give me a head's up. What the fuck are you good for anyway? You're no fuckin' good, that's what. No fuckin' good. No good at all … Iza comin', iza comin'. I wanna take my time. Will ya let me take my sweet time, Daddy? Will ya? Ow! Ow! Ow! Oh Fred, not in the face. You promised, not in the face! . . . My, oh my, but you do have the smoothest, roundest cheeks, the sweetest crimson lips. And best of all, that smell of pre-pubescence that gets me out of bed in the mornin'. Lickety-split, the world's for shit. Ah, that was a good one. Can you turn it up a notch? I'za feelin' it. I'za really feelin' it. Better than Pappy's. Better even than Miles, I'd have to say. And*

I'm back in the world of upside-down, my feet on the ceiling, my head on the ground. Trump trumps mighty Caeser and the reveling can begin. There goes a pretty one. I could kill the filthy cancer-stick suckers in this den of iniquity for pollutin' his air, for makin' his pretty blond locks smell like an ashtray. I could kill his fuckin' parents for leadin' him through this tenth circle of hell, the one with the chain smokers bound by chains of braided tobacco leaves, forever being lit by matches that never go out. Little Jimmy got off on a tiny brown spot on the barmaid's panties. Don't do a damn thing for me, but put that spot on some kid's tighty whities and I'm off to the races. What the fuck! Where's that bank of elevators? This joint's as dizzy as that Irrgarten *at the Overlook. The mood elevator's the kind I really need. Time to elevate, elevate, elevate. Ah, now there's a mood elevator I could ride all night. Ain't nothin' that handsome young prince couldn't elevate. Keep my mind on higher things, right? Definitely worth scouting. Lemme just snuggle up real close ... brush by, even graze, even nod hello to mom and dad passin' by. Oh, hang on, hang on now! Oh mother of pearl ... Don't tell me. They're splittin' up! Mommy and Daddy want to gamble and the kid's bored. The casino's a snooze for him. Oh, thank you, God. Thank you for making the sun to shine on the righteous and the wicked alike. Halleleuyah! ... Uh-oh! Wait a minute now. Oh shit! He's at the fuckin' elevator bank I was just lookin' for and the red up-arrow just lit up and the goddam ding's gone off and he's*

gonna get away if I don't move my horny ass over there ...
Good thing there's a bunch of people waitin' to get on ... Ah!
There we go. In like Flint, just in time. Lord have mercy!

6

Mark Driscoll deftly lifted himself off his nubile young teaching assistant and rolled over onto his side of the bed. Inhaling deeply, he let himself melt into what he often called "the most peaceful fifteen minutes of a man's life." It was an oasis of postcoital serenity he badly needed, even if the expected fifteen minutes seemed to have shrunk down to around nine or ten lately. The demons of care and woe just could not be held off any longer.

"Are you okay, Mark? You seem so far away today," said Sabrina Denning, Mark's pretty, flaxen-haired partner, his first and—thus far—only violation of his marriage vows.

"I'm all right," he answered absently, "I've just got a lot on my mind these days." Not the least of the lot was the blanket of guilt the affair had draped over him. The fact that he truly loved Julie made it worse. Before the accident he could never have imagined himself straying, but the current, unrelieved stress his waking life had become, which of course included sexual deprivation, had driven him to it.

"Hand me that pack of smokes on the nightstand there, will you, babe?

"Sure … Hey, since when do you indulge in the venomous weed?" Sabrina asked, genuinely surprised. She knew "Professor Driscoll" to be a straight arrow with few to none of the minor vices, an anomaly among today's "hip" professoriat. That was the thing that had attracted her to him. Sabrina was basically an old-fashioned girl who had watched a thousand black-and-white movies from the 1940's growing up in the nineties and tended to develop a crush on any professor who bore even the slightest resemblance to Mr. Chips—from the original version with Robert Donat. Yet, as bright as she was, the irony that she had seduced her moral paragon never occurred to her.

"Since now. But I only smoke two or three a day. It helps me relax."

"That's the way it usually starts," Sabrina cautioned dryly, wrapping herself like a papoose in the bed covers to ward off the late-summer chill. "But before you know it, it's up to ten a day, then fifteen, then a pack, and you're hooked. That's how my dad got hooked after the divorce, and he's still trying to kick the habit. I know your circumstances are very different from his, but in some ways they're also similar—I suppose one could say that you too have suffered a kind of divorce, don't you think?"

Inwardly Mark winced at the girl's adroit insight. *I would pick one of the smart ones*, he thought, taking a long slow drag on his Marlboro. But at this point his deepening smoking habit was the least of his concerns. Before the accident his wife had never been far from his thoughts: her inner presence was always either a warm, cozy balsam or a gentle pulse of delight, depending on his mood. These days she was on his mind even more completely, now, however, in the form of a painful obsession made up of sadness, guilt, fear, dread and any number of other negative emotions by which he at times felt crushed. He often felt as confined by Julie's paralysis as he imagined she did. The affair was an oasis for him, a brief, occasional escape from the misery, but it came at a high price in terms of self-loathing, for Mark was by character pretty much the morally upright citizen Sabrina pictured him to be. He'd never committed a crime, not even a violation, had only once lost points off his driver's license (speeding home to get little Nate to the toilet), and had in fact done more than his fair share of volunteer work and neighborhood-watch service. It was through the latter that he became friends with his neighbor, Pedro "Pete" Gutierrez.

These days when Mark looked in the mirror he was repelled by what he saw: a man cheating on an invalid wife who was drinking more than he should and had now added smoking to his list of shabby behaviors. *How could I have sunk so low so fast? It seems like just yesterday I was as happy as any man alive! Dream job, terrific family, a life of books and keeping company with great minds … When was the last time I lost myself in a book for more than twenty minutes? Where did it all go?*

The worst of it was, of course, the sexual betrayal, which weighed on his Catholic conscience, an implacable inner force that had stubbornly stayed with him into maturity, ignoring all his "liberated" conscious efforts to cast off the shackles of organized religion. This meant that he didn't merely feel an honest sadness for Julie's sake over his own infidelity, but a lacerating self-condemnation on top of it, which had deep roots in Church and family. He would torture himself with the memory, retained from adolescence, of his father shaking his head solemnly when asked by a half-drunken friend at a large family gathering if he had ever strayed. *No. Never. Not a chance. My wife is all the woman I've ever needed or wanted.* Mark never once doubted the sincerity of his dad's denial. He felt its truth in his bones and painfully measured himself against it. He also knew his guilt over his own affair was compelling his effusive display of concern over Julie's condition and his prickly solicitousness over the management of her consuming physical needs. The aides, experienced as they were, knew well what "game" he was playing and were savvy enough not to cross him.

The thing is that Mark, a very bright, self-aware man, recognized all of this, right down to the aides' deft "management" of his guilt-driven anger, and hated himself all the more for it. He began to feel emotionally trapped no matter what move he made or what attitude he struck. Hence his increasingly frantic reaching out to cognac and cigarettes, and, of course, Sabrina Denning, for relief. But, like a Chinese bamboo finger trap, the more Mark struggled to escape through these pleasures, the more ensnared by guilt and shame he became.

So, of course, he did what most men do when stress makes them go all stupid: more of the same. In a gesture half randy and half desperate, he rolled back over against Sabrina, who was still bundled up in the covers, and began rocking into her hip with his pelvis in unmistakable body language. He cupped her sweet-smelling hair in his hand and inhaled audibly, as if it were his farewell fragrance.

"Hey, are you serious?" Sabrina laughed, with a look both quizzical and delighted. "I've barely caught my own breath and you're ready to go again? What is it with you today anyway? A few minutes ago I felt practically alone here, all by myself in a shabby motel room.

And now suddenly you can't get enough of me. Not that I'm complaining, but what's going on with you, sweetie?" Sabrina seemed genuinely concerned, and this sudden attitude of serious attention, which he wasn't getting anywhere else, gave her face a kind of innocent sensuality that spiked his already rising lust.

And he was on her—in her—again, with the energy of a man desperate to smash the chains of his own identity, no matter how briefly. He was entirely in the moment, grateful to be there, one with the rhythm of thrusting. He was all senses, fondling her smooth skin, her firm, supple breasts, redolent of the faintest scent of patchouli, stopping every so often to press his legs against the full length of hers, as if to spread the crucible of their genitals down to their toes. He throbbed with a lust that could only engulf her and they seemed on the brink of forgetting who, when and where they were, when, suddenly, … Sabrina's cell phone began buzzing and writhing on the nightstand. She had forgotten to turn it off. As immersed in the act as Mark had seemed to be, that infernal buzz was like the explosion of a bomb, blowing him out of paradise and revealing how tentative, how flickering, how paper-thin, that Edenic state he so furiously sought really was.

All his inner demons were now outside, sitting there on the bed with them, greedier than ever for his attention for having been forcefully repressed yet again. He reached for a cigarette in frustration while Sabrina took her innocuous call. As he lit it, he was again reminded of his recent financial profligacy—the butts and the booze, items that were far from trivial in the Driscoll household budget these days. Alas, he liked only the high-quality cognacs and armagnacs, which could run anywhere between fifty and seventy bucks a bottle, sometimes more; and as for the cigarettes! Forget it! They were fast becoming a rich man's vice. He felt he was selfishly throwing away money at precisely the time when the family could least afford it.

And again the blanket of shame and guilt descended upon him, now smothering him with the bigger, more ominous and threatening financial anxieties, as such catastrophic thinking never fails to do. The biggest of all, of course, was the massive expense of Julie's care and treatment. True, her health insurance from the university was covering just about everything for the time being: the various medications, the doctors, the aides, therapists and high-tech machinery; but it would not last forever and was being eaten up alarmingly fast. What would they do when it ran out? The disability payments she was getting were a pittance compared to the salary she'd had to give up, more than decent by academic standards. Now they were a one-salary family, the salary being his, which was less than hers had been, and that at a university not known for its largesse in this area.

"That was my roomie Jennifer," Sabrina said sheepishly as she turned her cell off and slipped it nimbly into her bag. "She wanted to know what I was doing for dinner this evening, and I didn't know what to tell her, since you said you might—"

"—Sorry, Sabby, I can't tonight," Mark said somewhat peevishly, clearly still unnerved by the interruptus abruptus. "I've got a meeting right after dinner tonight that I can't move." This was a fact. He was scheduled to meet with Julie's psychotherapist to discuss her mental-emotional condition and progress. Since Julie, by her own consent, was not to be present at this hour, which was in addition to her regular weekly session, it had to be held after hours as part of the doctor's evening schedule. Mark said nothing of this to Sabrina, merely informing her vaguely of "a meeting," and this curtly and with a degree of chilliness meant to punish her for his sudden "expulsion from paradise." Besides, he hated discussing Julie's condition with outsiders, even this intimate outsider; such conversations brought him no relief, serving merely to arouse his fear of others' pity.

"Oh, well, that's too bad. I just thought we might—"

"—Forget it!" he shot back, his face reddening as he realized how angry he sounded. "Come on, Sabrina," he continued, softening his tone, "you know my time is not my own these days. I'm lucky I can even be here today. I'm lucky I can be anywhere …"

"I'm sorry, Mark. I wish there were some way I could help you, something I could do. God knows, I don't want to become another burden …"

"Oh, no, no, sweetheart, don't think that. Don't *ever* think that. God, if it weren't for you, I don't know where I'd be … " and on he went in this apologetic vein, with a degree of sincerity to be sure, but mostly out of fear his emotional turmoil might be pushing her away. "Things will improve, that I promise you," he concluded firmly, having not the least idea how such improvement might come about.

The absurdity of his promise made him reach for the cigarette pack once again, his third in less than an hour. And like an old jukebox stuck on the same record, the sad song of his financial plight again raised its mordant inner wail, now quickly broadening out to become the plight that was life itself. Good God, how utterly gloomy everything was! If it weren't so damned close to the bone, he could almost laugh at it the way he used to laugh at those afternoon TV soaps his mother was hooked on when he was in school. It certainly had all the elements of a good soap: invalid wife, semi-motherless child, two-faced husband, devoted provider and caretaker by day, sexual rake by night. Stay tuned for another episode of *As the Stomach Churns*.

But this forced effort to raise his spirits through sardonic humor wasn't working and he found himself faced with the same cold, hard facts, unleavened by humor. Julie's condition was just not going to improve, at least not significantly. The accident had severed her spinal cord at the fifth cervical vertebra, "C5" in the lexicon, located at the base of the neck. How full of terror that innocuous anatomical expression had become for him. Before, he would have taken it for the name of some hot new energy drink for dehydrated football players. *Refill your tank with C5, the all-natural power tonic. Pick up a 6-pack today!* It meant nothing to him. Now the mere sound of those two syllables, C5, near paralyzed him with dread and foreboding. *C5. C5. Christ, it's just a letter and a number! Like V6 or B1 or C3(pio)!* But, of course, it wasn't like them at all. Unlike them, C5 meant that Julie had lost control of all fine-motor movement of her hands and fingers. Never again would she hold a cup or a fork. And she could dispense with the help of an occupational therapist, a specialist in rehabilitating fine bodily movement, since there was nothing to rehabilitate. She did retain a minimal degree of gross bodily movement, in and around the shoulders, and the services of a physical therapist were being used to optimize that, but the good woman had cautioned Mark from the start that he should not expect any improvement in the arms or hands. *She has a total C5 severance. That means complete immobility below the scapulae.* He'd been struck at the time by the therapist's use of the Latin medical term for the more ordinary "shoulder blades," reading it as her appeal to his scholar's objectivity, but he was nowhere near hearing her pronouncement with a scholar's neutral ear. He kept his cool for the moment, but it devastated him, even though it wasn't news. It threatened the tiny flame of hope he refused to let go out.

Again he felt overwhelmed by the cumulative cost of the various treatments. In his emotions there was no separating the "noble" human problem of care from the "crass" financial one of affordability, and it drove him crazy that the latter was forever tainting the former. There were the various specialist doctors and nurses; there was Hattie, who worked full-time; there were the two part-time aides who spelled Hattie on her days off and sometimes in the evening before bed; there was the physical therapist; and finally there was the clinical psychologist, a specialist in trauma-aftermath who charged top dollar for weekly sessions. This was not to mention the endless minor—and not always so minor—out-of-pocket expenses for over-the-counter medicines, supplements, gadgets, orthopedic clothes, special dietary provisions, and on and on.

What would happen when the insurance ran out, with the court case still unsettled? The drunk who had t-boned Julie was a local police captain, one of "Syracuse's finest," a well-connected man who could probably keep the matter tied up in litigation for a very long time. He,

Mark, would have to take over God-knows-how-much of the work himself. Was he up to it? Did he have it in him to morph into some kind of secular saint, devoted utterly to the wellbeing of another, even someone he loved? (He *did* still love her, didn't he? It wasn't just compassion, or even pity, God help him?) Would he have to give up all hope of a flourishing career in scholarship, of writing "the great book" on Blake's German alchemical sources he had always dreamt of? Hell, he didn't know; all he knew was that he was scared shitless. Then, suddenly aware of his own fear, he would crucify himself for worrying more about his own shabby ass than his poor wife's.

They both began putting on their clothes when Mark said, "We just have to keep on keepin' on, and sooner or later it'll all work itself out. Right, my sweet?" Mark managed to squeeze this out with the weakest of wry smiles, but it was a pathetic bromide that served only to darken the mood further.

"You're the professor," Sabrina chirped with an unmistakable note of sarcasm.

"Oh no, don't do that. Please don't do that."

"Don't do what?"

"You know, don't take that snotty ironic tone. That's not called for."

"Sorry. I didn't know I was doing it … Look, I've got to get going or I'll miss my two o'clock Comp. Lit.

class," and, giving herself the air of being busy collecting her things, she ended with a perfunctory peck on Mark's cheek and a quick "Call me, okay?", and out the door she skipped.

7

The strains of the muted trumpet died away, followed by a smattering of applause from the weary dozen or so patrons at the Blue Rooster, a small jazz club in Manhattan's West Village.

"Thanks, everybody, and good night. Drive safely," crooned Dew Drop Davis, the combo's front man and spokesman. This was the musicians' cue to pack it in for the night.

"Hey, Santa, you wanna go get some breakfast?" It was the third time Art the drummer had invited the group's newcomer, one Samual "Santa" Claus, to join him and, if he again refused, would be the last. Santa was a "sideman" who played bass, a sideman being a type of itinerant musician hired to perform with a combo on an ad hoc, usually temporary, basis. He was the only whitey in the group, a tall, slim man of forty-six who had to bend over his fiddle to get the precise tone and phrasing he wanted. Decades of plucking and pulling and pressing those strings had given his fingers the tensile strength of a steelworker. He had, in fact, an overall wiry strength that showed in the way he lifted his bulky instrument by its fretboard with one hand, gently laying it inside its case just off-stage.

"Sorry, can't," said Santa, smiling as he picked up his case and headed for the back door. "I've got a date, believe it or not. Maybe next time."

"Yeah, next time ... next time," Art grumbled to himself under his breath. "Fuck next time, and fuck you, and fuck the high horse you rode in on!"

"I *heard* that," Santa laughed, pushing open the door, "something about a horse?"

"Oh *my!*" Art screamed and let out a shattering guffaw. "These walls got ears. Can't say nothin' 'round here!" And again a laugh that could pierce steel followed by his trademark staccato rimshot.

Art, however, was dead-on. You had to whisper to keep anything out of earshot of Santa. He had the heightened senses of a predator, which is what he was. Vision sharper than 20-20, able to read a license plate half a block away; hearing that could pick up a baby's cooing on the floor below; and those fingers, such fingers. Three of them could crush a beer can but those same three could as easily, with the subtlest gradations in pressure, bring out a dozen different tones on the bass. Beauty in the beast, you might say, though, truth to tell, Santa was quite easy on the female eye and could have had his choice of any number of jazz groupies—if he'd had the slightest interest, which he did not. His tall, slender stature could have modeled the stylish clothes he always wore—the high-collar leather jackets, the cashmere pullovers, the black designer T-shirts, often under a linen sport coat, the latter his chosen attire for this night. All punctuated by the fashionable amount of facial stubble.

And it was a face that turned heads, of both genders. A manly face, sculpted and aristocratic, with high cheekbones and a strong jawline that tapered at the chin, the whole framed by a thick shock of dark, ruffled hair, tousled over his forehead just a tad. And he had that killer smile available whenever he needed it, the smile that made his blue eyes twinkle with delicious mischief, the smile that had disarmed scores of innocent little boys and lured them to their doom.

No question, Santa was a handsome devil by any standard. Though forty-six, he could easily have passed for thirty-five. His youthful looks and cool manner, laconic yet friendly, gave him a subtle, low-key charisma that made it hard for anyone to stay mad at him. Which is why Art shouted in his direction as he slipped out the door, "Go on, get yo white ass outta here, Mr. Claus. We'll catch you tomorrow."

But Santa was already off and walking briskly up Christopher St. towards the PATH subway station at 9th St. He covered the two long blocks rapidly and efficiently, turning his head neither left nor right. There was nothing to see anyway at that dead hour between the end of night and dawn. The streets were empty of pedestrians. An empty taxi whizzed by, speeding for no reason he could fathom. It was mild out on this October morning, even at 3:30 a.m., prompting Santa to slip off his sport coat and carry it on a finger over his shoulder. If he hurried, he could catch the 3:44 a.m. PATH train to Hoboken and grab a couple of hours' shuteye before heading over to St. Aloysius.

The ride under the Hudson was soothing, the clacking and swaying of the train lulling him into mild spasms of pleasure as he looked forward to the events of this special morning: the waiting, the scanning and, finally, the spotting of the boy he had chosen, a fourth, possibly fifth, grader named Danny—Danny with the luminous blue eyes, the brown bangs that swept seductively across the top of his brow, the apple cheeks, the pouting lips. The boy was exquisite, a vision of puerile loveliness he had been watching and tracking intensely for almost two weeks now. Every school morning around ten minutes of eight, Danny would walk, and sometimes run, right by him on the sidewalk, backpack-bound, eager to join his classmates who would be heading en masse into the school's imposing gothic-style entrance. St. Al's was a fine Catholic grammar school run by the Sisters of Charity, good women who worked tirelessly to instill in the children a respect for the body, that "Tempel of the Lord" they each inhabited, but a respect that was way beyond their lustless, prepubescent understanding. This fact titillated him and, more often than not, drew him to the assembly yards of religious schools. The natural innocence of the boy, oblivious as it was to Sister's incessant propaganda for chastity, was a potent aphrodisiac for him. What greater thrill than to be the one to shatter that innocence.

But such fantasies were often disturbed by ghosts from the past, early memories which, ironically, were seed causes of those phantasies but that tended, when they intruded now in the present, to douse his pleasure, making him irritable and moody. Suddenly he stomped down hard with both feet on the subway-car floor, free to do so as he was its only occupant. "Fuck … fuck, fuck, FUCK!" he shouted, with such vehemence that spittle landed on the coat draped over his lap.

But his outburst only served to immerse him the more deeply in the stream of memory that now carried him along. Memories of the lazy, sultry summers and mild winters growing up in New Orleans' Mid-City district—the tiny shotgun house with the paper-thin walls and the even thinner privacy, the stolen streetcar rides on Canal St., the Christmas-tree bonfires on Orleans Avenue with everybody throwing fireworks into the blaze, creating an extravaganza. His father once beating him bloody for upping the ante with a Molotov cocktail, which had caused a fierce explosion and a flare-up of the fire that maimed a bystander. *Come here, you little, good-for-nothin' pissant! This time you've really gone and done it. Now we got trouble with the law. I'm gonna kill you! Whap! How's that feel, huh? Feel good? I'll just bet it does. Caught you with the buckle real good that time, did I? Serves you right, you stinkin' pile of merde you, you flamin' tortue! Whap! Whap! I curse the day you'ze born. You ain't never been nothin' but an affliction to me! If the Gulf wuz bourbon, wouldn't be enough to make you tolerable. Y'even make me hate the music, the sweet music, the one decent thing left me since I quit playin'. Whap! Even Miles hisself sounds like a horny tomcat out on the back fence these days. I don't know why I even bother playin' the 'Blue' anymore. You miserable, little sombitch! Don't you go crawlin' and snivelin' in the corner there! Don't you try and get away from me! How you think you gonna hide in this piece-of-shit cigar box we livin' in now?* . . .

It was still pitch dark as he emerged from the subway exit onto Hudson Place and River St. at the southeast edge of Hoboken, the mile-square city of restaurants, bars and way-overpriced condos on the Hudson. Everything was dormant, the shops and eateries dark, the newsstand shut tight. Quickly he crossed the empty cobblestone street heading towards Washington St., the town's main drag and primary shopping strip. It was just a few short blocks from there to the white, balconied three-building complex that contained his condo, across the street from Church Square Park, roughly in the middle of the city. He knew he was lucky to be staying at the Hudson Central Plaza, which, though a midscale residence that had seen better days, was still way beyond his means. He was subletting the modest efficiency apartment for $800 a month from a musician acquaintance he had met and played with for a few weeks at a Charleston jazz club years earlier. That was in his salad days when he was just starting to find his chops on the bass. "Sixto" Jackie Flave, a dexterous clarinetist from Manhattan away at the time on a southern vacation, was so named for the six toes on his right foot which he compulsively tapped six times on any downbeat. He took a shine to the good-looking kid from "New Awlins" and told him to look him up whenever he got to the Big Apple. Now Sixto was again "on sabbatical," this time somewhere in Georgia, and was more than happy to have "the kid" house-sit for him. $800 was a pittance for a flat that ran a cool $2,200 a month.

Sixto provided just the sort of adult relationship to which Santa gravitated. He was an acquaintance, a "contact," certainly not a friend. Santa had no friends, not because he was unpopular—quite the contrary, people were drawn to him and sought him out—but because he studiously avoided friendship. It did not suit his purposes. Contacts, on the other hand, individuals, mostly musicians he would meet from time to time on his endless itinerary, were vital to him. And he had many contacts, strategically located all over the country, mostly in big cities ranging from Seattle, Portland and L.A. to Denver, Omaha and Chicago to various cities in his native south and up and down the east coast. He kept in touch with these contacts by occasional text messages and the once-in-a-while "thoughtful" phone call, always careful to keep himself just barely on the social radar of the musician acquaintance in question, striking a delicate balance between amiability and distance. For what he wanted from them was not human interaction, and certainly not the entanglements of friendship, but the resources of location and opportunity such contacts unwittingly provided. It was through a recent exchange of texts with Sixto, for example, that he learned the clarinetist would be leaving Manhattan—and his condo—for a few months. This tied in nicely with his own stay at the time in nearby Atlantic City, allowing him to maintain the northbound trajectory of his current "tour."

Viewed superficially, apart from its monstrousness, Santa's life was aimless, random, lonely. No family, no friends, not even a home to speak of—just a constantly changing room or two in which to drop his bass fiddle and sleep. The fact of the matter was, however, that there was nothing aimless or random about Santa's life. It was thoroughly organized, built around a single, monolithic drive, the need to satisfy which gave it something close to an absolute force, and that force was more than powerful enough to crush any vestigial needs for human companionship. Every aspect of his life was planned out with obsessive care: the itinerary, the length of stay in a given city, the place of residence, the locations of schools and playgrounds and sports venues in the general vicinity of that residence, the securing of a hide-out for the enactment of the ritual, the scouting of victims, the days—sometimes weeks—of watching, spying, eavesdropping, the final selection, the setting of a date, the longed-for date on which the ritual could finally be enacted. Rituals generally have a religious significance, and this dark, horrific ritual was the mirror image of that, having the significance of an anti-religion. It was carried out with the same focus, the same mental absorption, the same surrender of personal intention that the medieval saints displayed who flagellated themselves before the cross. Like any phenomenon, even the totally one-pointed mind has both its dark and its light phases.

One may well wonder how a man in the grips of such an all-consuming drive could possibly restrain himself long enough to do such meticulous planning. Was he not, after all, an animal, a rapacious beast in thrall to an implacably lustful appetite? To this common-sense question one can only answer *yes and no*, because it fails to appreciate the significance of the planning as a kind of extended "foreplay." Again, in terms of ritual, as a prelude anticipating a moment of transcendent bliss. Indeed, the planning itself partook of this bliss, was in and of itself pleasurable, and no more to be hurried through than the fine wine and delicate escargot preceding the entrée of a sumptuous meal.

The Hudson Central had four elevators, one currently out of service. Riding one of the working three up to the seventh floor, he got out, turned right and let himself into the second door on the left. It was a small apartment, basically one room with an alcove-type kitchen. Sixto had left the refrigerator well stocked with beer. Famished after a gig as he always was, he made himself a cold-cut-sandwich, washing it down with a bottle of Stella Artois. Then he took off his shirt and collapsed on the sofa, pulling a quilt up over his lanky frame and setting the alarm for 6:50 a.m. He just lay there in a quasi-meditative state. There was no question of sleeping; the slowly mounting tingle of lust made that impossible. His only aim was to nurse that tingle by focusing his bare attention on it, neither ignoring it nor stimulating it, just letting it take its own course. The alarm was only intended to relieve him of the distraction of watching the clock.

He waited patiently in the van, parked midway between the school and the boy's house, two blocks either way. The optimal distance for a successful grab. He sat at the steering wheel, facing away from the school in the direction from which the boy would come. It was 7:43 and his eyes were poised falcon-like on the sidewalk in front of him. His fingers massaged the wheel in involuntary anticipation.

Ah, there he came at last, half a block away, ambling along by himself! This was a stroke of luck since the boy often walked to school with a buddy or two. His left hand gripped the front strap of his backpack as he tugged on it, trying to center the pack, which was too loosely set. Santa hopped out of the van and walked around its rear to the sliding side door at curbside, moving as casually as his excitement allowed. He felt intensely alive, the pursuit every bit as quickening as the catch. He opened the door and slid it back, pretending to search for something on the floor, all the while keeping a sharp peripheral eye trained on his approaching prey. When Danny was almost there, Santa stood up, took a deep breath, turned to the boy and went into his well-rehearsed spiel:

"Hey there, Danny! How about my luck, huh, running into you here on your way to school?" As he spoke the words of a "family friend," he carried out the critical motor actions with the requisite split-second timing, putting his arm around the boy's shoulder and "affectionately" pressing him to his abdomen as he applied the hidden chloroform-soaked handkerchief to his face.

"I was just on the phone with your dad on my way over to ..." he continued, as Danny slumped and Santa deftly scooped him up into the van, laying him down gently on the well-cushioned floor, the rear seats all having been removed. He pulled the door shut and stepped smartly around the front of the van (careful not to be too quick about it), hopping back into the front seat and driving off, away from the school. It all went so smoothly, so smartly—greeting, hug, bonhomie, drug—the boy never had a chance. And no one had seen a thing.

He headed south through Hoboken towards lower Jersey City, careful as always to obey all traffic signs. He turned west up the Holland Tunnel exit ramp and onto U.S. route 1/9 south. He was making his way arduously to the Pulaski Skyway, through some of the heaviest morning rush-hour traffic on the east coast, stretching under the Hudson from lower Manhattan to Jersey City. Also, the road on the Jersey side was, at one juncture near Journal Square, like a ghastly roller coaster ride, repeatedly looping up, down and around grease-smeared neighborhoods of urban blight —junked cars and trucks, abandoned auto parts, generators and dreary shanties.

(It was precisely this area that inspired the somewhat unfair parody of New Jersey's state motto, "The Garbage State.")

To complicate matters, he heard a soft moan coming from the boy in back. The drug was wearing off. But he was undaunted by any of it, for he had carefully planned and practiced the short drive and explored its destination many times, in all kinds of traffic, all kinds of weather. He didn't know the general area well but he knew every inch of this particular itinerary. As for the boy, he was actually glad to hear signs of life; it relieved his anxiety over a possible overdose. After all, death was supposed to close the ritual, not open it.

Finally he made his way onto the Skyway, that imposing gigantic spider leg of bridges stretching across the Passaic and Hackensack Rivers to Newark. But he wasn't going as far as Newark, slowing down about halfway across the Skyway for the Kearney peninsula off-ramp. Down the long exit he drove into an area dotted with trucking companies and truck-repair garages. No one lived there; it was strictly for freight haulers and their eighteen-wheelers, suitably located beneath the overarching Skyway. In other words, it was perfect. Also, it was only a stone's throw from the reedy brackish marshes of the southern peninsula, an ideal area for getting lost—or losing things, as Tony Soprano could attest.

As he slowly angled the van around the marshes, careful to avoid heavy swamp, he watched the boy in the rearview mirror, trying to raise himself up on an elbow. How lovely, how classical, he looked reclining there, tousled brown bangs sweeping his eyes, cheeks flushed with confusion, full lips like rose petals. Finally his eyes met Santa's in the rearview mirror as the latter pulled the van into a nook in the reeds with sufficiently solid earth. This particular location too was the result of a process of meticulous micro-planning for which no detail was too small.

He pressed the button for the CD-player on the dash and out streamed those six provocative base notes of "So What," answered by the two notes on the trumpet. Call and response—an elemental musical trope, a kind of seduction. He slipped out of his seat into the cleared-out area of the rear, stretching out right next to the boy.

"Where am I? What am I doing here? Who are you, mister?"

"It's okay, Danny. Just relax, take it easy. I'm a friend of your dad's from work. Since I was in the neighborhood when I phoned him, he asked me to pick you up from school and bring you home. Mom and dad made a snap decision this morning to take an Indian-summer vacation in the Poconos and they sent me to get you while they pack for the trip."

As he said this, he casually brushed back the boy's bangs, which further confused him, vacillating between the need to believe the man and a mounting apprehension.

"They did? They didn't tell me anything."

"As I said, it was a snap decision."

"But what happened—to me, I mean?"

"Well, you fainted as you approached me on the sidewalk. You must've skipped breakfast or something this morning. I caught you as you fell and loaded you into my van here to wait for you to come to."

"But what are we doing *here*? ... Where are we anyway? ... I want to go home! Take me home, mister!" The sedative after-effect of the drug was still strong, preventing his nervous system from keeping up with his by-now strong sense of alarm.

"That's exactly what I intend to do, Danny. But let's just hang out here for a few minutes, can we, and give you a brief rest and your folks a chance to finish packing and loading the car. That'd be the considerate thing to do, don't you think?"

This struck the boy as reasonable, and, more importantly, benign, temporarily allaying his fears, causing him to forget for the moment the bizarre circumstances in which he found himself. A considerate man, a man mindful of others' needs, wouldn't harm him, would he? The lingering effects of the drug inclined him to answer to himself: no. And then there were the man's suave, youthful looks, the careful grooming, the charming, ingratiating smile, the barest tinge of a southern drawl—all (by design) suggesting the very antithesis of the leering, drooling fiend of urban legend. The boy finally let himself take a breath.

At this point, Santa sensed from experience that this was as cooperative as the boy was likely to become, which gave him the green light to drop the ruse and proceed to the pleasure at hand. He placed his hand gently on the boy's shoulder, a stereotypical first move. The boy allowed it. In his heart of hearts Santa believed that if a boy did not flinch at this, there was at least a chance, however remote, of his allowing the entire seduction, if not to some degree participating in it. This had been his great good fortune once long ago, in New Orleans, and ever since he had longed to experience that special bliss of mutuality—deluded though it was—again. Eagerly, hungrily, he took the occasional boy's non-resistance as an expression of willingness, ignoring its obvious significance as a variation on the Stockholm syndrome. Blindly, desperately, he wanted his boys to love him. It was the grandest of all fool's errands, dooming him to abysmal frustration, for, in the moment of that one-way embrace, his body knew, even if his mind refused to, that non-resistance and willingness were entirely different worlds.

But the limpness of the boy's possum-playing did not last, for some instinct suddenly made him snap to and try to pull away. Gently he drew the boy to him and nuzzled him face to face. Ah, the feel and fragrance of those peach-fuzz cheeks. The lips so close, so inviting. The sweet breath of budding youth. He took it all in like the elixir it was for him, quickening, inflaming his senses to paroxysms of bliss almost beyond endurance. He wanted to weep. He felt close to a mystery—the mystery of the mingling, the inseparability, of pain and pleasure. He felt free of himself, free of his accursed existence, free of this rotten world.

Tenderness and lust contended together in his breast. He almost felt he could refrain from the act itself, be content with the depths of feeling he had already plumbed and somehow now withdraw, restore the boy to his life and move on. But lust pressed on implacably, fiercely, stinging him full-force with darts and pricks of ecstasy, rendering him existentially impotent, and the tenderness gave way, as it always did, to the blaze of carnality that obliterated everything but the drive for total possession. This was the moment in which he knew, again—it always surprised him—that, even more than to be loved by a boy, he needed total control over him, love's depraved sublimation. He realized anew that a boy's resistance could be an even sweeter, finer elixir than his willing, indeed eager, surrender. The sense of total control over an opposed and terrified living body, its complete domination, gave him a matchless thrill, and his awareness too that the boy, even in his terror, somehow appreciated the absolute quality of this moment, both of them knowing, as it were, together, that power here was the whole world, almost no matter who possessed it— this awareness spiked the feeling beyond ecstasy itself, to the brink of a dark *unio mystica*. Even death itself must now be anticlimactic.

When he was finished, he pulled out and stretched out on his back next to the boy, who lay on his stomach, naked and whimpering, his head turned away. He lolled in the afterglow, but only for a few minutes; the remainder of the ritual, indelibly fixed as it now was, roused him to act smartly and swiftly. He rolled back over onto the boy, who seemed at first to shudder but then just lay there. Gently, caressingly, he messaged the boy's neck and shoulders, smoothed his hair and kissed him tenderly on his left ear. After a moment, he brought his hands loosely together around the boy's neck, from behind. Then, wrapping one hand around the smooth neck and placing the other firmly on the forehead, he snapped adroitly in opposite directions. It was like cracking a walnut. The boy was dead; it was over.

Just as he always entered his boys from behind, he always killed them from behind as well—*a tergo*, as his

Jesuit ethics professor used to say in one of his frequent titillating examples of catechistic sins of the flesh. He could not abide eye contact at the moment of death, because he was not a murderer at heart but only out of necessity. In this way the hot shame of murder was a bit cooled by its facelessness, not entirely unlike a drone pilot who drops his payload on "he knows not whom" from an electronic console thousands of miles away.

He reached forward and grabbed the reinforced plastic garbage bag from the glove compartment, then drew it carefully over the still, small body. He always used the bag, rejecting out of hand a direct dumping of the naked corpse, as this would have offended his deep, unconscious need of atonement. All he knew was that, since he had taken everything from it, he owed this body a decent disposal. It had to be neat, clean, orderly. The fiddle case, which was part of the exculpatory ritual, he lifted out of a sub-floor storage space, placing it next to the body. He opened it and laid the boy snugly into it, smoothing out the bag's wrinkles and giving the head a final soft stroke, then closing it and setting the spring locks.

And so it was that he carried his latest victim, concealed like all his predecessors in this "jazz coffin," into the tall reeds of South Kearney on foot, proceeding straight to the hidden grave he had dug deep in the marsh a few days earlier. He removed little Danny in his bag from the case and nestled him down into the hole. Then he took his tool-belt spade and filled in the hole with mud. Another death march, another secret buried—under the spider-leg skyway.

8

"**M**ore rice, Julie?" Hattie asked, holding the fork up toward her mistress, though not too close. Her piercing laugh caused the dining room chandelier to tinkle, obliterating Julie's 'No thanks.'

"I'm sorry, Miz Julie, I guess I'm just not used to calling you 'Julie' yet," Hattie said, shaking her head. "It still feels kind of uppity, like I was bulldozing my way into the family."

"No bull, Hattie" Mark quipped. "You *are* a member of this family and have been from the get-go. After all, if you were just part of the help, would we have finagled you into cooking dinner for us once a week? Absolutely not! We treat you with the same disregard with which we treat each other. That's family love. So, you see, you *must* be a member."

"Oh, go on now," Hattie laughed. "It's my pleasure. I love these dinner gatherings; it's so seldom we're all able to be together. Most evenings I'm just sitting at home watching the news and heating up the leftover Chinese take-out ... What's the matter, Nathaniel, not hungry tonight?"

Nate, sitting across from the aide, shrugged and continued playing with his food. He was not into the spirit of the family bread-breaking this evening; he had other things on his mind, like the two big tests he was facing tomorrow, in math and in social studies. He was a conscientious student, almost to a fault, some might say, and was anxious to get to his room and hit the books. What was really bothering him, however, was Mr. Becker, his math teacher, turning him down flat when he asked for a personal postponement of the test so he wouldn't have two on the same day. He had the distinct impression the teacher thought him a shirker, and this was preying on his mind. He hated being thought of that way, especially by a teacher he respected.

"Anything the matter, sweetheart?" his mother asked. "School go okay today?"

"It was all right, I guess," Nate answered, now staring at Duncan, who was perched on his mother's lap. Actually, he'd been sitting there on and off all day, as Nate, preoccupied as he was that afternoon, had forgotten to relieve the little guy of "guard duty" on getting home from school. "But I've got two major tests tomorrow—math and social studies—so I need to do a lot of studying tonight. May I be excused from the table?"

"Of course you may," Julie smiled at him. "And why don't you take Duncan with you. Who knows, maybe he can help you study, she added jokingly."

"Yeah, right," the boy scoffed.

"Oh, no, no, Nathaniel, your mother's right, absolutely right," Hattie interjected, putting down her table napkin. "Where I come from school children use things like stuffed animals and statues and pictures as icons—good luck charms, you might say—to help them learn. They sort of act like connections to knowledge—or maybe 'filters' is a better word. They help filter out all that is unimportant and steer the gist of it straight from your books into your brain where it sits 'marinating' overnight, so to speak. And then it comes pouring out onto your test paper in its richest flavor."

"Hattie, your marinade metaphor has spiked my appetite again," Mark quipped as he leaned towards the platter containing the Haitian steak dish Hattie had cooked for a second helping. It was a quick recipe requiring only brown sugar, cloves and sour orange. Mark was very fond of both Hattie and her cooking; he had come to depend on her, psychologically as well as professionally: She took the edge off the tedium of Julie's days and served as a buffer between them at certain awkward moments, such as when he would walk in after dinner following one of those late "ad hoc meetings" of the English department. He also knew Hattie needed to feel needed and was careful to shower her with compliments at every opportunity. "Hattie, this is the most delicious steak I've ever tasted!"

"Oh pooh, Professor Driscoll," Hattie said, waving her hand in mock protest, "you say that every time I make this dish."

"Well, I guess that just means it gets better every time you make it, wouldn't you say?" Mark replied with a big grin.

Again Hattie's cackle seemed to make the chandelier quiver. "Oh, you're a smooth one, Professor, that's a smooth line you've got there." Mark and Julie laughed.

And again, a distracted Nate asked to leave the table. He had decided not to bring up the matter of his concern over Mr. Becker's possible suspicion of his motives. He was learning to be more self-reliant, to not go running to his overburdened parents with every little personal problem. He knew they needed him to do more for himself now, to grow up a little faster than either of them would have liked, given current circumstances.

"Sure, slugger, go and study," his father answered this time. "And yes, do take Duncan with you. You never know. As Pascal's wager has it, better to believe and be wrong than not believe and be wrong, or something close to that. Besides, the alchemists of olden times in

Europe firmly believed in the power of certain amulets, and even of animal spirit guides? 'Totems,' they called them. So why not Duncan? If Hattie's as good a voodooist as she is a cook—and I have no reason to doubt it—then Duncan's the right study partner for you ... Go ahead, now. Off with you."

Yet another resounding chortle came from Hattie, partly in reaction to the compliment and partly out of delight in being mentioned in the same breath as that Pascal gentleman, who certainly must be somebody important. Gently she took Duncan from Julie's lap and handed him to Nate, who made off with him upstairs to his room.

Hattie began clearing the dishes, but Mark immediately placed his hand on hers, protesting, "Oh, no you don't. As chief cook and bottle washer, you are *not* a member of the cleanup committee. I'll take care of that."

"But Professor D., I'm sure you have important work to do. Please, just allow me—"

"—Absolutely not! It's true, I do have a bunch of midterm papers to grade, so naturally I'm looking for a good excuse to procrastinate. This one is perfect. You, my dear, are dismissed for the evening," he said with mock-snootiness, looking down his nose at her and shooing her away with the back of his hand.

"Well, all right, I guess. Is there anything I can do for you or get for you before I leave, Julie?"

"No, Hattie," Julie answered, "you've had a long day and need your rest. Besides, I'm in good hands here with my two men, so off you go."

"Yes, ma'am," the aide nodded and left the room to get her things before heading home.

Both Mark and Julie followed her exit with their eyes, as if in anticipation of their privacy. Something between them was in the air.

Ignoring the dishes, Mark sat down next to his wife, covered her folded hands with one of his and smiled warmly. "Sweetheart," he began, "you know that, among all our other problems, we have this nasty ongoing suit against that police captain to deal with. It's just been dragging on and on with one continuance after another and we have no idea when we'll be getting a firm trial date."

"A settlement is out of the question, I suppose?" she said, turning her wheelchair so as to face Mark more directly.

"The lawyer says they're not offering anything near what your condition calls for—not to mention the man's clear culpability. The department is even disputing the breathalyzer test results, claiming the equipment may have been defective, or misused or something. Can you believe it? . . . In any case, it's all a lot of legal mumbo jumbo meant to drag the process out ad nauseam, in the hope, I'm sure, that at some point we'll just cave out of exhaustion and frustration and settle for less … The bastards! 'Serve and protect'—yeah, right. Tell me, who's getting protected?"

"Easy, Mark. What's the point of speculating on their motives? I doubt very much they're as diabolical as you're imagining," Julie said, smiling wryly.

"Don't forget, Julie," he went on, ignoring her, "they're 'town,' we're 'gown.' The locals have always been wary of us liberal, commie, pinko eggheads up on the hill here. As my T.A. Eric put it recently, 'we're met with overt civility and covert hostility.' It's a kind of classism and right now I'm afraid we're on the wrong end of it. They're not going to make it easy for us."

It pained Mark deeply to bring these matters up with Julie, which he felt could only add to her burden. It added to his own burden of shame and guilt as well: after all, even though Julie had been earning more than he before the accident, he was still, in his own eyes and by the light of his own conditioning, "the man of the family," the provider, and, as such, should be sparing his poor wife all concern over money, financial security, the future, etc. But the fact was, he couldn't, for the simple, embarrassing reason that he was almost financially incompetent; Julie was, by default and by natural inclination, the bookkeeper in the family. He had never had the slightest interest in, nor aptitude for handling, money, in any of its forms—CD's, IRA's, even checking accounts. They all baffled him. Oh, he was able to write a check all right, but balancing the checkbook was her job. The net result of all this was that he relied utterly on Julie's practical savvy in making all big financial decisions. The irony of it, to which his pride was blinding him, was that Julie, for her own self-esteem, would have welcomed any problem, personal or otherwise, that Mark saw fit to bring to her. She felt his scrupulous efforts to spare her the slightest concern over anything were misguided and not doing either of them any good. And so it was that she was all ears, and all empathy, now, in this moment, as Mark struggled to express to her his worries over their financial future. She loved him for his candor, for his courage to rely on her.

"Don't worry about it, hon" she consoled. "We're not going anywhere; we can afford to wait them out."

"But that's just it, babe. Can we? Can we really? We're going through the no-fault money like water. Soon we're going to need the big bucks coming from that judgment, don't you think?" He asked her this, torn by conflicting feelings of anxiety and chagrin. He needed assurance, needed it for some semblance of financial peace of mind, and there was no one else to give it. But then she was happy to give it, for his sake using words that perhaps ventured beyond what she secretly thought prudent: "Not to worry, sweetheart, the case is open and shut. I don't think they'll get another continuance and we've got a barracuda for a lawyer. We've just got to be patient and hang in there."

My God, he thought, *look who's telling whom to be patient and hang in there. Have I ever had to say that to her, ever, even once? No, not even once!* And he lashed himself yet again over the tryst with Sabrina, knowing full well that he didn't have it in him to end it.

Gently he brushed back a blonde lock from her forehead, then softly squeezed her hand, noticing as he always did its peculiar feel, now so akin to an inanimate object.

"Well, I think I'll go out onto the deck for a quick smoke and then I'd better get to those dishes," he said, smiling. "They're not going to do themselves." He immediately regretted using that particular cliché with its oblique reference to her helplessness. But she either didn't pick up on it or, more likely, just ignored it, turning her chair to head for the living room and a little private time before bed.

As she rolled herself into the spacious living room with its soothing blue damask drapes, a haven from which all electronic devices had been banned except for the little-used TV, she was feeling a lingering distress whose source she could not pinpoint. It had been there all day, hovering on the fringes of her awareness, and now, all other distractions having fallen away, it came to the fore. She sat there for a while staring at the filigree pattern in the center of the oriental rug, just feeling her malaise with the fingertips of consciousness, without trying to analyze it or trace it back—just inviting it to disclose itself. This was a sort of meditational approach to problems she had read about and been practicing for a while. Her condition was, in any case, inclining her more and more these days to the interior than the exterior life, to the life of non-verbal awareness and sensitivity, to the inner life of things; and she was just now beginning to perceive the aura of the enormous riches contained therein, beginning to sense the border of an awareness that had no firm boundaries.

But on this particular evening the interior approach was yielding nothing; her mind was like the static of a radio stuck between stations. So after a while she gave it up and went back to the default mode of ordinary thinking and examining. Her first thoughts were of Mark and the stress he was obviously under: his worry over her condition, the mounting debt, his stalled career as a scholar, Nate's well-being, and on and on. But then she had just been with him in the dining room, letting him air his anxieties and soothing the edges off them, or so she hoped. She somehow felt it was not the pressure Mark was under, severe as it was, that was troubling her now, that he would be all right as long as he could rely on her inner strength and sympathetic ear. And these she was ready to offer to the full, especially since there was so little she could do for him now sexually, beyond watching him pleasure himself. (And if he sought relief from the physical craving with another woman, could she really blame him, as long as he remained faithful in his heart?)

But if not Mark, then who, or what? It occurred to her that this elusive sense of distress was not new, that it had crept into her on several occasions in recent weeks. It was always the same, identifiable by its mystifying quality, its apparent baselessness. She recognized it more by what her intuition ruled out as a cause than by what it ruled in.

On impulse, while puzzling over it, she rolled over to the foot of the stairs, looked up and called out, "Nate! Nate, honey!" Hearing no response, she repeated the call, upping the volume a notch. Again silence. The third call was loud, intense, urgent.

"Yeah?" Finally she heard the muffled response from within his room and breathed a sigh of relief, without knowing why.

"Nate, come out for a minute, will you, please?"

Nate's door flew open and he leapt out to the upstairs bannister, leaning his bulky social studies text on it and draping himself over that, his thumb still inside the book keeping his page. He liked to read his textbooks while pacing his room—it helped him concentrate—and when called out would usually bring the closed book with him, thumb in place.

"Nate, don't put all that weight on your thumb. You'll bruise it."

Instantly he pulled the stressed digit out and began flapping it up and down as if in severe pain, yelling out, "Ooh, it's broken! It's busted! It's smashed! I'll never play Chopin's 'Minute Waltz' again!"

"What do you mean?" she replied, playing along, "You've never played it before, so what's the big deal?"

"Oh yeah, right. I forgot," he said, rounding out the shtick. "Anyway, I'm sure you didn't call up to check on the condition of my thumb, Mom. What is it? I've got so much studying to do."

Suddenly, Julie realized she had no good reason at all for interrupting Nate's homework session. "Yes, I know," she said, "and I'm sorry, kiddo. Actually, I was just testing my voice, seeing how loud I'd have to call out for you to hear me from inside your room. Turns out it's much louder than I thought ... Another boon from the calamity that keeps on giving," saying this last more to herself than Nate, who was already pacing up and down the upstairs hallway, having resumed his reading of the chapter subsection on *Jazz Culture of New Orleans*.

9

Mark strode into his classroom in H. B. Crouse Hall, ignoring his students, and went straight to his desk, slamming his books down on its sterile lacquered top. He looked like a man with a bone to pick, and indeed he was: He had just read an office email from the Dean informing him that a student had complained to him about "Professor Driscoll's increasingly frequent tardiness and missed classes." The student, of course, remained anonymous, in line with college policy, but Mark had a pretty good idea who the malcontent was. He was sitting right there in front of him on the left fringe of a group of some seventeen juniors and seniors, the majority English majors, who made up his class for "ETS 401: From Blake to Byron."

"Mr. Katz," Mark queried without looking at him, "according to William Blake, what class of beings enjoys residing in hell?" Evan Katz was a tall kid from the Bronx with a shock of bushy black hair who took sadistic delight in using his superior intelligence to needle his professors. He was a sort of teenage Norman Mailer type; quick-witted and articulate, he seemed, like Mailer, prepared to spar with anyone, with either his words or his fists. Pick your weapon. He also had literary pretentions and doubtless also the talent to back them up. Rumor had it he was writing a novel. Mark had taken an instant dislike to him two years earlier when he signed up as an English major, and it seems the dislike was mutual.

"Well, Mr. Katz? *Cat* got your tongue?" Mark beamed an arrogant smile to the young man as he tossed off this quip, aware that Katz had caught his pun on the German meaning of his name. But Mark picked the wrong day to mess with the Young Turk, whose tongue was in top form.

"Oh, possibly all of us masochistic students sitting here in this class, Professor Driscoll."

There was an immediate outburst of laughter, along with some trailing oohs and ahs, as the class reacted with spontaneous admiration to Katz's stinging riposte. Some simply admired the guy's cheek, while others not only admired him but also pitied Mark. He had taken one on the chin and felt totally disarmed, or at most half-armed, in the battle of wits. He realized that verbal jousting with Katz on this particular day could lead to no good. So he did the only thing he could, giving the upstart kid a smirk, gently withdrawing from the skirmish and returning to the question at hand. But now he was frazzled, knocked a bit off center, and no longer feeling confident of making his lead-off point stick the way he wanted it to.

So he did what an insecure professor usually does when he senses he's losing the class's good will: He answered his own question, a strategy that rarely goes well: "In *The Marriage of Heaven and Hell* the poet tells us that devils love it in hell because they are at home there; they're in a place that nurtures and encourages their evil desires; they're right where they belong. Angels, on the other hand, despise and fear hell."

"So, is Blake saying we should toss morality overboard and act on all our evil impulses?" asked a minion of Katz's sitting next to the master.

"No, not exactly …" Mark answered hesitantly. "It's subtler than—"

"—Because that would make him just another libertine, like de Sade. And a society of libertines—"

"—No, no, you're missing the point here," Mark protested, but it was too late because Katz then piled on with, "And how do you read that other outrageous pronouncement of Blake's, 'Sooner murder an infant in its cradle than nurse unacted desires?' To me this clearly advocates stopping at nothing—even infanticide—to clear a path for satiating one's personal cravings. Don't you see it that way, Professor?"

"Well, no," Mark stammered, cursing Blake's shock-effect ambiguities under his breath. "What Blake's really saying there is that we have to find a way to relate to our own dark or shadow side, to come to terms with our rejected selves and all the energy tied up in its seething urges. You know, that we're not just paragons of virtue ..." And on he staggered, laboring hard, and largely unsuccessfully, to bring home a coherent, convincing argument and move on, as quickly as possible, to something else.

By the end of the hour, an exhausted Professor Driscoll had decided that in future he would remove *The Marriage of Heaven and Hell* from the course syllabus and replace it with *The Songs of Innocence and of Experience*, completely ignoring the fact that the latter collection was every bit as mystifying and morally provocative as the former.

He took the elevator up to the department's common room to grab a cup of coffee. On entering he found the room engaged in its usual midday buzz of faculty and T.A.'s, plus a few undergraduate students courting the one or the other. Informal one-on-one conferences were being held at the long table in the center, brown-bag lunches were also being eaten there and the Xerox machines lined up against the walls were all going full blast. Bill Reinhardt, a Milton specialist with whom Mark was friendly, was operating one of them and gave a friendly greeting as Mark passed by. "Professor Driscoll, how's your morning going?"

"Oh, I've had worse, Bill; I've had better, but I've had worse," Mark replied wanly, patting Reinhardt on the back just as he spotted Sabrina sitting by herself in a corner. He headed straight over to her. She was correcting quizzes and hadn't seen him come in.

"Well, aren't you the diligent little worker bee? So early in the day and so busy," he said smiling.

She looked up and gave a snicker. "Well, we can't all keep the banker's hours of a professor now, can we?" she teased.

He sat down next to her and sighed audibly, a signal inviting her to ask him what was the matter. But she didn't take the bait, pretending rather to be immersed in the work. He would have to ask for attention directly, which somewhat annoyed him. Deep down he knew that she was losing her idealized image of him, that his clay feet were starting to show with all the stress. He resented her for pulling back from his vulnerable side, which he had risked allowing her to see in recent meetings in the expectation of evoking her empathy, her nurturing capacity. But he was ignoring how young she was, how naturally oblivious she still was to the world of adult suffering, and, while she was by no means entirely lacking in empathy, he also recognized that he was witnessing the slow, sobering death of a crush.

However, he also chose to ignore his own recognition and press on. He felt out of options. "By the way, Sabby, do you know that fellow, Evan Katz, one of our brighter majors?"

"Who doesn't? Everybody around here knows Evan."

"Oh, really? And how's that, pray tell?"

"You must have heard about him. He's one of the gods—maybe *the* god—among undergraduate intellectuals—smart as a whip, brilliant really, writing a novel. And he's read *every*thing. Even the graduate students give him a wide berth," she said laughing, as she gave the quiz on top of the batch a grade of "76" and circled it in red, then giving Mark her full attention.

"I see," Mark said, pretending to be impressed. "Actually, I do know him somewhat. He's a student in my lit class, and you're quite right: he *can* be a bit of a challenge. Not that I mind that, on the contrary, but—"

"Ah, I get it now," Sabrina broke in, nodding several times as if something was suddenly crystal clear. "You've been 'katztrated,' haven't you? ... Poor boy! Don't let it get you down. Fortunately, the trauma is quite temporary, and anyway you're in good company ... So now another faculty member is added to the list of Katz's intellectual victims. Let's see now: Katz: 3, English Department: zero!" she chirped, writing the score in the air with her magic marker.

"Oh, come on, Sabrina," Mark protested, hoping the flushed feeling in his face wasn't showing. "Give me a break. The guy is a raging narcissist. He's in love with himself and his own prodigious learning. He wears that cultured veneer like a crown—'King Evan I' is who he is, and we're all his mediocre minions, I suppose. He's insufferable! I can't stand the bright ones who seek only the intellectual joust, always looking to measure lances, if you catch my drift. They never ask a question in good faith; there's always a dagger hidden between the words."

"Easy, Mark, easy. Take a breath," she urged him, momentarily dropping the snarky attitude. "This can't all be about Evan Katz, can it? Just don't let him get to you; he's not that big a deal," she soothed.

"Oh, I know. It's not really him; he's just the straw bending my camel's back. Actually, sometimes I do feel like Nietzsche's camel, alone in the dessert, straining under the load that's been strapped onto me ..." Then he stopped himself, not wanting to get too maudlin too often with her, even though he knew in his bones that no restraint, no strategy of any kind, was going to reverse the inevitable dire course of their liaison.

He switched tacks: "Anyway, today's class was supposed to be one for the highlight reel, the first grand climax of the course: I was all set to reveal Blake to them as a sort of proto-Freud—you know, a great intuitive psychologist a century before depth psychology even existed. Blake knew all about the evils of repression and I was going to shock them with his outrageous pronouncement in *The Marriage of Heaven and Hell,* 'Sooner murder an infant in its crib than nurse unacted desires,' and then triumphantly explain to the class that the poet is using exaggeration, an extreme case, to warn us a la Freud and psychoanalysis of the harm we do ourselves by denying the presence of these dark, anti-social urges lurking in all of us. You know, the idea that repression doesn't tame the demons; it just makes them stronger. But, of course, Katz just had to preempt my neat little scheme by bringing up Blake's line about infanticide ahead of time and turning the whole discussion in the direction of ethics and the amorality of poets and how Plato banned poets from the republic and all that kind of insipid crap. Jesus Christ! ... The thing is, I knew he didn't give a flying fuck about a single thing he was saying, but I just got so bogged down in his sanctimonious—not to mention hypocritical—arguments, and the endless back-and-forth, you know, that I completely blew my shot at presenting Blake as a heroic and very modern thinker—someone far ahead of his time."

"Oh, don't worry about it, hon, you'll get another chance, if not with this group, then the next," she said in a tone that struck him as cheerily dismissive, stuffing her sheaf of quizzes into a leather pouch and standing up. "Well, I'm off to the library. Got a seminar paper to work on … Later." And off she went. No "Got time for a quickie today?", no "When can I see you?", not even a "Call me." He watched her leave the common room, turning her pretty head as she exited and calling out with a giggle to someone in the corridor, to whom she then apparently rushed.

Slowly Mark got up himself, not sure what to make of his chat with Sabrina, yet knowing in some remote corner of his mind exactly what to make of it. He walked to his office, collected a few books and materials for working at home and headed for the stairs. He rarely took the elevator down, even though it was six flights. As he hit each landing, he would habitually glance out the big gothic window onto the main quad below. Now, as he passed the third-floor window after looking out, he was suddenly stopped in his tracks, feeling the emotional equivalent of a swift punch to the solar plexus. He stepped back, cautiously, slowly, deliberately, and looked out again.

And there he saw it, the confirmation of all his symptoms of doubt and anxiety. Down below, strolling diagonally across the quad, was a chilling sight, a grim specter, a knife-twisting vision the likes of which he could never have imagined even in his moments of deepest despair. It was Sabrina, with none other than Evan Katz, the two of them casually strolling across the sunny green, immersed in lively conversation, he doing most of the talking, animated, crowing, gesticulating, she listening with rapt attention, laughing at each, doubtless witty, remark, each *bon mot*, as Katz would have called it in his snide, smug, arrogant French. Mark had to turn away, gasping for air and bracing himself against the adjacent wall in defense against his mounting panic. It wasn't merely that they were strolling together, damning enough though that was; it was that he couldn't think of a single reason to doubt that the object of their private little laugh fest was ... he.

10

The sun was already beating hard against the plain white tombstones, though it was only ten in the morning. The two elderly ladies lingered behind the other mourners who were moving towards their cars parked nearby. They stood together in their frumpy black shifts over the freshly dug grave, into which the unadorned pinewood coffin was now being lowered. They talked quietly and wore sunglasses to protect themselves from the glare coming off the ubiquitous white.

"I'm lucky I was even able to get him in here," the shorter woman said, shaking her head in disgust. "Holt isn't much more than a potter's field, you know. Thank God I found that burial insurance policy, cuz if you don't get into Holt, I don't know where you go. So that's at least one thing he *did* take care of. It don't surprise me none either cuz he was always sayin' as how he wanted to be buried in the same ground as his idol, Buddy Bolden—the best damn horn man Bourbon Street ever did see, he'd always say. Although, it's funny cuz I don't think he could be layin' much further away from the man than he is. Buddy's sort of in the middle—way over there, see, the biggest monument in the yard. The only grave in the place above ground, too, looks like."

"Sure does, but tell me, Constance, how're you holdin' up?" the taller woman asked, changing the subject. "I'm so sorry you had to handle all the arrangements for Fred by yourself, but, as I told you on the phone, I just couldn't get away yesterday, what with Jack havin' to go up to Baton Rouge for his chemo and all. I'd've given anything to be with my baby sister yesterday. You know that, don'tcha?" she said, giving her sister a squeeze around the waist.

Constance dried a tear with her lace handkerchief and replied, somewhat absently, as though talking to herself, "Well, it's strange, so strange. I'm certainly glad it's over—not just the illness, the cirrhosis, the alcoholic breakdown, the D.T.'s at the end and so on, but the whole marriage, the whole damn life. It's like wakin' up from a lifelong nightmare. Today, when I go back into that house, for the first time it'll be my place and I'll be my own woman. Can't remember when that's ever been. So, from that angle, I guess it's the end of an age of war and the beginning of peace. Still—and this is the strange part," she said, turning to her sister, "as much as I hated him and as scared to death of him as I was, there's somethin' in me that actually misses the bastard." She uttered the word "misses" with a quizzical emphasis, almost as if she were amused by the grotesque paradox of it. "For all his rottenness, for all the beatin's he put on me and—God forgive him—on poor Sammy, I miss that no-good bum, I really do. Don't make no sense at all, does it? The worst of it, though, is the powerful hate I bear him for what he did to my boy—no matter that Sammy was as tough as he was and never showed no weakness, never begged for mercy, not even once. I can't tell you the guilt that haunts me over that, and will follow me right into my own hole in this field … I know, I know, I should've taken the boy and run away to one of them shelters for battered women, but there was always somethin' holdin' me back, I don't know what it was, don't ask. Maybe my crazy feelin' for him kept me hopin' he would change—so that's on me all right. Plus, my job at Loyola forced me to leave Sammy with him during the day, for years. God knows what happened in all those thousands of hours I was away, but I just couldn't quit. *He* wasn't bringin' in no money and, besides, I wanted the free tuition for Sammy that the employees got as a benefit. I wanted Sammy to get educated so he could get out of here one day. And, well, he's certainly done that, and then some. I can't remember the last time he called. And I can rarely reach him. His gigs keep him so busy."

"I imagine so," the sister said wistfully. "Must be goin' on eight or nine years since *I* seen the boy."

"The *boy*, as you call him, is all of forty-six years old," Constance chuckled, and the two sisters shared a wan laugh as they carefully stepped away from the grave, arm in arm for mutual support. Just then, as they turned to go, an odd rush of wind came out of nowhere and swept over the gravesite, ruffling the black veils of the two women and causing them to hold fast to each other. It was gone in a flash.

"My word, where did *that* come from?"

"Must be some weather comin' in off the Gulf," Constance mused. As she said this, she spotted out of the corner of her eye an odd object, tiny and solitary, lying on the ground, not more than a hand's breadth from the grave opening. Its pinkish color set it off against the grave's bright-green felt border.

"What's this?" Constance asked, bending over to pick it up.

"Must've come in on that gust," the sister speculated.

"Sorta looks like part of one of them voodoo dolls they sell over to Marie Laveau's, don't it? Maybe a finger or a leg," Constance speculated as she turned it over and examined it. The pink, clothbound digit was about two inches long, sealed at one end and ripped open at the other, as though pulled from the doll's hand and thrown away. The cotton stuffing, of a reddish hue, protruded slightly from the open end.

As the two women walked away, Constance discarded the tiny effigy on the path, whereupon a second gust of wind, this one milder, instantly rushed by, pushing the thing along the ground and blowing it straight into the grave. Taken aback, Constance stepped back to the hole and peered over, to find it resting on the middle of the coffin lid. She looked up and thought for a minute, finally noticing the gravediggers, in their soiled green uniforms, standing discreetly off in the distance, chatting among the gravestones. Further down the path sat the backhoe, idling, waiting.

She walked back to her sister and again took her arm, and the two women strolled in the opposite direction, toward the exit of this poor man's City of the Dead.

11

He could see the masts of the yachts looming over the boathouses and the scruffy pines in the marina. It was his first time in Newport, on a brilliant and balmy late October afternoon. He was impressed by the chic shops and bistros in the refurbished brick buildings on Thames Street, one of the oldest and most historic main streets on the East Coast. He walked north on "Tames," as the locals insisted on pronouncing it, his fiddle case in his left hand and a piece of note paper in his right. On the paper was scrawled "Higby Jazz Café and Eatery, 13 Higby St." He came to a corner and turned right onto Higby, instantly spotting the big cup and saucer on the café's sign overhanging the narrow sidewalk.

On entering through the heavy oaken door, he stood still for a moment, waiting for his eyes to adjust to the dim lighting. "I'm looking for Rick Esposito," he said finally to a tall, gangly youth in a white server's apron coming towards him.

"Oh, Rick's in the back room. The band's on break from rehearsal right now, but I'll see if he's busy. Who should I say is asking for him?"

"Tell him it's Sam Claus, aka 'Santa,' will you? He may be expecting me."

"Sure thing. Say, did you say 'Santa?' 'Santa … Claus?'"

"That's right. Every day is Christmas for me, pal," Santa said laughing. It was his usual rejoinder. He was never bored or irritated by people's reaction to his name. On the contrary, it tickled him. It helped break the ice and set a congenial tone. Such things were important.

While waiting for Rick, he took off his black leather jacket and looked around the barroom, which adjoined the spacious dining room with its band platform in the far corner. Through the open double-door he could see two or three musicians hanging around inside, chatting on break. The place had a sort of tacky, upscale elegance, with a maritime décor; the barroom had a huge ship's wheel on the wall opposite the bar and several paintings and murals of seascapes on all the walls. Also seashells and fishing nets were hung here and there. It was not to Santa's taste, but then neither was the smooth jazz repertory that identified the group, named after its leader, Rick. On the grapevine Rick Esposito was known as a poor man's Chuck Mangione, a Mangione wannabe, down to the long hair and scruffy beard, who played soft trumpet as if it had sand in it. Some people liked the effect; as for Santa, he would put up with it because he needed the job.

"Hey, you must be Santa!" Esposito beamed, coming out of the back room and extending his right hand. "Nice to meet you. I'm Rick Esposito. I've heard a lot about you from Manny." He was short, slim and forty-ish and had on a PawSox jersey over raggedy jeans.

"Nice to meet you, Rick … Oh yeah, Manny and I go way back. We played New Awlins, St. Louis, Chicago and I don't know how many other places together, back in the nineties and early aughts," Santa said smiling broadly, thus commencing the slick and, by now, almost unconscious process of ingratiating himself with a prospective employer.

"You'll have to tell me all about it," Rick said, turning towards the back room and waving Santa to come along. "Come on, let's make ourselves comfortable while we talk."

They entered a small, plain room with a cluttered desk in one corner, a refrigerator in the other, and a round wooden table and chairs in the center. Rick motioned Santa to take a seat. "Soft drink? Beer? Whiskey?" he offered. "We've got it all."

"Thanks, I'll have some bottled water, if you have it," Santa answered.

"Ah, very good, Mr. Claus. Excellent! You've passed the first test of your interview," Rick laughed, retrieving a bottle of Poland Spring from the fridge.

"You forget," Santa replied smoothly, "I'm a seasoned sideman. I could smell that one a mile away. But you needn't worry, Sir Richard, I never touch the stuff."

Rick laughed loud and clear from his gut, already half under the spell of Santa's charisma. "That's Sir *Rick* to you," he said, enjoying the banter.

"So tell me, Santa, what brings you to our fair city? Not many people come to Newport in the Fall. The jazz fest is in July. Shouldn't you be traveling in the opposite direction?"

"Well, sure I should," Santa said agreeably, "but I guess in some ways I'm a contrarian. Like with the seasons, for example. I go north in the winter and south in the summer. You see, I grew up in New Awlins with all that heavy heat … I got used to the heat—I had to since my folks couldn't afford an a.c.—in fact, I even came to love it. It seems the sweltering somehow stirs my creative juices. But strangely, the same thing goes for the cold, for the frigid north. I love the cold too. The snow invigorates me and wakes up my musical instincts, just in a different way from the heat, but with the same intensity, the same … well, passion, I guess. What can I say, Rick? I'm weird. I love extremes."

"Speaking of creative juices, how about a little audition, for the second—and last—part of your interview?" Rick quipped. "Now don't misunderstand, Manny's okay is enough for me, see, but I just want to get a sense of your style, your game, so to speak. Besides, I only own a small part of the joint and my partners insist I do it."

"Hey, no need to apologize for doing your job, man. I'm glad to oblige," Santa said affably, taking his fiddle case from the aproned youth who had brought it in from the barroom.

"Let's go into the dining room so I can introduce you to the rest of the Higby Street Heat, okay?" Rick said, explaining to Santa on the way that their regular bassist, Brownie Biggio, had had to take a four-to-six-week leave to take care of some personal business, that Santa's timing was just perfect, and so on.

There were handshakes all around as the four players sized up the new man. All looked visibly impressed by the studly new arrival in the cool black turtleneck. There remained only the audition itself, which Santa, with great skill, nailed as he had scores of others before. He plucked and thumped his way brilliantly through the opening chords of "So What," supporting Rick on the trumpet.

Rick waved him off after about a dozen bars, saying "Hey, nice chops, Christmas man! You've got some digits there. We've got a nice long gig here; then we hit the road for a while. When can you start?"

"How about right now?" Santa said obligingly, and the drummer, Ted, a boyish-looking, curly-headed Irishman, shouted, "Yeah—all right!" and clapped his approval. The others laughed and followed suit.

Handing Santa a sheaf of charts, Rick informed him that they were an eclectic mix of mostly smooth-jazz and fusion tunes, favoring Mangione and Alpert, but also a few of his own compositions, thank you very much, such as the slow, soulful *Autumn Riffs* and the more up-tempo *Newport Rhapsody*, both of which he claimed he was in the process of negotiating to have published. Santa took the charts, acting duly impressed ("Oh, wow, that's terrific"), but he was well aware that Rick was probably just one of the thousands of pipe-dreaming, self-promoting artists he had met on the circuit.

Santa joined in for the second half of rehearsal and had no problem fitting in. Around five Rick called it quits, sent the group home and came over to him, asking, "Say, Christmas man, how are you fixed for accommodations?"

"I'm at a motel a few blocks from here—the Osprey, I think it's called," Santa answered, shutting his fiddle case and putting on his jacket.

"Well, why don't we drive over there and pick up your stuff? You can stay with us for the few days it takes you to find something more settled," Rick said, slapping Santa on the back.

"Oh no, I couldn't impose—"

"—No imposition at all, man. I'll just give Gemma—that's the wife—a quick heads up from the van. She just loves it when I bring home stray sidemen every once in a while. It feeds her maternal instinct. Mind you, we've *got* two kids, but I guess it's just not enough for her. I tell her jazz men can't afford large families, but she's not buying it. So, c'mon, you'll be doing me a favor," Rick said amiably, heading out the door. Then he added, "I'm just glad we got ourselves a top-shelf bass player." Santa felt flattered.

They drove in Rick's aging van the few blocks to the Osprey where Santa quickly packed his suitcase and loaded it into his own van. Rick explained that Santa was to follow him in the van up to Providence where he and his family had an apartment in the northern part of the city. It would be about a thirty-five mile drive crossing two bridges in heavy rush-hour traffic. "Of course, it'd be nice to live closer to work, but rents around here and even in Portsmouth just north of here are out of sight. So here I am, a jazzman commuter, would you believe? Now *that's* fusion, ain't it?" Rick bellowed from the gut, shaking his head while holding his shabby black fedora on with his hand.

Santa laughed too. *Seems a nice fellow,* he thought, *content with his lot. If he has Mangione-scale ambitions, it doesn't show. I think I'm gonna like him.*

"Say, Rick, can we stop somewhere at an ATM machine so I can get some cash? I'm a little low," Santa said, patting his jacket vest pocket. Having only himself to support, Santa had no substantive financial issues. He was smart and had made a couple of canny investments to amass ample checking and savings accounts. This, plus the money he earned from his gigs was more than enough to finance his "unorthodox lifestyle." Except for clothes, he wasn't a spender. Possessions and financial security held no interest for him. They weren't what he was after. Saving for the future meant nothing to him. There *was* no future.

"No problem," Rick said. "There's one on Thames a few blocks up from here. Follow me." And up they drove, stopping briefly at the ATM machine, then leaving Aquidneck Island heading west across the bridges to the mainland. On the stretch up I-95 north to Providence, they hit the brunt of rush-hour traffic and for a while it was stop and go. This gave Santa a chance to take in the exquisite Fall foliage at the peak of its radiance. The reds and oranges and golds and yellows adorning the rolling hills were vibrant and seamlessly blended. *Magnificent,* Santa thought, but he didn't leave it there, as he normally would, didn't leave it at the stage of simple, innocent observation, spontaneous impression. Instead, a second thought came to him, totally unbidden but perhaps impelled by his aesthetic reaction to the foliage: *Could I be so bad if I'm capable of such a sensitive response to nature?* Whereupon he immediately scolded himself: *Stop that sentimental bullshit! That's not you. Introspection is not your game. Keep your mind on the business or pleasure at hand. Always! The rest is for bourgeois fools.*

The two vans managed to stay together on the run up the interstate. It took a good hour to reach the exit for North Providence and cover the brief stretch up Admiral Street to a modest but well-kept apartment complex that Rick called home. The sign read Glenwood Apartment Homes; it was a cluster of pretty two-story buildings with white-over-gray clapboard siding. Each building housed four families and all were arranged around a common outdoor area with amenities such as barbecue pits, a small playground and an off-street parking area. It gave easy access to a park, a nearby village and public transportation to downtown Providence.

"Well, here we are, Santa. Home sweet home, huh? Come on, let's go meet the wife and kids. She's Gemma and they're Nick and Sarah," Rick said, leading his guest up four trellised stone steps and into the vestibule. He walked straight to the end of the short ground-floor hallway, knocked on the door of 1B on the right and immediately went in without waiting for a response, Santa following close behind.

Inside was a scene of domestic tranquility. Sara sat at the kitchen table doing her homework while her mother, who stood at the stove on the other side of the table, was busy emptying a box of rigatoni into a pot of boiling water. She looked toward Santa and smiled as she dried her hands on her apron.

"Hi, hon, this is our new bass player, Santa—Santa Claus, believe it or not," Rick laughed, still tickled over the oddity of it.

Mother and daughter "aahed" together—predictably—and Santa held out his hand to both ladies, affecting a "ho, ho, ho," which he never otherwise did, except in very special circumstances. This was one of them.

"Nice to meet you both. It's very generous of you, Mrs. Esposito, having me over like this on such short notice," he said to Gemma, who played her wifely role with, "Oh, it's nothing at all. Glad to have you, Santa. There's always room for one more. I just hope pasta with Italian sausages and meatballs is to your taste ... Oh, and please call me Gemma." She was a short brunette of olive complexion, with somewhat thickish yet pretty Mediterranean features. Her daughter looked just as her mother might have looked at eleven or so.

"Thank you, and, please, not to worry, …Gemma. I love Italian cooking. This area seems to have a lot of Italian restaurants."

"Yes," she said, "Italian and Portuguese. Around here you always have a choice between *salsiccia* and *linguiça*," she quipped with just the right intonation, as if she knew the languages well. Those terms were foreign to Santa but he guessed their meaning.

"All this talk about food is making me ravenous," Rick said, looking down the hallway towards the bedrooms in the rear of the apartment. "Where's *mio figlio bello*," Rick said, not to be linguistically outdone. "Let's conclude the intros and chow down, what say?"

"Oh, he's in his room playing video games with Luke. I'll just go get him," said Gemma, padding down the corridor towards one of the two bedrooms. She opened the door, called in and, a moment later, out came the two boys, Nick and his friend Luke. Santa's eyes went first to Nick, who was about nine or ten and a male version of his sister—mother and children basically shared the same face. Santa thought him pretty but consigned him instantly to the "off limits" category, made up of boys he either knew personally or who were related to someone he knew. Such consignment was automatic, a reflex, and had nothing at all to do with attraction, or the absence thereof, or with real-world practicality or probability. Nick was out, end of story.

But then his eyes alighted on Luke, and Santa instantly felt as though struck by lightning. There before him, out of the blue, totally unexpected, stood the most beautiful boy he had ever seen. A vision of comeliness, he almost seemed to have an aura about him. The still-small body, average in height and slight of build, carried a head of such surpassing loveliness as to rival even the most ravishing female beauty. The hair a tousled dirty blond, its bangs approaching the delicate, only faintly arched eyebrows; the curve of the peach-hued cheeks, so soft and full yet firm, framing the light blue, almond-shaped eyes that melted Santa the first time they crossed his; the finely proportioned, just slightly upturned nose specked with freckles on either side of its bridge, the whole crowning lips of such savory delicacy as to cause Santa to wince internally with desire.

"Santa, this is my boy Nick and his good buddy, Luke … ah, Luke … Sorry, Luke, what is it again?'

"Hofmann … Luke Hofmann," the boy pronounced, a little shyly, looking up at Santa as he did. The voice, though still pre-pubescent, had a bit of a husky timbre to it suggesting puberty close at hand. Santa almost took a step back in self-defense. The closing line of a short story he had once read by some German writer popped into his head: "Beauty is terror." For the first time he felt he fully understood the line.

"Very nice to meet you both," Santa said, extending his hand as he reminded himself not to hold Luke's hand any longer than Nick's.

"Yeah, they're school buddies, in the same class, I think. Aren't you guys?" Rick asked.

"Yeah," Nick answered. "Fourth grade, Mrs. Ehrlich. He sits behind me, so he can cheat on tests over my soldier," Nick quipped, with a snort.

"Hey, you're the cheater, man, not me," Luke protested, laughing as he gave Nick a little push. The laugh, and the sweet smile that followed it, sent a sharp thrill down Santa's spine such as he hadn't felt in a long time. His senses hummed with excitement and he felt at some pains to maintain his even demeanor. He would not even have described his feelings as sexual. Later that evening, as he lay in bed, he would search in vain for the right word.

"What school do you boys go to," he dared to ask, well aware that even such an innocent sounding question was risky.

"Kaplan Elementary," Nick answered. "It's about three blocks from here. We walk it together. I pass by his house every morning and pick him up," he added with some pride.

"Ah, I see," said Santa, silently thankful for that choice piece of information.

"Listen, gang, can't we continue this fascinating chitchat as we move toward the table?" Rick interrupted. "I've gotta eat!"

They all repaired to the table for an enjoyable meal of spaghetti, meatballs and sausage, with a loaf of fresh Italian bread and a tossed green salad on the side, that is, right after Gemma called Luke's mother and got her okay for Luke to eat with them. During the meal Santa tried not to look Luke's way too often, but it cost him considerable effort, the more so as he caught—or thought he caught—Luke smiling at him once or twice, doubtless out of a boy's normal admiration for an adult who seemed to like him, to take an interest in him. Santa, however, as perceptive as he was, had trouble distinguishing that sort of response from the desired one, the one from libido, he always hoped for.

After dinner, Santa helped with the cleanup and dishes, impressing his hosts with his gallant side. Then everybody was off to pursue other things in other rooms, leaving Santa and Rick alone in the living room with the remaining near-half gallon of red dinner wine. Santa was resigned to a few hours of banal chitchat; he accepted it as part of the price he had to pay for an opening into the local community. And considering the gold he had already struck, he was actually feeling gratitude towards his host and his host's son. Besides, at bottom Santa rather liked Rick and his exuberant personality and therefore didn't mind so much the corny jokes and poor man's wit. It let him relax a little and worry less about giving himself away through some stupid faux pas, an anxiety that made most social occasions an ordeal for him, a necessary evil, with the chronic effect of slowly driving him more and more into himself and away from the circle of humanity. He was aware of this isolationist tendency of his and took pains, with only partial success, to counteract it, accepting invitations like Rick's when he would rather say no.

But if he was tempted to think Rick Esposito a blustering buffoon who couldn't put two thoughts together, he was disabused of this view when Rick, in his verbal meanderings, came to tell of a recent incident involving the combo. Santa's ears immediately pricked up: "Yeah," Rick said, "that was a nasty business, one I hope I never have to repeat. But you can't let your players get away with that crap. I mean, if it had been mutual, or if the waitress had come on to him, I would've turned a deaf eye, so to speak. But he was harassing the poor girl, even groping her during sets. I had no choice. And we've done without a trombone player ever since. There's just something about trombone players, you know? But it balances out because I put the word out on him over the grapevine and I don't think he's worked the circuit since ..."

Santa's first thought was that Rick was probably telling him this as an oblique way to impress upon him the importance of respecting the rules for the group. The translation was: If you're going to fool around, be discreet about it or you're out of here! Suddenly, despite the chianti, Santa was a tad less relaxed, a tad more wary, than he had been at the beginning of their chat. Clearly the group members, above all Rick, kept a watchful eye on one another's "tendencies."

Later, Santa lay in Nick's freshly made bed, the boy moving into his sister's room for the night. Of course, he let his imagination run wild about Luke, trying to picture him in the most lustful attitudes and positions, dressing him this way and that, inventing a dozen scenarios, all culminating in mutual ecstasy. At length he was compelled to pleasure himself so he could get to sleep. But sleep still did not come easily. For one thing, he was aghast at how ready he was, with respect to Luke, to dismiss his own cardinal rule about going after boys he knew. (The risk was enormous and would trouble him for the duration of his stay in Rhode Island.) For another, he was frustrated by his inability to picture Luke's cherubic face to his own satisfaction; it remained annoyingly vague, tantalizing, elusive, probably owing to the newness of the acquaintance: the neural pathways of familiarity were not yet laid down. But what he did know as clear as day was that he was in love with that face, however dimly pictured, and that soon enough, over the coming days, it would imprint itself on his memory firmly enough. This compensatory awareness, overshadowing his misgivings about pursuing the boy, at last allowed him to drift into an uneasy sleep.

The next day was a busy one for Santa. Though he had the day off, he had to find a room as quickly as possible so he could gain some distance from the Espositos and avoid being socially associated with Luke. An occasional visit at Rick's, perhaps involving an accidental encounter with the boy, would be all right, but from now on all sightings of Luke must fall into the category of stalking, or as Santa preferred to call it, "scouting."

On the lodging front Santa had very good luck. He decided finally to flip open his smartphone and give Airbnb a try and was amazed at how simply and easily it all worked out. Within an hour he had found a decent efficiency in an apartment block in downtown Providence for thirty-five bucks per night, available on a biweekly basis. It had a new queen-size bed, a remodeled kitchenette and a flat-screen TV, and was only a five-minute drive from I-95.

By two that afternoon he was completely moved in and ready for the second item on the day's agenda, which was to do an initial recon of Kaplan Elementary School, located three blocks from Rick's place, which meant he had to be especially careful not to be seen by any of the Espositos. The school was a short drive uptown from his new address and he immediately found an adequate lookout spot on a knoll across the street from the entrance, from which he could observe the children as they streamed out on dismissal at 2:30.

He waited calmly, patiently, resolutely, as they came out whooping, screaming and chattering in droves, clumps, clusters, pairs, and, here and there, singly. The littlest ones were picked up by parents waiting in nearby cars; most boarded the yellow busses idling in wait in the school's wide circular driveway; some of the older ones, fifth and sixth graders, headed home on foot. It was these whom Santa focused on, scanning the face and figure of every single exiting boy with his eagle's gaze, waiting, expecting, hoping. Suddenly the thought arose that he might not recognize the boy, his mental picture being too weak. This caused him to contract and recoil in some pain, but, dismissing the thought as coming from need, he soon regained his equanimity and resumed the scouting.

Finally, when it was down to stragglers and Santa was beginning to think he had missed the boy, his patience was rewarded: Out the glass doors he came with his buddy Nick, both toting backpacks and jumping around like young colts that had been penned up all day. Santa breathed deeply and just watched, moving only his head, and that very slowly.

Over the next several days, Santa established his usual scouting pattern: on days off, watching the boy, or usually the two boys, twice as they arrived at and left school, on rehearsal days being there for the arrival only. He changed his lookout spot frequently, today the knoll, tomorrow a fast-food restaurant window, the day after, if he could find a good parking space, his van. He took precise notes on arrival and departure times, followed the boys home from a discreet distance to observe their lingerings along the way and their deviations from the homeward course, and even managed to identify their teacher, Mrs. Ehrlich, a striking young blonde woman with a gymnast's muscular yet shapely body.

Meanwhile the Higby Street Heat were lighting it up with their new bass player. Santa on bass and Ted on drums formed a rhythm section of rare synchrony—people said they were "happenin"—and, after a few weeks, the dinner crowds at the Café began to pick up. Rick, who was delighted with this development, had Santa over for drinks and/or dinner about twice a week in an effort to make the new man feel at home.

Naturally his and Luke's paths crossed more than once at the Espositos' apartment during that period, but Santa was always careful not to be overly attentive to the boy, never to fawn over him, and, at times, even to feign a greater interest in Nick and a relative disinterest in his friend. At the same time, Santa had the uneasy feeling that Luke was not at all deceived by these tactics, that they might even be a dead give-away to the boy, who every now and then would catch Santa's eye with a sly, knowing grin, causing him to lower his head in a mixture of pique and embarrassment. Santa's first thought, tinged with paranoia, was that, if Luke knew, then it must be obvious and the others must know too! But further interaction persuaded him of the more reasonable conclusion that they were all—Rick, Gemma and Nick—blissfully ignorant, and that Luke knew only because in some deep nether region of his consciousness he felt himself to be the object of an intense passion coming from Santa. There was just no hiding this from the beloved. By the same token, however, the boy had no accompanying sense of the danger of this situation. He felt only the charm, the fascination, the vaguely erotic thrill of it.

One cool, sunny afternoon, after Santa had taken up his usual post on the grassy knoll opposite Kaplan Elementary, he realized he had left his phone, which he needed for its clock, in the van. As he turned to walk back down the knoll to where the van was parked across a field, he was stunned to find Luke just standing there on the knoll about fifteen feet away.

For a while he could only stand there himself, riveted to the spot, unable to speak. Rocked by the shock of exposure and by feelings of fright and confusion, he instinctively looked away in various directions, half expecting the entire community to be in on this extraordinary "gotcha" moment. Then, slowly gathering himself, he finally let his gaze rest on that achingly beautiful face with its hypnotic almond blues, which were gazing straight into his—innocently, though perhaps not entirely innocently. Santa hadn't allowed himself a good close-up look at that face for weeks, and the shock of this sudden boon gave the moment a powerfully seductive charge.

The boy was wearing jeans and laced-up brown loafers (rather than the obligatory Adidas), topped by a black and pepper-gray turtleneck sweater that cradled his head like the crown jewels. A lock of his sandy hair hung over his brow like a stray leaf. He smiled at Santa, but this time honestly and openly, without a trace of the naughty irony of earlier days.

"Luke, what are you doing here?" Santa asked, unable to hide entirely the sheepish tone in his voice.

"I saw you standing here from my classroom window," the boy said. "It's not the first time. I've seen you here before."

"You have, have you?" Santa laughed nervously. "Well, you certainly have sharp eyes. I figured I was quite hidden at this distance." This last remark was an admission of sorts, ordinarily to be carefully avoided, but some instinct told Santa to go with it.

"Oh, I have very good vision, 20/20 the eye doctor said. Anyway, today I decided it'd be fun to sneak up on you from behind. So I ran out the side exit and snuck around to the back over there, and then I climbed up here quietly while you were watching the front doors. Neat, huh?" the boy declared proudly.

"I'll say it was neat," Santa smiled. "I have 20/20 vision myself, you know—better than that even, and I never caught a trace of you. Well done! But, tell me, Luke, what do we do now?"

"What do you mean?"

"Well, I mean, you caught me, right? Game over. Now you could run along on home or go over to Nick's house or something, or maybe we could just hang out for a while, together, maybe go for ice cream. What do you think?"

The boy looked at Santa with a quizzical expression reflecting naïve curiosity, budding puppy love and a host of inner stirrings he could not have identified. Santa should have been ready for his next question, but then, he was smitten himself:

"What game were we playing, Mr. Claus? ... Why do you want to hang out with me?"

Santa couldn't be sure whether the boy was asking genuinely, in good faith, or perhaps playing him, or whether it was some strange mingling of both, of openness and deceit, such as a child might be capable of, but the very ambiguity of it intensified his ardor. *Is it possible I've hit the lottery here?*

"Oh, please, Luke," he answered. "just call me Santa, okay? There's no need for formality between us, is there?"

"I guess not."

"But to answer your question," Santa said, leaning casually against a tree trunk and brushing back his own dark locks, "I want to hang out with you because I like you. You're my type of guy." He wondered if Luke would catch the ambiguity of the compliment.

"But why do you like me? I'm just a kid—"

"Just a kid, he says!" Santa laughed, as if to the foliage overhead. "To be perfectly honest with you, Luke, I've always preferred the company of children to that of adults. Kids are honest; with adults you can never be sure."

"Yeah, I guess you're right. But when you say 'like'— that you *like* me—do you mean the way I like Nick or the kids at school—well, *some* of the kids at school—or my dog Mugsy—like *that?*" As he put this most perceptive question, Santa was again mystified by the issue of the boy's sincerity. Was the kid baiting him? Until he knew one way or the other, Santa decided he must maintain an element of ambiguity himself. Another game, delightful in its own right: "Of course I like you the way you like Nick or the other kids or Mugsy, Luke—plus in my case there's another element added to the mix."

"What's that?" Luke asked.

Santa felt he needed to answer truthfully, in a broad sense, while yet withholding the full thrust of it. He searched his mind for some euphemizing analogy. "Tell me, Luke, have you ever been attracted to a girl in your class?"

"Only once—Melissa Farley. She's nice."

"Tell me, would you kiss her if you had the chance?"

"Hmm," Luke hesitated, "maybe I would. But I wouldn't want it getting around to the other guys."

"I know where you're coming from. But the thing is, see, that's sort of the way I like you."

"You do?" the boy asked, complimented and astonished that a grown-up could like him in that special way of liking that occurred between boys and girls his age.

"But we're both boys. Doesn't that make us gay?"

Santa laughed heartily. "Well, I guess it makes *me* gay, my friend, but your case is not clear. Assuming you do like me—and by the way, do you?" Santa interjected quickly into his own remark, aiming to catch the boy off guard.

"Yes."

"Well, I would say you're probably just going through a phase of same-sex attraction that is completely normal for a boy your age," Santa assured him, keeping the explosion of joy he had experienced on hearing the boy's answer entirely to himself. "Soon you'll be into girls exclusively and that'll be that ... But meanwhile I don't see why we can't enjoy liking each other, do you? . . . But, just as you wouldn't want it getting out to the other guys, we wouldn't want this getting out to others either. They just wouldn't understand."

The boy nodded assent, adding, "My dad wouldn't. He hates gays." Then he blurted out cheerfully, "I'm ten, you know. My parents held me back a year." With this he smiled up at Santa, removing all doubt from the latter's mind that the boy was ready for an amorous adventure. Santa could hardly believe that, for the first time, he was actually seducing a boy and not just grabbing him.

He extended his arm out and over the boy's shoulder and gently, tenderly, drew him to his chest, keeping his arm there in a semi-hug.

"You smell good," the boy said, his head pressed against Santa's midriff, as he breathed in a blend of leather from his jacket and the Bay Rum aftershave Santa favored.

"Thanks. You smell good too."

"I do? But I didn't even shower last night."

"It's got nothing to do with hygiene. Boys your age always smell good whether they've showered or not."

The two of them walked down the knoll and across the field to Santa's van, Santa keeping his arm around Luke's shoulder. Thus began over the days that followed the strangest of interludes for both child and adult, a forbidden rendezvous, a proscribed erotic apprenticeship in which both master and apprentice were assuming roles that were brand new to them and totally unexpected, but in which both took dizzying delight. They would meet at odd times, always careful not to arouse curiosity or suspicion—for an hour after school, or during Luke's lunch hour on Santa's days off, or during Luke's band practice when he could sneak away, and there was even an occasional morning or afternoon truancy on Luke's part, which gave them extended leisure. Usually, when time was short, they would hole up in Santa's van; occasionally there would be time to sneak off to his apartment; and once, when they were feeling especially giddy and up for the thrill of danger, they crawled into an area of thick brush in a nearby city park and surrendered themselves to their most lustful impulses not more then fifteen feet away from lunchtime strollers.

In an odd way the tryst had a positive effect on Luke's self-esteem: It felt good for a boy who, despite— or perhaps because of—his striking beauty, struggled with self-confidence, to be desired by a man he looked up to. He had always suspected his father resented his pretty, girlish features and would much rather have had a rough-and-tumble defensive lineman for a son. Santa made the boy aware of the value and power of what he did have to offer. Moreover, Luke enjoyed the esoteric quality of the relationship, the knowing of secret, forbidden pleasures and behaviors of which his friends and possibly even his parents had no notion. He felt superior to the mainstreamers. Unawares to the boy, of course, these "fruits" of the tryst were all the more indelibly imprinted on his outlook, that is to say, on his character, by virtue of being accompanied by sexual pleasure, almost in the manner of the conditioning psychology that links the reinforcement of learning to reward and punishment. What greater pleasure to bolster self-esteem than sexual pleasure?

For Santa the tryst also bestowed totally unanticipated benefits, quite apart from the intense sexual rapture itself. For once he was not merely taking his pleasure but sharing it as well. However modestly and briefly, he felt, perhaps for the first time ever, a sense of communion, a sense of the vast possibilities of a non-predatory relationship, a *human* relationship. This, of course, aroused in him tender, protective feelings towards his beloved, feelings that complicated things and made him profoundly uneasy, because he knew that soon he would be forced to exit this little utopia of two by cutting its population in half. He tried not to think about this, invoking his *carpe diem* mantra more frequently and more ardently than usual.

One afternoon, as they were sitting on a park bench in the afterglow of another flirtation with the risk of exposure, Luke asked, "Are you gonna be staying around here, in Providence I mean?"

The question cut Santa to the quick, stirring up as it did all the feelings of imminent doom—for the boy, and therefore for himself as well—he had been trying without much success to suppress. For he was totally with the boy.

"I'm afraid I can't, Luke. I'm gonna have to be moving on soon. Don't worry, you'll be all right … Try not to think about it."

"But I *do* think about it. I don't want you to leave. Why can't you stay? Don't you like it here? Newport is a nice place."

The boy's eyes were tearing up, more beautiful than ever in their limpid sadness. Santa was so moved, and at the same time so upset at being moved, that he got up, looked around reflexively, and motioned wistfully with his head for the two of them to head back to the van. He did his best to comfort the boy as they walked, but the hypocrisy of his own words almost choked him. He was bristling with self-loathing and had to endure the slings and arrows of his amoral inner judge who kept carping at him, "Fool! You brought this on yourself."

One evening after dinner, his homework done early, Luke told his parents he was going out to play with the neighborhood kids. He ran down to the corner and hopped right into the shotgun seat of Santa's van and off they drove down I-195 in the direction of Portsmouth, a town on Aquidneck Island just a few miles north of Newport. When they came into Portsmouth on the local road, Santa slowed down as it was hard to see the signs at the crossroads. When he found the one he was looking for, he turned right onto Corys Lane and entered the campus of Portsmouth Abbey School, an elite boarding school for grades nine through twelve run by Benedictine monks. He had scouted the place, of course, and knew it well, even in the dark. He kept moving west, past the campus itself, soon coming to his destination, the Green Animals Topiary Garden, a preserve of larger-than-life animals sculpted from evergreen shrubs, overlooking Narragansett Bay. It was past seven and dark, except for some minimal florescent lighting, and the garden was empty of human traffic.

They parked and got out. Santa led the boy onto the grounds displaying the meticulously shaped green animals: camel, elephant, giraffe, tiger, antelope, and on and on. Luke was bedazzled; he'd never seen anything like it.

"Hey, this is better than a regular zoo! No cages! Wow, these animals are so big you can walk under their legs. Come here, Santa," he laughed as he placed himself directly under the gigantic giraffe's mid-section with some two feet to spare. "Man, this is fun! Thanks for taking me here."

Santa smiled wanly and slowly moved under the giraffe next to his beloved. He was trembling a little and trying hard not to betray it.

"Isn't this fun, Santa? Don't you just love it? And it's like our own private playground after dark," he said excitedly, hugging Santa around the waist. Santa stood there, resting his strong hands on the boy's shoulders and looking away, his face a twisted mask of pain and conflict. *God help me! Show me the way! I can't bear this any longer!*

The van pulled into the same corner spot it was in when the boy came aboard.

"You'd better hop out and get in the house fast, Luke. Your folks'll probably want an explanation. Make it a good one, okay?" Santa smiled, mussing the boy's hair.

"Don't worry, I can handle them," Luke wise-cracked, getting out and slamming the door shut. "See you tomorrow, on the knoll, okay?" he said, smiling through the window.

But he did not see Santa on the knoll the next day, nor the day after that, nor ever again, anywhere. Within a week Santa settled accounts with the Higby Street Heat and left Newport, heading northeast.

12

"**It was a small** but lavish country residence, a tiny palace nestled in a faraway valley. The prince and princess had decided to spend their first summer there as a married couple. They had made the three-day journey there with a small staff of seven servants. The days were lovely and flew by without a care; they were spent doting on the newborn royal son, a healthy boy with strong lungs, as well as engaging in vigorous outdoor activities. The young couple swam in the nearby stream, hiked up and down the surrounding hills and often went fruit-picking for guavas, plantains and granadillas. It was a splendid and much-needed interlude for them, away from the bustle of the town and the main palace. They had plenty of time to themselves, and especially time for each other, performing light household chores together during which they learned to cooperate, in this way coming to know each other beneath the surface.

"One day, toward the end of their country idyll, the sun suddenly disappeared just past noon, covered over by a roiling sea of dark, angry clouds. On this day, the prince happened to be away on a fishing expedition with six of the seven servants. The princess stayed at home with her baby, both tended to by the remaining servant. As the winds picked up, becoming fierce, and the rains came down in blinding swarms, the servant rushed about the little palace, slamming doors, closing shutters and securing the outdoor furniture.

"The princess retired to the royal bed chamber with her infant, who had just been nursed at the breast and was ready for a nap. As she laid the tiny child in his cradle and covered him with swaddling, she noticed that the chamber door, which opened onto the garden behind the palace, and beyond that to the forest, had been carelessly left open. Hurrying over to the door to close it, she was stopped in her tracks by a tremendous inrush of wind, rain and fog. These seemed to make way for an enormous rounded shape that slithered up to the threshold, poked its scaly head inside and shoved its way through the doorway and into the room.

"The princess backed away and stood there frozen in terror, mouth open wide. She couldn't take in what her eyes were seeing and believed she must be suffering a nightmare. The creature, huge, green and armored with scales the size of coach doors, finally managed to get its entire body into the room, all fifteen feet of it, but not without scraping its sides bloody on the stone doorframe. This, however, didn't seem to bother it as it quickly scanned the room before lowering its fiery gaze on the infant slumbering in its crib. Deeply it breathed in that fragrance of newborn innocence, sounding like a hurricane gale as it did. This was what it had come for, its profound sense of smell an unerring guide.

"The princess remained rooted to the spot, her fevered imagination awash in chaotic images of dragons and basilisks and many other monsters as told of in the received ancient tales of the elders. Still, she had no idea what it was and nothing to compare it to. But the instant she saw the great green beast rest its covetous eyes on her child, she came to her senses and dashed over to the cradle, placing herself between it and the behemoth. The great beast raised its hideous head and roared a roar that shook the rafters, almost seeming to ridicule the young mother's protective instinct. Then, as it rolled out its ghastly tongue to sweep up its prey from the cradle, the woman pulled from her hair a long knitting needle and raised it to strike at that foul projection. But the beast was agile and instead used its massive tongue to swat her across the room and into the wall, where she slunk down dazed. Now there was nothing standing between predator and prey. All seemed lost.

"Just then, the royal bed began to rumble and shake, as if possessed by an invisible spirit. Finally, out from under it, on the side opposite the beast, there rose up a serpentine shape that more than matched the beast in size, although its appearance was very different. As it reared up high towards the room's domed ceiling, it shone magnificent in a white hue that was transparent and crisscrossed by a diamond pattern of brilliant burnt sienna. Involuntarily the princess thought of the beautiful boa snakes she had seen in the jungles of her native land, but they were all very small, rarely more than eighteen inches long. This splendid colossus towered over the shabby, dingy green beast, which now renewed its attack on the royal son, aware that it had one last chance and only one. But just as it again flicked its tongue towards its prey, the white boa seized that cursed organ with its sharp inward-curving teeth, ripping it from the beast's maw in one mighty yank. The beast roared in pain and humiliation, and then lunged at the noble boa across the bed. But the boa moved swiftly and gracefully aside, almost like a matador, then turned smartly to grasp the beast's scaly neck in its needled maw while deftly wrapping its luminous coils around its body. As it squeezed, a brown fluid hissed as it flowed from the beast's eyes, snout and mouth. Squeezing a little tighter each time the beast exhaled, the boa before long crushed the life out of it.

"After undoing its coils, the noble boa picked up the shrunken beast in its mouth and carried it back out of the bed chamber through the still-open door into the garden, its sides now scraped even bloodier than they had been on entering. Both disappeared into the forest, leaving the princess with quite a tale to tell her husband that evening. And the royal son had slept through it all."

"You sure can spin a yarn, Hattie. You should list 'raconteur' on your resumé," Julie quipped. It was evening and the two women were enjoying a cup of tea together in the family room, which was now Julie's makeshift bedroom.

"That's one of the many stories I grew up hearing in my neighborhood in Port-au-Prince," the aide explained. "Fables or legends, I guess you'd call them. Of course, there are no giant snakes in Haiti, at least not anymore. But it shows the complex role, the helpful role, mostly, that animals, and especially stories and myths about animals, play in the imagination of my people. And while I would like to think I've outgrown all of that, that I'm now somehow more educated, more 'Westernized,' those stories still stay with me and continue to—what's the word—*resonate* way back in the dark corners of my mind. They make me a little superstitious, I have to admit, in *spite of* myself.

"That's why I wish you would humor a crazy old woman, Julie, and take to heart Nate's advice to let

Duncan keep watch on your bed, so to speak, while you sleep. I mean over your inner as well as your outer wellbeing. I know it sounds silly, but I trust that boy's instincts and I do have this … lingering feeling about animal spirits. And it certainly can't hurt … Oh, I'm sure you must think me a fool!" As she spoke these words, Hattie had Duncan propped up on her lap and was smoothing the little ape's artificial black fur with her index finger. She stared at his eyes, which were mere slits of white bisected by arcs of brown and black under a protruding ebony monobrow. For a stuffed toy his look was not at all friendly. If you examined him closely, you saw that he was neither cute nor cuddly. So much the better, thought Hattie.

"No, Hattie, of course I don't think you a fool," Julie assured her, wishing she could put her own hand on the aide's. "Actually, I think it's charming the way you have one foot in and one foot out of your people's superstitions. That shows you're growing. And come to think of it, how are you or the Haitian people any different from us Americans, with our lucky rabbit's feet and our black cats bringing bad luck when they cross our paths and our dogs that stay at the master's sickbed to guard against evil spirits. We may be scientifically and technologically advanced, but far less so, I think, in our personal beliefs. We still haven't come entirely out of the forest. Totems die hard, I guess, if they die at all."

"Julie, I think you're being generous," Hattie replied. "What you say about Americans may apply to the poor and uneducated classes, to rural folk who live in some degree of isolation, but certainly not to the mainstream of educated people, city people, people like you and Mr. Mark."

"One would think so … yes, one would think so," Julie mused, "but I'm not at all sure of that. I'm not at all sure that our education and our sophisticated city ways are not a pretty thin veneer—and I mean 'pretty' in both senses, 'very' and 'attractive.' A thin veneer covering a seething cauldron of dark drives, urges and terrors. I'm telling you, sometimes it feels like barbarians at the gate in here," she said, looking down at her own breast. "I guess to an extent I'm a Freudian. The conscious mind, the mind's educated surface that we strive so hard to cultivate, functions not only to help us negotiate the world 'out there,' the physical and social world, but the world 'in here' as well—the world of the self, for lack of a better word, a world that is as strange and foreign to us as some remote jungle in the South Pacific.

"My own current situation has brought this home to me in a way I could never have appreciated before. After all, you could say that as a paralytic I am very close to being trapped inside my own interior world, the world of thought and feeling and imagination. I would even say that *it* poses more of a challenge to me, more of a threat frankly, than the outer world of body, movement and objects. After all, basically I can still move away from what I don't like 'out there,' however slow and crude and torturous that movement be, but no matter where I go, that other, inner, world goes right along with me. And since my outer world is now so shrunken, my inner world becomes so much more significant. For the most part, it's where I live these days. That's why it's so important for me to stay on the best terms with it, so to speak, to make sure we continue to 'get along,' especially during my down periods when it's hard not to think, 'Oh, screw it all! Why bother? What's the point?'"

"Oh, Ms. Julie—*Julie*, I mean—I know it's hard, terribly hard, but you mustn't think that way," Hattie said, trying not to show her distress.

"I appreciate your concern, *dear* Hattie. I know it's that of a friend, but—and forgive me for saying this—that's like telling me not to think of a pink elephant, you know?" Julie laughed at this paradox, and at what struck her in that moment as the general futility of her life.

"My God, Julie, I wish I could just wave a magic wand over you and—"

"—Oh, Hattie, what's the point?—whoops, there's that question again!" Julie said, and burst out laughing, and the aide cackled right along with her, both enjoying the taste of freedom that comes when two friends realize their own profound silliness together.

"But there *is* an upside, Hattie," Julie continued, "and that's my meditation practice. It often brings me consolation; sometimes it gives me a sense of expansiveness and freedom that lifts me out of the prison of this body—for a while at least. Also, it gives me an inkling of … of *my*stery—I don't know what else to call it—of depths upon inner depths to be explored, way deeper than the chaotic Freudian territory. And I had no clue of any of this while I was in a mobile body … My God, Hattie, see what it took to get me to slow down and look inside myself? A catastrophe!"

"Well, I don't know much about Freud, Julie, but I do think that's a very interesting way to look at it," Hattie enthused. "Though I must say it's a sad judgment on the rest of us, if a person as bright as yourself must suffer such a—"

"—Oh please, Hattie, I'm not special, believe me. And besides, meditation is certainly no panacea. For instance, it certainly hasn't shed any light on this wretched uneasiness, this low-level anxiety, that's plagued me over the past few weeks. There's just this vague sense that something's wrong, something that matters, something quite apart from me, or my situation, or our run-of-the-mill family problems. It nags at me, it sneaks up on me almost every day, and often right in the middle of a meditation, or just after. Yet it has no content, no object or target, and it doesn't seem to point in any particular direction. It's free-floating, as they say. I don't know what to do with it, what action to take, if any. The only thing I'm sure of is that it's not about myself, at least not directly."

"Anxiety is usually about the future, Julie, wouldn't you say?" Hattie counseled. "Regret is over the past; worry is over the future. Maybe you'll just have to be patient and wait; maybe your meditation will reveal the source of the problem to you in the fullness of time, at a time when you're ready to deal with it. In fact, maybe it's your meditation that has alerted you to this 'uneasiness,' as you call it, in the first place, dug it up from those inner depths you spoke of, and so you will have to trust whatever power is guiding that meditation to guide you through the rest of the process."

Julie sat motionless, carefully considering Hattie's words, and finally burst out with "Hattie, you're amazing!", slowly shaking her head in disbelief. "You should charge extra for psychotherapy, or guru healing, or some combination of both." Again Hattie cackled, throwing back her head with its shiny black locks. Her cackle was as therapeutic as her words.

Just then Nate walked into the room, drawn by the cackling like a moth to flame. "Hey, you guys, would you mind keeping it down in here," he said in mock-censure, "I'm trying to concentrate on history. Ugh!"

"'Ugh?' Nathaniel, 'ugh?'" Hattie chided. "Don't you know how important history is? What period are you studying?"

"The colonial period."

"Oh, that's wonderful! Do you know, Nathaniel, that both our countries were once colonies?"

"No kidding. Yours too?"

"Absolutely. Haiti was ruled by the French just as America was by the British."

"Really? Were the French as nasty as the British?"

"Oh, I'm sure they were. All colonialism is based on greed, and greed makes people violent. But you should take pride in the story of your country's birth, Nathaniel. It was the birth of a people's freedom, which is a wonderful thing."

"Do you really feel that way, Hattie," Julie asked, a bit cynically, "even knowing that America itself became a colonial empire later on?"

Hattie looked at her in astonishment, the whites of her eyes bulging. "Well, Ms. Julie, nothing lasts for*ever* now, does it?" she finally crowed and let out another cackle such as to twirl the ends of an early patriot's moustache. Composing herself, she added, a little apologetically, "But seriously, Nathaniel, you need to know something about history if you're gonna be an educated person."

"Yeah, I guess so, but it's so boring. Just names and dates and governments. I wish I could watch it on the History Channel. Now that's cool! I love the Nazis—I mean, I love *watching* about the Nazis and Hitler and all on those old films with the lines running through them."

"Well, those old films are very important, sweetie," Julie said. "They help document the atrocities—the bad things—that took place during that time." As usual these days, Julie was walking a tricky middle path between giving her boy too much and too little information. She would often feel uncomfortable when judgments of discretion entered into talks with Nate, fearing that her own trauma had somehow skewed her sense of discretion. What was too much? What too little? Was it better to say that "many" Jews were murdered or that six million Jews were murdered? Or was the question simply absurd? She didn't know. In coming to know with terrifying clarity how dangerous and how fragile life was, was she overprotecting her son, keeping him an orchid in a hothouse? She didn't know.

Just then Nate noticed Duncan resting on Hattie's lap. "Now here's a guy who could whip those bad old Nazis," he joked, picking the little fellow up and making his furry little arms punch like a boxer, knocking off Nazis left and right as in a video game. "Ksh, ksh, ksh," he would say with each punch, adding the requisite sound effects. Finally he put Duncan down, not on Hattie's lap where he had found him, but on his mother's."

"See what I mean?" Hattie asked, smiling at Julie.

13

It **was after lunch** but not yet time to go in to class. There were twenty minutes or so of free time to play some pick-up basketball in the schoolyard. Nate, Jamie Poindexter and another boy leaned patiently against the concrete sidewall of the school building behind the basket, waiting to take on the winners of the current game. It was three on three; loser of the point takes it out; five points wins. (The games had to be short so that they could squeeze three or four of them into the available time.) Nate was standing a few feet apart from the other two, sweeping a bit of litter back against the wall with his sneaker. Just then, as he looked up, he felt a terribly sharp pain on the left side of his head, just behind his temple.

Stunned, he looked down and saw a robin's-egg-shaped rock, half an inch wide, lying near his left foot, and just next to it a few drops of blood he realized were coming from his own head. As he rubbed the sore spot, he picked up the rock to examine it and then panned to his left to identify its thrower.

He needn't have bothered.

"What's the matter, Driscoll? Got a headache?" taunted a familiar voice coming from a cluster of boys standing close by. It belonged, of course, to his nemesis Rensky, who now emerged from his rat pack, tossing up and catching another, similar, rock in the palm of his hand.

"Let's see now. What should I do with this one?" he said, looking around and pretending to suddenly light on Nate, who was now holding a handkerchief to his temple and staring daggers at Rensky.

Smart kid that he was, Nate realized he was in the lion's den and could not count on being rescued by a grown-up this time, at least not soon enough. He had to think of something fast. Sure, he was angry enough to attack Rensky, but he knew a head-on attack was likely to end badly for him, Rensky having the arms and shoulders of a blacksmith's son. Deftly scanning the area to see if there was any advantage available to him, he spotted Greg Gronda, an oversized defensive tackle on the local peewee football team, standing just behind and to the right of Rensky, with his back to him, talking with two or three others. Gronda had two inches and at least twenty pounds on Rensky.

Nonchalantly turning left, Nate strolled towards the corner door of the gate, as if to leave. When, by his rough geometrical calculation, he came to the right spot, forming a straight line connecting himself, Rensky and Gronda, he turned swiftly to the right and ran full-speed straight at Rensky, who, taken by surprise, froze in his tracks and could only watch. With all the charge he could muster, Nate hurled his seventy-pound body right at Rensky's navel, assuming the form of a cannon-ball in mid-flight. He had seen plenty of feet-first karate landings in movies but, being untrained, did not trust himself to perform one successfully then and there.

In this he was wise because, as a human cannonball, he hit his target accurately and with full impact. Rensky was knocked back hard into Gronda, who, books flying, was sent sprawling, making a four-point landing face-down into some unidentified viscous liquid spilled over the macadam surface of the yard. Nate, who had gotten the least of it, jumped up immediately and put on a horrified expression, so as to give the impression—to Gronda—of being a shocked and surprised bystander who had had nothing to do with the collision.

Slowly staggering to his feet, Gronda turned to see Rensky doing the same. Looking then at Nate, who was looking at Rensky while shaking his head, as if to say, "Man, you must be suicidal," Gronda took the cue and punched Rensky flush in the face, sending him down for the second time in thirty seconds. This time, however, poor Rensky had help getting up—from Gronda, who then punched him a second time. As the defensive tackle bent over to "help him up" again, the shrill whistle of the schoolyard monitor pierced the air and everybody froze. Quickly drawing his own conclusions as to what had happened, the monitor grabbed the two delinquents by the arm and marched them off to the principal's office. Off they went, to the chortling, cackling and sniggering taunts of all those bystanding boys who were not Rensky's minions. They laughed on two counts: one, it tickled them to see the real instigator, Nate, get away with it; after all, any subversion of authority was cool, wasn't it? Two, the monitor, a short stick of a balding teacher in his forties, was leading away perhaps the two burliest kids in the school, one, Rensky, built up from weightlifting, the other, Gronda, just born big. Each looked as if he could have brushed the monitor off his shoulder like a fly.

Meanwhile, the basketball scrimmage had ended and the winners, now of three in a row, called out "Next victims, please!", throwing down the gauntlet to Nate and Jamie. "These three guys are good. I've seen them in PAL basketball," Jamie whispered to Nate as they and their third, a wisp of a kid named Marty who was even skinnier than Nate, lined up in front of their opponents on the court.

"Fine," said Nate, feeling his oats after his splendid take-down of Rensky, "I'm feelin' it. I'm up for a challenge. Let's show them how it's done." After a final dab at his cut scalp, Nate stuffed his blood-stained hanky into his back pocket. Then, crouching slightly and holding his arms out, he took up a defensive position before his opposite number, a short kid with good ball-handling skills. He had on a backward baseball cap, a gesture Nate was inclined to read as arrogant and which therefore piqued his lust for conquest.

The kid put the ball in play, passing it to a taller kid to his left. That kid tried to pass it right back to him, but Nate, in a lightning reflex action, intercepted the pass and flipped it to Jamie under the basket for an easy chippie shot. This took the opposing team by surprise, snapping them to attention as they instantly upped the quickness and aggressiveness of their game. It didn't help. Nate and Jamie were in a zone and could do nothing wrong. Marty was there for window dressing and because the rules required it; he was more observer than participant. On one occasion he did assist Nate on a layup: Jamie had passed it to him and he stood there at mid-court balancing the ball on his finger tips as Nate whizzed by him, scarfing the ball up and driving in for the basket.

At this point Nate realized that something was happening to him, more specifically to his body, something wonderful and mysterious. He was undergoing a growth spurt, both physically and in terms of skill. If not for the game, he probably wouldn't have noticed it. But he did notice it, noticed it right in the middle of play, and he basked in it. It was as if some bodily tumblers had all at once clicked into place and he could function on a new, higher level. He no longer felt any strain or need for extra effort in laying the ball up on the backboard for a bank shot. He could simply and smoothly roll it up there off his fingertips without having to push it. Also, he was feeling a new confidence in taking his set shot, and even his jump shot, this usually being the last to come for a kid, requiring as it does the complex coordination of jumping and shooting.

But there he was, shooting jumpers, graceful, feathery, effortless jumpers, the way it's supposed to be. His passes, which had always been good, were suddenly faster, sharper, defter. In fact, Jamie, who prided himself on reading his pal's basketball mind, was surprised in this game by a pass that came at him like a Nolan Ryan smoker, causing him to bobble the ball and thus blow an easy point. But apart from that, the two played together flawlessly, with no-look chest and bounce passes—one even behind-the-back from Nate—and shooting bordering on unconscious and stifling flypaper defense. It was almost as if they were one player in two locations.

The other team was psychologically defeated about halfway through. And Nate put the final nail in the coffin with a game-ending twenty-foot jumper that he knew was going in the instant it left his fingertips. And so it did, hitting nothing but net. Swish! Final score: 5 to zip.

The two teams high-fived each other, an essential part of the ritual, and Nate, normally a self-contained kid who despised all bragging and lording it over a bested opponent, had all he could do to suppress the urge to grin broadly. It was a natural response to the feel of his own burgeoning physical powers. But he took hold of himself and said the obligatory "Good game" to the others, not begrudging them the respect due "the worthy opponent."

The warning bell rang, signaling a return to class, and both front and side entrances to the building suddenly became like two massive vacuum-cleaner heads sucking in the surrounding debris. Nate and Jamie lagged behind, in no particular hurry, wanting only to bask in the glow of victory a while longer. "Dex, were we on fire or what!" Nate exulted, putting his arm around his bigger, taller pal's shoulder as they strolled across the yard towards the side door.

"*You* were on fire," Jamie laughed, wiping the beads of sweat from his brow. "I was still warming up when it ended. But we sure beat the crap out of those guys, huh?

… Say, what got into you there anyway. You almost took my head off with that one pass. Whadja do, double down on your vitamins this morning?"

"Nah. I don't know, I guess I was just really feelin' it. Suddenly I felt I had range, you know? Command over my shot. For the first time, I think, I wanted to shoot more than pass. And I guess I was still all juiced over that business with Rensky. Boy, Gronda really let him have it, didn't he? Every punch felt like it was coming from me."

"He had it coming to him," Jamie smirked, his voice dripping with contempt. "Man, I hate that guy! You must *really* hate him, huh?"

"Well, I agree with you he had it coming. I only wish I could've dished it out myself, you know? But I'm still a year or two short; I still have to count on brains more than brawn. But maybe my upped game is a sign I don't have long to wait, you know?

"But as for hating Rensky—well, I don't hate him. Don't get me wrong: he is definitely the biggest pain in my butt, but I don't hate him."

"But how can you say that, Nate? He never picks on *me* and I *still* hate him! How can you not?"

Nate stopped walking and turned to Jamie, who also stopped. Screw being late, Nate felt he had something important, something quite "grown-up," to share with his friend. "Look, it's like this," Nate began with knitted brow, handing the basketball to Jamie so as to free up his hands to help him make his point. "I don't hate Rensky because he doesn't hate me. Not really."

"But how can you say that? That's nuts! He's always pounding on you. Tell me that's not hate, okay?"

"Yes, it's hate all right, but it's not for *me*. It's not against *me*. It's not really being directed at me *personally*, see?"

"No, I don't see. That rock he threw didn't hit anybody else's head, just yours."

"Look, Dex, what I'm trying to say here is that … shit, this isn't easy … is that Rensky, er, Rensky hates what he *thinks* I am, not what I really am."

"I'm sorry, what he *thinks* you are? What does he *think* you are?"

"Oh, you know, a stuck-up kid who sticks to himself and can't be bothered hanging out with kids like—well, like *him*. You know, there are other kids besides Rensky who feel like that about me—and about us—about you and me—as if we think we're too good for them. See, they don't really know us, do they, so they can't really hate us. You can't hate what you don't know. But you can hate what you *think* you know, say, a false picture of the real thing. Thank God, Rensky is the only one who needs to *do* something about it."

They had reached the side entrance where Jamie flipped the ball to the yard monitor, who stood at just about eye level with him and chided, "Better get a move on, boys, if you don't want to be marked tardy." The two went in, Jamie with sweat-soaked head lowered deep in thought, Nate wondering if he had made himself clear.

"So, you see?" Nate summarized, "That's why I can't say I hate Rensky. He doesn't hate the real me, so why should I hate him? I hope I never have to hate anybody. It's too hard."

As they walked to their lockers, Jamie kept his eyes on the shiny laminate floor, carefully weighing what he had just heard, impressed with the reasoning of his friend, which was subtler than he was used to hearing. He had some thinking to do, about Rensky and others.

14

Luke was a fluke! *I must be a kook to juke with a duke. No more a dat shit! Gimme the peons to pee on, the ones wut tickle me, tingle me, tinkle me. Everythin' south of the border—never higher. The higher the wire, the more you catch fire. I'll show you how low I can go. Back door in the grass, down and dirty, and out it comes, bustin' through a kid like you. I'll lay you away before you can say my holiday name. So come over here and fan my Yule log, will ya? Mark it, Quincy, mark it. It be blazin' 'fore long. Jess like Daddy's hand 'cross my cheeks, hot and heavy. Whop! Whop! Whop! Harder, man, harder, and soon you be breakin' somethin'. Or bringin' somethin'. Then I'll be all jiggy-boned, huh? All jiggy bones, 'cep for one, all loosey-goosey, 'cep right here where I'm gettin' strong. A love supreme, dat's what it seem. That's Daddy's song, I pass it ong. I make it even purer, it's too much for the endurer, than his death there's nothin' surer, for this love there is no curer. The boss is stoned, the stoner's boss; I'll say no to your*

171

joint 'cuz it's no great loss. See, weed is not my kinda seed 'cuz this one's drug is a cute li'l bug jess layin' all snug on a big thick rug. Lemme do ya, hon, we'll spread dis love from heav'n above, unless the evil one discove what Christmas love is still made of. Then the jiggy's up! Santa is Satan with n in da middle; let's get it on, boy, and high diddle diddle. Oh, wait! There's one scootin' behind the popcorn stand, watchin' the poppin' that ne'er be stoppin', and I be coppin' a feel from behind. Gotta be careful 'cuz mama and papa may be nearby; ask me no questions, I'll tell you no lies. "Come over here, Sammy, you lyin' ta me? 'Cuz if you be fibbin', I'll pull out your tree." Guess I better be goin', such a long way to go. But one thing I'm not is a lousy no-show. And so many Miles to go before I weep, and so many Miles to go before I sleep. Sleep the fevered sleep of the damned.

15

*I*n ... *out* ... *one* ... *in* ... *out* ... *two* ... *in* ... *out* ... *three* ... *Oh shit, not again! This fucking feeling will not leave me in peace! It just plops itself down in the middle of my mind every time I close my eyes and start deep breathing. It's like a stupid tune you can't get out of your head, like "It's a Small, Small World" or "Santa Claus Is Coming to Town", but even more obnoxious because I don't have a clue where it's coming from. It's really spoiling my meditation, which is one of the few independent activities left me. I don't know what I would do without it, but, damn it, how long is this maddening dread going to hang around? If only I had some sense of what it's about, maybe I could process it emotionally, but it's still a complete mystery. Apart from the fact that my life is changed forever—and not for the better—everything seems about normal. I suppose it could be some post-accident depression, but it's really not depression I'm feeling so much as uneasiness, nervousness,* *anxiety, dread, like I want to jump out of my skin ... God, it's miserable.*

Gathering the loose strands of her concentration again, Julie resumed her breath-counting, but it went no better than before. The uneasiness was there again—or rather still—dead center, and the more anxious and resistant she became over it, the more recalcitrant the feeling grew. Intuitively she knew she wasn't going to get anywhere this way, but she was still too much in the grips of her need to "shine" in meditation, to have it go "well," like teaching a good class or writing a good journal article, to step back and take a breath, so to speak. She was still too much under the spell of the American bitch goddess, Success.

On it went like this for a time, her purest intention to begin meditation as a tabula rasa inevitably leading her back into the same morass of dread. The harder she fought it, the worse it got. The wry observation occurred to her that it was every bit as impossible to move this feeling out of her mind as it was to move a finger or toe of her alien body. On days when she was too tired or fed up to fight or when common sense happened to get the upper hand, she still felt frustrated because *that* sort of "tainted" meditation wasn't what she wanted. It seemed that whatever she did or didn't do just led down the same blind alley.

One morning, as she was about to leave her make-shift bedroom in disgust, Mark walked in looking for a book of poetry he had left there the evening before which he needed for class. It was a gray, blustery morning, of the kind that makes Syracusans shudder over the thought of impending winter. Julie stopped her chair in mid-roll and looked up at him, noticing how fine he looked in his brown corduroy sport coat, after having just shaved his weekend stubble. He, noticing her smile, felt good about it but could still detect her troubled spirit just behind it. Moreover, he thought she looked pallid sitting there in her chair, her blonde hair and unmade-up face emphasizing the wan complexion. She reminded him of those tubercular salon ladies he had seen in much nineteenth-century painting, who cultivated their pallor for an effect of delicacy and refinement; he ascribed her condition to her current routine, which with the recently plummeting temperatures was almost entirely restricted to indoors. *She needs to get out of this house for a while. I've got to devise some sort of family outing. But what?* he wondered.

"Say, hon," he quipped, hoping to cheer her up, "have you seen that volume of Sheets and Kelly I've been carrying around lately?" He loved spoonerizing the names of the immortal Romantic lyrical duo, Keats and Shelley, that way—but only at home, never in class. She laughed and tsk-tsked him, as she usually did, and told him it was under the pile of Sunday Times newspaper sections on the leather couch. He went to retrieve it and, while flipping through it on his way back, said, affecting nonchalance, "Everything okay, my sweet?

"You mean, apart from the fact that my meditation process is for shit, I'm bored out of my mind and I can't move anything below my neck?" she said in an attempt to sound flippant and blasé but which didn't come off that way.

Jesus, I've got to start paying closer attention. How could I not know she was hurting this bad? he thought, shaken by his own enormous capacity for denial. The matter of the affair didn't even occur to him. "Oh sweetheart, you're suffering and here I am worrying about two dead white poets," he said, trying to give solace and amuse at the same time. He still loved her, loved her deeply despite everything, and felt the sinking pain of frustration over his impotence to help her in any significant way. Holding her coffee cup to her lips, fluffing her pillow, carrying her from couch to chair to bed and back, day in and day out—how paltry all these tiny little services seemed to him in this moment.

"Look, babe, I've been thinking about it: how about we all take a vacation over the upcoming holidays, say, to the Caribbean somewhere. Aruba, maybe, or Puerto Rico or the Virgin Islands. You know, sun and sand and Pina Coladas with fresh coconuts. I don't think either of us has ever been on a tropical vacation, have we? What do you say? We'll bring Hattie with us, of course."

"Oh, I don't know, Mark. I really don't think so, as much as I'd love to," Julie replied, angling her chair to face him squarely. "Our financial situation is still unstable, and we have no idea how the insurance issue is going to turn out. I think we'd better hold off on vacations for a while yet." He saw her smile was gone, replaced by a drawn expression, which pained him. He wanted to put his fist through the wall.

"Come on, hon," he pleaded, "this is one of those times when you just have to throw caution to the winds! A stay at the beach isn't a luxury here; it's not some extravagant gesture. It's something we *need*. We *all* need it. It's like a mental health day—call it a mental health week."

"Oh Mark, what good would lolling on the beach do me—assuming, that is, I can still loll—if all I was thinking about was money and how we were wasting it sipping ten-dollar pina coladas?" The mock-decadent picture she painted angered him until it struck him that they had switched roles: For once she was the one worrying about spending. This scared him a little, because if Julie, usually so intelligent yet so easygoing about money, was suddenly concerned about the family budget, well, there must be a damned good reason for concern. He suddenly felt buffeted by conflicting feelings, clashing attitudes, discordant values. There was nothing to lean on, no rock to cling to in a roiling sea of battering waves. And then, as sometimes happens when a couple senses it is close to rock bottom in the relationship and things cannot possibly get any worse, they do. Julie passed a remark, totally innocent in itself, that unleashed a fury in Mark he had no idea was there. She said, "What I really need is to get back to work, to write something, to feel useful again."

"Come on, Julie," he flared up. "Why can't you just forget about the work for a while and give yourself the leisure you need to heal and adapt to new circumstances. It's not as if your scholarly resume would suffer if you took a year off, you know. It's already thick enough to choke a gorilla, for Christ's sake," he snarked, nodding towards Duncan, who sat in the chair tucked in on Julie's side, placid as ever.

All at once, Julie's eyes were ablaze with a fury at least equal to his: "Oh, I'll bet you'd just love it, wouldn't you, if I put the work aside and then just sort of drifted away from it altogether. Become an ex-scholar. Oh, she had such promise! Actually, maybe that's not such a bad idea, because then I'd no longer have to put up with your annoying sulking over my superior productivity. We'd both be deadwood." Her chest was heaving with labored breathing, almost giving the appearance of moving on its own. He, of course, could see she was in some distress, her pale cheeks having taken on a deep flush of pink, but it was too late to back off. He had to stand his ground on this one. It was just a question of which insult to answer first.

"I don't sulk," he retorted, glaring at her. "And I don't know how you can say that. I've always supported your research—Christ, I'm your biggest fan. When I think of all those evenings I stayed home with Nate so you could get away to the stacks for a few hours ... And just because I don't rush into print with every little jot and tittle I scribble down on paper doesn't mean I'm less productive. I prefer to let an essay mature for a while before putting it out there."

"*Mature* for a while?!" she repeated, mockingly. "Is that how you're glossing it these days? Well, in that case you must be holding back some real graybeards. You'd better let them out before they crumble to dust on your hard drive!"

He found that last sling so outrageous and yet so funny that he didn't know whether to roar back at her or roar with laughter. So he did nothing, just standing there with an idiotic half-smile on his face. She too was out of ammunition, depleted of hostility, and already feeling silly for an outburst she recognized as way over the top.

"Oh, Mark, forgive me," she implored, tilting her head a little to the left, the only gesture now left to her for expressing regret in her profoundly impoverished body language. He was moved. "I didn't mean any of that nonsense," she continued sheepishly. "I don't know where it all came from ... Wait, correction! I think I *do* know where it all came from. It's my meditation. It's been going so poorly for weeks now. I seem to have lost the ability to concentrate. Whenever I start to count my breath, this feeling of dread just drapes itself all over me, blankets me, so that I can see or think of nothing else. I'm telling you, I'm at my wit's end over it, especially since meditation has come to mean so much to me. With my external life now so diminished, it gives me access to the other half, you know, the inner half, or at least it used to ... Besides, it's one of the very few things I can still do for myself ..."

The tiff instantly evaporated from Mark's mind, and he was already down on his knee in front of her chair covering her hands, which were folded in her lap, with his right hand and wiping a tear from her cheek with his left. He ached for her in sympathy and was, perhaps for the first time, in awe of her strength, her heroic perseverance, in soldiering on as she had been all this time since zero hour. He felt oddly grateful for their quarrel, for it was like an axe taken to what had become the thick ice of their polite and perfunctory behavior towards each other. The marriage was alive again and flowing with fresh emotion. He wanted nothing more than to offer her some real help and, what is more, he felt he now had the inner resources to do just that.

"You know, sweetheart," he began, "I've been giving your meditation problem some thought lately, aware as I am of the trouble you've been having and how much it means to you. But I just couldn't come up with anything worth mentioning ... until just now while you were fretting over it and all of a sudden this short little tale from Hasidic lore popped into my head. Something out of Kafka, I think. Funny, but I hadn't thought about it since I first read it in graduate school. But it did impress me at the time. It's short enough to paraphrase, so I'll give it a try. It's called "Leopards in the Temple":

> Leopards break into the temple and drink to the dregs what is in the sacrificial pitchers. This happens over and over again. In time they learn to calculate it in advance, and it becomes a part of the ceremony.

"Oh my God, Mark, that's wonderful! That's marvelous!" Julie shouted, tossing her head back and laughing.

"Well, pithy to be sure, but I don't—"

"—No, no, love! You couldn't possibly know ... You see, that is the very same thing Hattie told me weeks ago when I was complaining to her about the problem, but in my self-absorption I had totally forgotten it. Of course, she made the point in a totally different way, without the symbolism of parable, but it comes down to the same thing. She said I had to trust the process, that maybe that nasty feeling is sup*posed* to be there, that maybe the meditation itself is presenting it as something I must deal with. I have to make the terrifying leopards part of the ceremony, so to speak, the 'ceremony' of my meditation. I have to bring them in, befriend them, to have any chance of understanding them."

"Of course," Mark seconded, "since understanding is the first step of transformation, in this case the trans-formation of leopards, i.e., hostile forces, into powers of the Self, to be used at will, this being the ultimate goal of any alchemical experiment," he added, pleased with himself for having steered the conversation towards his own scholarly obsession, but even more for having told her something to buoy her spirit.

"Well, since I've now been given the same advice by two mentors—*three*, I suppose, if you count Kafka—I guess I'd better start taking it seriously, don't you think?" she said, shaking her head to flip a lock of hair into place.

"I most certainly do," he replied, leaning in to give her a gentle hug, followed by a long, open kiss that reminded both of them of the old days. "I know it's not the easiest thing to do, my love," he went on, "but serious self-inquiry, which is what I believe all meditation is, is always going to involve some suffering, sometimes rock-bottom suffering. You just have to get through it as best you can, without pushing it away. I know you can do this; you'll learn to manage the inner world with the same grace under pressure you've used to manage the outer. You're becoming an artist of your own life," he smiled, nuzzling her before getting up and checking his watch.

"Well, I'd better be off. I'm running late for class." He picked up the poetry book and headed for the door.

"Hey," she called out to him when he was halfway there, "why don't you leave the office a little early today, so we can work on some 'research' together here at home … if you catch my drift."

"If you're pitching, I'm catching," he laughed, heading out.

From then on Julie was determined to make "the leopard" a part of the ceremony. She resolved to avoid or fight off the menacing dread that was "spoiling" her meditation no longer. On the contrary, she invited it in, made room for it in her mind and body as best she could. At first, of course, she found this extremely difficult, going against the grain as it did; it violated all her cherished ideals of meditation as a state of serene and relaxed equanimity, impervious to all "the slings and arrows of outrageous fortune."

But she persevered, and over the next several days she allowed the feeling to take over her meditation sessions completely, to do with and to her whatever it wanted, which made "it" very happy, but, paradoxically, also took some of the edge off it, enabling her to work with it better. She began to study it, to watch it quietly and minutely, almost as if it were a mantra or a Zen koan, for in truth it *was* a koan, not the artificial sort assigned by Zen masters to students, such as "Show me your face before your parents were born," but a koan from her very life, a life koan, which always has a vital, compelling quality to it that is lacking in the ones found in the manuals.

In the beginning the feeling was just that: a feeling, something to be felt rather than seen. But in time, as she kept her outer eyes closed but her mind's eye open and poised, she began to discern some sort of visual component to the feeling. The inner visual field at large was, to be sure, dark, but it was not empty. It was filled with all sorts of shapes and textures and colors flittering and skittering across the stage of consciousness. The feeling itself, however, was evolving into something of a mysterious protagonist, a pitch-black, shapeless blob that held the stage against a slightly less black background, as if it were playing the character of an intruder skulking around a darkened room.

As a mutating shape in this cosmic mindscape, the blob changed in precise accord with each permutation of the feeling: as the feeling waxed or waned in intensity, the shape expanded or contracted like a black balloon. If the feeling diminished to a low ebb, the blob flattened; if the feeling disappeared, as it sometimes did when she became otherwise distracted, so too did the blob, only to return the instant she realized she had forgotten it. The blob never ceased to move and change, yet over the days and weeks that followed, she noticed that it seemed to be settling into one particular shape more than any other: the shape of an arch. She knew enough to resist the temptation to interpret this as, say, the arch of a church nave or a castle or a gateway to an old medieval city. All such readings simply generated an endless chain of narratives, taking her away from the thing itself. So she ignored them all, focusing doggedly, solely, on the morphing process, fortified by her deepening faith that it would reveal itself, in its full significance, in the fullness of time.

One mid-morning, she found herself alone in the house. Nate was at school, Mark was at a department meeting, Hattie was out running some errands and the alternate aide was late but expected at any minute. She was sitting comfortably in the living room, in the path of an incoming sunbeam, and enjoying the solitude, which she realized was the first such delight she had known since zero hour. No one around! No TV or radio blaring. No washing machine or drier churning. No busy bodies rushing to and fro, no purpose-driven voices invading her space. The perfect opportunity to meditate. Softly she closed her eyes, which flitted just a bit before settling, and took a few deep breaths to center herself. Before long the blob appeared, at first shapeless and featureless but soon enough shifting into the shape of the now-familiar arch. A black arch. Against a less black background. For a moment or two, she did the usual, simply observing the arch and feeling the feeling as presented. But after a while, she found herself, with no deliberate intent, scrutinizing this black thing before her mind's eye, looking for minute features, tiny distinctions, that might be tucked away within the general figure. The arching line itself, for example, was not perfect: if one thought of the arch as the upper half of a circular clockface, then there were tiny indentations at ten and two o'clock, and just above each indentation a tiny outcropping. Moreover, the horizontal baseline of the arch, the semicircle's diameter, had three minute breaks in it, dividing it roughly into quarters. She had no idea what any of this might signify, if anything.

Over the next few weeks, as she continued studying it, she began to note vague wisps of linear features inside the arch, as if her eyes were gradually adjusting to a dark theater: she saw that there were parallel vertical lines, no fewer than two, topped by a slightly convex horizontal, possibly indicating a concentric arch within the arch, or perhaps a rectangle. The thing also began to variegate itself into a field of more and less dark planes, giving the heretofore flat surface a quality of rounded depth. She felt that something was slowly revealing itself, but intuitively she refused to let her longing to know push the process.

Then one day, as she was examining the bottom quadrisected diameter with the utmost care, she thought she could see that the two inner quarter lines were themselves quadrisected. Two four-part forms next to each other, like two packages of black Lady Fingers ... Fingers ... Fingers ... One would almost think they were ... the fingerlike toes of two feet. Oh my God! That's it! Duncan! It's Duncan! Staring straight at me!

She reeled with delight. There was no doubt. Her every fiber, transcending its paralysis, told her she was right. And it was as if the final revelation, so ardently wished for, now threw an exposing light back onto the figure in her imagination, bringing it to full clarity. There he was, the little devil, the neckless head, the body-length arms, the slitted eyes below the monobrow. The four-toed feet made him anatomically incorrect, but then he was a toy, wasn't he, not a mock-up of a specimen. Though now revealed, he was still as black as pitch, which brought on paroxysms of laughter as it struck her that, in this case, darkness illuminated was still ... dark.

She felt empowered and basked in the enjoyment of what she took to be her first substantive accomplishment since zero hour. But alas, her triumph was short-lived: She soon realized she hadn't a clue as to why Duncan should appear to her this way, why this stuffed monkey that was sitting right there with her should assume so important a place in her psychic life. Also, hours later when her euphoria over the revelation had cooled, she found to her dismay that the feeling of dread that had sent her on this meditative quest in the first place was still there, perhaps even more painful than before. Her heart sank with the somber awareness that she wasn't finished, that she had merely reached a way station in a daunting process apparently meant to take her far deeper into herself, into the depths of the inner sea of good and evil. It would probably get a lot worse before it got better ... *if* it got better. What would become of her? She shuddered.

But there was no question of backing out now. She was committed to seeing the ordeal through to the end, come what may. So she marshaled her psychic resources and poised herself to resume her meditations, from now on with Duncan for inner company, for, despite being exposed, he did not just go away but insisted on staying on for the ride, wherever it might lead. On some days he would appear to her inner eye from far off in the distance and remain there for the duration of the session; on others he would move in close to within the intimate distance of a conversation partner. She had no control over any of this, neither his location nor his behavior. *The spirit moveth as it listeth*, she recalled from the King James Bible of her Methodist childhood. Sometimes he would sit in the lotus position right beside her and seem to meditate along with her. Was he meditating on *himself*, as she was? Was he meditating on *her*, forming a sort of symmetry like that of opposed mirrors reflecting each other ad infinitum? Sometimes he sat facing her, sometimes his back was to her, sometimes he sat at a right angle to her, or an angle in between. His size in a given meditation was protean and unpredictable, just as the blob's had been: he could manifest as his familiar eighteen-inch stuffed-toy self, or grow to the size of a macaque or a chimp, or even a full-size hulking gorilla, pacing the space before her, beside her, around her, his impossibly wrinkled knuckles scraping the ground and steadying him as he moved. The only thing she could predict was his presence; he was always there within. In this sense too he reminded her of a Zen koan: once it gets inside you and grips you, as the masters say, you can neither swallow it nor spit it out. For relief, you have no choice but to solve it.

One November morning, after listening to Hattie read her a passage from *The Gateless Gate*, the signature koan collection of Rinzai Zen, she settled in for her daily meditation. After closing her eyes and deep-breathing for a while, she recognized that something was different, radically different: Duncan was there as always, but this time he was not set against the usual less-black background. On the contrary, he was bathed in a sea of light—warm, quickening, effulgent light, light that filled a space that was otherwise totally bare. No walls, no floor, no ceiling, no exterior, nothing but Duncan and she herself, in a world of light. Oddly, she was not put off by the absence of familiar, or for that matter *any*, surroundings. The light did all the surrounding and that suited her just fine. Calmly she watched Duncan, who was sitting (on the light!) perhaps twenty-five feet in front of her and slightly to the left. He was hunkered down with his back to her but at an angle that allowed her to see just the barest outline of the right side of his face. He seemed to her serene, as did she to herself. It occurred to her that they could stay together that way, indefinitely.

Suddenly there was a flash of light so brilliant as to make the light it illuminated seem pedestrian by comparison. Like a shot she felt herself propelled forward and slightly leftward into the body of Duncan, the instant of their fusion fizzing and hissing like an electric wire downed in a summer lightning storm. She felt euphoric, ecstatic, mighty—she was Queen of the Universe ... And then she woke up.

She had fallen asleep during meditation and been dreaming.

16

Skeeter Michelin shivered in his heavy plaid mackinaw against the fierce November wind whipping down York St. He was raised a southern boy in the States and had to laugh every time it struck him that he couldn't be more out of his element up here in Ottawa. He stepped up his pace and was thankful to finally reach and pull open the heavy Country French door to the Bourbon Bar, one of the less frenzied pubs in the city's Bymarket section. The burst of warm, 40-proof air that hit him was salving; at the same time, he winced at the few flurries still clinging to his coat.

Instantly he spotted his old friend at the far end of the bar, hunched pensively, it seemed to him, over his glass. Moving towards him, his one still-gloved hand upraised, Skeeter called out in a firm tone of greeting, "Sammy, Sammy Clause, you old dawg from the shotgun days! My parish buddy!" But Skeeter was taken aback when he got no response and thought, for an instant, he had the wrong man. That is, until Santa happened to turn his head to the right and break into a smile: "Hey, Skeet, how's the boy? Good to see you, pal."

"Jesus, Sammy, don't do that to me. When I didn't see you react, I thought I'd lost it, that I'd have to check back into Bedlam for a few months," Skeeter said, sitting down, shoving his gloves into his coat pocket and rubbing his hands together vigorously.

Santa laughed. "Apologies, my friend. I guess I just don't respond to 'Sammy' anymore. I'd say you're about the only person on the planet who still calls me that."

"Oh, come on now," Skeeter protested, "There's your folks and all the people in the neighborhood." At the same time he raised a finger to Julien, the bartender, whom he knew well, and indicated he wanted the same thing his friend was having.

"Been a while since I been home, Skeet."

"Ah, well, I'm sorry to hear that ... Say, what is it you're drinkin' anyway," Skeeter asked, nimbly changing the subject.

"It's still Pappy's," Santa answered, taking a sip.

"Yikes!" Skeeter said, feigning shock. "That's a little rich for my budget, Sammy ... Oh well, I guess just one little ol' Pappy's won't hurt."

"The fact is, I gave up drinkin'—oh, I guess it must be about fifteen years now—but I decided to make an exception tonight, you know, for old times' sake," Santa said, raising his glass in a toast.

"Well, fuck me, you old teetotaler," Skeeter laughed, noticing how little, if at all, his friend had changed since their last meeting, also in Ottawa, some five years earlier: same matinée-idol looks, sort of Valentino-esque, thought Skeeter; same thick, dark, youthfully spiked hair poised over those prominent cheek-bones. The raised leather collar of his camel's hair windbreaker ringed by the toney black-cashmere scarf gave him the sheen of an ad straight out of *GQ*. Skeeter, by contrast, looked older to Santa, much older than his forty-eight years: his olive Creole face was starting to curl up into itself, his hair was down to a few squirrelly strands crossing an uneven dome to meet in a gray mullet that hung limply down the back, and there was an alarming sallow hue tainting the whites of his eyes. Also, his fingers looked arthritically gnarled as he reached for his Pappy's, probably the outcome of four decades spent pressing trumpet valves.

They clinked glasses and looked forward, these two lifers, to getting reacquainted. There was a lot of catching up to do. Skeeter Michelin was, in truth, not only Santa's oldest, but his *only*, remaining friend. They had grown up in the same shotgun neighborhood in New Orleans, "shotgun" referring to the style of the tiny, twelve-foot-wide houses in which the city's working poor lived. It was said that if you opened every door in

193

a shotgun house and fired a shotgun through the front doorway, the blast would fly cleanly to the other end and out the back. Fred Clause actually tested this theory one Friday night after overindulging in the Pappy's: Alas, the test was a failure, the shotgun shells blasting a hole two feet wide in the back-bedroom wall, fortunately just *before* his poor wife was ready to crawl into her bed.

Skeeter lived across the street, one shotgun to the left. The two boys grew up suffering the mutual terror of violently alcoholic fathers and abjectly submissive mothers, a bond sealing their friendship from early on, one not unlike that of a "band of brothers" in combat. When one old man was on the warpath, his kid would run across the street for sanctuary. When both were, the boys would meet in the street and find some mischief to get into, often itself violent. Both of them left home in their teen years, going their separate ways and becoming professional jazz musicians. The current era of social media enabled them to reconnect some two decades later. Skeeter was the perfect "friend" for Santa, one he didn't see more than once every few years, and then briefly, and to whom he was absolutely unbeholden.

In fact, in this particular moment it was the other way around: "Listen, Sammy, I'm sorry about the gig fallin' through," Skeeter said, turning serious. "My boss had penciled in some other bass man without tellin' me, some friend of his from Toronto. The guy can go either electric or acoustic; the scuttlebutt is, he once played with Dizzie … Anyway, I'm awfully sorry, getting you up here to the north pole like this for nothin'. Tell me, how can I make it up to you?"

Santa turned on his stool and looked his old friend square in the face, his eyes darkly twinkling as he raised his glass. Then, breaking out into a big, broad grin, he reassured him, "Now don't you be worryin' about *that*, ol' buddy. For the few days I'll be stayin' in these parts, I've got plenty to keep me busy."

"Well, I'm very glad to hear that," Skeeter said, relieved. "Of course, you'll come over for dinner one evening, won't you? Marie would love to see you." Marie was Skeeter's reason for settling in Ottawa. A pretty, raven-haired girl of French Canadian and native American ethnicity when they met at one of his gigs fifteen years earlier, she agreed to marry Skeeter on condition that he stay in Ottawa so she could live near her family. Skeeter agonized over the decision for weeks before deciding that love was more important to him than music, not to mention climate, for if asked for a list of his top five North American cities for *not* having a successful career in jazz and *not* living the good life, Ottawa would have been right up there near the top.

"I'm afraid I'm gonna have to take a rain check on that, Skeet. You see, I'm in the middle of negotiating for a job in Toronto. One of their guys is in town doing some scouting and I'm gonna need to be available for meetings at any time. When you told me on the phone the other day that there was no job here, I set up the interview. You know how it is; you lived on the road for years—a traveling sideman just like me," Santa said, affecting resignation, even as, in raising his glass, he lay his other hand on his friend's forearm with genuine affection. He was so skilled by now in mixing truth with falsehood; it was almost an unconscious reflex.

The two friends reordered and carried their drinks to a booth along the back wall for more privacy.

"You look good, Sammy. Nice threads. You always did have an eye for fashion, even in the days when you couldn't afford a pair of socks," Skeeter joked. The eyes of both men glistened with that slightly moist, far-away look that comes when a note of nostalgia is struck between lifelong friends of common origin, especially when "the good old days" were bad. "So tell me, anyway, how've you been?"

"Oh, you know me, Skeet. I'm in it for the music. I go wherever it takes me."

"Really, Sammy? You mean you've never been tempted to settle down and have a family? A good-looking guy like you—I can't believe some sweet, young thing hasn't struck your fancy."

"Plenty of women have struck my fancy, Skeet, just not my libido," Santa said, surprising even himself with a witticism that was also half confession. As a rule and for obvious reasons, he never referred to his own sexuality in conversation, nor to his style of gender relations, even obliquely as here. But he was going on forty-seven years of age and perhaps beginning to feel, though not yet consciously, the utter loneliness and desolation of his chosen path. Was he "leaking" to Skeeter some deeply buried need for connection, for being recognized for himself, hideous warts and all, and not just the cool-jazz persona he had cultivated so meticulously over the years? If a psychotherapist were to ask him this, he would no doubt laugh in his face, for, as intelligent, and even educated, as he was, Santa possessed little self-insight or awareness. His subtlety of mind was reserved for his sexual obsession and for the music, that seductive art of the ear "beyond good and evil," which meant that the most he could ever articulate about his personal psychology would be a certain sense of general malaise that crept over him every so often, more and more as the years went by. Right now, for example, in this moment of what passed for Santa as intimacy, he had no idea why Luke should have just popped into his mind, the boy with whom he had shared something real, however predatory and vile that relationship might appear in the eyes of society.

"Libido … Li*bido*?" Skeet asked, puzzled. "That's a college word, Sammy. All my books have pictures in them. Does it mean what I think it means?"

"I'm afraid it does, my friend. I only have eyes for the boys." There it was, another half confession, this one only half aware to the confessant himself. The ambiguous sense of "boys," male children versus "The Boys in the Band," was Santa's way of leaking his secret safely, knowing as he did which sense Skeeter would take.

"Geez, Sammy, I would never have guessed. I mean you never let on or anything … Lucky thing you live in the jazz world where anything goes."

"Yeah, but that's the thing, Skeet: You see, I *don't* really live in it, do I? A couple months here, a couple weeks there, and it's off to the next gig. Don't get me wrong, that's the way I've played it, that's the way I've wanted it, but maybe it's starting to feel a little old." Catching the bartender's eye, Santa raised his empty glass towards him and made a circle in the air, indicating another round for them both.

"By the way, Skeet, the drinks are on me, and no backtalk please." Unused to alcohol, Santa was feeling decidedly tipsy; he was also feeling a common symptom of that state, the impulse to talk, though not without a silent warning to himself to watch his words. He was wrestling in his mind with the question, How do you open up *a little*?

"Say, Skeet, how'd you get that name, anyway?" Santa suddenly asked, emptying his glass and feeling jolly all over.

"When I was little," Skeeter waxed nostalgic, "I was always buggin' my folks for somethin' or other and they just started callin' me Skeeter, like the damn pesky swamp skeeters you can't get away from down there. Later on in teen years, the meaning of jacking off got tacked onto it—I mean, what teenage dude isn't a skeeter, right?—which made it double the fun for me. Eventually I just gave up tryin' to ditch the name … But you're a whole different ballgame with 'Santa,' aren't you? Now there's a nickname a dude can live with, right, Sammy? The gift that keeps on giving."

"Yeah, that's me all right. Every kid's dream. The old bastard pinned it on me. He liked the band Santana— you know, the jazz fusion element—and he'd yell at me 'Hey Santana!' whenever he wanted me to put the record on the hi-fi. Eventually he shortened it to 'Hey, Santa!,' you know, and over time, I guess, everybody else latched onto it. And the rest, as they say, is history."

"Ah, I see," Skeeter nodded. "Oh, by the way, Sammy, I'm sorry to hear about your daddy."

"Sorry? What's to be sorry about? He's there and I'm here. That's a *good* thing," Santa cracked wise, all smiles. His eyelids were drooping just a tad.

Skeeter, in mild shock, sat up straight. Could it be his friend hadn't heard? He *did* say he'd been out of touch. He had better proceed with caution. "Sammy, is it possible you haven't heard your daddy's passed away? … "

Santa was looking Skeeter straight in the eye. The smile was gone; his face was of stone.

"God, Sammy, I'm sorry to be the one to break it to you. It happened just recently. Cirrhosis. My mama told me about it on the phone, must be about a month ago. She was at the funeral there with your mom and your aunt who came down from Prairieville … Sammy, I'm so sorry!"

"What for?" Sammy shot back, looking now at his glass, then remarking venomously, "I wondered why the world was feeling like a better place recently. Must be because he's out of it." With that he took a deep, sullen swig of his replenished Pappy's, emptying the glass and almost slamming it back down on the table. A few heads turned.

"Look, Sammy," Skeeter said "I know you had it much worse than I did. My old man would at least dry out once in a while and give us some peace. Besides, I had my brothers to take some of the heat off me, and after he broke Bobby's arm that time divin' over the dinner table at him, he stayed on the wagon for two years. You never got that kind of relief, I know. With you it was a constant grind, day in and day out. I have to hand it to you; how you came out of that hellhole without getting totally bent out of shape, God only knows. – But you know, Sammy, I'm thinkin' that there's always a silver lining somewhere, even in a hellhole, and in our case it's the music. It's our bastard old men who introduced us to it—to Miles and Bix and Dizzie and Buddy and Satchmo—and started us playin'—

"—He showed me a little fingering, I'll grant him that, but no more than that," Santa said grudgingly as he looked away, as if wanting to take back what he had just given. "All I ever needed to know about acoustic base I learned from John Casey in three semesters at Loyola. The man was a genius; he once toured with Wynton, you know, and he had his own combo in Chicago. But then the drugs got him, just like all the others. Now *there's* an addiction and a death I *can* mourn," Santa concluded, the Pappy's morphing his voice into something close to a cynical snarl.

With that remark Santa's inner red flag went up as he realized, in his drunken haze, that he had lost control of his mouth to a dangerous degree. This, of course, was the other reason he had long ago chosen sobriety, apart from the disagreeable dulling of his senses: He needed to keep his wits about him at all times. So when Skeeter suggested a nightcap, Santa politely declined. They engaged in some further small talk about New Orleans and jazz, after which Santa slowly got up, focused his eyes and then walked carefully and deliberately over to the bar where he paid the tab. When he returned, the two friends put on their coats, Saks Fifth Avenue and Mickey Finn's, embraced and headed out.

They stood huddled against the entrance, bracing themselves against the stabbing wind. "By the way, where you stayin'?" Skeeter asked.

"I'm over at the Marriott, on Kent."

"Nice, very nice," Skeeter responded in an exaggerated tone, unable to conceal a note of jealous snark. "I've played a few gigs there. That's the only way I'd ever get in."

The two friends wished each other well, turned and walked in opposite directions.

Three evenings later, Santa stood at the end of the check-in desk in the main lobby of the Marriott Hotel glancing at a complimentary copy of the *Ottawa Citizen*. He was wearing his camel's hair coat again, on this occasion, however, with a natty red satin scarf, neatly tucked in. He chatted casually with a dark-complected young concierge of Indian descent bearing the nametag Arnav who stood behind the desk leaning against the sleek brown-mahogany sidewall. There was a lull; most guests had checked in by now and were at dinner. The lobby was all rather severe squares and rectangles, not unlike a

Japanese Zen monastery; it was bathed in a lemon-hued light, as reflected off the bright tan floor tiles and leather furniture. It was nearing eight p.m. and the spate of glass exit doors onto Queen St. were like so many ebony squares set off by the recessed ceiling lights.

"Dining out this evening, Mr. Clause?" asked the young concierge.

"Yes, Arnav, I think I will. Tell me, what's the word on the Fish Market Restaurant up on York and William?"

"Oh, very good, sir, one of the best in the Bymarket area, I would say. Many of our guests give it a big thumb's up."

"Thanks. Sounds like the place for me."

Just then an elevator door opened and out walked a matronly lady wrapped in a brown parka with a faux fur collar. Her ample girth, and the clack of her high heels on the tile floor, obscured the diminutive figure trailing behind her, who suddenly darted out and sped past the woman in his navy-blue Nikes. He was a boy of about nine in a blue Toronto Maple Leafs hoodie that sported a big white leaf right in the middle. His hood was up but the pretty, brown ringlets framing his forehead were still visible. The face was cherubically round, dotted with freckles just under the eyes, and he flashed a big smile as he sped past the desk on his way out, in response to Arnav's friendly greeting, "And how is Master Ethan this fine evening?"

"Good!" He stopped himself abruptly in mid-sprint to reply.

"And are we off again to fetch mother and dad's evening coffee."

"Yep."

"And which one will it be tonight, Starbucks or Dunkin' Donuts?"

"Tonight's Dunkin' Donuts," he chirped, skipping out the glass door into the glittering nightlights of Queen St.

"Sweet kid," Santa remarked to Arnav and smiled, looking down at his newspaper.

"Yes, very sweet," the concierge agreed. "He comes from a prosperous family. The Doyles. The father is an investment banker in Toronto. They stay with us two, sometimes three times a year. Very nice people. Yes indeed, very nice."

Santa, of course, already knew not only this about the Doyles, but more, much more. He knew, for example, that Robert Doyle often came to Ottawa on business, bringing his wife and young son with him whenever his schedule was light. He knew that Mrs. Doyle—Dorothy—had once been a fashion model for the Sutherland Agency in Toronto, which explained the boy's comely face. He knew, about Ethan, that the boy was not only pretty but, almost as important, polite to his elders. How did he know this? Simple: It was the lady who had exited the elevator first, Ethan a respectful second. This deference, a product of good breeding, upped the boy's "hotness rating" considerably in Santa's eyes, and nether regions, for what was more gratifying to lust than the seduction of youthful virtue.

The fact is that Santa had had his eye on young Ethan from the moment he and his parents checked in four days earlier; they came in during a lull as he, Santa, sat in a lobby easy chair with a direct view of the desk, scouting prospects from behind his newspaper. Santa watched, and waited, waited, listened and watched, and his patience was rewarded when he at last felt sure he understood the Doyle family's pattern of post-dinner behavior: They dined in the hotel restaurant every evening from seven to eight, then retired to their suite on the sixteenth floor, room 1624 to be exact. Twelve to fifteen minutes later, Ethan would come back down alone to fetch his parents' coffee at one of the shops across the street.

Santa had managed to confirm the consistency of this routine through subtle, "disinterested" questions about Ethan put to Arnav a few evenings earlier, further concealing his motives by feigning curiosity about other guests who had checked in without children. To the concierge Mr. Clause was just an avid "people watcher" with whom he could enjoy spending a few minutes chatting over the desk around dinnertime.

But, of course, like any performing artist, Santa, when he was scouting, was a master of the illusion of spontaneity, of seeming to react to the events of the moment, when in fact his every look, word, gesture and movement enacted, even as it concealed, a meticulously calculated agenda. Since first spotting the boy when the family checked in, Santa proceeded, over the next several evenings, to take up watch in the same lobby chair facing the desk, not directly, of course, but from an oblique angle. (All directness was strictly avoided.) As he observed the boy on his first solo coffee run, his heart began to race with the realization that he had discovered a possible opening for a grab. From that moment on his intelligence bent itself intensely and entirely to working out the minutest details of a plan and anticipating every conceivable mishap. It was an extremely tight window: no more than the few seconds it would take the boy to exit the coffee shop, cross the sidewalk carrying the brew in a cardboard holder and step off the curb into Queen St.

Santa knew immediately that the key incident would be a "bump and drop," which involved his standing behind the open rear gate of his parked van and "accidently" bumping into the boy just off the curb, causing him to drop the coffee, and then bending down with him to see if it was salvageable. While the two of them were down and obscurely busy between parked cars,

Santa would press the chloroformed handkerchief over the boy's face, slip him deftly into the van through the gate and take off. Dangerous, yes. But also very doable. He just had to make sure his crouched body hid that of the boy during the grab so as to block the view of any passing pedestrians. As for passing drivers on Queen St., he would take his chances with the cloak of deepening darkness.

It was always the tedious aspects of a plan that presented the greatest danger, since they invited boredom and the consequent temptation to cut corners and be slipshod. Santa knew this very well and always forced himself to keep his concentration poised even during the most mundane planning exercises. In this particular instance, the tedium came with working out the locations and maneuverings of the van. The intersection of Queen and Kent where the Marriott stood was heavily trafficked and parking was usually difficult to impossible. On three successive afternoons, Santa had to sit in his van in a nearby restricted zone for some two hours, observing the pattern of parked cars as they came and went, in order to be sure he would be able to park right in front of Dunkin' Donuts during the critical moments. Precision of location was a must. And even then, there was no guarantee the boy would cross the street from precisely behind his van rather than from between two other cars, or, for that matter, from the corner. Nor was there any guarantee he would enter Dunkin' Donuts at all that evening, since he seemed to enjoy—or perhaps his parents enjoyed—alternating between Dunkin' and Starbucks. (On this evening, as it turned out, he was in luck on both counts.)

So in any grab there were always incalculables; the important thing was to anticipate all contingencies as carefully as possible and be ready to abort at even the faintest indication that something, no matter how seemingly trivial, might be going awry: an early or late arrival by the victim, a grab scene at which something seemed out of place or missing, a nearby occupied car or a car, occupied or not, whose motor was idling. Santa was also a master of self-denial when called for. There was always the next time, the next grab.

Santa knew that Ethan Doyle was at this moment standing at the counter in the Dunkin' Donuts shop across the street waiting patiently for his order. He folded his *Ottawa Citizen*, inserted it into his coat pocket and said to the concierge, "You can hand me my fiddle case, Arnav. I want to make sure I get to the Fish Market while they're still serving." The concierge bent down behind the desk and lifted the case up by its handle with one hand, easily handing it over to Santa.

"The case is very light, Mr. Clause. I'm guessing it's empty." It was; Santa had brought the empty case to his room to vacuum its felt lining and tighten its snap locks, then stowed it behind the front desk while waiting for the boy.

"Not for long, Arnav, not for long," the jazzman quipped darkly as he headed for the exit, whistling the saucy trumpet entrance of "So What." The thought occurred to him that he had not played Miles's music even once during his trysts with Luke. He wondered why.

17

As the writhing cloud beds pass over the thickly forested mountain, they are tickled by its peak, releasing their vapors in the form of droplets that cling to the branches and ferns and moss below. *Life is good up here. Plenty to eat for everyone, so there's no struggle, no competition. We don't even need a water source, since the plants are always drenched in the stuff. And the trees are low enough to eat from without stretching. Silverback says we've got to leave our tree bed today and move down the mountain to where it's warmer with the cold season coming on. I hope he doesn't take us too far—I'm tired from breaking up all those fights yesterday among the little ones. God, how they chase each other around. Big Ears in particular can be such a nuisance; he's always teasing his little brother, picking on him, especially when he knows I'm busy or not looking. He needs a good cuffing. Ah, here's some thick shoots full of juicy pulp. Umm, delicious. I'll call those sleepyhead boys down for breakfast. Harumph! Nothing!*

Harumph! Harumph! *What the …? Oh, I know: I'll bet they got a little tipsy gorging on that berry juice last night and are sleeping it off. Damn! You just can't leave them alone for a second.* Eeee!!! Eeee!!! Eeee!!! *That should do it. Yeah, here they come.*

Later, heading down the mountain. *Tough climb down through all that thick brush, much more for me than them. Can hardly see the ground beneath this dense green. Good thing we're coming out into a clearing. Oh, there they go, those reckless little devils, scampering every which way, released from forest captivity, thrilled to be running free … Uh-oh, trouble! Sonovabitch! There it is, over there. I see it, half hidden under those carefully arranged leaves and twigs: one of those camouflaged rope traps. Thank God they're away from it. Let me go stand by it nonchalantly and test them, see if they've learned anything from all my teaching. I'll just put my foot on the loop. There! Ah, here they come. Good, you see it, don't you? That's right, one of you step on the taut branch while the other undoes the loop. Careful, Big Ears, hold that branch steady now, otherwise your brother is a goner! All right. Very good! Very good! It's nice to know all those lessons weren't wasted, not even on Big Ears. Still, my heart is heavy. A thousand warnings, as many warnings as there are trees on this mountain, cannot protect them from the ten thousand traps of all kinds that lie in wait for them, wherever they go. Some of our troop, who've been to the other side of the mountain, the side where the sun goes down, say it's even worse over there—more traps, bigger and better traps, more dangerous traps, better hidden traps. They say most of them aren't even meant for us. But that doesn't make them any less deadly. And the lower we go, the worse it gets. It seems there's no mountain high enough to lift my spirit.*

18

It was mid-afternoon on an overcast Sunday in early November, the day of the first SCO or Syracuse Children's Orchestra concert of the school year. This was the event carefully selected by Mark for his invalid wife's "coming out." The venue, the downtown Civic Center concert hall, was familiar and, with one significant exception, wheelchair friendly; the crowd would be filled with parents and fellow academics who were friends; and Nate would be on percussion for most of the program. Julie agreed with Mark and Hattie that it was time to take the plunge.

And so the three of them arrived together in the family sedan, parking it in a special area on the Center premises reserved for musicians, staff and special-needs patrons. Nate, who had to be there early, had gotten a lift from a friend's parents. The one exception to the hall's accessibility to the disabled was the long escalator most patrons were required to use to ascend to the main orchestra level. This problem was obviated in Julie's case by one of the private elevators Mark had reserved, which took them up to just outside the right-side entrance. Julie, rejecting the offer of a sidewall box as unnecessary "pampering," insisted on rolling down the wide, thickly carpeted right aisle to about the fourth row where she parked, in the aisle, next to her husband and her aide who took the first two seats. For this kiddy concert seats were occupied only back to about the twentieth row, mostly by parents and siblings.

The trek from the car to her seat in the concert hall had been for Julie nothing less than a gauntlet of well-wishing and expressions of sympathy. Halfway along she came oh so close to turning her chair around and fleeing back to the safety of the domestic womb. Hattie was invaluable here, running interference with amusing side quips about this one's dress or that one's undress and resting her hand comfortingly on Julie's shoulder, a hand she couldn't feel but knew was there just the same.

Just before Hattie took her seat, she unobtrusively tucked Duncan onto Julie's lap, just under her coat, which she kept on during the performance. A little psychological edge—it couldn't hurt. They sat for a few minutes, Julie taking in the hall's sleek modernist style with its geometric masses of red, black and brown. She was feeling an odd mixture of proud expectation—after all, this was her son's performing debut—and agoraphobic nervousness, fully exposed as she was to the stares of so many who knew her but hadn't seen her since "B.A."

She tried to concentrate on the program, which Hattie read to her. It was an extremely demanding one, she thought, very heavy on the classical, featuring virtuoso pieces by Wagner, Elgar and Tchaikovsky—the overture to *The Flying Dutchman*, the grand "Pomp and Circumstance" march and the brilliant majestic finale of the Russian's *Fifth Symphony*, respectively. The only lighter fare was a medley of street-dance numbers from *West Side Story*, which, though ebullient in spirit, was actually no less demanding on the orchestra with its complex, syncopated jazz rhythms, just the sort of tricky business to trip up a novice percussion player.

Julie was nervous for her son. She knew he'd practiced hard and hadn't missed a rehearsal, but *still*. Finally, the teacher-conductor came out on stage and mounted the podium. He had the perhaps unfortunate fate to be called Mr. Wagner, which his players, of course, germanicized into Herr Wagner, pronounced "Vahgner," behind his back. He raised his baton, held it poised for a few seconds, and finally gave the downbeat. The program opened with part of a slow suite by Bach, calculated to get the players warmed up and ready to rock, so to speak, with the stellar music to come. The Bach piece relaxed Julie a bit, though not entirely. Hattie, attuned to the slightest permutations in Julie's condition as she was, picked up on this residual unease and vowed to keep half her attention on her charge for the duration of the concert.

The show went stunningly well from Wagner through Tchaikovsky, the young players seeming to gain in confidence, ensemble skill and subtlety as they moved through one difficult piece after another. Even the jazzy dance rhythms of Leonard Bernstein were tossed off without a hitch, Nate making every snare-drum entrance right on cue.

Still, despite the virtuoso playing, Julie somehow couldn't shake her nerves. That feeling of dread she had wrestled with for weeks in meditation was upon her with a vengeance. She focused on it yet again, now with an attitude of demanding to know why. Why? Why here? Why now? What the *fuck* is it?

And the instant she silently imploded with the f-word, it came to her, with the power of a revelation, that the dread she was feeling in this moment was not her own, not her own at all, but her son's! It had never been hers, always been his. She was feeling Nate's fear, as it rumbled up and down his intestines up there on stage; in this specific moment, it was his fear of the snare-drum part the orchestra was approaching as the grand finale of the program: the snare drum as featured in the closing section of Shostokovich's *Twelfth Symphony*, a percussion passage requiring enormous dexterity, off the charts in difficulty, a challenge for even the most seasoned professional drummers.

Built as he was to keep problems to himself, especially lately in view of his mother's condition, he never once mentioned his concerns about the Shostokovich in the months of rehearsals for the concert. Yet in this moment Julie knew, beyond all doubt, that she was experiencing Nate's fear—not a sympathy fear, not a mother's fear, but the very fear that was right now overloading Nate's nervous system. The distinction was subtle but profound to Julie. It was as if Nate in this moment were an extension of her own body and not his own person. But how could this be, she demanded. By what arcane power? What secret knowledge? And again a revelation comes, now itself a process like that of a thread being unraveled from a sweater: She looks down at her lap and sees the bulge in her coat being made by Duncan. *That's it! The connection, the key to it all, is Duncan! When he's with me, touching me—even though I can't feel him—he's acting as a conduit connecting me to Nate's feelings. I'm actually feeling whatever Nate's feeling as he feels it, as it unfolds, and reading those feelings maybe even more clearly than Nate is able to since I'm somehow still myself and have some distance from them. It's the oddest thing—I'm Nate and myself at the same time, and it's all made possible by a third party: Duncan. Go figure! ... So that's what that dream of me fusing with Duncan meant that I had weeks ago. It must have predicted or prefigured this moment I'm having right now. And the oppressive, tortured quality of all those meditations must have been meant to alert me to the suffering Nate was experiencing about the upcoming concert and is going through to an extreme right now.*

The Shostokovich came off well, even brilliantly. Nate was sharp, nimble and, to all but the most discerning ears, flawless. There for each and every entrance, instinctively marshaling his anxiety and pressing it into the service of his art. The crowd was stunned into silence by the final gigantic crescendo, Nate's long and furious drum roll bringing the piece to a colossal crashing end. Finally someone clapped, breaking the spell, and the house, standing as one, erupted in wild applause. Nate, as a featured player, was asked to stand for a solo bow, during which the audience intensified its applause to a level best described as fierce, half their attention on Nate and half on Nate's mother.

Julie was overcome with relief, and filled with pride and love for her son. The tears slipped down her cheeks, ignoring her efforts to hold them back. What could be more wonderful than this, her own paralysis reduced to a mere inconvenience in this moment of her son's triumph over profound adversity. This was the price of great artistic achievement and it was so well worth paying.

Yet, at the same time, vaguely rumbling underneath all the excitement and high emotions, there remained, still, a whisper of that same, now so familiar, dread. Again she looked down at the bulge in her coat that was Duncan and realized that her deep connection to this cartoonish monkey was still far from completely understood, still far from totally revealed, even with all she had learned in the few moments she'd spent sitting there in the aisle. Beginning with her dream weeks earlier, her dawning awareness had been like a row of florescent lights flipping on in her mind, one after the other, but stopping in front of that last, still unlit, tube. *Oh God, when will that last light blink on and what will it illuminate? And what will Nate, and Duncan—this strange, unfathomable link between us—, have to do with it?*

The crowd began to head for the exits, but many made a detour over to Julie to offer congratulations. "Wonderful performance! ... Nate the star of the show! ... You must be very proud!" And on and on in that vein. Julie did her best to appear gracious, but the excitement of the concert and, even more, of the extraordinary triadic insight that had come to her during it, so deeply foreboding as it was, was taking its toll. She began to experience difficulty breathing and shortly thereafter started to cough. She tried to suppress these symptoms, but that only worked for a few minutes; she thought, with the sort of idiocy that can afflict even the brightest among us in such circumstances, that it might be all right to risk her life for the sake of social propriety. But, of course, that was no good, and, the moment her chest began to heave as she gasped for air, Hattie and Mark went into action, he spreading his arms in front of Julie to herd the well-wishers together and signal an end to the social niceties and she crouching down at the wheelchair to help Julie calm down and try to catch her breathing rhythm.

An usher, a plump girl in a navy blue suit carrying a rolled-up program, pushed her way through the onlookers, using the program as a weapon, and announced that 911 had been called and an ambulance was on its way. Julie was busy trying to get enough air but heard with extraordinary clarity all that was being said around her: "Will she be all right? ... What do you think it is? ... She obviously wasn't ready for this. How could they ..." Inwardly she had to chuckle at the spectacle she was making of herself and her own foolishness in trying to suppress its onset. *You're getting what you deserve, girl!* she chided herself amiably.

Mark managed to push the rubberneckers a ways up the aisle away from his wife, but that was the best he could do. Doubtless under the spell of their own ghoulish curiosity, most of them simply refused to leave, even after being "encouraged" to do so several times by Mark himself. Finally, two darkly uniformed men, the older a paramedic, the younger an EMT, came striding smartly down the aisle steering a yellow gurney that parted the onlookers like the Red Sea. As the men, alerted to Julie's condition, placed her carefully on the stretcher, the paramedic barking terse commands to his apprentice, she noticed the traditional Asclepian patch the former wore on the shirt of his uniform over his heart—the light-blue six-pointed Star of Life, in its middle the white serpent entwined around the white healing staff. The macabre irony of the symbolic serpent crept over her, the snake whose venom sometimes kills and sometimes heals, the uncertain outcome of all illness and its medical treatment. But she felt oddly calmed, even amused, by this ground-zero situation, this being-placed precisely at the crossroads of life and death. There was nothing to worry about, really, nothing more to be done; either the one or the other would prevail, and, in a strange way, it was really none of her business. Her coughing eased.

With swift efficiency they slid her through the rear double-door opening of the white ambulance with the red stripes. Mark hopped in after her; Hattie would collect Nate, take the car and meet them at the ER. The ambulance driver, the third member of the team, turned on the siren and pulled away towards the Upstate Medical Center, which, thankfully, was only five or six blocks from the concert hall.

Through it all Julie remained acutely aware of everything going on around her, the cushy, high-tech style of the ambulance interior, the mingled smell of bleached sheets and medicine, the bleating siren, her husband's clammy hand on her cheek, and, above all, the terse, impersonal communications of the tech men as they performed their expert movements and well-practiced procedures, setting up the oxygen, listening through the stethoscope, reading the patient's O2 saturation, hanging the saline drip, and a myriad of other things. *We're coming in with a thirty-four-year-old female quadriplegic who's having difficulty breathing. Her heart rate is accelerated and she was having coughing fits, but they seem to have abated. We're monitoring her vitals and giving her saline … No, I don't know. It's hard to tell … We'll be there in a minute.*

Who are they talking about, she wondered.

19

The charcoal van cruised southwestward along Ontario's King's Highway 401, through a rural section with low rock formations hewn out on either side. The departure from Ottawa had been uneventful, just the way he liked it. By evening he would be in Toronto, one of his favorite cities in North America for both work and play. He was approaching Kingston and began seeing signs for Alexandria Bay and the Thousand Islands area on the U.S. side of the St. Lawrence River and wondered casually whether that neck of the woods was worth checking out. *Nah. I'll stick with the big city. Much easier to get lost.*

Mother Nature, however, had other plans. The skies had been blue and sunny, though cold, when he left the Marriott and headed south from Ottawa, but once he got onto 401, cloud masses began rolling in from the West, turning celestial blue into dreary gray in a matter of minutes. All weather passing through this border area

came from the Canadian northwest, so if you were heading into it, the changes could be fast and furious. He
was unaccustomed to these capricious shifts in winter
weather patterns typical of the North Country and felt a
little disoriented, as if he were driving into some kind of
fog-filled carnival funhouse.

But it soon ceased to be fun. Flurries quickly turned
to heavy snowfall, morphing in its turn into blizzard
conditions, the ground-zero state the locals referred to
ominously as the "White Shadow." He looked out the
windshield, unable to see anything beyond the hood of
the van. He put the windshield wipers on maximum
speed and found it made no difference. Either there was
nothing to see out there or what there was to see was
hidden in a white dessert without features. Either way
he had no choice but to pull over and stop, just in front
of another stopped car on his right he was counting on
to have found the shoulder lane.

He kept the motor running for a while for its heat
and flipped on the van radio, fishing for a local weather
bulletin. It was not hard to find: ... *heavy lake-effect snow
presently blanketing the Kingston area and heading quickly
east across northern New York State and Vermont ... the
heart of the storm further west near Toronto, causing several
closings of Highway 401 between that city and Montreal
... all unnecessary driving to be avoided ...*

He sat there undecided. And again nature decided for him. During the five minutes he took to consider his options, the blizzard passed, the clouds parted and out popped the sun smiling brilliantly down on a thin veneer of snow, as if the previous twenty minutes had all been a bad dream. He looked around incredulously and shook his head. But he wasn't going to play Russian roulette with the weather and reconsidered his earlier dismissal of the Thousand Islands region. It was not a winter resort to be sure, but a pleasant enough place to stay while he waited for the weather to clear. At most a day or two.

He drove across the vertiginous Thousand Islands Bridge, a single lane each way, south to the customs booths, passed through without fuss to stateside and then, reading his GPS on the dash, looked for signs for New York State Route 12, which ran along the south bank of the St. Lawrence. This he drove for a few sunny miles into Alexandria Bay, the only town in the area he'd ever heard of and, in his mind, as good a reason as any to stop there. He had no trouble finding, and settling on, the Riverbank Resort Hotel, which was the town's largest by far. He'd had a visual on it from the road two miles back and just kept his eyes on it until he pulled into the parking lot in front. It was a four-story build-ing that looked like an immense, whitewashed house-boat, giving the impression of being docked at the south bank. The hotel's facade faced away from the river, thus allowing all guests in balconied rooms on the rear wall an unimpeded view of the beautiful St. Lawrence and its "Thousand" tiny islands. The most notable of these was Heart Island, which featured a magnificent Rhineland castle built around 1900 for his wife by George C. Boldt, millionaire proprietor of the Waldorf Astoria Hotel in New York City.

He requested such a room at registration, for one night with an option for a second, and was given one without issue, this being the resort's off-season. Which, however, did not mean the place was empty; on the contrary, there was a fair number of guests relaxing in the lobby, mostly young people on get-away weekends (it was Saturday). In fact, the desk clerk, a tall, thin, blond fellow with pockmarked cheeks named Arthur, who was trying, without much success, to grow a pencil-thin moustache, commended to Santa two gala hotel events scheduled for that weekend: a leisurely boat ride through and around the islands, with a stop at Boldt Castle, and the opening of the ice-skating rink, which was the frozen-over swimming pool surface just off the hotel's façade. It was too early for skating, but the hotel wanted the publicity that would come with an opening attended by more than just the hotel staff. Santa feigned interest in both events, as usual, in order to make small talk with the clerk and assess him as a potential dupe, in case anyone "of interest" should appear on the scene.

But on this day it was just perfunctory; he wasn't planning on any adventures in Alexandria Bay; all he wanted was some downtime. As he grabbed his keycard and bag and headed for the elevators, his ears were pleasantly assaulted by the world-weary strains of a bluesy jazz piano, coming from the bar-restaurant just off the main entrance. *That's either Bill Evans's ghost or his reincarnation. Yeah! The aching, abandoned mood of* Moon Beams. The track being reproduced was "It Might as Well Be Spring." He loved the unobtrusive bass accompaniment of Chuck Israels on the album. It was one he cherished, a 1962 classic, and, as he stepped into the elevator, he suddenly felt his short stopover at the Riverbank Resort might be looking up.

He checked into his room on the third floor; it was decent enough but it had the faintly shabby look and musty smell of faded grandeur, with heavy, old, gold-embroidered drapes and a lumpy mattress and pillows long past their expiration date. The bathroom was little more than a phone booth. Still, there *was* that balcony with the fabulous view, and he *did* love the cold, so he rubbed his hands in anticipation of a couple of nice sits out there. He looked out the window onto the river and saw that the sky was once again hidden by massive, drooping cloudbanks and that it was starting to snow again. *How is this possible?*, he wondered, as only a tourist could.

He showered and lay down for a nap, intending to sleep for an hour at most. He slept for two-and-a-half. He sat up, swung his legs over the side of the bed and reflected. *The road is draining. My predilection is draining. Life is draining.* He dressed for dinner, donning his killer ensemble, a navy blue blazer with a white knit turtleneck. He studied himself in the mirror; his handsome face was adorned with two days of stubble, just the right amount for today's fashion. After primping at the mirror for a moment, he left the room and stood by the elevator. The ding dinged, the doors opened and he stepped inside, joining two women, one an attractive, thirtyish blonde, the other an older woman, similarly handsome, who could have been her mother. From the corner of his right eye he could see both women stealing glances at him on the way down. He still had it. This was the primary value women had for him: as a gauge of his own attractiveness. As long as the girls continued to pay attention, the boys would too. Thus the logic of his narcissistic fantasy.

He left the elevator, crossed the lobby and entered the dimly lit restaurant, the Jacques Cartier Room, buoyed by this little shot of self-esteem. At the same time, he felt a subtle weariness of needing it—yet again. Was there no end to need? And what was it exactly that he needed? To be desired? Desirable? To be loved? Was it the velvety feel of young flesh? The transcendent orgasm? An explosion of cosmic bliss enabling him to throw off this mortal coil? Was he seeking the spiritual in what was universally regarded as depravity? These and similar questions were like so many dead weights pulling down on his consciousness. They wearied him; they gave him headache.

It was going on seven p.m. and perhaps half the tables in the big room were occupied by guests who were either reading menus or already dining. The agreeable thrum of chatting filled the air. The hostess led him to a table for one placed against one of the massive arched windows of the room's west wall, with a moonlit view of the river. He settled himself, opened the menu to the inserted list of chef's specials, topped by the *Grilled Black Cherry Glazed Quail with Cognac Whipped Sweet Potatoes*, and ordered a ginger ale.

And that's when he heard it, again: the tinkling of the lounge piano. Only this time it was not the silken airs of Bill Evans that wafted over to him, but of Chopin. A gorgeous, shimmering melody, one he knew. Could it be the same player? Unlikely, considering the ocean of difference between the two styles. He knew, of course, that Benny Goodman "crossed over" and that Wynton played Bach concertos and sonatas, but these were extraordinary musicians. He could not conceive of such a talent working a hotel lounge.

He had to find out. He stood up, took his glass in hand and made his way towards the melody, which came from a parlor grand at the far end of the room. The light being so low and the room colors so muted, he had no clear impression of the pianist until he was almost there, and was surprised to find, sitting at the keyboard, a dark-haired, boyish-looking fellow, in his late twenties at most, whose appearance instantly reminded him of his own at that age. The only significant difference was that the young man was shorter and of smaller stature. He looked to Santa like some cherub incarnate as he swayed on his stool in rhythm to the delicate melodic phrasings of the composer, his eyes closed, his face and frame mirroring every nuance of Chopin's aching beauty. He had no awareness of Santa's presence. Until well after the lingering notes of the final pianissimo chord went silent.

Finally he looked up to see Santa smiling down at him.

"That was beautiful."

"Thank you."

"Chopin, wasn't it? I know the piece well; I've known it my whole life and have always loved it, but I can never remember the name of it."

"That's because Chopin, sublime poet though he was, used mostly banal technical designations for his works, titles like "Opus 25, Number 8," or *Fantasy in F-minor*. Who can remember?" A sympathetic response. Santa felt drawn in.

"So, what's the designation for that little gem you just played?"

"That was the 'Opus 10, Etude—or Study—Number 3,' he answered in a pensive tone, momentarily placing his hands together against his lips. "Anyone who hears this piece is instinctively drawn to it, even if they don't care a fig about classical music. Chopin himself exalted its exquisite melody above all his others. He said it came directly from God and that no composer could expect such a gift more than once in his lifetime."

Santa was taken by the young man, who spoke with a faint accent and impressed him as highly cultivated and refined, yet who carried his erudition very lightly, as light as the tune of "Opus 10, no.3." Like Santa, he wore a dark blue blazer but with an open-collared pale pink dress shirt. He gestured towards one of the stools surrounding the piano, inviting Santa to sit, then commented, "You must be a music-lover, a *Kenner* of the noble art of St. Cecilia, as the Germans would say. Most people don't know Chopin from shinola."

Santa smiled and sat down, resting his ginger ale on a coaster and extending his hand as he introduced himself. "My name is Clause, Samuel Clause. No need to mention that people call me 'Santa.'"

"Jirak. Karel Jirak," the pianist responded. "People call me Carol, and there's not a damned thing I can do about it." He laughed, a soft, precise, yet full-throated laugh, itself musical, though carrying a weary tinge, as if he'd made this self-deprecating quip too many times to count.

"Well, I'm sure you can imagine the kind of razzing *I* get," Santa said in sympathy.

"Yes, certainly. I'm afraid we both carry labels— identities, really—that make life a bit uncomfortable, don't we? You're a fat, jolly holiday icon in a red suit and I'm a combination gay hermaphroditic transsexual." Again the soft, musical laugh.

This warmed Santa, won him over a bit. A young man so gifted yet so palpably frank in the way he believes others perceive him. How open was he, he wondered. He decided to probe a little.

"Do I detect a wisp of an accent in your English, which, by the way, is otherwise flawless, even elegant?"

"Thank you very much. I take pride in my English, which is my second language. My first, of course, is Czech. My father moved us to America when I was ten. Usually that's young enough to acquire a second language without accent, but, alas, in my case the grafting only took ninety-five percent." As he spoke, he began to play again. It was "Embraceable You," a lounge standard by Gershwin, a song he said he liked and could play easily while continuing to chat.

"Your accent is charming. I hope I'm not embarrassing you by saying so," Santa said, intending to ingratiate himself.

"No, not at all. And again, I thank you. I'm afraid my father is not so enamored of it as you. When I was a teen, he hired tutors to drill that last five percent of Czech out of me, but, as you can see—or rather, hear—it didn't work."

"Sounds like a lot of misdirected effort to me."

"Well, you see, he's a composer, and like most composers, he's also a perfectionist. I, thank heaven, do not carry the curse of perfectionism. It's enough that I bear the consequences of *his*—the sins of the father, in biblical terms ... On the upside, his driven personality took him to the top of classical-musical life in Prague. He became executive director of the Dvořák Symphony Orchestra in the early nineties, which led to his getting an offer he couldn't refuse from the Setnor School of Music at Syracuse University. He's the director there— that's right, the head honcho. And the rest, as they say ... But enough about me. Please, tell me something about yourself. How did you come by your love of Chopin?"

"Well, that particular piece—that ... etude, wasn't it?—I heard as a small boy almost at my mother's knee, I guess you could say. She played it all the time on an old 33 LP—that is, unless my father was on his third or fourth bourbon and demanded I take that 'sissy stuff' off and put on Miles—that's Miles Davis and his sweet trumpet in *Kind of Blue*." He was feeling a strong impulse to return the young man's candor in kind. Still, *Tread carefully here!*, an inner voice warned.

"Yes, of course. Miles Davis is a god to me as well. *Birth of the Cool*—I mean, when I first heard it on a friend's CD player in Prague, it was like *my own* birth. He, and some other jazz masters, were the main reason I was more than willing to leave my home and my friends to come to America … I've never regretted it. I'm taking advantage of the remitted tuition for children of faculty to get my Master's in performance and composition at S.U. This gig here is for chump change, but I actually enjoy lounge playing very much; it allows me to play a lot more jazz than I otherwise would, you know?" He looked up and smiled at Santa as he put the last flourishes to the Gerschwin tune.

"Well, you know," Santa said, purring a bit—he knew this would be the final icebreaker—"when I checked in a few hours ago, I was quite taken by the Bill Evans number I heard coming from here as I passed by, and as I heard the Chopin just now, I said to myself that can't be coming from the same player. They must have hired two—I mean, come on, *really!*"

"Guilty as charged, on both counts," Karel beamed.

"Well, that's fantastic, and especially for me, you know, since I'm a jazzman myself—"

"Ah, I thought as much," Jirak exclaimed, laughing. "I actually spotted you right off, but I didn't want to be presumptuous. Tell me, what instrument do you play? *Where* do you play?"

"Well, I'm what they call a sideman, which, in my case, amounts to an itinerant bassist. I'm on the road a lot, moving from gig to gig. I just follow the work and the money. I have no ties," Santa said coolly, brushing a bit of imaginary lint from his sleeve.

"Fascinating!" Karel said in genuine wonderment. "A soldier of fortune, a throwback to the wandering minstrels of medieval times."

"Well, yes, except that I don't serenade highborn ladies swooning on balconies," Santa quipped, proud to have shown his learned young acquaintance that he too had a bit of cultural refinement and at least a rudimentary sense of music history. After all, three semesters at Loyola U.—a fact he did not neglect to insert into the conversation—were not a weekend seminar.

Jirak chortled and depressed the keys for another tune, something uptempo by Herbie Hancock. The management insisted on only the shortest of breaks between numbers. The conversation, however, continued unimpeded.

"So, Santa, living the sort of quasi-Bohemian life you do—life in the clubs, on the road and all that—you must have seen many strange and wonderful things, no?"

"Yes, many. But then, what strikes *you*, or rather most people, as strange may be no more than *de rigueur* to me," he replied, pleased with himself for having snuck in that French expression, even though he wasn't quite sure he had used it correctly. Still, either way, French always helped when conversing with the educated class. The other voice in him was, however, aroused and whispered, *Careful here. You're approaching dangerous territory!* He took a sip of his ginger ale, which he had not touched till now.

"Well," Karel said, after sipping from his glass of sparkling water, "that certainly sounds provocative. What exactly do you mean?"

He looked Karel in the eye for a brief moment, shifted on his stool and said, "My friend, there are so many gifted artists in my business, brilliant musicians, a few even touched with genius, but there is also a dark and dangerous side, a constant procession of very fucked-up individuals: drug addicts, alcoholics, thieves, sexual degenerates—even murderers. And some of the worst of them are some of the best musicians. There's just something about music and musicians, you know?"

"Oh yes, I know," Karel quickly agreed. "It's the old Romantic myth of the mad musician in league with the devil, selling his soul in a Faustian bargain for an endless stream of creative energy. I do believe there is much truth in it. While I've known a few unhinged graduate students, I have nothing like your worldly experience, which strikes me as amazing. You've actually lived what I've only read about. I envy that."

"Don't be too quick to envy me, Karel. You don't know me at all." *Red alert, man! Back off! Back off!*

"This is true," the young pianist said thoughtfully. "But I *can* tell you this: It is not only musicians, though they may lead the pack. It is artists of any stripe, practicing any art. There is always this ambiguous relationship of the true artist to conventional morality, as if he were put on this earth precisely to push moral boundaries back, rearrange them, and sometimes even transgress them in what seem to us the most depraved and destructive ways, for mysterious purposes—social, psychological, evolutionary, spiritual, who knows?—purposes that may remain mysterious even long after a given artist has passed on ...

Santa was riveted by the discussion, drinking in the young pianist's every word. He couldn't remember the last time he had felt this alive, this involved, in the give-and-take of a conversation. He felt that, somehow, something of great importance was at stake.

"The history of art is replete with fascinating examples," Karel continued as he signaled the manager that he was now on break. "Going all the way back to the ancient Greeks, who sanctioned erotic man-boy relationships, something we can no longer even wrap our heads around today. Then there's Caravaggio, the great early-Baroque painter who was probably bisexual and killed a rival over a prostitute both men coveted. He also painted portraits of pre-pubescent boys with whom he was sexually involved.

"And the list goes on: there's René Condillac, a pre-revolutionary goldsmith in Paris, who sold his bejeweled creations to rich Parisian aristocrats and then mugged them on the streets at night, sometimes killing them, to get his art back. Tchaikovsky prowled the back alleys of Paris in search of boy prostitutes and was tortured by a secret passion he had for his young nephew Bob. The twentieth-century French poet and novelist Jean Genet, born the son of a prostitute, lived the life of a petty criminal before turning to art and political activism later on.

"There's a fascinating feature, by the way, to the case of the jeweler Condillac. It concerns one of his greatest creations, a magnificent diamond-studded pendant he made on commission for a certain Countess D'Arceau. It was in the shape of a violin because she loved the sound of that instrument above all others. The thing is, it opened up like a little case, and when she opened it, she found a tiny effigy of her young son inside. She was delighted because she hadn't asked for that feature; Condillac added it on his own."

"Why do you think he did?" Santa asked, mesmerized.

"Who knows?" Karel replied. "Maybe he was a pedophile as well as a murderer. It's not impossible. Psychoanalysis links the shape of the violin to that of the female body. When the pedophilic artist seals the boy in the violin case, the boy with whom he identifies, he is symbolically regressing him to the status of a fetus, thereby expressing his desire to return to the womb. Or some such nonsense.

"In any case, that particular woman paid dearly for it, well beyond money. One night, as she was strolling home with her husband after a chamber concert, they were both attacked from behind. The count was merely rendered unconscious, but she had her throat slit. The pendant was, of course, taken."

"So that means the jeweler was a murderer and possibly even a pedophile, as well as a thief," Santa summarized, as though it all made a neat and pretty picture—ghastly, to be sure, but neat and pretty all the same.

"Well, we're just speculating here. But I wouldn't be at all surprised. 'Stranger things …,' as they say," the pianist snickered, intoning a few soft chords. "In any case, I think there are far more pedophiles among artists than in any other group of professionals. Just think today of the British composer Benjamin Britten, or, on the pop scene, J. D. Salinger or Woody Allen or Michael Jackson. About Jackson, by the way, I don't think he actually sodomized boys or had any real sexual contact with them. He really just wanted to be with them in bed, to cuddle, you know? It was part of his pathetic attempt to turn *himself* back into a boy, to regain his lost innocence—the Romantic project, right?—as were all those cosmetic operations on his face that backfired on him, leaving him looking like a freak. Michael Jackson was a perverse modern Romantic."

Santa sat still and remained quiet, trying to process all that was being thrown at him by this young polymath. He was being given a glimpse of a world he knew little about, but a world that, he felt, promised to throw new light on his own existential situation, to put it in a context he hadn't known was available. Again, the voice said *Oh no, not that! That's madness! Banish the thought!* But it was too late, and who knew if he would ever get the opportunity again. His whole being ached to put this question to Karel. Again, he shifted in his seat, now looking down at the piano keys, cleared his throat ever so slightly and asked, "Has there ever been a sexually deviant musician, a pedophile, say, who was degenerate enough to murder his victims? ... What do you think?"

Karel looked at him. "A pedophilic child-murdering musician? Hmm ... I really don't know. But I wouldn't doubt it. I'm sure there have been such types, God help them. Why do you ask?"

"Oh, just curious. Not to mention the fact that I am one myself."

"One what?"

"Performing-artist pedophilic murderer." Santa said the words entirely without tone or affect. But when there was no response forthcoming from Jirak, who merely gazed at him blankly, he finally covered his tracks with the broadest grin he could muster. The young man eyed him for another moment and then burst into laughter. "That's one strange sense of humor you've got there, my friend." He looked down at the keyboard, put his hands to his head and swayed from side to side on his stool, as if straining under a mental burden.

"So *there* you are!" The words came from a lilting female voice from behind, instantly bursting the hypnotic bubble of the conversation. It was the waitress who had brought Santa his menu and ginger ale when he first sat down: a plump, pretty brunette in her early forties, who had a habit of giggling after most of her remarks to male guests. "You went and disappeared on me, you naughty boy! Would you like me to move you over here?" she asked giggling?

"No need," Santa replied, "I'm already over here."

The giggle became a peal of laughter, from all three of them. It was Santa's best jest in a long time.

"Seriously, though"—more laughter—"just bring me a ham and cheese sandwich to go, will you? I'll take it up to my room." Santa slipped her a few bucks and off she went.

"So, what's the next watering hole for our wandering minstrel?" Karel asked teasingly, noodling a few pianissimo bars of something jazzy, even though he was still on break.

"Oh, probably Toronto," Santa mused, "although who knows when? Last time I looked, it was total whiteout out there. Even this afternoon the radio said 401 was closed in several areas. It's probably buried by now."

"Say!" Karel said, clapping his hands three times, "I have an idea! Why don't you go south instead, not a lot, mind you, just a little south—to Syracuse? It would be different for you! Off the beaten big-city path. There are a lot of jazz clubs and bars there; I'm sure you can get work if you decide to stick around for a spell ... And, you know what? I'm going to give you a very nice letter of introduction to my father ..."

Santa already had his hands up indicating "Slow down."

"No, no, it's no problem, no problem at all," Karel insisted. "He should meet you; he'a a jazz aficionado himself. I'm sure he would like you very much. I'll leave the letter at the desk for you. You can pick it up there in the morning when you check out ... And look, if you

stay in Syracuse for the holidays, I can join you there—
you know, I'll be on Christmas break with plenty of
downtime. I'll show you around, show you the School
of Music. They do have a jazz department, you know.
Maybe you'll make a few useful contacts. Who knows?"

Karel was in such a spasm of enthusiasm over the
prospect of meeting up with him again that Santa simply smiled as he listened to the proposal. There was no
point in offering excuses against it, even though at that
moment he had no intention whatsoever of abandoning
the snow-covered 160-mile stretch of Kings Highway
401 leading to Toronto.

They chatted for a while longer, about indifferent
things, just enjoying each other's company.

Next morning at the checkout desk, Santa asked if there
were any messages for him.

20

The Varsity Restaurant, on South Crouse Avenue just off campus, was astir with lunch-hour traffic. Normally by one-thirty p.m. one could count on a modicum of seclusion there, but today, a rare day of sunshine in November, the students poured out of their dorms for purposes of seeing and being seen.

Mark sat in a side booth nursing his coffee, his coat collar up, trying to keep a low profile as he waited for Sabrina. His mind was on the task at hand and he didn't want to be pestered by students or colleagues as he mentally prepared for it. Earlier preparation consisted of the two or three belts of bourbon he had taken from the pint bottle he kept in the locked bottom drawer of his office desk. He couldn't believe what he was about to do and he needed a little liquid courage to do it, for today was the day he was determined to break it off with Sabrina. Julie's collapse at the concert had brought him to his senses, broken the spell, so to speak, and, although she was recovering nicely at home with no apparent after-effects of lasting significance, he now fully realized the absurdity of his escapist affair with Sabrina. He could not, *would not,* continue to bifurcate his focus this way, living two lives, neither one very well; he loved his wife and simply must be there for her, all of him, come what may.

None of which meant that he was looking forward to this last tryst with Sabrina. On the contrary, he dreaded it, dreaded cutting the cord of emotional dependency on her that he had spun over these recent months. Getting off Sabrina would be like getting off booze or cigarettes. It is one thing to realize that a certain addiction is no longer viable, but quite another to act on that realization.

He was tempted to run outside for a quick cigarette, but just as he decided to do just that and was getting up, he saw her push open the entrance door. He waved to her and slowly sat back down, observing her as she made her way over. *Of course,* he cursed to himself, *she would look radiant in her North Face ski jacket and red stretch cap, cheeks all rosy from the cold, stepping lively with that sexual energy unique to her. Don't make it easy on me now! Don't make it easy!* Gracefully she sidestepped a bunch of students rushing for the exit like a herd of buffalo. He felt bereft in the groin, his determination momentarily faltering, but then his head, the one on top, reasserted its insistence. *No wobbling now! This must be done.*

"Hi," she said smiling, sitting down across from him, facing the cafeteria line behind him.

"Hi, Sabby. How's it going?" He sipped his coffee, by now cold.

"All right, I guess. I'm deluged with work," she moaned, pulling off her cap and smoothing a strand of her lovely blond hair with her hand. He found the gesture enchanting. "I've got fifty student papers to read and my own research paper due in a week. Other than that, I'm swimming in free time ... How about you? How's your wife doing?"

"Julie is coming along nicely. She's stable. Thanks for asking." Absently he searched his coat pockets for something, unable to find it.

She thought she detected a whiff of alcohol on his breath. Ordinarily she would have asked him about it. Not today.

"Listen, Sabrina, there's something—" he began.

"—Mark, I think we should stop seeing each other," she blurted out, looking him straight in the eye.

For a moment they both just sat there stunned, their world suddenly turned on its head. Mark was utterly flustered, not knowing whether to finish what he was about to say, not at all sure he had heard her right.

"What? Not see—?" he asked incredulously.

"—Oh, sweetie, it's not you, it's nothing to do with you," she hastened to assure him, clasping his hands with her own after neatly shoving his coffee cup aside. "It's my circumstances. I just don't have the time or energy for an affair right now. You know what I'm up against. I can't believe I've managed it this long."

"An *affair*? Is that what we've been having—an *affair*?" he asked, deliberately emphasizing the tawdriness of the word. Already he was feeling the swell of anger in his tone, even while simultaneously enjoying profound relief over his release from the burden of cutting the cord himself. He didn't know whether to hug her or pummel her for beating him to the punch.

She slowly withdrew her hands from his, searching her mind for a kinder way to frame her point. Obviously she hadn't given the matter as much forethought as he had.

But he now had the offensive and wasn't about to give it away. "Please tell me, Sabrina, is there someone else?" He knew she wouldn't lie to him "by comission," the opposite of omission. If he asked about it, she would tell him. She was like him in this way.

When she didn't immediately deny it, rather ruefully looking down and then to the side, he knew and instantly pounced: "Well, of course you have my sympathies, sweetheart, carrying on two *affairs* simultaneously. That would break the back of any doctoral candidate, not to mention the front." He was astonished at the corrosive quickness of his own acid tongue, lashing out at this girl who had just done him a huge favor. Yet he felt unable to stop. "May I ask who the lucky beau is with whom I've been sharing your considerable charms?" Even he himself felt this was uncalled for. He removed the animus from his voice as best he could, affected a humbler demeanor and asked, "Is it anyone I know?"

Again, she lowered her head, prompting him to respond in shocked disappointment, "So it *is*. So it *is* someone I know." And with that the despised image of Evan Katz surfaced in his memory, sending a sharp pang of betrayal through his gut. It was the ghastly memory of her walking off with him across the quad that day after class, the two of them laughing it up, probably at his expense. "Oh no, Sabrina, not Katz! Say it isn't so!" he all but mewled at her.

She looked at him with an odd mixture of defiance and sheepishness. "We're really just friends. I'm two years older than he is ..."

"Two years, schmoo years! The hormones want what the hormones want! *Et tu, Sabrina, et tu?*" he bellowed. They both realized that half the joint was listening in and hunched down low into their coat collars.

"It's not that way, Mark," she almost whispered. "He appreciates my sensitivity to literature, to poetry ..."

"Oh, I'll just bet he does," Mark oozed in his snarkiest tone. "*From Poetry to Panties*—that'll be the title of his first book, don't you think?"

"I'm sorry, I don't appreciate the sarcasm," she said, getting up to leave. "And besides, it'll be his second book. He's already working on his first."

Feeling a surge of panic, Mark put his hand over her wrist, at first too firmly. Then, loosening his grip but not removing it, he changed masks and pleaded with her, "Wait, Sabby, please don't go. Don't leave like this … I apologize; I don't know what came over me. I realize I have no hold over you, no claim on you, but …" He was desperate to score a point, to salvage something from this encounter, not even knowing what, and this desperation forced his mind down into the pond scum of social esteem: he wanted to impress upon her the folly of her choice, to make her aware that she was "settling" for a mere undergraduate student when she already had a professor, but he couldn't think of a way to make the point that didn't sound absurdly jealous, and therefore humiliating, so he just went on dithering. "Anyone but Katz, Sabby. Anyone but that arrogant twit!"

"Come on, Mark. He's really a nice guy when you get to know him. He's extremely intelligent, he's well read, he's witty and has a great sense of humor—and he's kind and honest. He has many of the qualities that attracted me to you."

"Thanks. God, that sounds so 'past tense.'"

"Sorry, I didn't mean it to ... Then again, maybe I did. Look Mark, we've always known this was a 'friends-with-benefits' type thing—you know, no complications.

He wasn't sure what "friends-with-benefits" meant specifically, but he'd heard the students throw the expression around and didn't like the sound of it. Too brokered for his taste. Suddenly he was feeling his age, which was actually helpful. It made it easier for him to let her go when, a few minutes later, she used the excuse of having to review an oral report for an upcoming class to get out of there.

As he watched her slip out the glass doors, the sun hitting her hair at a perfect angle, he took the last sip of his coffee. It was ice cold.

21

Although the ride down I-81 from the border was new to him, it turned him inward, as there was little to attract the eye in the late-autumn countryside of upstate New York. The trees were bare and the road was straight, running through flat terrain, the same flat terrain that crossed the border up into Canada. This is how it felt to approach Syracuse from the north in the cold season: you went neither up, nor down, nor around, just straight in, through snow-powdered fields, like a missionary entering his long-suffering frigid wife.

Inward, however, in the sense of into the realm of self-reflection, was the one direction Santa had steeled himself never to take. From early on he had cleverly adopted the Zen prescription of rooting his consciousness firmly in the present, in *this* moment, in the kaleidoscope of passing experience. He had conditioned himself never to think about himself, never to entertain notions of who he was and why he did what he did and whether what he did was good or bad. That was all useless speculation that could only lead to doubt and dithering, whereas all the great Zen masters extolled *action*, the complete pouring of oneself into everything one did, however the world might judge it.

The problem was, however, that, since his understanding of Zen had never got beyond the books he read, he had substituted the *idea* of action for action itself. This was the error of intellectualization, which all true students of Zen learn to recognize and overcome. Unconsciously, in order to rationalize what he did, Santa was substituting a convenient map of reality—the *idea* of action—for reality, or action, itself, and, like most defense mechanisms over time, this ruse, this self-deception, was starting to fray at the edges. Lately, at down times such as now on the road, he would find himself day-dreaming about his life, trying to shape it in his mind like a lump of unformed clay into some kind of narrative framework. But such reveries always brought him up hard against the central question of identity: *Who is the protagonist of this story? Who the hell am I after all?*, at which point he would suffer a rude awakening and quickly reapply the Zen prescription of mindfulness, now more and more with a barely perceptible tinge of desperation.

Without realizing it, Samuel "Santa" Clause had, by this juncture in his life, maneuvered himself into an increasingly untenable spot between the proverbial devil and the deep blue sea. As an intelligent man well into middle age, he was naturally entering that mature phase of life in which the need to summarize one's experience, all of it, and evaluate it in some way, to put it in some sort of perspective, was powerfully asserting itself, but, at the same time, that very need was being fiercely suppressed by his long-held, self-imposed directive to "stay in the moment."

The stronger the need became, the more he found himself day-dreaming about "the big picture," the panorama, of his life. And "the moment?" Gone, who knows where?

As he drove past the village of Black River, just north of Watertown, a curious passage from Kafka floated into his mind, something a professor once read to him in a literature class at Loyola. Its strangeness had struck him at the time, for reasons he couldn't begin to understand. It was one of Kafka's parables, called "The Watchman," and was very short, short enough to remember almost verbatim, and he now began to recite it to himself, just as he pulled into the left lane to pass a slow-moving pickup:

> I ran past the first watchman. Then I was horrified, ran back again and said to the watchman: "I ran through here while you were looking the other way." The watchman gazed straight ahead and said nothing. "I suppose I really oughtn't to have done it," I said. The watchman still said nothing. "Does

your silence indicate permission to pass?"

He still had no clear understanding of the parable's meaning, but, as he passed beneath a sign for a nearby elementary school, he felt a shudder at an ominous-sounding pronouncement that was forming in his mind: *No one ever gets away with anything.*

Also, on this lonely drive, on this gray autumn day, he began to be assailed by an ever so slightly fevered need for reasons, for answers to why-questions, just the sorts of questions he had always managed to dismiss with his pseudo-meditative posturing. The sorts of questions that, if engaged and entertained at length, could get one deeply mired in the quicksand of one's own mind. He thought of Karel Jirak, charming, debonair, gifted musician that he was. He had so much enjoyed their conversation, coming away from it with a strange sense of gratification for knowing that he was still capable of appreciating adults for themselves and not just for what they could do for him or for the sensuous beauty of their children. And couldn't one say the same, more or less, of his relationship with Luke? He had loved Luke and let him live, at considerable risk to himself. That had never happened before.

Was it possible he was changing? Certainly that primordial craving at the center of his being was not. Perhaps change was coming from those frayed edges at the perimeter of his defenses, from the outside in. This thought brought him up short, sobering him, bringing him back to "this moment, here and now," where he was bent on staying.

But reflection and the zones of time, present, past and future, had, on this occasion, been let loose for too long and were even more bent on having their own inning. And so he asked himself, among other things: Why was he taking Jirak's advice and going to Syracuse, a town that, so far as he knew, had little to offer. Small, provincial, close-knit—not at all the sort of place he would have chosen on his own. So, why? Was it because of Jirak himself? Did he really, seriously, intend to meet him there over the holidays? To "hang out" with him? Is this what he really wanted? If so, why? Certainly his feelings toward the pianist were, however keen, no more than platonic. Was this, then, a sign of change in him, of expanding and deepening social needs?

And why did he pick up Jirak's letter of introduction to his father, something he'd had no intention of doing and that had totally slipped from his mind, that is, until he was passing the hotel desk on his way out and suddenly thought of it. *Why* had he suddenly thought of it? Just then, right there at the desk? So far as he knew, there was absolutely nothing the old man could do for him, professionally or personally. So why? And with this "why" another line from Kafka moved across his inner eye like words on a printed page, words expressing Gregor Samsa's profound relief at his family's rush to get help that would free him from his imprisonment in an insect body: *He felt drawn back into the circle of humanity.* Was he a subhuman creature, an insect? Was he seeking some reentrance into the circle of humanity? Was he making the Jirak family his circle, even though they were no more than an abstraction to him? Were they to stand in for his own?

Questions all, for which he had no answers, not to mention the fact that he believed in neither the one nor the other. All Q and A, however lofty or noble, was a fool's game, he fiercely insisted to himself. But was his insistence still out of that old rock-hard conviction, which he fancied to be grounded in his own pellucid vision of the here and now, or was it this time out of a need to shore up a foundation that had just now passed through a tremor, possibly its first?

He riveted his gaze on his surroundings, as if they were some sort of lifeline out of the quagmire of self-awareness. But there was little out there to draw him out of himself, certainly not the drab roofs and domes and spires of the city of Watertown, which now appeared on his left, nor the inevitable sign for the local mall, here named after the Salmon River, passing by on his right. He felt a bit unfairly deprived.

Finally, though, a sign appeared that did catch his attention: Syracuse 72.

22

Julie wasn't sure what to think or how to feel about her recent "episode" at the Children's Orchestra concert. On the one hand, she thought such an undemanding outing should have been well within her powers; on the other, she felt her astonishing discovery of the mystery of Duncan might have been enough to unhinge even the healthiest and heartiest of souls. What was she to make of it? It challenged her view of the world, of the very structure of reality, on a fundamental level, the level of common sense, not to mention all her empirically grounded academic training, and she was loathe to mention it to anybody for fear of being considered a mental as well as a physical cripple.

So, for the time being, she would keep it to herself. But how it seethed within her, day by day! How it joined her to her son at the hip, so to speak, at times most uneasily, such as when Nate would experience strongly negative feelings—the angers and sadnesses and anxieties of everyday life. Those feelings seemed to resonate through her mind and body more clearly even than her own. Wasn't this too much Nate? And why was this "gift" visited upon her? Was it even helpful, or was it some sort of neurotic or pre-psychotic sinkhole on a preternatural level of mind?

The only assurance she had was that her "fit" at the concert had been little more than a false alarm. She was home now and feeling fine—at least on the physical level. But were such "fits" something she had to start dreading every time she rolled out the front door? Please, God, no!

It was just after breakfast, and as she sat in the kitchen trying in vain to concentrate on the *New York Times*, its front page propped up in front of her on a small lectern, in walked Nate looking, as usual, for his lunchbox. The school bus was due in a few minutes.

"In the fridge, sweetheart, in the fridge—where it always is."

He grabbed the box and was heading to the hallway closet for his coat when Julie asked him to sit with her for a moment or two.

"Sure, mom, what's up?"

"Oh, nothing special. It's just that I have all this time on my hands now, so I'm becoming a busybody mom, sticking my nose into all my family members' affairs," she laughed.

"Oh, really," said Nate, setting his lunchbox on the table and resting his chin on it, then cracking wise: "So what else is new?"

"Ooh, you little devil, you," Julie said, feigning outrage but plainly proud of her son's quick wit. "I ought to have Hattie come in here and give you a paddling for me. She's my paddle now, you know."

"I know," Nate answered, tongue firmly in cheek, "and that's just the way I want it. I couldn't pay Hattie to spank me. Believe me, I've tried."

"Is that so, you little scamp!" she laughed again, unable to sustain the indignant pose. "Watch out, I might have to call up Luca Brazzi and have him come over here to make you an offer you can't refuse. How do you like them apples, huh, wise guy?"

Nate widened his eyes and put up his hands as if facing a gun, made an explosive guttural sound from the back of his throat, clasped his hands to his chest and collapsed from his chair down onto the kitchen floor—"dead." After a few seconds, he convulsively shook his limbs, a last gasp, the final throes, and then just lay there stretched out—*really* "dead."

"Oh my goodness!" Julie cried, playing along, "This is wonderful. Now that I've gotten rid of the kid, I can go back to the soft, cushy life I used to know and love, b.n.—that's 'before Nate.'"

"Mom, you don't mean that!" Nate croaked, suddenly coming back to life. At nine he could still intend the words more as a question than an assertion. Recognizing this ambiguity, Julie's heart ached for him. "Nate, honey, come sit up here next to me and tell me how it's been going for you lately, you know, with all that's happened in recent history." She didn't want to be any more explicit than that.

He flopped down on a chair up close to her and noticed Duncan perched there on her lap, on guard as usual. He slow-motion-punched the little guy, smiling at his mom as he did so; they were at about eye-level with each other. She had on her orange and blue S.U. sweatshirt, which he liked. The sound of the washing machine kicked in from the laundry room. Hattie on the job.

"Everything's okay, Mom. Really," he said. "You don't have to worry about me." He meant it.

"Well, who else should I worry about?" she replied, widening her eyes. She was learning to use her various facial muscles to carry out the expressive gestures formerly performed by her hands, arms and shoulders. She would, for instance, "shrug her eyes" instead of her shoulders, as now, to indicate frustrated ignorance. Her head, of course, did all the pointing, and even her nose, availing itself of various tweaks, had amassed a modest vocabulary of contrarious reactions.

"Tell me," she continued, "how was Stephanie's birthday party yesterday? Did you have a good time?" Stephanie was a classmate whom Julie knew Nate to be sweet on, and Julie had, via Duncan, strongly registered her son's unusually intense feelings of pleasure and joy at being in the girl's company during the three hours of the party. She was now furtively probing Nate for particulars to corroborate yesterday's emotional "reading." She needed such corroboration, as she still couldn't quite believe in the validity of her new paranormal "gift." Such things, after all, only happened in movies or supermarket romance novels or on *The Twilight Zone.*

"Yeah! It was great," chirped Nate. "I pulled a yoyo out of the grab bag—the best prize in there."

"And was Stephanie glad you came?" Julie asked, gently steering the conversation back to the matter at hand.

"Oh, yeah. She even wanted to dance with me, but I told her I didn't know how, and she said she could teach me. So she did. It was fun ... Girls ain't so bad, I guess," he concluded, brushing his blond bangs back with his hand. Seeing this, Julie wished to God she could have done it herself.

"*Aren't* so bad" she corrected, smiling.

"Right. That's what I said."

"No, I mean ... Oh, never mind. Listen, tell me, how have you been getting along with that Rensky boy

lately? Is he still trying to bully you?" She had registered a strong anger and fear response from him a few
days earlier, not having a clue as to the cause. She now
guessed Rensky and hit the jackpot.

This, of course, was maddening. Her son's feelings
themselves were always crystal clear to her, but external
circumstances of time, place and causality remained a
mystery. There was no clairvoyance, and it frustrated her
no end that she could see inside her son but not outside
or around him. *Christ, if you're gonna give me an inside
view, give me the damned outside view to go with it, okay,
so I might actually know what to do—or have someone else
do—if it ever came to that!*

"Oh, Rensky's okay," Nate said, soft-peddling the
issue. She could tell he was lying, probably to protect
her; the same emotional upset, now coming from his
memory of the event, was echoing in him and, thanks to
Duncan, who sat right there between them, was coming
through to her loud and clear. "I had a little run-in with
him the other day—no big deal."

"What do you mean, 'no big deal?' What was it?"

"Nothing really. He and his goons tried to grab
me after school and drag me off to the parking lot so
he could pound on me, you know, hidden between the
cars—"

"Oh my God, Nate!" Julie cried, throwing her head
back and rolling it in alarm.

"No, no, Mom, it's okay! Really! It's okay! They didn't do it. Mr. Iacobucci, the history teacher, stopped them. He was getting into his car and saw them drag—I mean, pulling me and broke it up."

Julie shook her head vigorously and craned her neck from side to side, as if trying to use the animate parts of her body to quicken the rest of it, as though she believed that regaining the lost control of her body would somehow be enough to solve the problem of Rensky. "Nate, sweetheart, this can't go on. I want a meeting with the principal and ... oh, what's the boy's name?"

"Leo."

"—a meeting with the principal and Leo's parents. We've got to get a handle on this."

"No, Mom, please," Nate implored, laying his hands over hers, feeling their cool lifelessness. "Let's not do that. Look! I give as good as I get with Rensky. Sure, he's bigger and stronger than me but I'm faster and smarter. I'm his match. Really, I am. I'm telling you, I can handle it."

Nate's basic, almost organic, confidence, which was deeper than his fear and which he conveyed in such an assured, adult tone, belied his young years and comforted her profoundly. She felt its steadiness, its strength, and her own response to that strength, and was amazed. In that moment she let go a little bit, let go of her precious little darling, just a smidge, allowing herself to bask in the pride of his nascent independence.

"All right. We'll put that on hold for now," she purred. "But if anything else—"

"—Don't worry, Mom. You'll be the first to know," he interrupted her with an exaggerated pretense of concern, jumping up from his seat. "I've gotta get going. I'll miss the bus."

"Oh, let the bus go today, sweetheart. Dad can drop you off on his way to work. I'm so enjoying our little chat."

Just as Julie uttered the words, the yellow bus pulled up outside, all puffing and farting and squealing like a stuck pig; it waited the mandatory ten seconds and pulled away. At the same time Mark shambled down the stairs and into the kitchen, grabbed a cup from the cupboard and poured himself half a cup of coffee, black no sugar. He was wearing his thick-wool Irish sweater and looking quite autumnal. "Wasn't that your ride you just missed, slugger?"

"Yeah, but I'm skipping school today. I just don't feel up to it," Nate joked, holding his "fevered forehead" and coughing up a storm.

"Is that right?" Mark asked, feigning grave concern as he put his cup down. "Oh, my poor young Lochinvar! You just don't feel up to it … You … don't … feel … up … to … IT!" And with that Mark pounced on his son, tickling him all over and making him squeal almost as loud as the bus. "*Still* not feeling up to it, my boy? *Still* not ... ?

"Stop! Stop! I'm feeling better! A lot better! I'll go, I'll go already!" Nate laughed and shrieked in his reedy nine-year-old's voice, then slumped on his chair seat and hung limp like a rag doll.

"Well, you'd better get a move on, slugger, if you're expecting a ride from me. I have to run; I've got office hours at nine this morning before my noon class."

"Oh, do you really have to leave so soon, Mark?" Julie asked in a faintly plaintive tone. "Nate and I were having such a nice little chat. We were hoping you could join us."

Mark immediately read Julie's tone as a thinly veiled expression of her loneliness. She was surrounded by loved ones who were constantly leaving her. True, they always came back, but only to leave again soon after. He felt a stab of guilt and regret when he found himself comparing her, against his will, to the pet dog that barks all day long in an empty house after his owners leave for work. "Hon, any other day and I'd be more than happy to stick around. We could all go to IHOP or Denny's for a late breakfast. But this morning I'm scheduled to meet this student, a freshman coed, who's having trouble adjusting to living away from home for the first time and is very depressed. I'm worried about her. I need to talk to her and try to decide if she needs professional help. Otherwise, you know ..."

"Of course, of course," Julie said, smiling supportively. "I'm sure we can get together later in the week, or even next week. No biggie." On the contrary, Mark secretly felt that his wife's loneliness was, indeed, a biggie, that it was, in fact, what had impelled him to let go of Sabrina. It was time for him to start acting on his own motives. He must not lull himself into thinking that Hattie, wonderful as she was, was enough for her day in and day out. She needed more of *him*.

"Definitely!" Mark said with emphasis. "It's already on my calendar."

Husband and son each gave her a peck on the cheek and headed out. She wheeled herself into the living room and watched through the picture window as they climbed into Mark's Honda Accord and drove off.

Mark was already running late and also had to go a bit out of his way to drop Nate off, so he was playing fast and loose with lights and stop signs.

"Easy, Dad," Nate warned jokingly, "we don't need another accident ... One is more than enough."

Mark was taken aback by his son's sharp tongue, with its barb of gallows humor, and took the warning to heart. "You're absolutely right, Nate. What am I rushing for? So we'll both be a little late. No biggie, right?"

"Hey, *no biggie*! That's mom's favorite expression. You stole it!" Nate crowed in mock-rebuke.

"What? Are you calling me a thief? A common thief? Why you …" roared Mark as he reached over with his right hand in the shape of a claw—for tickling—and went for the boy's mid-section. But Nate was ready this time and, using his lunchbox as a shield, smushed his thin, lithe body hard against the passenger door, just out of reach of the dreaded claw. This followed, of course, by the taunting mockery coming from one who presumes himself safe from danger even while remaining close to it, the taunting, five-note singsong "*Hm*, hm, hm, *hm*, hm!"

This was just too much! Mark threatened to pull over, pretending to search furiously for a parking space on the crowded rush-hour boulevard. Finally spotting one and slowing down, he bellows, "Argh! The jig is up for you, my savory young morsel," as if he were the ravenous cannibalistic giant straight out of "Jack and the Beanstalk." The boy undoes his seatbelt, threatening to open the door and jump.

"All right, all right now," the giant relents. "Don't bail from the beanstalk. It's a long way down. I'll let you off this time with a warning," he growls, waving his giant index finger, the dreaded tickle finger. "But the next time you use that rapier tongue of yours on me,

I'll cut it out and use it to flavor my little-boy soup. Capeesh?"

"Giants are rarely Italian, Dad. Italians just aren't big enough."

"Oh," says dad apologetically. "I haven't measured any lately, but I'm guessing you're right … Hey, wait a minute! You just used that tongue again!"

They enjoy a good laugh. Mark wends his way slowly along Salt Springs Road, bordering the Lemoyne College campus, on his way to Smythe Elementary.

"You know, slugger, I've been meaning to ask you …" says Mark, suddenly turning serious, "about mom and how you're getting along with her." He turns off the car radio to underscore his point. "What I mean is, how *you're* doing vis-à-vis mom … Oh, jeez, for an English teacher I guess I'm not using the language very well—"

"No, no, Dad. I know what you're getting at—I think."

"You know, it's been so hard on all of us since the accident; God, it's impacted all our lives profoundly. We're not even close to processing it, forget about being over it, forget about so-called "closure," which seems to be the American ideal for processing grief … Anyway, I'm not just concerned about mom—I mean, obviously for the time being her condition requires the most attention from us, the most energy—but I'm concerned about you too."

"No need, Dad. I'm doing okay."

"Yeah? Are you sure, kiddo? It's a lot for a kid to handle. What am I saying? It's a lot for a *grownup* to handle! I know, I *am* one—well, almost." Nate laughed and undid his seatbelt as Mark was given the signal by the lady crossing guard to turn left into the school parking lot.

"There's just one tiny little thing," Nate said, a bit tentatively. Hearing this, Mark pulled into a spot in a remote corner of the lot so he could listen, undisturbed by the drop-off traffic. "Oh, what is it? Tell me," he asked, putting the gearshift in park and turning off the engine.

"Well, you know how mom is not supposed to get upset because of her condition, right?" Nate began, flipping the handle of his lunchbox up and down.

"Yes."

"Well, I try not to upset her because I don't want her to get sick again, the way she did at the concert, and go back to the hospital."

"That's the idea, slugger. While mom's in rehab, we have to take special care to preserve a tranquil atmosphere around her. So we mustn't go running to her with every little problem that arises, like an empty Cap'n Crunch box or a pair of missing socks. You've got Hattie for that. Or better yet, yourself. You get that, don't you?"

"Sure I do. But it's easy with things like cereal and socks. The thing is, sometimes I'm not sure where the line is between small things and big things. Like today, she asked me how it was going with Rensky—you know, the kid who's always on my case? I wanted to tell her that the guy's a real hemorrhoid and I wish he'd leave me alone … But then I didn't. I just didn't want to upset her, so I pretended everything was all right. I mean, it *is*, sort of; I can handle Rensky. Still, it would've been good to talk with her about it."

Mark reached over and wrapped his arms around his son, pressing him to his breast, as if to infuse him with full and equal measures of love and strength. "Oh God, slugger, I know how hard it must be for you; it's hard for me too. We're both in the same boat. But we'll paddle together, one oar each—no, wait, that would just drive us around in circles!"

Mutual guffaw. Mark could never resist riffing on his own metaphors, even, perhaps especially, in intimate moments. In his mirth he accidentally hit the horn and got a nasty look from a father in a passing drop-off car.

"Seriously, though, I want you to come to me with personal issues like this, more than you've been doing, and more than I've been encouraging you to do lately, if I'm to be honest about it. We'll work mom back into it too, slowly; after all, who's to say that getting her take on our problems isn't more therapeutic for her than pretending there *are* no problems?

"Yeah. I don't think she believed me anyway when I told her everything was all right with Rensky."

"See? There you go," said Mark, waxing optimistic. "Rensky's helped us gain perspective here. He has some use after all."

"Oh, I wouldn't go that far."

23

McNifty's Bar & Grill is a popular watering hole on the corner of Burnet and Tisdale in Syracuse, just off the section of beltway that bisects the city east to west. As a literal corner bar, it has a V-shape with the entrance at the point of the V. As you enter, you face two rooms: to the left is the pool table and access to the restrooms; to the right is the bar itself and the surrounding area with tables, about a dozen of them. The tables are themselves styled as rectangular mini-bars, seating six to eight patrons each; they are bolted to the floor and feature top-rail moldings of burnished oak. A nice touch. In the upper-right corner of the V sits the diagonal step-high platform on which music groups perform—rock, country, jazz. The wall behind them is crammed with autographed glossies of groups that have played there, many with colorful names in the requisite bad taste, such as "Supergush," "Nasty Cate," "The Finger," "The Jugsuckers."

The overall décor of McNifty's is perhaps best described as early "more is more." Not counting the occasional falling-down drunk, the floor is the only surface in the joint not filled with curiosities. Even the ceiling has various WWI-vintage model aircraft suspended from it. All walls are virtually hidden behind shiny black-and-whites, borderline-obscene rhyming quatrains, caricature drawings of longstanding patrons, and out-of-place—and therefore *in*-place—objects such as a gumball machine, a vending machine dispensing chocolate condoms and a long wall panel upon which are mounted ten clocks showing the time of day in ten second-tier U.S. cities comparable to Syracuse: Rochester, Tucson, Baton Rouge, Colorado Springs, Grand Rapids, and so on.

The wall photos are not just of musical alumni; they also attempt to evoke a nostalgic feeling of old Syracuse, a beleaguered city whose idyllic past outshines its bleak present. Enlarged photo prints of downtown's pre-war Clinton Square, an old-time steam locomotive chugging down Salina St., or a horse-drawn mail wagon parked in Fayetteville mingle with pictures of happy blue-collar workers leaving grungy factory yards or an S.U. coach blissfully raising a hard-won trophy. Shots of celebrities who are sons and daughters of the city, or who at least attended its university, abound, and include the same faces to be seen on the walls of any nostalgia bar in town: Dick Clark, Tom Cruise, Richard Gere, Alec Baldwin, Joe Biden, astronaut Eileen Collins, Jim Brown, Ernie Davis, Rod Serling and Phish drummer Jon Fishman. Scores of other worthies also adorn the walls at McNifty's, but these are the crème de la crème.

It was around 9 p.m. on the Saturday night before Thanksgiving week, and the joint was already jumping at McNifty's. Given the fact that the place's V-shape left little room for the dispersal of noise, customers were forced to absorb a midnight-level din three hours early. Only the most strident voices could make themselves heard, these and the frequent piercing shrieks of ladies who had already had one too many. It was bedlam at the bar. Party time! The massive chalkboard calendar on a sidewall above the bar, which showed the month's schedule of entertainment, listed that night's group as Don't Fret, a local jazz combo just starting out.

The group's front man, a young singer-guitarist named Jack Eastwood, had placed a want add in the *Syracuse New Times* for a bass player and, within three days, Santa was once again gainfully employed. While checking into a Red Roof Inn near downtown earlier that week, he had picked up a copy of the alternative weekly and immediately phoned about the ad. He gave Eastwood his resume and references at the audition but sized him up as someone to whom they would not matter much, someone who went by his ear alone.

The combo was small, consisting of four members: Jack, Santa, Ross at the piano and Mookie, an emaciated bearded fellow with a patch over one eye, on drums. It was little more than a rhythm section. They were coming off a break after their first set, which had gone well, which is to say, the crowd was still sober enough, and therefore polite enough, to listen. Now it would be a different story.

Not that they didn't expect it. The group, green as they were, were already well acquainted with the perils of playing in a tightly-packed barroom rather than in a more spacious adjacent room built for live entertainment and/or dining. In McNifty's everything happened in the barroom. Santa was more than prepared for the routine assaults of such a venue: being crowded by bystanders and jostled by bypassers, drowned out by raucous shouting and laughter, and mildly jarred by the crash and tinkle of glass every ten or twelve minutes. These things were par for the course and his years of experience had totally inured him to it all.

However, on that particular evening something else happened which, while not especially unusual in itself, had consequences for Santa that were far from routine. The table closest to the performers was no more than five feet away from their platform. It was occupied by six young men and women, presumably three couples, who were enjoying themselves and, doubtless owing to the half dozen or so tall glasses of draught beer they had each drained, contributing more than their fair share to the overall racket. Two of the men wore dress shirts with rolled-up sleeves and loosened ties and looked like young professionals. The third couple, who sat nearest to Santa, looked like wannabe Hell's Angels, he long-haired and unshaven, sporting a blue bandana and black leather vest, she stuffed into tight, tattered jeans and high leather boots. Despite the contrast in style, there seemed to be no culture clash among the six of them. They interacted seamlessly, thus giving the impression, correct or not, that they were all of the same professional class, with the two "Angels" merely playing dress-up for the evening.

The others called him "Lance," and he was big enough and brawny enough to carry such a name without fear of ridicule. He had the sculpted, fiercely handsome face of a Viking and laughed louder than his companions—much louder; it was a husky and power-ful laugh with a violent edge to it and, to an onlooker, might inspire as much intimidation as geniality. She had thick, pouty lips and long blond hair down to her ample bosom, which pressed invitingly against a sweater of red-dish purple. They called her "Lorrie." Lance and Lorrie, giving new meaning to the expression "power couple."

The trouble started when Lorrie became aware of the eye candy on bass for Don't Fret. She immediately swerved ninety degrees on her barstool so she could give her full attention to this Adonis in the tight black tee shirt. It tickled her to realize she could almost touch his right hand as it strummed those sexy strings, strings providing beat and rhythm to a slow, sensuous R&B number written by Eastwood himself. No matter that Lance and everyone else in the room were obliterating the strains coming from the platform with their crushing din; Lorrie only had ears for the bass notes, and eyes for the bass player.

Totally aware of this not-unfamiliar situation and alert to its potentially dangerous complications, should Lance suddenly take notice, Santa carefully kept his eyes off the woman to avoid encouraging her. But this passive tactic had its obvious limits and, in due course, Lance did indeed come to notice Lorrie noticing Santa. At first he seemed merely to smirk in his arrogance, as though thinking, *That's rich! There's no way she could prefer him to me!* But it wasn't long before his eyes began to take on a paranoid squint as they pinballed back and forth between his woman and the handsome bass player. He stopped laughing, stopped mixing it up with the other two couples, homing in on the two of them, bent on finding evidence that it was the musician who had started the flirtation.

As it always does, the paranoid search for evidence bore its poisonous fruit. Lance quickly convinced himself that Santa was the instigator here, taking the latter's occasional glances at *him* as evidence of taunting and gloating, rather than as indications of the anxious concern they actually reflected. Repeatedly Santa felt the burning focus of the Viking's ferocious stare, which began to linger on him longer and longer, seeming to morph into some humanoid laser beam ever more tightly locked into place. But alas, the woman's stare also lingered longer, the result being that Santa began to feel himself the object of alternating glances of love and hate, each repeatedly neutralizing the other in a furtive dialectic of madness. A triangular drama was playing itself out here to which Santa was contributing nothing but his appearance. *Looks* can *kill! And they can* get *you killed!* he thought grimly.

His mind turned to possible tactics for aborting the drama before it could reach its potentially ugly climax. He knew he was safe from any confrontation for a little over an hour, the length of time this set would continue. That also meant, of course, that Lance had another hour to stew in his paranoid bile. In any case, Santa had plenty of time to think. Making a run for it was out: much too shabby, not his style at all. Using the group members as a phalanx of protection, especially without their full knowledge and consent, also held no appeal. It wouldn't be fair and they might well resent him for it afterward.

No, he was totally on his own in this one. Which meant, as he well knew, that, one way or another, he was going to have to face the Viking. Of course, he had endured such one-on-one shitstorms before on the jazz circuit, but never with a man of Lance's intimidating stature. The massive frame, the steely gaze, the piercing voice of stone, the take-no-prisoners persona. Everything about the man signaled to other men *Stay out of my way. Don't mess with me!*

Santa kept a close and steady eye on his antagonist, but only peripherally, without seeming to, giving the impression of being lost in the music while subtly observing about him whatever he could to gain any possible advantage. He noticed that, despite his impressive musculature, Lance had a bit of a paunch, which he would carefully pull in whenever he stood up but absently let out when slouched on his stool. This meant that he was probably not a fitness buff, or, if he did work out, neglected his abs in favor of his arms and pecs. A good thing to know. At one point he watched the Viking's ambivalent reaction to Lorrie when she teased him about his paunch by playfully poking him there with her little index finger. He laughed all right and it was loud, but there was an unmistakable hollowness to its ring, as though he'd much rather have slapped her around for her insolence. He then quickly drained his half-full glass, perhaps attempting to drown his pique, but then slammed the empty glass down on the table loud enough to cause neighboring patrons to turn their heads. Of this and more Santa took careful note.

When the set finally ended, Santa leaned his fiddle against the wall and casually stepped off the platform heading for the restroom, making sure to keep his gaze straight ahead as he passed the Viking's table. But though his eyes were restricted, his ears were trained like radar on any shuffling of stools that might be heard to his rear. And, as he expected, there immediately occurred a grotesque scraping sound directly behind him, which needed no interpretation. About halfway across the room, Santa caught a glimpse of the Viking trailing him in a gilded mirror perched on the wall behind the bar, just above the array of scotch and whiskey bottles adorning the backbar. *So it's going to happen right now. That's good—no time to overthink it. Just a quick review of the key moves I've got to make, with maximum speed, power, precision. Yes, yes, that's right. I've got it. Okay, here we go!*

Santa knew the layout of the privy, which was essential to his plan. Its outer door, accessible from a narrow corridor extending along the upper left arm of the V, opened into an interior space housing both Ladies and Gents toilets, ladies through a door directly to the left, gents through a door straight ahead about ten feet. To get to the toilet, then, a man had to push through two parallel doors, one following hard on the other.

Walking nonchalantly and pretending to be oblivious to the threat coming after him, seeming blissfully unaware of anything amiss at all, Santa pushed open the outer door and stepped in. As the door slammed shut on its spring behind him, he lurched like a cat through the inner door, which slammed shut in turn, and braced himself in the toilet's inner sanctum for his attack.

Then, hearing an angry, heavy hand bash the outer door open, he flexed his own hands and fingers and made a loose fist with his right, the hand capable of inflicting the greater damage, given the awkwardness of the cramped space and that hand's superior strength. His bassist's fingers, as hard as spikes, were poised. The instant the inner door opened, Santa let loose with a straight-ahead karate punch to the Viking's gut that had the force of a piston stroke.

If Santa was aiming for maximum shock and awe, he got it, the Viking doubling over in a spasm of exquisite pain. Giving him not a second to gather himself, Santa then grasped Lance's thick golden mullet with his right hand, easy enough to do in the latter's bent-over posture, and, slipping his left deftly under the man's belt in the back, proceeded to use the Viking's upper body as a battering ram against the unforgiving front of the porcelain sink a few feet to the right. A single, full-strength blow was enough. The thud was muted and sickening, leaving Lance in a crumpled heap on the wet and fetid tile floor.

Santa stood over him and quickly checked himself out in the mirror above the sink. Then he washed his hands and ran a comb through his hair.

Just as he turned to exit, the outer door and, right after it, the inner, sprang open and in stumbled a beefy, young beer-drinker in a loose flannel shirt who almost tripped over Lance on his way to the urinal. Attempting to focus his bleary gaze on the motionless body as he looked down while swaying precariously, he let out a guffaw that almost caused him to collapse on top of it.

"Son of a bitch couldn't hold his liquor, huh?" he laughed, fumbling to open his fly.

"Guess not," Santa answered, heading out, avoiding any further exchange and hoping the fellow's inebriated state would compromise his memory.

Santa took a quick right down the corridor away from the bar and stepped outside McNifty's rear entrance. Lingering there in the raw, damp dark on the top step of three, he scanned the small parking lot to ascertain his degree of privacy. Not a soul to be seen among the rows of rust buckets and pick-up trucks, the only movement a stray snowflake here and there. He stood there listening to the muffled din from the raucous crowd inside— the waves of laughter pierced by shrieks, the odd strains from the jukebox, a cacophony mitigated by the smooth whirr of passing traffic coming from the beltway nearby.

Slowly he turned around and just let his forehead lean against the diamond glass panel in the middle of the door. Its coldness felt good, even purging, for he suddenly found himself engulfed by a wave of disgust he knew was only tangentially related to what had just happened. It wasn't that it bothered him to hurt the Viking—on the contrary, the asshole got what he deserved. Besides, if he could live with murdering children, how could this be more than a trifle? No, it was what the incident, and others like it from the past, were coming to mean to him in a larger, existential sense; it was the sort of consideration he was lately finding himself less and less able to fend off, as if life itself were beginning to demand some sort of accounting from him. The utter stupidity of the incident, its emptiness, its unrelatedness to anything beyond itself—intuitively he felt it as an absurd movie trailer of his life, a grim summing-up that revolted him, and he began to feel the anxiety, the claustrophobic panic, of knowing that there wasn't a damned thing he could do about it.

He walked over to his van, got in, and, strictly on impulse, pressed Karel Jirak's number on his cell.

"Hello?"

"Hello, Karel. Santa here."

"Santa." A moment of silence as if Jirak were considering the odd name. "Ah, of course! Santa—Santa

Clause, no less! My intimate at the Riverbank piano bar recently."

"Well, I don't know if 'intimate' applies, but yes, it's me."

A hearty laugh at the other end. "Don't give it a thought, my friend ... Hey, it's good to hear from you. I was hoping you'd call, but I wasn't expecting it so soon. This is delightful."

"Well, for some strange reason, I've taken your advice—"

"You'll have to forgive me; I'm always giving people advice. What particular counsel would you be referring to?"

"You remember, don't you, when you told me I should get off the beaten track—you know, one big city after another—and try the slower pace of a smaller town like Syracuse? Well, here I am!"

"You're kidding! I never thought you'd take it seriously. Are you really in Syracuse?"

"Absolutely. I've been here for a few days. I took a room at the Y and I'm already working with a jazz group here at McNifty's Bar and Grill. Do you know it?"

"Do I know McNifty's? Are you kidding? It's a Syracuse landmark. The quantity of beer I've consumed there would fill a small swimming pool."

Santa feigned a chuckle.

"But, listen, Santa, I'm not in Syracuse, unfortunately. I'm up here at the Riverbank for the weekend, earning my keep. But I will be coming down to Syracuse next week to spend the Thanksgiving holiday with my family. In fact, I'll probably drive down on Monday morning. Why don't we meet for a drink somewhere Monday evening?"

"That sounds fine," Santa said, trying to sound enthusiastic. Yes, he wanted to see Jirak; why else would he have called him? Yet he was sharply aware that he was setting a kind of precedent here: He almost never allowed himself the potential entanglement of a gratuitous acquaintance. Too risky. He wondered what was happening to him. Whatever it was, he felt vaguely threatened by it, though no less compelled for that.

"Good, very good!" Jirak chirped. "But let's not meet at McNifty's, okay? That would just be a busman's night off for you, wouldn't you agree?"

"Absolutely," Santa answered, uneasily conscious of repeating himself. "But I'm the new guy in town, so I'll leave it to you to pick the gin mill."

"With pleasure, my friend. Why don't we meet at Chez Charlene's? It's a cozy little spot in the alleyway behind M street, about a block down the S.U. hill … Let's see now, you take—"

"No need," Santa interrupted. "I've already got it on my phone's GPS. I'll be there. Is around seven good for you?"

Karel answered that seven was perfect, and they did indeed meet at the agreed-upon time and place, the piano man enjoying a liquid dinner of several "perfect Manhattans," made with two parts rye whiskey, one part sweet vermouth and one part dry, and Santa nursing a ginger ale. The single matter of significance to come out of the meeting was Karel's invitation to Santa to join him and his family at their home for dinner on a date between the holidays to be determined. Santa accepted with sincere gratitude.

24

he next day, Tuesday, found the Driscoll family busily engaged in preparations for Thanksgiving. Mark came straight home after teaching his class to help Hattie with the house cleaning. Julie helped both of them with the baking of cookies and pumpkin pies as best she could, keeping an eye on the timer and taste-testing the results. When Nate got home from school, Julie told him to clean his room and make it habitable for at least two male cousins who would be staying over, after which he was to make himself available for other services. A pumpkin almost as big as a wrecking ball was set out on the front steps to the main entrance, just beneath a huge cutout of a turkey pasted onto the left of the double doors. The turkey dropped a cardboard egg if you pulled a string.

They wanted to get as much done as possible before family members began trickling in. In this, alas, they were not entirely successful as Aunt Liz arrived on her usual Tuesday afternoon, picked up from the airport again this year by Mark, who taxied her back and promptly installed her in an easy chair next to Julie. It was understood that Julie would occupy her sister with conversation so as to keep her out of the way while the others worked. Of course, no one had thought to ask Julie if she was happy with this arrangement, for, although she loved her sister dearly, the woman was a world-class motor mouth who left no gaps in her run-on commentary on the state of the world for others to fill. But Aunt Liz was given a glass or two of red wine to sip and Julie half a glass, the god Bacchus thus taking the edge off a situation that could have become a bit oppressive for Julie.

By late afternoon, having done yeoman service as an auditor, Julie felt more than justified in excusing herself for a nap. She smiled at her sister, did a smart 180 in her chair and rolled into the family room, while the second aide, Hattie's assistant, who now came only three afternoons a week, set the Shoji screen in place. This, of course, left Mark and Hattie totally unshielded from Aunt Liz's non-stop tongue. Mark, however, cleverly kept topping off the good woman's glass with merlot, so that it wasn't long before it occurred to her that Julie had had a capital idea: An hour's nap was just what the doctor ordered after her cramped coach-class flight. Whereupon she was shown to her bedroom upstairs, the same one she always took, her bags placed, also as always, on the cedar chest at the foot of the bed and a set of towels and wash cloths laid out on the comforter.

The projected hour-long nap wound up three. Aunt Liz awoke refreshed, in time to join the family for a dinner of "with everything on," just delivered from TGIP, a fledgling chain that was the brainchild of a cadre of S.U. business students.

"Mm!" Aunt Liz effused, halfway through a slice, the first of three, which helped explain her Rubenesque figure. "This pizza is really good. Better than anything I've had in Davenport. The sauce, generally, west of Chicago is too sweet, but then it improves again in Denver, goes sweet again in Utah and then picks up in Nevada. Probably because of all those Mafioso types in Vegas and Reno—you know, they've got to have their tomato sauce just like it was in the old country. Even California—"

"—I *like* it sweet," Nate interrupted his aunt, half intentionally.

"Well, then you can join my ex, Nate. He also has the taste of a nine-year old, which is fine if your nine years old, not forty-two. He's addicted to anything sweet, you know, especially Brandy Alexanders, banana daiquiris, grasshoppers, mojitos and just about anything else with sugar in it … used to be he'd even add sugar to whiskey and bourbon and cognac and even wine, believe it or not. Of course, he matured somewhat when he hit thirty: he learned to appreciate alcohol 'straight,' without any additives. Then he was really off to the races and I was off back to Cedar Rapids to regroup ..."

Involuntarily, everyone took a deep breath. Even Nate seemed bewildered. Aunt Liz, her doughy cheeks bulging, her ample bosom heaving, smiled radiantly at all of them, as if they were her humble subjects. Her smile was not unlike her sister's, only with much deeper dimples.

Next morning just before noon, things suddenly got lively. Mark's brother David arrived from Staten Island by car—passenger van to be precise—with wife Moira, their three children, all around Nate's age, and the beloved family terrier Sparky, who had keenly disappointed Mark by not passing away to doggie heaven in the intervening year. Sparky, as if intuiting Mark's disappointment, commenced one of those nasty, staccato barking jags little dogs are so adept at, the kind that give one a three-Excedrin headache, standing directly over Mark's shoes and looking straight up at him. Mark, doing his best to greet the arriving family amidst the cacophony, was furtively using his foot to shove Sparky out of the way, which, of course, only succeeded in enraging the little fellow and upping his volume.

They all moved quickly into the house to greet Julie and Aunt Liz who were anxiously awaiting them. The relatives had all seen Julie in her chair before today, so there was, so to speak, no ice to break on that score. Still, there was a palpable sense of uneasiness at first as they all seemed, without intending to, to encircle Julie in the kitchen, as if she were some sort of exhibit in the round.

Gradually, however, everybody relaxed as Nate took his cousins up to his room to play video games and the grown-ups sat around the kitchen table drinking coffee and catching up on recent family history. Before long, Carmella Gutierrez from across the street popped in to ask what she could bring to tomorrow's feast, was told the obligatory "just yourselves," meaning her, husband Pete and several children, and took that as a signal to bring the dish she had already decided to make anyway. Pressed by all to sit down, she joined them for a cup of coffee. Before long husband Pete came looking for her and swelled the festive circle even further. It was starting to feel a little like the salon Driscoll of old.

Julie sat at the table chatting amiably, fielding the expected inquiries into her condition from all sides with all the grace and good humor she could muster. Mark made sure to stay close to her and help out with witty euphemisms on occasion when the well-intended questioning struck him as a tad morbid or intrusive: "The wheelchair is cutting edge; they're coming out with a sports model next year … It's got a cool name: the C5."

After a while the company split up, Carmella running back across the street to check on her own cooking, the men retiring to the living room to surf the channels for football and basketball offerings, and the ladies lingering in the kitchen to discuss their own concerns, centered mainly on the children. The latter were blissfully absorbed in Nate's PlayStation paradise upstairs. It had turned rather cold and blustery outside, so there would be no practice-putting on the lawn or sipping of wine on the deck that afternoon. But wine was fine inside or out, and there was plenty of it to go around, so it didn't matter.

Moira Driscoll, a trim, petite brunette with a terse manner not unlike that of her terrier, was tickled as always to see Aunt Liz, and the feeling was mutual. They enjoyed each other's company at family gatherings enormously; they were relatives who, in different circumstances, would still have chosen each other as friends. Liz, especially, had a weakness for Moira's acid tongue, which, when fired up by Pinot Noir, left no family member unscathed, and Moira doted on Liz's appreciation, which usually expressed itself in ear-shattering cackles. "Oh, leave the men alone!" Moira would snap. "Leave them to their inane TV sports, their beer-belching and their scratching."

Shrieks from Aunt Liz. Julie enjoyed it too, though she knew Mark didn't belch or scratch, at least not in company.

"My kids all hate school. I'm telling you, they're *this far* from another Columbine. I check their coat pockets for firearms every morning," cracked Moira after a healthy slug of Pinot Noir, followed by another glass-tingling cackle from Aunt Liz. The wine was going down smoothly; things were warming up in the kitchen.

Julie was sitting between Moira and Aunt Liz, savoring the banter. She more than held her own in the general give and take of conversation but was too smart to try to mix it up with someone like Moira, whose dry, cynical wit, usually tending towards the dark side of things, could "kill" in any comedy club on open-mike night. Julie was content to sit there, relaxed in her chair, every so often taking a small sip of white wine from Hattie or one of the others.

Duncan, as usual, was nestled on her lap. The little fellow was rarely seen anywhere else these days, ever since that momentous Sunday afternoon concert when she realized that his mere physical presence on her lap, despite—or was it because of?—her lack of physical feeling, gave her immediate access to Nate's ongoing emotional life.

Every day the irony of it struck her anew: physically anesthetized, yet, emotionally, transcendently alive, given full access to the rich inner life of another—her son no less! She still hadn't told anyone about it, not even Mark or Hattie, there being no urgency to do so as far as she could see. Then too, she was still far from coming to terms with this mystifying ability herself and wanted to avoid all arguments with the "empirically-minded" types who made up her social circle.

More seriously, Julie had been struggling from the first with strong feelings of ambivalence towards this new power. While it was wonderful to be able to know in any given moment how her son was feeling, frankly, she didn't always want or care to know. If a little knowledge was dangerous, unlimited knowledge was more so. A second sight could be oppressive, in the way that a repetitive melody can get caught up in a brain loop for a period of hours or even days and drive someone batty. And while it was true that the obvious solution to this oppression was simply to have Duncan removed from her lap, thus cutting off the conduit, she was loathe to do this out of good conscience, for fear of "missing something important."

So she kept quiet about it, as about so many other things that had burdened her over the first fifteen months of her new, profoundly reduced life. One of those things, of course, was that persistent, underlying feeling of dread over, she knew not what, that deep sense of malaise that had driven her to try meditation in the first place. It was an affliction that not only did *not* disappear the day her inner Duncan manifested, resolving her long series of protean dreams, but was in fact fueled and fortified by that resolution, as though she were peeling off internal layer after layer of defensive pain on her way down to some unimaginable abyss of horror. The wine and the warm ambience of family had dulled the feeling for the moment, but even now, whenever her mind went to it, there it would be, in the wings of consciousness, waiting patiently for her attention.

At around five o-clock dinner was brought in from a nearby take-out restaurant. This freed up Hattie and Mark to continue preparations for tomorrow's grand spread—baking more pies, washing and cutting up vegetables, roasting chestnuts, putting out cut-glass trays of chocolate mints and candies and stuffing the big bird with Julie's special blend of meats and spices, the chef herself supervising. Mark carried out these "extra duties" attentively and efficiently but, at the same time, felt somewhat harried by mixed emotions: On the one hand, he very much wanted to give Julie as nearly normal a Thanksgiving as he possibly could; on the other, he feared that this attempt to reproduce a facsimile of "normality" might, paradoxically, have the opposite effect of pointing up to her just how abnormal things really were. But he forced himself to bracket all of this mentally and carried on as best he could.

After dinner Julie wheeled herself into her darkened room to get away from the others for a while and be alone with her thoughts. It had been a long day for her, to be followed by an even longer one, and she was fading a bit. Duncan was still in her lap, which meant the line to Nate was open, but she was only half paying attention—that is, until a sudden blast of anger hit her like furnace heat, a blast she instantly recognized to be his. This was nothing new to her; she had had a few such "transmissions" from Nate since the "opening"—only a few, to be sure, as the boy was not especially prone to anger. So she knew enough not to react precipitously, but rather to simply take a deep breath, sit there and wait. Whatever it was would either pass or he would come to her with his complaint. In case it was the latter, she turned her chair around to face the kitchen, away from her view through the glass doors of the treetops, barely visible now in the deepening night. Within seconds she could hear her son's familiar breakneck stomp down the stairs, followed by "Where's Mom?" Directed to her room, he came shuffling right in, totally oblivious to her need for a moment to herself.

"Mom, Jason won't give Robbie the controller, and it's Robbie's turn. Will you tell him to?"

A feeling of pride surged through her as she realized Nate was complaining on his little cousin's behalf, not his own. "I think you'd better take this one to your father, sweetheart. I'm sure he'll straighten it right out for you."

Nate looked around. "Why are you in the dark?"

"Because it's soothing. I have a bit of a headache."

"Oh, I'm sorry," he said, smoothing her cheek with the backs of his fingers before walking out. It was the best thing she had felt all day. She rolled herself over to the threshold and signaled to Hattie with a glance to come into her room. She'd had enough for one day and wanted to turn in early.

On cue, a collective "Aah" from all present filled the dining room, as Mark and Hattie carried in the carved-up *pièce de résistance* on two huge platters, one piled high with white meat, the other with dark. Everybody was seated around a long rectangular table, made longer with the insertion of two extension leafs to accommodate a dozen diners in a pinch. The children sat at a separate card table set up nearby. Mark made a brief toast to welcome the gathering, followed by his annual joke about his favorite kind of turkey. But this time, when he tried to follow up as usual by tapping his drumstick and asking, "Is this on?", he was promptly hooted down. "You know what you can do with that stick," suggested his sister-in-law as an afterthought. "Tough audience!" he allowed sitting down, to no one in particular.

The mood was convivial. Moira, sitting next to Aunt Liz, fell to taking side-mouth pot shots at her husband's lack of flair for romance, thus exemplifying the principle of equal criticism for both Driscoll brothers: "They don't call them mechanical engineers for nothing." Cackle from her rapt listener. Julie sat at the head of the table, on either side of her Mark and Hattie. They sat nearest to the door to the kitchen, the shortest, easiest route for the wheelchair. Mark was feeling deep satisfaction over having pulled off such a major event for his wife; Julie, for her part, was grateful and brimming with affection for him, nuzzling him often with a soft kiss to the neck whenever he would lean towards her. She knew how hard it had been for him. Hattie watched all this discreetly and happily, feeling more a part of her adopted family than ever. She couldn't imagine being anywhere else. David, sitting right beside the kiddy table, was mystifying the little ones with the paradox of the Chinese bamboo finger trap, inserting his index fingers into either end of the little cylinder and easily pulling them out. Of course, when the kids tried it, they just got more stuck. It is questionable whether David's explanation to them in terms of helically wound braids and compression of biaxial strands was enlightening. The Gutierrezes, at the other end of the table, were enjoying themselves explaining the niceties of their Texas-Spanish mother tongue to a young, unattached S.U. professor of

Spanish, Javier Testa, whom Mark had invited since he had nowhere else to go.

The long table was decked from end to end with myriad heaping platters of vegetables and other side dishes, all prepared by the two sous chefs under Julie's close supervision. There was zucchini squash; there was cauliflower cooked Italian style; there was asparagus cooked in flour and egg, and Brussels sprouts sweetened with cherry sauce, and garlic mushrooms, and extra stuffing and, of course, the obligatory cranberry sauce, alas from a can, which went untouched except by Professor Testa. There were also two baskets of bread, one French, the other Italian, freshly sliced and toweled, placed at opposite ends of the table, along with several small plates of butter sticks and wedges of camembert, brie and munster cheese, set out at room temperature.

For starters, there were also four uncorked bottles of wine on the table, two each of red and white, whose contents decreased almost visibly during the first serving. This was, of course, in inverse proportion to the rising volume of animated chatter and laughter, the latter coming most audibly, at times piercingly, from Aunt Liz and tickling her tablemate Moira's fancy no end. But Aunt Liz's cackle could be infectious if the general mood was right, and today it was. Before long, the entire room was whooping it up, laughing, joking, chatting, eating, drinking, all with the gusto of epicures at their last meal.

And then, within thirty seconds, a profound pall was cast over the general merriment as everyone there stopped what he or she was doing or saying and all heads turned towards the head of the table. There sat Julie, suddenly being ministered to by Mark and Hattie. It wasn't clear what was happening to her but everyone's gut registered "not good."

"Let's get her into the kitchen. There's more room," Mark urged. He and Hattie wheeled her out, Nate, Aunt Liz, Moira and David following close behind, the others remaining standing at their places, napkins in hand, faces etched in worry.

Hattie had already phoned 911 and an ambulance was on its way. Mark was crouched down between sink and fridge in front of the wheelchair, holding Julie's hands and urging her, in the calmest voice he could summon, to try to relax and just breathe. Help was coming. All would be well.

Julie was looking at Nate, down on one knee beside her, trying to tell him something, but the words just would not come out the way she wanted them to. "Do' worw ..." was all she could manage, and that with a terrible struggle. The left side of her face had a profound droop to it, as if some perverse force of gravity were sucking it down, trying to pull it away from the rest of her body. Since she was quadriplegic, it was only this droop and consequent slurring of speech that signaled the crisis, causing Aunt Liz and Mark and even Hattie, sitting nearest her, to be slow on the uptake. Liz, with whom Julie had been chatting when it all began, mistook her sister's initial garbling as a sign of one too many sips of white wine and even kidded her about it. "Hey, kiddo, you're dropping half your consonants. Is Hattie keeping track of how many sips you've had?" Julie, herself unaware, tried to smile at her sister's good-natured impertinence, but could not produce more than a half-smile—literally. That's when Liz noticed the grotesque distortion of her sister's lower face and alerted Mark and Hattie.

"She's stroking," Hattie pronounced, now in the kitchen, confirming what most were already fearing. Julie was leaning her head to the left, trying to form a phrase with a mouth that seemed only to mock her. "Ma heh … ma heh …," she kept repeating. Hattie soon decoded this as "my head hurts" and quickly stepped over to the sink to make Julie a cold compress.

Just as she applied it to Julie's forehead, gently holding it there with one hand, with the other stroking her beloved ward's hair, the doorbell rang, followed by a robust rapping on the front door. It had taken a mere seven minutes for the ambulance to arrive. It took less than that for it to depart, Mark once again hovering over its precious cargo in this latest nightmarish commute to Upstate.

25

"**So, Nathaniel, let's** check out this lunch menu, shall we, and see if there's anything on it we especially like. I'm sure you're quite used to reading menus by now, aren't you?'

"Oh, sure. It's easy. I just look for cheeseburger … Hattie, why do you always call me 'Nathaniel?' You're the only one who does. Everybody else calls me 'Nate,' except for Aunt Moira; once in a while, she calls me 'Nathaniel' too."

"Hm. That's a good question. An astute question. I think it's because I'm trying to make myself special to you in some way, and this is maybe one little way to do that."

"You don't have to make yourself special, Hattie. You already *are*. Especially now with mom back in the hospital and all."

Hattie felt a pang of love for him for his naïve honesty in admitting that his love for her was based primarily on self-interest. He needed a Mom, damn it, and she would have to do. After all, was any relationship of a nine-year-old boy to his mother really any different? Yet, at the same time, she sensed in Nate a certain maturity, a certain independence of will or spirit belying his young years, doubtless forced on him, at least in part, by his straitened circumstances. But she really didn't know, couldn't know, since her acquaintance with the boy dated only from the accident.

It was the café section of the Wegman's on Genesee St. in DeWitt, the jewel of supermarkets in upstate New York with its subdued lighting and upscale prices. She'd pulled him out of school for lunch and a private little tete-a-tete to see how he was holding up with his mother now in intensive care and no firm release date in sight. She knew that just asking Nate how he was doing would not cut it; he had learned the lessons of emotional stoicism only too well; she would need time, and privacy, to probe and get him to open up.

It was noon and the popular café was bustling, but Hattie had secured a table in the far corner away from the traffic and the din. She had hoped they could sit outside as the weather was unusually mild for late November, but angry, dark clouds were rolling in from the West. Three high school girls, deciding to cut school-cafeteria lunch, were giggling—discretely—over their own truancy at the next table. An old man fussing over a slice of pizza sat at the table on the other side. A waitress came and took their order, Nate ordering the cheeseburger, medium rare, and Hattie the chicken salad sandwich on rye.

"I've been wanting to do this, Nathaniel—have lunch with you, that is—for some time now, but preparations for Thanksgiving and everything else left no time. Where *does* the time go?"

"Tempus fugit."

"Come again?"

"Tempus fugit. That's Latin for 'time flies.' I learned it in Language Arts. Some dead Latin guy—Vito or Vigil?—said it a long time ago, like, I mean, *thousands* of years ago. Latin is dead too."

"My goodness, Nathaniel, what an educated young man you're becoming, learning dead languages and all. So, how *is* school going these days, anyway—I've been meaning to ask you? How's Dex?"

"Dex is Dex. He's fine. He's always the same, 'cept he gets fatter. He loves strawberry Pop Tarts ... and 'everything' bagels ... and soft ice cream—you know, the Dairy Queen type."

"Oh my! Carbs and sugar, the downfall of us all," Hattie replied, fingering a charm necklace that lay on her flawless ebony skin, setting off her fulsome décolletage. "Tell me something, Nathaniel. Does it bother you that Dex is overweight?"

"Well, no, not really, 'cept he might lose some of his speed on the basketball court and other teams might start knocking us off," Nate quipped, his eyes resting now on the three girls at the next table, who were giggling up a storm and looking very fetching in their maroon blazers, which were adorned with the white seal of some Catholic high school.

"Yes," Hattie agreed in a musing tone. "Plus, it's not healthy, is it, being too overweight. It takes a toll on the body." As she sort of floated these words with a faraway look, she raised both hands behind her neck and deftly undid the clasp of her necklace, collecting it in her left palm. Then she let the eighteen-inch chain hang down vertically from between her thumb and forefinger, holding it out to Nate. It was made up of Haitian animal charms, a collection of tiny effigies of a dozen or so bird and mammal species native to her Haitian homeland, most of them endangered such as the golden-winged warbler, the rhino iguana and the solenodon, a small rodent with an elephantine trunk. But Hattie ignored these and went straight for the Antillean manatee, the lovable sea cow linked by sailor legend to mermaids and sirens because of its long tail. Carefully, almost surgically, she pulled apart the tiny ring attaching it to the yellow gold chain and slipped the little figure out. Placing it in her palm, she circled it daintily with her index finger, smiling warmly at Nate as she did so.

"Do you know what this is, Nathaniel?"

"I don't know. It's some kind of sea creature, I guess. It looks a little like a walrus, only with its face pushed in and no tusks."

"This is a manatee. It *is* a sea creature, so you're half right. I grew up with these in the Caribbean Sea near my home. Everybody in Port-au-Prince loved these gentle giants. Sometimes they would hug the shore and we'd see them when we went to the bay beach, or we'd see schools of them from pleasure boats or fishing boats. Today, though, it's rare to spot one. They're getting scarce."

"I think I've seen them on TV, on the Animal Channel," Nate said, taking the charm from Hattie's palm and scrutinizing it.

"Nathaniel, will you do me a small favor?"

"Sure, anything."

"Will you give this manatee to Dex? You don't have to tell him it's from me. Just give it to him, will you?"

"Sure, if you want me to ... How come?"

"Well, manatees are supposed to have a special connection to Agwé, the loa, or, as you would say, god of the sea, a Haitian god. Agwé protects sailors and all marine life, even pirates. See how the manatee's tale curves down?" she said, tracing the curve with her finger. "That grounds him in Agwé and in Agwé's wisdom. Give it to your friend, will you, with the encouragement that he eat more fish and fewer hamburgers. Who knows, maybe it'll work."

"Okay, I'll give it to him in school tomorrow … But Hattie, what about me?"

"What do you mean?"

"Don't you have a special charm for me too?"

"Nathaniel," she said in a mock-scolding tone, "you already have all the totemic protection you need—in Duncan. And he is so much more powerful than anything on my necklace, what with all the years you two have put in together. Why, you two have common roots. You don't need a manatee or anything else. Okay?"

"I guess. But Duncan really belongs to mom now, doesn't he? I really don't have that much to do with him anymore."

"Come now, Nathaniel! Oh ye of little faith. Do you really think a spirit as big and powerful as Duncan's is only able to protect one human being at a time? He watches over the whole family and God knows who all else," she said warming to the subject, widening her eyes as she made a sweeping gesture with her arms. "Even over me, I'll bet," she added, cackling with glee.

They finished their sandwiches and sat there nursing their diet sodas, neither of them eager to leave. Nate sensed that Hattie had something important, something "heavy," to tell him and Hattie could tell by his relaxed, lingering attitude that he was aware of it. This in turn put her at ease. She needn't rush, needn't struggle to hold his attention. "Nathaniel, speaking of your mom, I've been thinking that you need to be brought up to date on the current situation." It struck her how coldly objective, how clinical, the words rang in her ear as she spoke them, but there was really no other way. "Has your father told you anything about your mom's condition?"

"Not too much, only that she had a stroke and her recovery will be very slow. He said we all need to be patient." He was staring her straight in the eye as he sipped the last of his Pepsi, as if to say, "Go ahead! Tell me. I can take it. No matter what you're going to deliver, I won't flinch … Oh, God! How messed up is this gonna be?"

"Well, that's certainly true. With strokes great patience is absolutely necessary. It's a long, slow recovery process," she seconded, straightening her posture a bit. "But here's the thing, Nathaniel. When we go visit her in the hospital this evening, I don't want you to walk in and expect to see your mom just as she was before the stroke—"

Oh God, no! How much worse can she get he thought as he felt the rumblings of hysteria deep in the pit of his stomach. Still, his face remained a sculpted calm.

"You know …," Hattie went on, reaching across the table to cover his hand with her own and immediately second-guessing the gesture: She didn't want to appear too concerned. "You know that with stroke the brain's speech center is affected. For the moment—and I stress *moment*; it *is* temporary—your mom is not able to speak. Also, you'll notice as soon as you see her that the left side of her face is drooping considerably, especially her mouth. She should have at least partial recovery from this too. It all depends on how the tests come out. We'll know a lot more in a few days."

"When will she be coming home?" he asked tonelessly, as if he were asking the time of day.

"We don't know yet, Nate. We'll know better when the tests come out. She was given an MRI—that's a test that provides images of the brain—anyway she had the MRI when she first arrived at the hospital. It showed them where the clot was. Then they gave her powerful medications to break up the clot, dissolve it, before it could do any more damage … Oh, a blood clot is—"

"—I know what it is," he interrupted her a bit flintily. "It's coagulated blood." It did not escape his attention that she had called him "Nate," one of the very rare times. The abdominal rumblings surged up and into a state of painful anxiety. What could it mean that she would drop the comforting, mock-formal "Nathaniel" he had so come to love in favor of the give-it-to-him-straight "Nate?" A shudder passed through him, the only outer sign of it two blinks of his limpid blue eyes.

"To help during the transition period back to speech—I mean, since she can't write—she'll be trained to use a special device to communicate with us. I think it's called a BIC or—"

"It's called a BCI, a brain-computer interface. We learned all about them in science class. You get hooked up to a bunch of electrodes, which carry thought impulses of individual letters to a word processor, which then records the letters on a monitor screen. It's cool. They say it's a breakthrough of the mind-body barrier." He snapped the words at Hattie as though each one were a tiny missile aimed straight at her ignorance. He was angry at her, despite himself, for being the bearer of all this depressingly bad news. He wanted to hurt the messenger. Hattie guessed as much and took the attitude of allowing herself to be a target.

"Goodness gracious me, Nathaniel," she said with genuine admiration, "you're so well informed in so many areas! I think the nine-year-olds are taking over the world!" she joked, unwittingly seizing the entire room's attention again with another one of her delicious cackles.

As she laughed and let her glance linger lovingly on her young charge, it suddenly dawned on Hattie what her deepest reason was for taking Nate to lunch. True, she wanted to feel him out and get a sense of his current emotional state in light of this latest crisis in Julie's health; also true, she wanted to prepare him to encounter the most significant person in his life reduced almost to a condition of animal existence. But the deepest reason was to let him know, somehow, that she was more than ready and willing to take over the job of mother, should he, God forbid, lose his current one.

The problem was, she couldn't think of a way to communicate this to the boy, to let him feel the pure promptings of her heart, without sounding unnecessarily alarming or dire or opportunistic. Any way she might express the sentiment would involve speculation on Julie's death, and she could not risk exposing the boy to this. And so she was forced to accept the pain of what the psychologists call "benign suppression," the conscious and deliberate holding back of a profound wish, a desire—in this case maternal—coming from the core of one's being. She would not, under any circumstances, tell or indicate to Nate that he, in fact, had two mothers, one in reserve, and that the one in reserve was ready to take over at any time. She could only hope the boy knew this, felt it, consciously or otherwise.

"Oh my, Nathaniel, look at the time. We've got to get you back to school right now," she said, tousling his golden hair with her beringed hand as they got up to leave. Suddenly the girls at the next table had their heads together and were clucking conspiratorially, all six eyes trained on Nate's pretty profile as he walked past. He could see it all with his excellent peripheral vision, well honed from practicing no-look passes on the basketball court. Just for a moment the future looked bright.

26

No more than half an hour later on the same day, Mark Driscoll strolled into his noon lit class with a smile and greeted his students with a chipper "Good morning, all!" The reason for his upbeat mood, despite the recent spike in stress at home, was that he felt he had finally unloaded another burden he was carrying, almost as heavy, and that was his affair with Sabrina. All the anxiety and guilt that had, over the months, attenuated the sexual *frisson* to the point of diminishing returns was, at least for the moment, completely gone. Both his body and mind were feeling light and airy, playful, eager for new challenges. Not that he was ignoring or trivializing his wife's current plight—far from it, but he was wise enough to mentally bracket all that, for a time at least, and just allow himself to bask in the much-needed feeling of pride in having corrected a precarious moral and emotional course. He surprised himself in feeling little sense of loss over the affair with Sabrina, and in fact secretly wished her well. Was he deluding himself? Time would tell.

Today's hour was to be a relaxing one for him, as the syllabus called for him to play a CD of Tchaikovsky's *Manfred Symphony*, which, even leaving out parts, would take up most of the hour. In the previous hour, the class had finished its discussion of Byron's dramatic poem, *Manfred*, which tells of the titular hero's tortured inner life and tragic end. It was the last work of the semester. Mark liked to bring in musical treatments of literary subjects whenever he had the chance, especially since Romantic literature had inspired so many fine ones.

Typical of the Russian composer, the music was extremely dramatic and lyrical by turns; Mark was sure the students would "get with it." It follows Byron's closet drama closely in depicting the alienated hero Manfred's lonely, nomadic life wandering through the Swiss Alps, anguishing over the loss of his great love, Astarte, mainly through his own fault. He is plagued by guilt and self-loathing until being rescued and taken in by some mountain monks. But the reprieve is brief: In torment over actions that cannot be undone, Manfred dies as the monastery bells ring out.

Mark inserted the CD, Mikhail Pletnev conducting the Russian National Orchestra, and sat down behind the console. Right from the wrenching opening chords in the cellos, he knew he was in trouble. He felt something come to life deep in his abdomen and begin to stir uneasily. The students were still struggling to gather themselves and focus on the music and noticed nothing. As the music soon began to swirl upwards in the violins and engage the deep strings in a duel, a back-and-forth syncopation of furious antagonists, Mark was gripped by anxiety over these deep stirrings, which had begun so entirely unexpectedly. They felt powerful, primordial, and potentially beyond his control. He had never felt anything quite like this before, except perhaps long ago in early childhood, and was riven by uncertainty over how to handle it. He was starting to panic over the possibility of an emotional meltdown, right there in class, as the music soared in anguished frustration over Manfred's guilt and his inability—or was it refusal?—to gain deliverance even from the consolations of religion.

Mark could not know it then, but he would later come to understand that, in the innocent act of slipping in a CD, he had touched off the abreaction of an entire year's worth of repressed feelings: his wife's catastrophe, his guilt over the affair, his neglect of his son, his irrational anger towards his students. All of it rippled up his chest and into his throat, where he was able to block it with only the most painful contraction of his neck muscles. God, how it all ached to pour out of him right then and there, and he began nervously and furtively tapping his foot behind the console, as his mind cast about frantically for some face-saving strategy. He pulled out his handkerchief and pretended to attend to a sinus issue, at the same time getting up and heading towards the door, giving his best impression of a teacher who had meant to bring something to class, forgot to bring it, and must now go fetch it. On his way out he waved to the students, signaling them to stay with the music, that he would be right back, etc.

At this point the music was nearing the end of the first movement, the strings recapitulating the now dirge-like melody and the brass punctuating it with hammer blows. It was a horrific, infernal sort of beauty, with the ring of an unalterable tragic destiny. Mark still had his handkerchief up to his nose and, as he opened the door to leave, pretended to sneeze in order at least to take the edge off the force of emotion that was now erupting in him.

Fortunately, his classroom was adjacent to the men's room and he was able to slip in without being seen. He was thankful no one was inside, and, at mid-period with most people occupied, figured he had a good chance of having the place to himself. He went straight into a stall, locked the door and let out a roar of pain that would have frightened a bear. For a brief moment he *was* his expression, and nothing but expression, all else forgotten. Relief came swiftly, overwhelmingly, like the first dowsing of water from the fire hydrant that the firemen would wrench open for the neighborhood kids in his early summers. Then, as another wave rose up, he remembered that the walls were thin and that he needed to tamp it down a bit, modulate it, to avoid attracting attention.

Quickly the moment of blessed self-forgetfulness was over, but it had been enough to raise him from the dead. He threw some water on his face, dried it with a paper towel and checked himself out in the mirror. He saw gray flecks in his moustache he hadn't noticed before. Looking more closely, he decided he could pass for someone in the grips of a sinus attack. As he exited the restroom's successive double doors, he got a bit entangled with a student on his way in and felt a tiny spike of anger at him, as if to say, "Jesus, could you spare me the few minutes!" This told him he was back in control; it was safe to return to class.

And return he did, feeling like a man who had just thrown off a net of iron chains. Fleetingly he realized how relative the sense of well-being is: he had *thought* he was feeling fine when he first came into class; but next to this unsought emancipation, this sudden explosion of joy, it was a poor man's bliss indeed. But then he sensed the truth of the old saw that comparisons are odious and that his best bet was just to leave it alone and get on with it.

Closing the door behind him as he stepped back into class, he recognized the lilting Spanish-style melody of the Russian's second movement. He let his eyes rove among the students and concluded that most of them were charmed by it, going by their body language at least, heads resting dreamily on palms or tilted slightly to one side. A few slackers were buried in their I-pads, of course, in defiance of his express banishment of the damned electronic gremlins from class. Realizing that he was getting short on time, he walked over to the console and moved the CD ahead to well into the symphony's finale, to the orchestral fortissimo, the final spasm of Manfred's anguish just before the entrance of the soothing strains of the organ announcing the poet's ultimate release in death. He let the finale play out, thinking to himself that he still didn't feel composed enough to lead a discussion of the music as an analogy to Byron's tragic hero. He needed a ploy, a ruse, to give himself another minute or two to settle down. *Ah, yes, of course* he thought.

"My very good friend in the music school, Tony Jirak," he began, "likes to rib me for my predilection for Tchaikovsky, who always wears his heart on his sleeve— all that lush emotionalism, you know? But I told him I'll never apologize for it. I told him I thought Tcaikovsky's early death, probably by his own hand, was, and remains, a profound loss to music-lovers the world over, comparable to Chopin's death, or even Mozart's … All those entrancing melodies that never got to be written!" he lamented, looking down and feeling a deep sense of loss.

"I *love* Tchaikovsky," one of the female majors sitting up front blurted out spontaneously. She was a slim brunette, pretty, with her hair pulled back in a pigtail. Mark was more than happy to hand the ball over to her. "I've loved him ever since I took ballet lessons as a little girl. I still get goose bumps whenever I hear *Swan Lake*. It makes me want to do split leaps."

"Well, far be it from me to stifle a terpsichorean impulse, Sarah," Mark quipped. "I happen to have a CD of *Swan Lake* in my office. If I run and get it, will you please be my guest," he added, sweeping his hand gracefully across the front of the classroom. Sarah giggled and all at once became self-conscious, her cheeks reddening, and shyly declined the invitation, which got a big laugh from the other students.

Which is when Evan Katz concluded that all this folderol, however charming, was a little too warm and fuzzy for his taste, and decided the time had come to put into action a plan to bait the good professor that he had been harboring and keeping in store for the end of the semester: "Professor Driscoll, there's one thing that bothers me about Manfred, both the character and the poem. I wonder if you could illuminate the matter for me."

Katz's slightly snooty and patronizing tone put Mark immediately on guard. But by now he was feeling good, strong, in command of his faculties—in fact, better than that: A certain relaxed euphoria was setting in. If Katz was looking for some intellectual jousting, he—Mark—was ready to provide it.

"For the life of me," Katz continued, "I can't figure out exactly what Manfred's problem is. I know he's a typical 'Byronic hero' and all that and he doesn't really need a specific issue or problem in order to go around all depressed and guilty, just spewing gobs of Romantic *Weltschmerz* all over those beautiful Alps. But why do you think it is that Byron declines to give us at least *some* personal psychological specifics here, something we can relate to or identify with? Especially the guilt. Why the hell is this guy so crushed by guilt? I mean, if it's just the general state of the world that drives him bonkers, well then he's really a weakling, isn't he, hardly a hero in any sense. It seems Byron is giving us a sniveling neurotic, wouldn't you agree? A pathetic wretch who should just curl up in a corner somewhere with his banky. In fact, maybe all this 'Byronic hero' stuff, and Byron's own social swagger and flouting of convention, is really a mask, a cover-up, for what I would call his pusillanimous Romantic neuroticism."

After firing off this stunning opening salvo, Evan Katz sat back, assumed a serious expression and stroked his chin, giving himself the air of a man who was deeply troubled by something and lost in profound thought over it. Of course, nobody in the room was fooled by these theatrics, least of all Mark. Katz was definitely up to something but what was it? Until he had a better sense of his intent, Mark thought it best simply to go along with Katz's line of reasoning, which did, after all, carry some weight in the canons of scholarship, being as it was a caricature of a tradition of criticism of the Romantic poets, namely, that they were wimps, thin-skinned escapists in search of a transcendental world that would replace this paltry one the rest of us manage to put up with.

"Well, as I'm sure you're aware, Mr. Katz"—he'd taken to addressing Katz with "Mr.," while remaining on a first-name basis with everyone else—"there is a wing of scholarship that agrees with you, one of the leading champions of your point of view being Aniela Jaffé, a protégée of the psychologist Carl Jung. She regards the Romantic hero type as basically an escapist, someone whose quest for a higher world, a metaphysical Eden or Shangri-La, is really no more than a high-toned ratio-nalization of his repugnance for this one ... Now, I don't necessarily reject Jaffé's critique out of hand—"

"—No, no!" Katz interrupted. He was having none of Mark's olive branch: "What I'm getting at is, the guilt, the guilt. There must be some reason why Byron leaves the underlying cause or causes for such profound guilt vague. I mean, it *kills* the man, for God's sake! It's very mysterious, don't you think?"

Mark just stood there, regarding Katz intently, waiting for him to answer his own question and finally, so he hoped, lift the veil on his nefarious motives, whatever they might be.

"I mean, Byron was far too great a poet to commit such a gaffe deliberately," Katz reasoned, "which to me means that it was *not* deliberate."

"I'm afraid I don't—"

"Well, we know that Byron wrote the poem in 1817, shortly after going into self-imposed exile in Switzerland following a scandal involving his failed marriage ... failed because of an incestuous affair he was carrying on with his half-sister."

There was an audible gasp from the class. Mark felt a new uneasy stirring from below. He shifted his stance.

"I mean, come on!" Katz almost bawled, getting himself into quite a lather. "Adultery! And incestuous adultery at that! I think Byron's guilt over the sexual relationship with his sister was too much for him to bear. With *Manfred* he was trying to exorcize the demon, but the demon was so powerful that he couldn't even identify it, give it a name in the poem. It remains simply a dark, mysterious void in the poem, a vague Germanic

Weltschmerz, and we readers just go on scratching our heads over it."

The son of a bitch! I can't believe this. He's found a way to stick the knife in over my affair with Sabrina. I wonder how much she's told him. He's scolding me right to my face, right now, right here in class in front of my students, and only he and I know he's doing it. I'm Byron the adulterer. He's got all the power here; he can say whatever he wants to me, really rub my nose in it, as long as he does it through the surrogate of Byron and Manfred, through the ruse of literature. It's brilliant, the bastard!

All at once Mark was a spectator—of his own student's dramatic performance, which was not quite finished: "Adultery! Sexual intercourse between a married person and a person who is not his spouse ... Excuse me, *his* or *her* spouse. A heinous betrayal! It undermines the family, the most sacred institution of society. It makes the adulterer a social outcast. Byron tried his best to turn his sin into some kind of special prerogative of poetic genius. Poets and intellectuals play above the rules, as it were. Their creative gifts exempt them. Blah, blah, blah. It didn't work though. The poem's botched attempt both to disguise and exorcize the poet's sin is the evidence that it failed. It became Byron's personal object-lesson on the limits of poetic license. The strictures of society are there for a reason, and woe to him—or her—who flouts them ..."

Katz rambled on in that vein a while longer, while Mark stood there transfixed.

The prick is a poseur! He's posing as a moralist! As if he gave two shits about adultery as a moral issue. He's feigning concern over Manfred-Byron's adultery as a way of getting in his digs about me. That's clear from his harping on the adultery, even to the exclusion of Byron's incest, easily the "graver sin." And there's not a damn thing I can do about it. My hat's off to you, smart boy.

At the first significant pause in Katz's diatribe, Mark looked at his watch and said, "Oh, look at the time. Class dismissed." The students filed out, passing by Mark at the doorway. They all looked at him, most even smiling—except for Evan Katz, who strolled by with his eyes straight ahead, wearing the slightest trace of a smug sneer.

Well done. And well deserved, I must confess. That is my karmic punishment. My karmuppance, you might say.

And, mirabile dictu, he did indeed feel a little purged, which allowed him to take it all in stride.

27

Santa drove his van through the baroque wrought-iron gate, which had been left open. Following the directions Karel Jirak had given him, he continued slowly for about a block along the paved path that snaked through a copse of maple, oak and fir trees towards the house. When he came in sight of the house, his mouth dropped open. It was much more mansion than house, a Victorian Gothic mansion to be precise, with a huge four-window cupola on the second floor, several arched gabled windows in front and a wrap-around porch. Although the whole place was lit up like a Christmas tree, there was just enough natural light left to make out its basic color as classic royal blue.

Santa looked for a place to park and found a small, square paved area on the lakeside of the house—Skaneateles Lake, that is—a scenic and exclusive region about twenty minutes southwest of Syracuse. In fact, peering down the tapered lawn to the embankment, he could see the long shadows of the trees cast upon the water as they flittered with the wavelets. *Well, what have we here!* he enthused. *A castle on the lake. I should've taken my classical music studies more seriously.*

He parked, got out and looked around. There was one other car on the pavement, not quite new, probably belonging to another guest, he thought. *I wouldn't be surprised if the fleet of family cars is kept in some massive garage, probably underground.*

Santa knew what he was in for—a night of splendor, refinement, impeccable taste, a night among the moneyed intelligentsia of Syracuse. Just his few meetings with Karel had alerted him to this. It was clear to Santa that Karel admired his father and felt driven to reproduce his success in the classical-music profession. *My God! Sanity between father and son! Nothing more than cutthroat competition. What an evolutionary leap!*

He walked up the stone steps to the broad landing in front of the tall double doors, clapping his sides and his gloved hands together. It was a cold, crisp, gorgeous December evening, not yet the bone-chilling sort for which Syracuse was infamous that would doubtless arrive with the Christmas holidays. Just the sort, though, that perversely appealed to his southern boy's blood. He looked around again: Everything was in repose. He tried peering inside through the clear perimeter of the frosted glass doors but could only make out a portion of elegant black wall sitting on white molding. There was no one to be seen; he would have to make his entrance, a fashionable quarter-hour late, with a minimum of advanced scouting.

He pressed the bell and heard orotund chimes ring out a vaguely familiar phrase from a piece of classical music—Czech music, he guessed, but couldn't be sure. He heard footsteps quickly approaching the door; it was Karel. Through the clear strip of glass, Santa could see Karel reaching for the handle, impeccably dressed in a blue blazer and gray slacks, virtually identical to the ensemble he himself was wearing. They both also had on open-collar shirts. He was already beginning to feel comfortable.

"Santa! Welcome! Welcome to our humble abode!" Karel crowed with self-conscious irony as he carefully pulled open both doors. "Come in, please, come in! I see my directions have served you well." A beaming smile on his face, he then opened his arms wide for the warm embrace his Slavic blood demanded, and Santa allowed himself to be swallowed up in the smaller man's grip, but only for the briefest moment.

"Come, come, my friend! Let me introduce you to my father and our other guests. He's been most eager to meet you, ever since I told him about you—my father, that is." Karel led Santa through the short, chic black-walled foyer and into a magnificent living room, which, though quite large, was crammed to bursting with furniture and curiosities that breathed Victorian: There were thickly upholstered sofas of dark wine-red fabric and ornate, high-backed chairs, all framed by walls dazzlingly busy with lush, tasseled draperies and oil paintings depicting dramatic mythological motifs, these interspersed with embroidered tapestries telling of other legendary events which Santa could not quite make out. There were settees and loveseats and end tables with vases of flowers on them. Two aspects of the room's décor stood out, however, even from this charming chaos of objects: three lancet windows, stretching from wainscoting to ceiling, facing front and matched by three lancet mirrors adorning the wall opposite them; and two wooden gargoyles of the finest hand-carved detail guarding the room and mounted on symmetrical fluted posts that framed its entrance.

The wall opposite the room entrance was entirely hidden behind built-in oaken shelves of books from floor to ceiling. In the corner stood a leaning ladder on a trolley for access to the highest shelves. Most of the books were multi-volume sets of collected writings, mainly of literary masters (Proust, Flaubert, Balzac), but there were also a few shelves at the end of the wall near the ladder that were stuffed with musical scores and manuscripts. These were the only works that were neither hardcover nor handsome; otherwise the collection, exhibiting so many gilt-edged book spines, made a brilliant impression.

Santa, it seems, had entered an aristocratic museum of Western culture that would have awed any commoner with an intellectual ego. And Santa *was* duly awed, though of intellectual ego he was blissfully free. Then too, he'd hardly had time to take in a fraction of it all, as his eyes were instantly drawn to one of the two guests, a blond boy of about nine or ten wearing black jeans and a black- and cream-colored panel shirt that set off his pretty head just so. Santa was immediately smitten, unable to resist letting his eyes rove up and down the boy's small stature for several minutes while the introductions were being done. He had trouble keeping his attention evenly divided.

"Santa, let me introduce you to my father, Antonin Jirak," said Karel, doing the honors as they all stood in the middle of the room. Santa thought his friend sounded a tad nervous, as indicated by his heightened accent (now at 10%) and the formality of his expression.

"Father, this is Samuel Clause. 'Santa' for short. We met recently at the Riverbank during one of my dinner serenades. I've told you about him."

"Ah, yes, of course! Your jazz musician acquaintance. Welcome, Mr. Clause. It's a pleasure to meet you," said a tall, erect, well-dressed gentleman with thinning wavy hair combed straight back and a graying pencil-thin moustache. He was holding what looked like a snif-ter of brandy in his left hand and an expensive Cuban cigar, gold paper ring intact, in his right. Speaking with a distinct Slavic accent that was even more charming than Karel's, he found it necessary to put his cigar in his mouth in order to shake Santa's hand.

"Oh, please, make it 'Santa.'" They shook hands and Santa took a step back, pretending to make an appreciative survey of the lavish chamber in all its splen-dor, at last bringing his eyes down to rest again on the boy, finally acknowledging the boy's father with a brief nod.

"Thank you, Karel. I'll take it from here," Professor Jirak said, casting an ironic smile at his son. "Santa, please allow me to introduce to you my esteemed col-league at the university, who is also a dear friend—and his young son ... This is Mark Driscoll and Nathaniel Driscoll ... Mark, Nate, this is Santa Clause ... no, no relation, Nate, I'm sorry to say." All five of them laughed loudly, which is to say, a bit self-consciously, and hands were again shaken.

"Mark is a professor of English literature," Antonin continued, laying his cigar down in an ashtray and brushing a bit of ash from his smart gray twill suit, "spe-cializing in the Romantic period." Santa and Nate eyed each other quickly, both enjoying the maestro's quaint Slavic pronunciation of the words "professor" and

"Romantic." "I myself 'profess' Romantic music, especially from Eastern Europe—Russian, Czech, sometimes Scandinavian. We get into a lot of arguments, Mark and I do, about poetry and music and how the two relate, or don't relate, as the case may be, and, of course, Mark adores Tchaikovsky while I can't abide the man's mawkish emotionalism, and, of course, I condemn him for his pedophilia ..." The maestro spoke these words more harshly than he had intended, and so used a sip of his cognac as a cover for scanning the others' eyes to see what impression they had made.

Santa's face was impassive, though inwardly, at the mention of the word 'pedophilia,' he had snapped to, of course; he had been only half listening while engaged in pondering the near absence of physical similarity between Mark and his son, the father tall and dark but otherwise fairly unremarkable in looks, his boy, however, a cherub of the first rank, who would need only wings, he thought, to attend on the throne of the Almighty Himself—if there *were* an Almighty.

They remained standing there a while longer, exchanging pleasantries, until finally the maestro said, "Santa, what can I get you to drink ... and please help yourself to some of these hors d'oeuvres," stepping as he spoke towards the small wet bar standing near the corner of the long wall. Next to it stood a sideboard displaying trays of several different delicacies. Santa noticed Jirak senior walked with the quick, deliberate pace of a businessman, rather than that of a man strolling through his own garden of art.

Santa, of course, did what he usually did when offered alcohol during a happy hour: he accepted a small glass of white wine, from which he sipped sparingly. For the evening at hand he wanted his senses fully poised.

They all found their seats, Mark and Nate on a sofa, the others on plush surrounding chairs. Santa put his glass down on the ornate, bow-legged coffee table around which they were all grouped and popped a mint into his mouth from one of the two cut-glass candy bowls on either end of it. When Nate followed suit a minute later, Santa smiled at him and felt—justifiably or not, who can say—the budding seed of a secret comradery between them.

"So, Santa," the maestro began, puffing grandly on his cigar, "Karel tells me you lead a sort of vagabond existence, moving from place to place, from one jazz group to another. I must say, it all sounds rather exhausting."

"Oh, I'm used to it, Professor," Santa said with a wan smile. "I've been doing it for most of my adult life. It has its compensations."

"Such as?" the maestro prodded, puffing away.

"Well, for one thing, I'm free and beholden to no one. I can come and go as I please."

"Yes, that's for sure, but one might read that as just a euphemistic way of saying I'm all alone, all by myself. Tell me, do you ever get lonely?"

"Father, don't you think that's a bit personal? You've just met the man ..." Karel interrupted, his blushing cheeks reflecting equal parts embarrassment and pique. To cover himself he speared a shrimp on his plate with a toothpick and raised it to his mouth.

"Forgive me," the maestro said, looking at Santa and then at each of the others in turn, "I tend to be a bit brash, a tad impulsive perhaps, like a character out of Dostoyevsky, or so I was always told by my deceased wife, God bless her soul. And now my son has taken up that monitoring role in my life, bless him."

"Oh please, don't give it a thought, Professor," Santa reassured him. "That question's been put to me a thousand times. I've come to expect it on first meetings, and the fact is, I've thought about it a great deal ... The answer is, I think, that old saw, the one that says there's a difference between loneliness and being alone. I'd put myself in the second category." As he said the words, Santa tried hard to reinforce them with a chuckle, but something deep within was stirring up an irritation, a sort of restlessness that reached up into his neck and shoulders and made him feel ever so slightly hypocritical. This, in turn, caused him some alarm, as if, for once, he sensed he was lying not just to the others but to himself as well. After all, why was he here? Why had he come to Syracuse?

He became a little flustered, just enough to lose his train of thought and break off his commentary. The maestro came to his rescue by turning to Mark, and to another subject: "You're a jazz aficionado, aren't you, Mark?"

"Oh, yes, since high school at least," Mark chirped. "In my sophomore year, a classmate lent me an LP— that's this thin black disk with grooves in it that was once used to hold music," he quipped, turning to his son for effect. "It was Dave Brubeck's *Quiet as the Moon*. I was a big Peanuts fan at the time—still am, in fact—and when I heard Brubeck's rendition of "Linus and Lucy," well, it opened up a whole new world to me."

"Yes," the maestro seconded, "it's amazing how the most commonplace, even trivial, event can spark a profound awakening in a man. You see a commercial with a cartoon version of a Valkyrie in it on the television and you're led to Wagner. You listen to, oh … that overstuffed American tenor, Mario Lanza, belt out the "Song of India" on YouTube and it's welcome to the enchanting world of Rimsky-Korsakov and the Russian nationalist composers—"

"—There's no need to point out that Lanza is American, father," the son interrupted in irritation. "We are *in* America and they know who he is—or was." Santa was amused by Karel's pedantic correction.

"Oh, come now, Karel, that's a bit picayune, don't you think? … Anyway, tell me, Santa," the maestro then asked, turning again to the guest who seemed to interest him most, though he could not have said why. Was it his dashing good looks? His modest charm? Whatever it was, it was elusive, but all the more compelling for that. "Tell me, what turned you on to jazz?"

"Well," Santa said, resurrecting his Big Easy accent, "As Karel may have told you, I'm from New Awlins so it would've been hard to miss." They all laughed, including Nate, who turned to his father and asked, "Dad, where's New Orlins?", which provoked another laugh. As Mark explained to his son about regional accents, Santa was secretly feeling pleased that Nate was interested enough to ask. He also noticed with pleasure the smooth, gossamer down adorning the right side of Nate's neck, the side made clearly visible to him from where he sat by an end-table lamp. He had his 20/10 or better vision to thank for such subtle delights of the senses, delights denied to most of us. It reminded him why he generally avoided alcohol, or anything else that might compromise his sensorium.

"Yes, of course," the maestro observed with smiling aplomb, "New Orleans, the cradle of jazz. Louis Armstrong, Buddy Bolden, Jelly Roll Morton, and scores of others. You had so many models, so many masters, to stimulate you. Sort of like a boy growing up in Florence in the late fifteenth century, no? Masterpieces everywhere you looked. Not like the benighted cultural desert we live in today, eh?"

"Oh, father, it's no good complaining about that," Karel retorted sharply. "You know very well a particular cultural era cannot judge its own quality. There's no distance, no objectivity. It's like looking in a mirror and trying to catch yourself with your eyes closed." Professor Jirak was becoming visibly annoyed by what he felt were his son's niggling interjections, but, for the sake of his guests, he took the high road and held his tongue.

Santa, for his part, was enjoying Nate's mirthful reaction, barely suppressed, to the maestro's struggle to negotiate the name Jelly Roll Morton with its soft el's and r's, a formidable challenge to the Eastern European tongue. The reaction also included a broad smile—was it lingering—at Santa, which he returned in kind. We're they becoming co-conspirators, fellow covert operatives in the war against adult pretension and stuffiness? He hoped so.

The chatting went on until moments later when an elderly woman in an apron appeared between the gargoyles and announced that dinner was served.

"Thank you, Katerina," the two hosts answered in unison.

They all stood up, picked up their drinks and followed Katerina into the dining room. Santa let Nate pass in front of him on the way there so that he could furtively observe the boy from behind in leisurely fashion, leisurely enough to take in Nate's gate, in which he found much to admire—it was erect, poised, purposeful, in no way obsequious; it hinted at a keen intelligence, which for Santa enhanced the boy's desirability a great deal. Added to this was the boy's mature behavior in the company of adults, reflected in his ability to listen to their conversation politely and even give the appearance of being interested; no typical nine-year-old tactics of apathy such as blowing, humming, kicking the air or pestering his hosts with the question whether there were any video games on the premises.

This whole quality of maturity in a child was heady stuff to Santa, who as a rule never got personally close enough to his victims to appreciate it, Luke being perhaps the sole exception. It now embedded itself in the boy's physical beauty to make him, alas, a most appealing prospect for grabbing. In fact, thoughts of comparison with Luke had already crossed Santa's mind—involuntarily. Then, just as Nate sat down at the table—Santa made sure it was opposite his own seat—he performed this little-boy gesture that caused a sudden spike in Santa's libido: He tossed his golden bangs back with the most comely, nonchalant jerk of his head. This movement, totally unexpected, reminded Santa of a young colt romping through a meadow, suddenly throwing back its mane in instinctual celebration of its own vitality. (Perhaps he didn't realize it, but the few sips of wine he had taken—his first alcohol since Ottawa—had stoked the embers of his lust to a level of comfortable piquancy.)

Oddly, however, as soon as he began to take secret delight in the colt metaphor with its animal suggestiveness, that same restless irritation that had nettled him moments earlier surfaced again, filling him momentarily with annoyance and dissatisfaction. But he had no time to consider it now as the soup course was brought in: French onion topped by a thick cheese crust. There was a brief silence as they all commenced blowing on their hot soupspoons. Santa used the timeout to survey the dining room in all its opulence: the brocaded wallpaper lavishly embroidered in floral pinks, blues and greens; the velvet drapes with their tassels, ties and fringes; the double glass doors looking out onto some sort of stone terrace rimmed by a balustrade, the whole illuminated by faux old-style gaslights; and, most impressively, a two-tiered wrought iron chandelier hanging directly over the table, its tiny bulbs mimicking the flickering flames of a hundred candles. It all conjured a dazzling image of the kind of Victorian decadence yearned for by an aesthete who rued his birth as having come a century too late.

By the time the soup course was finished and the entre, of prime rib au jus with asparagus tips, was brought in and served by Katerina and a young man in a white coat named Frederick, the conversation was again in full swing:

" … The jazz one hears played in Prague is really first-rate, especially in some clubs in the old town," the maestro was opining. "There's the Jazz Republic on Wenceslas Square and the one … oh, what's it called, the one that virtually dared the Communists to shut it down, back in the fifties—Karel, you know the one I mean—"

"—The Reduta, father, the Reduta."

"Yes, yes, of course, the Reduta! Velebny and Hulan played there, you know," he said, turning to Mark, who nodded agreeably, although he had never heard of either musician. Then, in one of those abrupt changes of subject that the maestro seemed to enjoy inflicting on his guests, he asked Santa, "Tell us, Santa, which of the jazz greats do you favor? Who are your idols?"

The question, which Santa was expecting, nevertheless made him thoughtful and he took a moment before answering: "Well, as far as my own instrument is concerned, there are several I admire who stand out from the rest … there's Charlie Mingus and Ray Brown and … a fellow you've probably never heard of: John Casey is his name. He was my teacher at Loyola. He once toured with Wynton Marsalis—a wizard on the double bass, with fingers of steel that just danced across the strings." With his cool, concise, yet intense way of expressing himself, Santa had them all hanging on his every word, but his glance lingered longer and more often on Nate than the others.

"But for me, irrespective of instrument, there's really only one man, a unique genius who towers over all the others." A solemn hush filled the room as though they were awaiting an oracular pronouncement. "And that would be Miles," he said after a pause, well aware that the first name was sufficient. "Miles Davis and his magic trumpet. And I'll narrow it down even further: It's the album *Kind of Blue*, made in August 1959. And not the whole album either—just the first track, called 'So What,' where the master, with a mere two notes—no more than that, just 'daa da ... daa da,' over and over again—shuffles off all the rules and regs society has seen fit to load onto its members, crushing the life out of them, sapping all spirit, all play, all joy. It's just like call and response, okay? The bass throws out a series of calls or questions in a rising phrase: 'dum di dum di dum dum.' As if to say, 'What about this? What about that? What about the other?' And the trumpet answers each of them with that same simple, blasé 'So what!' ... For me, that is the pinnacle of jazz art, containing its supreme subversive power, its transcendent cool—all in a tiny nutshell of a phrase. Atomic power compressed into a binary nucleus ... When I hear it, I feel emancipated, I feel that nothing is beyond me, nothing forbidden ..."

The instant Santa noticed that they were looking at each other more than at him, he dialed down the fervor, astonished at the force of his own candor. "Anyhow, that's the way I see it," he said, rounding it off and looking for a way to lower the temperature of his remarks, which he thought to have found with the mild disclaimer, "Oh, I'm well aware that Miles Davis is not the greatest jazz trumpeter in terms of virtuosity or technique. Any number of others top him there—Louis Armstrong, Dizzy, Wynton—but for reaching that place where music morphs into something even finer, even purer, than itself—a purity that is somehow not the opposite of the impure—he stands alone ... for me at least."

Damn it he chided himself. His intent had been to turn down the heat, to mute the trumpet so to speak, and here he was blowing fortissimo in spite of himself. Silently he thanked the maestro for intervening: "That's very interesting, Santa. And come to think of it, Miles Davis is not even from New Orleans—or *New Awlins*, as the natives put it—is he?" A peal of laughter all around. "He's from the midwest if I'm not mistaken, and was based in a lot of different places—New York, San Francisco, sometimes even Europe—but never in ...

New Awlins! He represents cool jazz, which is a whole different strain, isn't it?"

"You do know your jazz history, Professor," Santa smiled. "Miles did, however, grow up in St. Louis, which is one of the first cities jazz spread to from New Awlins. So I'm guessing there was a drop or two of New Awlins in his blood as well."

"Dad, didn't Mom grow up in St. Louis?" Nate, who had been listening intently, suddenly interjected. Santa's gaze shifted instantly to the boy's face and lingered there, as it had done each time he had spoken up during the meal. *Astonishing poise, astonishing maturity* he thought. *He holds his own, unselfconsciously.*

"No, son," Mark answered, "she grew up in Cedar Rapids, which is about three hundred miles north of St. Louis on the interstate. You must be thinking of the story I've told so often about our trip—your mother's and mine, with Aunt Liz—to St. Louis years ago to see Miles in concert. That was long before you were born, kiddo."

"So your wife is also a jazz aficionado?" Santa prompted, in a sly effort to learn what more he could about the boy's personal circumstances. And what he now learned sent a shock wave of pleasurable excitement from his groin in all directions throughout his nervous system.

"Oh yes, very much so. I couldn't count the number of terrific jazz groups we've heard all over the upstate area in recent years, even here in Syracuse where the pickings can be slim. And we've made many trips to New York City and Boston, ostensibly to attend professional conferences and such, but in truth just to revisit some of our old jazz haunts ... Of course, all that's changed now. You see, my wife was in a terrible auto accident a little over a year ago. It left her more or less paralyzed from the neck down. Needless to say, we don't get out much these days ..."

"Oh, I'm so sorry to hear that," Santa consoled, giving his best impression of sincere concern, the tiniest part of which, however, he felt, disturbingly, to actually *be* sincere.

And it was precisely this almost but not quite insignificant note of genuine concern that now took hold of him and spoiled the rest of the evening for him. For it was just the latest trigger of that niggling irritation that had leached into his awareness to spoil several earlier moments of this pleasant, not to mention promising, evening. He was beginning to notice, and in noticing loathe, his own lies. This unfamiliar feeling of disgust over his own hypocrisy was something he knew he could not afford to entertain. It endangered his whole project, undermined his very *raison d'etre*. He then recognized the conflict as something he had been wrestling with at least since meeting Karel in Alexandria Bay, and that it had something to do with a nascent, heretofore ignored, indeed suppressed, need for human companionship. All of this now seemed to cascade down onto him like a raging waterfall and it was all he could do, as he sat there trying to take part in the table talk, to maintain his composure and at least seem attentive.

But then came the anger as his pride railed against his own weakness, this "weakness" of the milk of human kindness that was now insinuating itself into a heart he was sure he had buried long ago. He cursed the contrived stoicism of his lofty meditative posturing. Where was that stoicism now when he needed it most? It was no good being battered to and fro in a sea of roiling emotions. There was no way he could carry on if such a state were to become more than an anomaly, as it seemed to be doing. He must reassert his existential mastery of the moment immediately, starting now (when else?). It had stood him in good stead for decades, and would surely continue to do so. It was all up to him. This sudden inner cry for companionship, pusillanimous at its base, must be pulled back in on its own tether and smothered. Consider the boy! The beautiful boy! And all the other beautiful boys, of past and future, each one an escape route to freedom, that freedom that was knowable right within this trap that is our life. Indeed, the freedom that revealed this trap to be an illusion.

This pep talk, internally self-administered in no more than twenty seconds, did not restore his equilibrium to the point of unfettered re-involvement in the social moment; it merely enabled him to endure it. Karel, who had his own reasons for being less than affable during dinner, had picked up on Santa's momentary distractedness and managed as the table was being cleared to whisper to him sympathetically from behind his napkin, "Don't worry. You'll be out of here by ten-thirty, eleven at the latest." But Karel, in assuming that Santa's remoteness had just as much to do with what he felt to be his father's overbearing manner as did his own, could not have been further off the mark.

28

ativity, **native, native** *fluency, itty bitty native. Dat's what I got wit Nate. Natrally, natch, a natural he be. A natural be he, boo hoo, hi bye, good night and don't call me, let me call you. The mama's all plegic, she can't lift a finger. But then so was mine; over that we'll not linger. Mens insana in corpore insano. Dat be da Clauses, as sure as bat guano. Who be da boss here anyway? Gittin mighty hard to tell wit everbody jockeyin' for native dancer, to straddle the saddle, up shit's creek no paddle. Now I got Little Goody Two-Shoes crawlin' up my arse. What um gonna do wit him, huh? He'd have me lay off a god cause his mama's lost bod? Fuck dat! I listen ta him once, he'll have me for lunch. A house divided against itself and shit like dat. See, I know my bible. Oh sure, I may cherry pick the verse, but pickin' cherries ain't no worse. Dat's what I gotta keep in my head if I wanna get back to goin' ta bed. Nate's my bait. He's got da whole crate—a laddie Apollo, such a pleasure to follow. His face like the sun, his hair like*

*its rays, his light without dun, his body ablaze, superior fun
... Man, I can't sing his praise without feelin' adaze. How
much penile power can be packed into a few freckles framing
that little dip of a nose, on an axis with the inflatable nose
in his clothes, that hose of a nose, just for now in repose ...
If it's penile power you want, it's penal power you'll get, you
pitiful, pussified prick. I'll penalize that pissy li'l pipe till it's
too pooped to pop. "Pop" did I say? I'll pry it pull for pull till
it's past reprieve in my palm ... Oh, Fred, stop houndin' the
boy. You see what the Pappy's does to you. It brings out the
devil, the devil, it's true. Come over here, Samuel. Sit here
by me ... Ay yai yai, good is evil, evil good. The girls in the
country, the boys in the hood. What's good for me is beyond
all "should." I wouldn't change even if I could. But somethin's changin' me, it seems—not fist, nor stone, nor wood,
but something airy, deep and far from understood. It's like
I'm leaking lollipops—li'l reds and greens and yellows all
around, and lavenders, all on the ground. And lavenders
all on the ground. But mostly reds, those little crimson disks.
Their sticks in deep, too deep, tsk tsk. But the wine-dark
sea still swells in me, its mighty waves won't let me be, they
loom up like the sweetest ghee, so let's just stop ... and leave
it be ... and see ... and see ... and see ... and see ...*

29

NIH NATIONAL INSTITUTE OF NEUROLOGICAL DISORDERS AND STROKE

What is Locked-In Syndrome?

Locked-in syndrome is a rare neurological disorder characterized by complete paralysis of voluntary muscles in all parts of the body except for those that control eye movement. It may result from traumatic brain injury, diseases of the circulatory system, diseases that destroy the myelin sheath surrounding nerve cells, or medication overdose. Individuals with locked-in syndrome are conscious and can think and reason, but are unable to speak or move. The disorder leaves individuals completely mute and paralyzed. Communication may be possible with blinking eye movements.

Is there any treatment?

There is no cure for locked-in syndrome, nor is there a standard course of treatment. A therapy called functional neuromuscular stimulation, which uses electrodes to stimulate muscle reflexes, may help activate some paralyzed muscles. Several devices to help communication are available. Other treatment is symptomatic and supportive.

What is the prognosis?

While in rare cases some patients may regain certain functions, the chances for motor recovery are very limited.

Mark and Julie were sitting at the kitchen table after breakfast the morning of her second day home. Together they read the grim description from the NIH website on the laptop screen in front of them. Julie was not totally locked in; she could move her eyes and head, twitch her facial muscles and utter guttural sounds, but she could not form those sounds into anything intelligible. The stroke had severely impacted the language center of her brain, the so-called Broca's area, reducing communication to a mostly one-way affair. Of course, they already had an eye-blinking system going for answering yes and no questions—one blink for yes, two for no—but that left Julie with virtually no means of initiating communication and no way of expressing specific needs and desires. These were to be addressed via one of the new brain-computer interface technologies or BCIs that were now being offered to "locked-ins" at Upstate Medical Center. Julie had an appointment at the hospital for orientation and training scheduled for three days hence; in the meantime they would have to make do with one blink for yes, two for no, which they all quickly learned was a most laborious and tedious way of accessing a person's particular wishes, amounting to a sort of *What's My Need?* elimination game for locked-ins, but where the game was often far from over with the accumulation of ten "no's."

The "panelists," Mark, Nate and Hattie, had spent most of their waking hours since Julie's homecoming hovering over her like mother hens, doing their best to make their precious loved one comfortable but doing this so insistently, so feverishly, that the chief result of their efforts was merely to raise their own anxiety levels to the ceiling. Nate, in particular, was extremely clingy, unable to leave Julie's side for more than a few minutes at a time. The first thing he saw to whenever he came near her was the positioning of Duncan on her lap. He would prop the little guy up if he had fallen over or, if he hadn't, pick him up, slap him gently for dust, primp him here and there and place him back on Julie's lap, finally making minute adjustments in his angle.

Nate had been obsessively attentive to this task, which by now had become for him almost like an office, though without his knowing either the concept or its vital function in human affairs. He did it strictly on instinct and with an intuitive magical belief in its salutary effects on his mother's well being. This belief of his had somehow failed to be undermined by the present crisis but, on the contrary, was strengthened to a degree bordering on the superstitious, as if Duncan's importance in the scheme of things grew in direct proportion to Julie's deteriorating condition. When on Thanksgiving day Julie was being lifted onto a gurney to be wheeled out to the ambulance and one of the attendants had taken Duncan from her lap and tossed him into a corner of the kitchen counter, Nate immediately retrieved him and made sure to bring him along on his first visit to the hospital, where he installed him right next to her on the raised head of her orthopedic bed. And there he stayed for the duration of her confinement.

Julie, for her part, was just as anxious as Nate to have contact with Duncan restored, for she had gradually come to feel the mysterious access the little guy provided to her son's emotional state to be indispensable to her own equanimity. Thus it had been, increasingly and despite some initial resistance on her part, ever since that extraordinary moment of revelation of this intimate inner connection at the school concert. And it was as a revelation that she understood it, as something made dramatically clear by the removal of some obscuring barrier. Duncan must be actually sitting on her or at least leaning against her at all times. It was to her as if her growing uselessness and irrelevance to her son's outer wellbeing were being counterbalanced by an increasing interior symbiosis, a symbiosis whose interface was Duncan. The toy ape had made even more porous the flimsy boundary she had always felt to exist between her son and herself. He made her lose awareness of where she ended and Nate began.

All of this and much else besides were weighing heavily on Julie's mind, making her somewhat indifferent to Mark's and Hattie's busy ministrations. And they, of course, couldn't do enough for her precisely because there was so little they *could* do for her. Mark, having corrected his students' final exams and papers and turned in his grades by mid-December, was now on holiday break and therefore free to devote himself entirely to Julie's care. But when he retired now and then to his study to do reading for his research or work on a chapter of his Blake book, he couldn't sit for more than ten minutes without shuffling out with a book in his hand, his index finger inserted at the spot where he had just stopped reading, to see if there was anything she needed. And if he found her napping in her wheelchair, usually in either the living room or her makeshift bedroom, he would find it all he could do to resist the temptation to wake her up just to ask her if there was anything he could do for her.

It didn't help, of course, that this compulsion was being driven, at least in part, by a lingering guilt over the affair with Sabrina, a misery only compounded and intensified by a sexual longing that stubbornly refused to accept the end of the affair; the guilt, it seemed, would last as long as the desire for Sabrina seethed within him, frustrated though that desire was. No matter that that frustration was the freely accepted consequence of his iron determination never to slip again. Mark was one of those unfortunate lapsed Catholics whose conscience never "got the memo" about its owner's lapse and therefore grimly and with Draconian resolve continued to draw no clear distinction between inner states and outer behavior, between intentions and acts.

Hattie's attitude, while just as solicitous and attentive as Mark's and Nate's, was naturally also a good deal more objective and more focused on making Julie as comfortable as possible than on the possible salutary effects of any of the various therapies, physical or otherwise, she was facing. In other words, Hattie was now more concerned with palliation than cure, for she was convinced by both her instincts and her experience that Julie was, at this point, on an irreversible downward course. Of course, she kept this conviction entirely to herself, seeing no benefit whatsoever in sharing her sober realism with the others. There was plenty of time for that.

Knowing Julie as she did in both personal and clinical depth—she'd been her primary caregiver for over a year now—she knew in any given situation what to do and when to do it: when to approach or awaken her and when not to, when to nudge her to further exercise and when to slack off, when and which way to dress her, how she liked her meals prepared, how she liked to be fed (don't hold a forkful of food up to her; wait for her nod), how she preferred her meds to be given (counterintuitively: water first, pill second), how to use the utmost discretion in helping her with toilet functions—these and a thousand other miniscule daily transactions between them made Hattie by far the most pragmatically useful significant other in Julie's life. The other two were, after all, "men," in the derogatory though justified sense of the word used by American wives and mothers to describe the functional household incompetence invoked by the male members of many families to avoid chores. Mark provided financial support and both he and Nate provided constant waves of emotional nourishment, but just now it was Hattie who was of the greatest usefulness and the least bother to Julie.

On Julie's third day home following her release from the hospital, Hattie felt in her bones that it was time to probe her charge's state of mind beyond the superficial sphere of momentary bodily needs. It was a little past noon and she had just finished feeding Julie a small bowl of tomato soup, one of her favorites. As she lovingly dabbed her mouth with the napkin, she said, "There. Now wasn't that good?"

Julie blinked once.

Hattie then gripped the glass of water on Julie's tray while still looking at her and Julie again blinked yes. Carefully the aide lifted the glass to her lips and gave her a sip.

Julie gave a low murmur and the faintest nod, expressing satisfaction. Hattie removed her tray and put Duncan back on her lap.

"Is there anything else I can get for you, sweetheart?"

Two blinks.

"Are you comfortable?"

One blink.

Her face then taking on a thoughtful mien, Hattie paused for a moment and said carefully, "Let me ask you this, dear: Are you also comfortable in your mind? What I mean is, do you have at least a measure of peace of mind, given the ... trying circumstances you find yourself in?"

Here blinks would not do. Widening her eyes and lifting her head a bit, Julie gave a somewhat animated hum, which Hattie, correctly, took to be an acknowledgment of the deliberate understatement contained in her shrewd question: *Trying circumstances! Boy, you got that right!* But then she narrowed her eyes and, contracting her face ever so slightly, tilted her head from side to side as best she could, conveying that they both knew there was no simple answer to that question, indeed, that even if she *had* the full power of speech, she would still not be sure how to answer.

All this was perfectly clear to the devoted aide and friend, who needed no nuanced verbal explanations. She was subtly attuned to the ebb and flow of Julie's emotional state, and in particular to the current of tension that had been singeing her inner life for months now. What she didn't know was the cause of that tension, and that was mainly because Julie herself didn't know, still didn't know, even to this hour. It was mystifying, the more so as it became ever more pressing. All Julie had was an overwhelming sense of the inevitability of it all, the conviction that whatever it was was somehow preordained and must play itself out, and that there was no turning away from it. For all she knew, her whole life had been but a preparation for this moment that she felt to be imminent, a moment demanding from her an absolute stillness. It was a peculiar sort of comfort she drew from this inevitability, almost as if it cancelled out—and hence in a way freed her from—that other unalterable fact, the fact of her physical paralysis. There was, after all, no escape on any level from this impending denouement, whatever it might be; therefore in a sense all movement was irrelevant. She could just snuggle up to her own intense motionlessness and, ultimately, lodge herself in it. And wait.

One could say, therefore, that Julie was, in a superficial sense, withdrawing from her family; she was less and less concerned with their momentary presence or absence, their comings and goings, the more she strove to make herself available to this interior necessity, this shrouded purpose, which would not be put off. For she had known from the beginning that her unease was not a matter of self-concern but directed away from herself. At whom else, then, than her family, her loved ones? It was purely her inner bonds with them, bonds from the depths, that now commandeered the stage of her consciousness, crowding out all concern with ordinary social and physical contact, not to mention concern with her own comfort. She was well beyond that.

Moreover, and strangely, she was no longer lonely, afraid or depressed, no longer confused or plagued by uncertainty about the future, though these had been the roiling sea of emotions battering her immobile body since the accident, like storm waves pounding the post of a jetty. She was freed of all these, though serious, yet ultimately mundane concerns and would no doubt have been hard-pressed to say exactly how it was she *did* feel. It wasn't happiness, or gaiety, or delight, or even wellbeing, at least not in the ordinary sense of those states. No, it was more than any one of them, more even than the sum of them. It was the primordial vibrancy of being alive, the pure poised awakeness of mind and body (paralysis be damned), poised for the moment, pregnant with the moment, waiting to give birth to … it hardly mattered what. It would in any case be more life. She hadn't felt this way at any time since her confinement—indeed, she couldn't remember ever having felt this way before, this immersed in life, this swept up in its bracing currents. An idea occurred to her that she had read about in Jung in an undergraduate psychology class. He spoke of *enantiodromia*, a monster of a Greek word meaning literally "running into each other," a term he used for the tendency of things, especially psychic things such as emotions, to change into their own opposites. This generally happened, she recalled reading, whenever an emotion became lopsidedly strong, and eventually all-consuming. It would then flip over into its opposite. Sadness into bliss, for example. Julie believed she was experiencing some form of enantiodromia, and that suited her just fine. She felt beyond the constraints of even her own mind and body, phenomena she now regarded as, at least for the moment, trivial, and at once available to the Cosmos, an instrument of Cosmic Will, as it were. Though she was no longer a practicing Christian, still those old words from the Gospel of Luke came to her: *Not my will but Thy will be done.* It mattered not a jot that she had no clue to whom or what "Thy" referred. Could she have intuited on some level that the incarnation of this mysterious "Thou" was sitting right there on her lap?

30

He patted his mouth with the table napkin after finishing his complimentary breakfast of oatmeal mixed with raisins, nuts and a gob of honey. *Only the healthy stuff. No eggs, no butter, no carbs. Went slack for a while there. Sort of lost my way. Must rededicate myself to a Spartan diet, strengthen my resolve against that sort of erosion that just sneaks up on you unawares. THIS is who I am, not that, not some pathetic waif begging to come in from the cold. I thrive in the cold. The cold is my ether. North in winter, south in summer—that's me. But why am I thinking about this at all? It's diabolical the way your own mind is forever trying to corner you. Must deny myself all fondling of questions of identity. That never ends well.*

Diners in the hotel's breakfast room were sparse at this time of year: besides him, only a female graduate or professional student poring over a thick textbook at a corner table and an overweight businessman three tables over digging into a plate piled high with scrambled eggs, bacon and home fries. He'd relaxed for a few days following his evening at the Jiraks, taking leisurely drives around the city, familiaring himself with its primary northern and western exit routes. He wanted to be in Toronto for Christmas if at all possible, so it was time to get down to serious business. He took the elevator back upstairs to his room and sat down at his laptop. Once he had identified a "project," he always moved swiftly into the fieldwork and information-gathering phases, the latter usually beginning at the computer, particularly when he had some knowledge of the boy's background. Since there was no band rehearsal that day, he had plenty of time to search.

He googled Mark and Julie Driscoll. Table talk at the Jiraks and Julie's Facebook page told him all he needed to know about her. Meticulous researcher that he was, he read all her entries from the beginning to the present, noting that they only began in September of 2012, a few weeks after the date of her accident. Mark had no Facebook presence at all. This meant, he reasoned, that it was probable that neither of them was a social media addict, not surprising in view of their level of education. But their academic status also pigeonholed them as parental liberals in his mind, and therefore less likely than most others to be helicopter parents. (Of course, in Julie's case, this went without saying, although there was nothing preventing her from using a proxy.) This was good.

Next he dug up online, from the two school websites, the Fall academic calendar for Mark and Nate. *Christmas break begins at noon on Wednesday, December 23, for the boy and probably about a week earlier for the father. The mother's recent stroke means that Mark will likely be sticking close to her at home, or at the very least be preoccupied with her, and far less so with Nate. So there's a window there. I guess I know where I'll be around noon on the 23rd. But I mustn't forget about the Haitian aide. She's devoted to them and could be the uncontrolled variable here. Her Facebook photo comes in very handy.*

Nate, he had calculated from the city map, lived too far from school to walk, so he had already scouted the specific route of his school bus twice, both going and coming, and would do so at least one more time before the 23rd. He had driven his van slowly around the Driscoll's block starting at 7:15 a.m., carefully under cover of the neighborhood traffic leaving for work. (With few exceptions he never simply parked and sat in his car on a scouting mission. That was far too risky, especially in surburbia.) When the bus stopped for Nate between 7:28 and 7:30, he would pull up behind it as it resumed its route—preferably with a car between them—and follow it as inconspicuously as possible as it wended its way the two miles to Smythe Elementary.

Every so often he would turn off the route for a moment or so, only to make a quick K-turn and get back behind the bus, two or three cars away. Finally the bus would turn counterclockwise into the big ovular driveway in front of the school and take its place at the end of the column of identical yellow replicas. As it did, he would pull into the little parking area of the 7-Eleven down the block, at an angle precise enough to allow him to watch each bus discharge its precious cargo, but without concern over being observed since he was among several parents sitting in nearby parked cars watching their children, making sure they got into the building safely. He savored the irony of sitting among them.

At 2:20 on the afternoons of these scouting days, he would pull up to the same 7-Eleven store near the school and commence to watch for Nate at dismissal time, thus precisely reversing the morning ritual. Though the grab was to take place when school let out, he still deemed it absolutely necessary to follow the bus's route both ways and commit it to memory, not only on general principles of thoroughness but in order to prepare for an untoward event: a missed connection, say, at the grab site and the consequent need to play catch-up. As always, he took meticulous bus-schedule notes.

As it turned out, he was successful in spotting Nate getting off or on the bus upon each morning arrival and afternoon departure. But he also noted the corpulent Jamie Poindexter walking and chatting with him on most of these occasions; to be precise, always upon exiting the a.m. bus and one time getting on the p.m. He wondered whether that association might not be a complication on grab day. Would he have to find a way to separate the boys? But immediately he decided *no*, he would just take his chances and, if it came to such a pass, simply abort the "project" on the spot and head out immediately for Toronto.

He was astonished at how easy it was for him to come to this decision, as if it carried no more weight than whether or not to see a movie. He suppressed the strongly implied question as to the subjective value of what he was doing, the question of how much he still cared for the life, how much his heart's desire was still in it. Just as with questions of identity, questions of value— personal, not moral—must also be denied access to conscious awareness. As for morality, it did not exist for him as a value category. His bible in this was Nietzsche's profound critique of Christianity, *Beyond Good and Evil*, which he had pored over in college in a survey course of the great philosophers and whose subtle sense he had twisted over several painstaking readings into the strongest rationalization he could devise for the life he wanted to lead. Years later, when he discovered the wisdom of the East and meditation with its emphasis on the importance of remaining grounded in moment-by-moment experience, he realized he could let go of all tortured philosophical argument, all ideological ballast, and simply abandon himself to the sexual pull. *Ars gratia artis.* Art for the sake of art. Orgasm for the sake of orgasm. The existential act was its own justification; it needed no other. But was he still convinced? Or was his practice of unthinking mindfulness beginning to fail to protect him from his own creeping doubts?

Such doubts, all stemming from the nearly lifelong repression of his own humanity, kept drifting up into awareness from the periphery of this central zone of psychic blackout, like so many air bubbles from a deep-sea diver floating up to the surface. This, despite—or was it because of—his renewed commitment to the life he had embraced. It wasn't guilt of the ordinary sort, the guilt over violating society's strongest taboo, that assailed him but a more profound guilt, the gnawing sense of having betrayed his own deepest nature, now calling to him through these "thought bubbles."

Perhaps, too, at forty-six his libido was beginning to lose just the barest jot of its piquant edge, so that the heretofore blinding power of eros no longer quite obliterated all other concerns as it always had. Now there were whole days when he just wasn't interested. With diminution of interest, especially when that interest is one's very raison d'etre, comes self-questioning and with self-questioning anxiety. Santa's anxiety took the form of occasional, unpredictable spikes of dread, a twinge while shaving when suddenly he would feel an impulse to swipe the razor across his throat. Or an irrational fear that would sometimes come over him while driving the local beltway that his legs were about to become paralyzed, causing him to lose control of the van. Such moments, occasional though they were, left a distressing sense of foreboding in their wake when they did come, giving his renewed commitment to the life a subtle but unmistakable patina of hysteria, as if he were continuing this way less because he wanted to than because he was afraid to stop. This meant, of course, that he was fatally misreading his own dread and the guilt behind it, taking it as a warning to not "get caught"—whether by himself or another was not clear—rather than what it was: the precisely opposite warning to cease and desist from this ghastly psycho-spiritual suicide. And so he buried himself with ever greater ardor in preparations for grab day, some necessary, some not, checking facts, figures and conditions many times over, to the point where even he himself recognized with a sigh his own absurdly neurotic caution.

The brief span of days between meeting Nate and grab day seemed to him to drag on forever, but at last Wednesday, December 23, was upon him. Though zero hour was set for noon, he was up quite early to see to final preparations, showering and shaving, primping and preening, laying out his outfit of fresh jeans, a recently purchased orange and blue S.U. sweatshirt and white socks, topped by a Santana red jacket with a fleece lining, each item of apparel carefully chosen to accent an informal, youthful appearance, a subliminal suggestion to the boy that "I am one of you." He even planned to carry a backpack (with nothing in it but props: two books and a bottle of water), giving himself a rough-and-ready quasi schoolboy look. Nothing over the top, mind you, all quite downplayed, the entire ensemble designed to convey a vibe of camaraderie. He considered Nikes for footwear but promptly rejected them as excessive in favor of sturdy suede leather loafers. The sun was out, unusual for Syracuse at Christmastime, and there seemed no threat of snow, and hence slush, the enemy of suede.

He dressed and ate lightly in his room, an English muffin, a small bowl of prunes and coffee, like an athlete about to undergo the physical rigors of competition who wants to feel poised for anything. Finally, he brushed his teeth and gargled with Listerine, this last perhaps in the undying delusional hope of erotic reciprocity rather than out of any rational motive. The same could be said of his dabbing himself, just before leaving, with an after-shave scent, his own special blend of patchouli, cinnamon and vetiver oils. He had always loved patchouli, even as a kid finding it pungently hypnotic, and could not believe that it didn't necessarily have the same aphrodisiacal effect on others that it had on him. *How could it not* he puzzled.

He was standing over the bathroom sink as he thought this, looking into the mirror, gazing searchingly because he was not especially pleased with what he saw, nor had he been for a while now. He was still handsome all right, still possessed of those taut, high-ridged cheekbones and that killer smile, but something was missing, something had gone out of his face that he hadn't even known was there until it no longer was, a twinkle in the eye perhaps, a certain *plaisir de vivre* that was more than the sum of his facial features and had in fact given those features their aesthetic integrity and their carnal magnetism.

But then, as he left the inn at about 11:25 and strode briskly through the parking lot towards his car, he felt, suddenly, oddly relieved and, soon thereafter, delighted, to sense something of that old grab-day tingle again that he had always relied on to put a spring in his step, an exquisite frisson made up of the heady mingling of sex and danger. Then he realized that his depression of moments earlier was no longer there; on the contrary, a thick and delicious erotic current seemed to him to course through the cityscape, penetrating everything his eyes lit on—the parking-lot blacktop, the shiny deluxe cars filling its spaces, the noonday traffic whizzing by on Erie Boulevard. All at once he was feeling like his old self. *Ah. It's so good to have a grip again, to have finally come out of that funk I was in. You see, S., it was temporary, some subtle indisposition of the nervous system, a glitch in brain chemistry. I'm older now so I should probably count on these lapses happening on occasion. They go with the territory. The thing is not to be thrown by them.*

As he climbed into the van and turned the key, his mind felt sure, his awareness supple. He sat there a moment, adjusting his seatbelt and making a final review of his meticulously devised plan. A moment later, as he turned onto the boulevard from the Red Roof's access road, he reminded himself of the rare advantage that was built into today's grab, namely that he and the target boy had already met and, so far as he could tell, were on solidly amicable terms. This delightful circumstance was offering him the opportunity, equally rare, to stage an accidental meeting during which he would charm the boy and lure him into the van, thus eliminating the risk of any witnesses to a forced physical abduction. He turned left off the boulevard and drove up a long escarpment threaded with modest but well-kept single-family homes. It led on top to a broad ridge of land upon which sat W. H. Smythe Elementary School.

The noontime bell rang and all classroom doors were thrown open at once. The kids, stuffed into their insulated winter jackets of red, blue and yellow, poured into the hallway ecstatically like a plague of technicolor locusts in search of plant life. As they streamed out the glass doors onto the front pavement and headed for their busses, some alone, some in clusters of two or three, all ushered by three adult monitors, few seemed to notice that the sun had retreated and that the gray air was being lazily tickled by errant flakes.

One of the outside monitors, a strapping young black policeman called Mr. Horton who moonlighted as a staff worker at the school, was wearing a Santa hat whose peak was too loose and about four inches too long so that the white ball at the tip kept getting in his face. Not a single kid who passed by him failed to crack up while pointing this out to him, but he began enjoying the little farce so thoroughly that he decided to leave the fluffy ball there, right between his eyes. Perhaps he was enjoying the joke a little too much, amusing the little ones as he basked in their attention. This led soon enough to his becoming distracted and ceasing to attend to them collectively as he should. A tiny lapse in and of itself, one might argue, except that on this day he happened to be the monitor in charge of the right-hand third of the pavement area, the area with the most direct approach to the sixth in the line of the seven yellow busses, the bus that took Nate Driscoll and Jamie Poindexter home.

Back inside, Nate and Dex waited patiently together in the corridor for the crowd in front of them to ease out. Finally reaching the threshold, they instantly spotted Black Santa, some fifteen feet in front of them and slightly to the left, surrounded by about a dozen kids who were happily teasing and taunting him.

"Hey, Santa isn't black!" a tiny boy squealed up to Horton. The kid was almost invisible, buried as he was in a jumble of coat, hat, mittens and scarf.

"Who told you that, son? He is too," Mr. Horton mock-scolded the little accuser, pulling the kid's knitted red hat down over his eyes.

"Don't you know nothin'? He's whatever you need him to be," one of the older kids remonstrated with the little peanut, crudely attempting to mediate.

"That's all bullshit. There ain't no Santa Clause! Don't you know?" Thus a still older, taller child, perhaps just recently disillusioned himself and now feeling cynical about all things Christmas.

Witnessing this little Yuletide vignette from nearby, naturally Nate and Dex decided they wanted to have their own little moment of fun with black Santa. Nudging their way through the crowd and pulling up behind the innermost circle of the littlest kids, Dex looked down and began laughing at the pint-sized accuser who was feeling put upon by all the arguing and just stood there with his arms crossed looking grumpy. Dex picked him up and held him out to Mr. Horton, urging the peanut to give black Santa a good one in the chops. This put fear in the little guy's heart—a fistfight with someone who just might be Santa? I don't think so! And he began frantically arching his back to be put down.

Jamie obliged. The instant the tot's feet touched concrete, Jamie heard someone call out to him from the driveway curb area, "C'mon, Poindexter. Aren't you getting on? Remember, you owe me money."

"I owe *you* money?! You got that backwards, dude." And he scooted off toward the bus and his putative debtor, waving Nate "Later, bro" en route. Nate lingered a moment longer, enjoying the little kids enjoying black Santa, then turned away and headed cheerily for the bus which had edged up to the head of the line and was almost ready to pull out. Nate was about to break into a sprint when something stopped him in his tracks. He spotted a man crossing the pavement about fifteen feet in front of him, heading in the opposite direction to that of the busses. The kids rushed past him to their busses, both in front of and behind him, some carelessly brushing his trousers, but he just plodded along patiently, smiling down at them, patting this one and that one gently on the head. It wasn't the presence of an adult among the children that had stopped Nate; there were several other adults on the premises besides the monitors—parents, guardians, older siblings—waiting patiently in the crowd. It was the man's stature, his bearing, the way he carried himself—it was that these subtle qualities, hard to define as they might be for a nine-year-old, gave off a whiff of the familiar. It was that he recognized them, sensed he had encountered them before, and not long before, all blended together in the same person. Most important, he had liked them.

Just as the man passed him and left Nate gazing at the back of his Santana red jacket, it came to him in a flash: "Hey, mister, don't I know you?"

The man stopped, swiveled smartly around on his left heel and looked down at the little inquirer with an expression both kindly and quizzical. Then, leaning back, he squinted and cupped his chin in his hand, finally pointing down at Nate as if trying to coax his name into memory.

"You remember? Dinner at that big house on the lake? ... 'So *What*?" the boy prompted, aping the rhythmic way he had heard the title articulated at dinner, with a hard accent on the second note. All at once the man lit up with a rapturous smile, spread his arms wide and shouted, "Of course! *Nate*! Nate Driscoll!" He bounced a palm off his own forehead as if to mock his own dullness in not immediately recognizing a kid who was obviously so special. "Nate, my boy! Of course I remember.

I guess I was lost in thought. Par for the course with me … Well, come here. Let us have a look at you?"

The language he used in conversation with an unsuspecting target was always carefully crafted, never mindlessly improvised or thrown away. In making these particular remarks, Santa had two aims: one, to disarm the boy with flattery by using 'adult' expressions with him such as "par for the course." He had long ago noticed that most kids, especially the intelligent ones, were utterly charmed when a grown-up treated them as conversational equals. It happened so rarely; indeed, they were thoroughly conditioned to being talked down to, and so were already half seduced by such a subtle, oblique compliment. Two, by urging the boy to "Come here!" for a friendly hug, or at least a hearty pat on the shoulder, in a dissembled spirit of camaraderie, he was able to measure a kid's instinctive trust, at least in that moment. The more wholehearted the kid's response to that amiable "Come here!", obviously the better, the more easily, the seduction phase should go. In this Nate proved neither fish nor fowl: He took one step forward, smiled and held out his hand for a handshake. Santa learned little beyond the fact that it was a field of open possibilities. He knew Nate was a smart kid and that he would have to use his subtlest skills and play it very cagily.

"So, tell me, Nate. How's your family? How's your dad? And your mom, of course? I hope she's making a speedy recovery from her stroke." He nodded his noble brow once or twice as he spoke, his face etched in profound concern.

"Dad's fine. Mom's begun BCI training but it'll take time." His voice trailed off and he looked away as he mentioned his mother, cluing Santa that he'd rather not talk about it, not even to demonstrate to Santa that he knew what BCI training was.

Santa took the hint: "And what about you, Nate?" Deftly he dropped the boy's name more frequently than he normally would, but not so often as to be noticeable. This on the principle that using a kid's name endeared you to him. "How will you be spending the holiday break?"

"Oh, nothing special, with my mom and all ... " he said, again looking away. Then suddenly he perked up: "Anyway, what are you doing around here?" he asked with his child's disarming directness. Santa, of course, was ready for it: "Oh, I'm not staying too far from here. Just down the hill off Erie Boulevard. Actually, I was just walking back to my car from the Lemoyne campus," he said, pointing across the intersection to the spread of simple but stately brick buildings half hidden by clusters of maple and oak that comprised the Jesuit college. "Their audio archives have a fine collection of rare old jazz recordings going back to the early twentieth century. I was listening to some of the old masters. And I've taken a few LP's out for a week or so," he added, brightly patting his backpack over his shoulder. This was all made up. His backpack held nothing of value, and it was S.U., not Lemoyne, that had the valuable jazz archives.

"Got any Bix Beiderbecke?" Nate chirped.

"You've got to be kidding! That's amazing, Nate. You've actually heard of Bix Beiderbecke?"

"Sure, my Dad has a couple of his songs. But I only remember him because of his name: Bix Beiderbecke. It's funny. It sticks in your mind," he chuckled.

"Well, it sure does, doesn't it? And you know what? His middle name'll just kill you. Know what it is?" Santa laughed as he let himself fondle the lad's flawless face with his eyes, even taking carnal pleasure in the cold steam clouds carrying his words, wishing he could bury his face in those clouds right then and there.

Nate stood there open-mouthed, waiting for the bombshell.

"Would you believe: 'Beanbag'! Bix 'Beanbag' Beiderbecke!" Santa slowly enunciated, and the two of them had a good guffaw on old Bix. 'Beanbag' was made up. Nothing like humor to loosen a boy up. He thought of it as alcohol for kids. The trick, of course, was to know what was funny to *them*, not yourself. The boy was now primed for the intrusive move. This was, of course, the critical moment; everything hung on it: "Say, Nate, I have an idea. You mentioned the Jiraks's house earlier. Funnily enough, I was just on my way to my car. It's over there in your school parking lot—it's next to impossible to park on the Lemoyne campus. I'm heading over to the S.U. Music School to meet Karel, Karel Jirak. You'll remember him from dinner. Anyway, we'll be playing some of these old records over there, including old Beanbag Bix here, and then we'll probably jam for a while ourselves. Karel on piano, me on bass and *guess who* on drums? You see, I didn't forget you're the maestro of the drums, huh? What do you say? How about making us a trio? It'll be great fun."

A pleasant, stimulating tension coursed through his loins as he watched the boy react. It was like a roll of the dice, with roughly the same odds. Seduction, yes or no? He glanced around, irrationally wondering if there was any chance of a forced grab if it all went south?

When he turned back to Nate, he could read conflict in the boy's face, which was lit up by a smile yet also turned slightly aside and angled down toward the pavement, now being softly pelted by armies of flakes. An invitation to jam with two professional musicians, *adult* musicians, appealed strongly to the boy's vanity; he couldn't imagine anything being more "cool." And he did like Santa, and it wasn't as if he would be going off with a stranger; heck, Santa and his dad were practically friends, weren't they? Still, something in him, some vague and obscure reservation, gave him pause. It wasn't the parental taboos, drummed into him from the cradle, though they too carried weight and did assert themselves. No, it was something more personal, more intimate, something peculiar to this particular relationship. But Nate was far too absorbed in the moment, in the exquisite rush of Santa's flattery, to realize what was behind his own hesitancy: It was that he didn't entirely trust the adult-child equivalency of Santa's attitude, so much as he favored it and wanted it to be genuine. It was too glib, too facile, something that felt to him affected for a hidden purpose. Who knows, maybe there was no such thing as equal footing in relations between adults and children. But Nate only dimly, inchoately, sensed these doubts in himself, which gave his enthusiasm for Santa's invitation the stronger pull by far in the psychic tug-of-war between desire and caution.

"Uh, I don't know," he at last said slowly, absently rubbing a sneakered foot on the pavement to accelerate the dissolution of the alighting flakes, perhaps in lieu of dissolving his own hesitation. "I'd have to get permission from home."

"Well, of course," Santa quickly seconded. "That goes without saying. Let me just get my cell out of my inside pocket here …" He casually flung open the phone for speed-dialing purposes.

"Wait," Nate stopped him. "You've got our number on speed-dial?" he asked, his face beaming a satisfied smile, all doubt melting away.

"Oh, sure," Santa waved him off, as if to seal the obviousness of the fact in gesture. "Your dad and I exchanged numbers at the Jiraks, just as we were leaving. We've actually already talked, twice I think, if memory serves."

"Uh, I also have to tell my friend Dex that I won't be riding the bus with him today. He's already on it over there waiting for me," Nate said, pointing busward as he moved away towards it.

"That's fine. You go right ahead. While you're taking care of that, I'll give your dad a quick call and let him know what we're up to, okay?"

"Great!" Nate squealed gleefully as he broke into a short sprint over to the bus. He was far too thrilled by his good fortune to notice the red flags furiously waving to him from just behind Santa's diabolically specious words.

Santa turned his back to the bus about three-quarters in case the boy's friend should become curious to get a look through the window at his competitor for Nate's company. He also held his arm and cell phone up close to his ear, further obscuring his face as he simulated the call to Mark Driscoll.

Nate came sprinting back and Santa told him that permission from home was secured. Just then the bus carrying Jamie Poindexter pulled away, leaving just one, the one that had anchored the original column of seven. They turned the opposite way, this oddest of couples, and walked together the short distance to the school parking lot and got into the van. The entire scene was lost on the school monitor in the floppy Santa hat who had his back to it the whole time as he bantered with some of the kids who lived nearby and normally walked home and who therefore had time to linger.

As Santa pulled out onto Salt Springs Road and drove west towards the Syracuse University campus, the snow was falling heavily enough to require windshield wipers.

31

Hattie cast a quick glance at the kitchen wall clock on her way to bringing Julie her lunch tray, on it a bowl of beef barley soup, a piece of buttered rye toast and a sliced-up banana. *12:07. Half a day today. Nathaniel will be home from school soon.* She found Julie in her room, gazing through the glass doors out onto the hard, brown backyard sod, a sod no longer able to melt the flakes now beginning to hide it. She looked pensive and somewhat withdrawn. Hattie was worried about her, as this introversion seemed to be becoming her default mood lately. It was as if she were gradually drifting away from them, toward some secret, inaccessible isle of the spirit, less and less concerned with the things of this world.

She saw the food tray and turned her head away dismissively, gazing out again at the barren turf, as if suddenly discovering a sad and secret kinship with that gnarly wasteland. Hattie read the gesture easily and adjured her: "Now, come on, Julie. You've got to eat. Nutrition is even more important than your medications. You need your strength."

Platitudes all, except that the last one caught her attention as being especially compelling in this moment. She did indeed need all the strength she could gather for whatever trial she believed she was fated to undergo. She had better eat and eat well.

So she turned back to this true friend and famulus who had become so dear to her, dear beyond description, through all these months, through this entire ordeal, smiled and, breathing in the aroma of the modest meal, widened her eyes with feigned enthusiasm, as though she couldn't wait to dig in.

"Now that's the spirit, that's more like it, girl!" Hattie encouraged, gently lowering the food tray onto the wheelchair tray, both trays now sheltering Duncan who remained tucked in on her lap just beneath. As she opened Julie's napkin, Hattie wondered what it could possibly be that had flipped her charge's attitude towards the food so abruptly. It seemed much too easy.

She set the rotating stool down at an angle to the wheelchair so as not to block Julie's view, sat down and began spoon-feeding her the barley soup, her favorite. But even this charming little intimacy between them, one they both enjoyed every day, was feeling decidedly one-sided to the aide on this occasion. Again and again, Julie opened her mouth wide for the soup, as if she couldn't get enough, but kept her eyes, which struck Hattie as slightly glassy, mostly trained on the yard. There was nothing out there worth staring at, nothing moving but the falling flakes and windblown tree branches, Hattie thought. She also had a queer sense of the gray noon light pouring in through the glass doors as shrinking and gathering around the two of them like some scintillating yet oddly comforting vortex. *There's more going on here than her simple inability to communicate, or even a reaction of depression to that terrible fact. She's looking within, gazing at something deep within her own mind. She's lost to me right now, lost to all of us. All I can do is stay right here next to her, on the "outside," and be ready … but for what? God knows!*

At this point, Julie was completely oblivious to Hattie's concern. Indeed, she was hardly even aware of being fed, having consigned the repetitive act of opening her mouth to whatever was still functioning of her parasympathetic nervous system. All her energies were tautly focused on a hypnotic center point, a throbbing nucleus that seemed neither inside her nor outside, but hovering in some altogether different and rarefied dimension that included both but was identical to neither. Instinctively she knew that the worst thing she could do would be to try to wrench herself from this spell or rapture, whatever it was, out of some craven impulse to fall back into the comforting arms of "normalcy," whatever that was. No, her proper business was to stay with this process, wherever it might take her, and let the chips fall where they may. It seemed to carry its own validity, its own gravitas, right within itself.

Hattie fed Julie the last of the banana, gave her a final sip of water, wiped her chin and carried the laden tray back to the kitchen. Her brow was furrowed; she felt a strong impulse to do something but hadn't a clue as to what. On her way back to Julie's room she suddenly made a sharp left and headed up the stairs for Mark's study. She hated bothering him; there was really no manifest problem and she knew these past two hours had been the most undisturbed span of concentration on his research he had enjoyed in weeks. Yet she felt it couldn't be helped. Something was wrong and keeping it to herself was just not an option.

She tiptoed the three steps from the top of the stairs to the door of Mark's study, which was half open. Leaning in, she casually rested her left forearm high on the doorframe. The room was small, lined with crammed bookshelves on the upper half of three walls, and smelled of cigarettes, though she could see no physical evidence of smoking. "Mark," she said in her calmest voice, "you got a minute?"

"For you, Hattie, I've got two," he chuckled, getting up from his desk and returning a ponderous folio volume of medieval alchemical imagery to its proper two square feet of space on a bottom shelf behind him. Hattie had caught a glimpse of some elaborate design on one of its pages just before Mark closed the book, an ink drawing made up of concentric circles and a dizzying array of symmetrical and interlocking acute angles contained within them like so many spokes.

"Hattie, my dear," he laughed, pointing down behind him, "with that book I could rule the world—well, the world of 1450 anyway."

"Mark, I don't like the way Julie's been behaving lately," she said, stepping into the room and crossing her arms.

"How do you mean?" he asked, sitting down and gesturing for Hattie to take the other chair.

"Well, it's nothing specific, and she's not in any great discomfort, so far as I can see. It's just that she's so—what's the word ... *distant* these days, so removed. What's that expression? ... Oh, yes, out of the loop. You know? She seems to be withdrawing from us, from everything. Something inside her is pulling her into herself, and, of course, she can't tell us about it. But I have a feeling that, even if she could, she wouldn't. She's content to give simple 'yes' or 'no' responses to my questions, with no effort to ... to extend or deepen or ... or even emphasize with facial expressions or head gestures. And that's not like her, you know that." Compressing her fulsome lips into a frown, Hattie looked down at the desktop, littered with books and journals and sheaves of word-processed paper.

Mark sat back in his swivel chair reflectively, folding his hands behind his head, his face showing concern. "Well, I'm sure you can imagine how frustrating it must be for someone with a gift for language like Julie's to suddenly be entirely deprived of it—bereft, actually." But then he changed his tack: "But that's not to say I don't appreciate your coming to me and telling me this, Hattie. After all, you are an extension of my own eyes and ears" Hattie ignored the compliment, which she found slightly self-serving and entirely gratuitous. "I don't think frustration is the issue here, Mark. It's not that she *can't* communicate—though that's true enough—it's that she chooses not to and is content to use her 'locked-in' condition as a cover for that."

The subtlety of this distinction on Hattie's part poised Mark's attention and sent a shot of adrenalin coursing through his torso, rousing anxieties he'd been doing his best to ignore. He looked at his watch and said, "You know, Hattie, maybe this would be a good time for the three of us to have a little powwow," while getting up and stretching his shoulders. "Let's see if we can at least come to some sort of meeting of minds, if not words. If I'm to be honest, I must admit that I *have* noticed Julie's increasing reclusiveness of late, but I think I've been rationalizing it—or trying to, at least--as my own overly sensitive projection."

She preceded him out the door, turning her head back towards him with a slight facial grimace, as if to reproach him for dropping the professorial word "projection." He shrugged his shoulders and followed her down the stairs.

As they descended the lower half of the staircase, they came into hearing range of a desultory series of strange gutteral noises—grunts and groans and agonized whines—coming from Julie's room. Instantly recognizing the obvious, Hattie scurried down the remaining steps, Mark fast on her heels, and both rushed into Julie's room, to find her furiously tossing her head back and forth, this way and that, chaotically in every direction, adding heft to each thrust of her only moveable part with croaks and yawps, as if desperate to burst out of the double prison of her wheelchair and her own body. Hattie later remembered thinking she looked oddly like the head of a bird struggling to break free of its birth shell.

"My God, why didn't she sound the alarm!" they both shouted, almost in unison, referring to the other electronic feature of her head-operated wheelchair motor, a feature she'd never seen fit to use, apparently not even on this occasion. "Who knows," Mark muttered, bending down to her and gently laying his hands on her shoulders to calm her and make contact, "maybe the damned thing's not working, or maybe she forgot it's there, who knows? … Julie, sweetheart, look at me!"

Hattie was down on one knee on the faux Persian rug right next to Mark, both their backs to the glass doors, Julie still facing the doors as Hattie had left her just moments ago. "Julie … Julie!" Hattie implored, a tad too excitedly as she yielded momentarily to her own mounting panic. Without realizing it, she was mirroring Julie's head movements on a minor scale with her own, probably in an unconscious act of sympathy. "Julie, please, try to calm yourself, okay? Take a deep breath or two and calm down so we can ask you some questions and try to figure out what's wrong."

But Julie seemed not to hear; on the contrary, she appeared to turn up the intensity of her thrusting, her noises becoming even more primordial, more animalistic, more desperate.

After a while, Mark got to his feet and put his hand to his forehead as if trying to remember something. "Mark," Hattie said firmly, looking up at him, "Lets try and give her some water."

"Yes, of course," Mark answered. He went to the kitchen and filled a glass halfway, brought it back and handed it to Hattie, then crouched down to rejoin her at eye-level with Julie. Hattie tried several times to give Julie a sip but she was having none of it, willfully twisting her head this way and that, away from the glass. They looked at her closely, pleading with her and trying to soothe her, but no discernible order seemed to be emerging from the chaos going on above Julie's neck. Quite the contrary, her head swings became agitated enough to partially loosen the handbrake on her wheelchair. She was dribbling saliva and occasionally rolling her eyes back in her head, and the harder she fought against the dead weight of her own tongue to form speech, the more cruelly the feral sounds she emitted seemed to mock her.

Feeling all at sea, Mark took his glasses off and messaged his forehead for a moment, perhaps in hopes of prodding an insight. "What do you think, Hattie? This is totally unlike anything we've seen before, wouldn't you say? She's obviously in some kind of agony, physical agony I'd say. But then, how do we tell? It's like trying to figure out why a baby won't stop crying. Except that she—Julie, I mean—is aware of our frustration. That must make it twice as maddening for her."

By now Hattie realized that all their solicitousness was just wasting time, so she stopped talking and doing for a moment in order to observe. Finally, she answered, "I don't think it's physical, Mark. Julie doesn't react to physical issues this way; it's not her style; she's more the stoic type. And the only adequate external cause would be harm or danger to one of us. And since you and I are right here and all right, it's got to be ..."

"—Oh, please, Hattie. Don't go all Haitian on me now!" Mark barked in rising anger. "I need your best Western empirical self right now, nothing less, understand?"

But Hattie was undaunted. She was going with her gut, and this family—*her* family—meant far too much to her for her to be put off by a scholar's skepticism. "Mark, I've just got this feeling. It's strong. I've learned from experience to trust it. And there's nothing to lose here by doing so." Then she added with hesitation, "And you know, if my feeling does turn out to be right and we ignored it, and something happens to …, well, …"

This gave Mark pause. And while he stood there pondering with his hand on Julie's shoulder, and she, still in her hysteria, remained oblivious to all attempts to comfort her, there suddenly came into hearing the sound of a familiar motor from the street. As the sound grew to a roar, Mark shouted in triumph, as though celebrating manna falling from heaven. "The bus! It's the school bus! Nate's got half a day, so that'll be him!", and he rushed into the living room to the picture window to watch as his son's appearance proved Hattie wrong. But the bus did not slow down, not even a little, rather whizzing by their house plus another three for its next stop down the block, wheels squealing as always. What would Mark not have given in that moment to hear that hideous squealing of wheels in front of his own door.

Padding back into his wife's room, he asked, hoping, "Hattie, does Nate have anything going on after school today?"

"No, I don't think so. The Christmas party was this morning. The school is closing down for the holidays. There wouldn't be anything going on now."

"Did he say he was going to anybody's house after school, like Dex's?"

"No, he didn't."

"Shit!" Mark muttered. He removed his hand from Julie's jittery shoulder and glanced out the glass doors to see the snowfall thickening. "I'm gonna take a run over to school to see if I can find him. I'm sorry to leave you here alone with her."

"No, no, you go, Mark, and don't worry. We'll be okay," she reassured him, not at all sure herself. "I'll call you as soon as I know anything, and you do the same, all right?"

"For sure," Mark answered, about to go and grab his heavy jacket in the kitchen mudroom when they both realized that Julie had stopped her thrashing. In fact, she wasn't moving her head at all now but just sitting there, still as a Madonna statue, her eyes closed. It was only her labored breathing from all the exertion that gave evidence of her being alive. They were at a loss as to how to read this sudden change: Was it the resolution of one crisis or the onset of another? But there was no time to agonize over this with the worry about Nate's where-abouts now uppermost in their minds. In fact, it was Julie's crisis, if crisis it was, that was fueling their anxiety over Nate. The two were now inseparable.

Hattie could hear Mark pulling away from the house, his tires screeching like the rubber-burning start of a drag race. She turned back to Julie, unsure whether to try to rouse her or just leave her be. Never in her life had she felt so stupid, so helpless. For her own part, however, Julie was not feeling helpless at all. Quite the contrary, she had made a profound self-correction fol-lowing an initial panic response and repositioned herself squarely on the only course available to her, the only way she had of helping Nate, a way she had unwittingly been preparing for for months. For Hattie, of course, was right: All this upheaval in Julie was about Nate, and only about Nate. With Duncan nestled there on her lap, still tucked in beneath the wheelchair tray, serving as emotional channel, a current of sheer terror had sud-denly begun assailing her. It started the moment Hattie left her to return the lunch tray to the kitchen. Nate was in serious trouble and registering profound distress, and Nate's distress was Julie's distress, a terrible synergy all happening in real time.

Julie's first response had been the maternal-instinc-tive one of attack, this overwhelming all rational con-siderations such as her complete ignorance of her son's external circumstances and even her paralysis. Suddenly she felt herself bolting from her chair, running through the kitchen and out the garage exit. In reality, of course, she had barely moved her torso half an inch. Then, in a wink, feeling how utterly bolted she was to her chair, she returned to an all too familiar awareness of the gulf between urgency and reality, necessity and impossibility, and it drove her to distraction. She could neither move herself nor communicate sufficiently to get others to move for her. The very proximity and yet remoteness of pragmatic communication—so near yet so far—were maddening, not unlike the grapes of Tantalus, perhaps the most infernal punishment in ancient myth. How on earth could she convey to them that Nate was in dire straits, that her little boy was terrified, that she could feel his heart racing as her own? Did a monster have him in its clutches? She shuddered and shrank into herself, but then burst forth yet again with another onrush of the furious energy of impotence.

Finally, in that way nature has of always seeking balance and avoiding the prolongation of extreme conditions, Julie flashed on something, something that brought an abrupt end to her futile physical struggle. She remembered the throbbing center point of moments earlier and with it her conviction that she must remain true to that living nucleus no matter what, without so much as a clue as to its ultimate nature or intent.

Automatically she relaxed into her chair and drew a deep breath, and with that breath's brief moment of let-go, of utter purposelessness, came a cascading plethora of breathtaking epiphanies: To begin with, she realized that this crisis, this anguish, this despair, was what her nagging, months-long unease had been all about. *That* had been the hidden harbinger of *this*. It was also why she had been vouchsafed the gift of direct awareness of her son's every feeling, a gift she'd had cause to both treasure and curse since its first manifestation at the school band concert. This insight, in turn, banished all lingering doubt that Nate and his present peril, whatever it was, were at the center of it all.

She saw that her entire life of recent months had been an initiation and a preparation, a form of spiritual apprenticeship. She had been in a kind of training for precisely the ordeal that both she and her son were now enduring. Another realization ignited by this chain of insights was that her recent habit of meditation was part of her training. A practice to strengthen her powers of concentration, her sharpness of focus, enabling her to endure the unfathomable challenge facing her. Then came yet another link in the chain: She saw that her own internal psychic mechanism of repression had kept these powerful revelations out of her conscious awareness to protect her long enough for her to develop the psychological stamina to bear the unbearable. Any earlier breakthrough of insight, especially with regard to Nate, would have killed her, as she would have had to bear it over time. She was not meant to connect the dots until now.

This spectacular rising of Julie's mental curtain did not actually happen in linear fashion as it necessarily does in the stepwise telling of events here; it was much more akin to a cluster of inner explosions not unlike the near-simultaneous bursting of three or four fireworks against a darkened sky. The point is that the mobilizing effect on her was tremendous; she felt energy pour into her as if from all directions. Suddenly she knew what she had to do, she knew why she had to do it, and, most crucially, she knew she was capable of doing it. Within minutes her place in the world had changed profoundly from that of an impotent, and hence tortured, waif in a crisis to that of a woman about to go into battle confident in her own powers. She even entertained the fatalistic notion that her personal tragedy, her accident and corporeal life sentence—indeed her entire life—had all unfolded precisely as they had for the sake of this singular moment of total sacrifice. Let it be so, she thought, let it be so. It all felt compellingly, infallibly, right to her, and her heart filled with gratitude for this strange gift of self-sacrifice.

But there was much to be done, so on to work, she urged herself. She took a few deep breaths to center herself, balanced her head and neck on her shoulders as best she could and slowly lowered her eyelids. (It was a moment later that Mark and Hattie suddenly noticed she had become still.) The throbbing point was still there, in the center of her mind, waiting for her attention. It was alive, a living thing, and she now knew what form that life would take, indeed, had already taken. That omnipresence of her meditation almost from the beginning, that little conduit to the fluctuations of her boy's heart for almost as long. As she gazed at it with her inner eye, the point moved swiftly towards her from a distant inner horizon to the size of the little guy still sitting on her lap underneath the tray. Duncan, her faithful protector, had been with her throughout. Now she knew why Nate, with such uncharacteristic stubbornness, had insisted she buy him that day years ago at the airport gift shop.

Now she knew so many things that had heretofore been shrouded in confusion, hidden in the cloak of worry and personal need. She was no longer alone in her ordeal; now Duncan was with her, a stuffed toy gorilla on the brink of metamorphosis into a force of nature. And with him she set about the business at hand. With laserpoint focus she poured all her newly harnessed energy into those fierce black eyes beneath the overhanging ape's brow, until at some indefinable point the two eyes moved into each other, coalescing and becoming one, so that she was now, in effect, addressing a mandala, the most universal and powerful symbol of unity in world religious culture.

She gazed unflinchingly, intrepidly, into that fierce, dark mandala eye, fully confident that it was her ally in this life-and-death crucible, though she knew not the why nor the wherefore. Somewhere in the back of her mind, buttressing her good faith, was the reassuring knowledge she had of mandala symbolism in religious art and its potential healing power. Now a practiced meditator, she gave herself to the eye completely, without reserve, with total fervor, availing herself of that selfless courage unique to mothers. Before long its concentric circles all dissolved outwardly into one all-encompassing circle, which soon yielded in turn to a feeling of pure, abstract circularity—a circularity whose center was everywhere and its circumference nowhere. She was in a condition of total surrender, no longer knowing where or even who she was, mind off, body off, emancipated from the lifelong dual prison of man, so much more confining for her than most. After a moment there was no longer even any sense of circularity, much less of an eye, still less of anyone gazing into the eye. She had slipped into the welcoming embrace of the circularity, which soon deepened into a dense yet comfortable sphericity, and in the moment of that deepening there was no longer anything there at all, merely emptiness, a great expanse of space, glistening in cool twilight and utter freedom.

At length, yet in no time at all, coming back to herself and the confinement of the wheelchair, she felt poised, charged, ready to confront her destiny. Closing her eyes again, she spoke silently, urgently, almost in the solemn cadence of an incantation, to the little companion sitting on her lap: "Duncan, we must go ... We must save my boy ... We must save my son ... Take us to wherever he is ... The terror, Duncan, the terror ... Follow Nate's terror ... It's a lifeline ... Follow it there now ... Away, Duncan ... Away from here ..." These and similar invocations she silently chanted like mantras, over and over, pleading with the steel fiber of a mother's perseverance. She would not leave off as long as there was breath in her body. "Duncan, please ... Away from here ... The terror, Duncan, follow it ... Duncan ... Duncan ..."

With her eyes closed all this while, at some point outside time and almost imperceptibly, she found herself moving. But it was a strange kind of movement, as if, though progressing from one locus to another, from point A to point B, she weren't actually going anywhere at all. It was as if she were a still point and her destination were moving towards her, not she towards it. It seemed to her that whatever she was meant to face was heading straight for her, advancing swiftly along an axis of terror. A world of menace rolling unto her feet. All she had to do was wait.

32

The snow was now falling at a near whiteout clip as the van made its way cautiously along Genesee St., heading towards the Syracuse University campus. Already one saw the beginnings of drifts in the street near the curbs. He was concerned the boy might get suspicious that he didn't suggest calling off the jam session due to what looked more and more like a blizzard. So he turned on the radio and fished around for a station playing jazz in hopes of distracting him. Eventually he found one on the FM band playing an old Charlie Parker standard called "Bird of Paradise."

"There we go!" he said, affecting elan. "Now that's the real McCoy, Nate, don't you think? Old Yardbird and the sweetest sounding sax this side of paradise."

"Yeah, I guess so, " Nate answered laconically, looking straight ahead at the million or so flakes whisking by the windshield, its wipers now working at top speed to maintain visibility. The tentative note in the boy's response caused a slight tingle of distress in Santa's solar plexus and he pressed down on the accelerator as far as he dared to short of inviting slippage.

Turning left onto University Ave., the van tooled up the hill towards the main campus, occasionally skidding a little whenever traffic sped up. Under his breath he cursed his own negligence for failing to have his snow tires put on. *Just the sort of critical detail that'll bite you in the ass.* Finally he made it up to Waverly Ave., which borders the north campus, and turned left onto it looking for the entrance to the parking garage of the university's Sheraton Hotel. The Sheraton garage had been part of the plan from the start. Even though parking in the main campus lot, A1, would have been much more convenient, he knew that campus attendants were quite vigilant in spotting vehicles without parking stickers, particularly vans like his with out-of-state plates, and he would go to any lengths to avoid having his plate number fed into the system.

Of course, the downside to the garage was the now daunting trek on foot up the hilly, snow-swept front of the campus to the college of music. Would the boy balk at this? He pulled into the garage, took his ticket from the automatic dispenser and found an embarrassment of riches in a cavernous, almost empty facility. December 23 on an all but abandoned university campus. Who needed a hotel?

They trudged up the wide central walkway between the student center and the school of journalism, then making a right onto the brick pedestrian avenue, the entire campus now a smooth white blanket with few discernible features. Already their eyebrows and coat collars were caked with snow and their footprints were the only blemishes on the virgin white. Nate was quiet, too quiet, and Santa racked his brain for some further distraction. They were so close now, just a couple of hundred feet; nothing must be allowed to force him to abort the "mission." The physical hardship of the Syracuse winter made the boy seem all the more desirable to him, as if the cosmos were telling him, "Not without a fight! Not this one."

"The weather's bad, and getting worse. What if your friend doesn't show up?" Nate asked finally, as they approached the winding, brick-and-concrete stairway up the steep lawn to one of the music school's many entrances.

"Don't worry, Nate, Karel will be there. He's from Prague, which is snow country. A few flurries won't bother him." He had no idea whether Prague was snow country; he was betting Nate didn't either.

Before starting up the stairs, Santa looked up at the imposing neo-Romanesque building in front of them, a huge, old brownstone castle perched on a high bluff, making it the highest structure in Syracuse. Its design was exquisitely complicated by a panoply of high roofs, gables, dormer windows and rounded arches, but it retained enough Victorian Gothic features to create an overall impression of forbidding aristocracy, as if the stinging winds on the bluff were whispering to would-be visitors, "This far and no further."

The stairway itself was forbidding, consisting of twenty or so sequences of wide off-white-brick steps, three, four or five at a time (depending on the angle), connected by landings. With reinforced iron railings on either side, it wound its way up the steep, snow-covered lawn to the double-door entrance on top. The climb was an arduous one, even for students under normal conditions, all the more so today with the heavy snowfall, now becoming furious.

They had made it about halfway up the stairway and Nate had slowed his climbing pace almost to a halt, stopping now on nearly every landing to stomp his boots clean and look up at Santa, as if to say, "Really? More of this?" Again cursing the weather under his breath, Santa felt he had to act, to create a diversion that would get the boy up the remaining steps without protest and under his own power. He knew that once inside the castle, the prize was his.

Emboldened by a sudden idea, he leapt up the next group of steps, turned and looked down at Nate. Then with his left hand he scooped up a clump of snow from the concrete base of the railing, packed it into a light snowball and lobbed it softly at the boy with his right, hitting him in the shoulder. Nate just wiped the snow away and stood there.

"Come on, boy! Let's see what you got!" Santa laughed, betting Nate would respond to the fun challenge. After all, what kid didn't love a good snowball fight? He packed another one and threw it harder, this time hitting the boy near the crotch. His hunch was sound: Nate bent down, made his own snowball and threw it at Santa, who deftly moved just a smidge into its path in order to take the blow, shouting a loud "Oh!" and thereby giving the boy satisfaction and encouraging him to continue the assault. Which, alas, he did, chasing the "retreating" Santa up the stairs and pelting him several times while suffering little return fire.

At one point, after flinging a snowball with all his might and missing, Nate lost his footing on the slippery edge of the landing and started to fall backwards. Santa instinctively leapt down to the landing and grabbed the boy just in time, saving him from a potentially disastrous injury, if not worse. Even in "mid-rescue" he felt the strangest sensation as he wondered whether he was acting in Nate's interest or his own. It was just another fissure in a massive persona growing ever more fragile, letting in light for a mere instant, for the click of a camera shutter, then closing up again to allow business as usual to continue.

Soon enough all the frolicking got them to the uppermost landing, which opened onto a small terrace that led to the castle entrance. Santa brushed the boy off, then himself; then they went in. The doors were unlocked, here as in most other campus buildings, unlike the armed camps that the grade and high schools had become. They went up three steps to a wide, well-lit corridor on the second floor, which was the main floor, containing the suites of administrative offices. Not a soul was to be seen in the long corridor that traversed the building from front to back. Santa peered through a few office-door windows, noting the skeletal groups of staff, mostly women, hunched over their computers but doing more chatting and laughing than working, clearly anticipating an early day today.

Everything thus far was as Santa had envisioned: students and faculty gone, staff bare bones, rehearsal rooms empty and open to anyone who should wander in off the street of an afternoon. He relaxed a little. Of course, it also helped that he knew the building and all its rooms intimately by now, after the grand tour Karel Jirak had given him weeks earlier, which had been followed by several scrupulously detailed tours he had made on his own. He knew well the castle's high ceilings, its doorframes and floors made of fine oak and cherry wood and redolent of varnish, its exquisitely carved stairway bannisters and posts, its splendid red-patterned carpeting that seemed to cover every square foot of floor. The building's interior was as warm and welcoming as its exterior was forbidding. But he knew its exterior as well, even down to its magnificent bell tower and the times of day at which the bells tolled adumbrations of Christmas carol melodies. Just that very noontide they had rung out "Santa Clause Is Coming to Town."

"Karel said to meet him in rehearsal studio 508, which is three flights up. They've got a piano in there. Come on, this way!" Santa said, striding briskly down the corridor ahead of Nate, as if he couldn't wait to get into the cool, cool world of Miles and old Yardbird. He reached the main staircase near the far end of the corridor, waving the boy on as he began to climb. He was indeed as excited as Nate perceived him to be, but that excitement had nothing to do with the cool of jazz and everything to do with a nine-year-old boy's wintry-cool pink cheeks. It was the heat generated by *that* cool he was after.

"But you didn't bring your fiddle," Nate shouted after him, running to catch up. "How are you gonna—"

"—Not a problem," came the answer a beat quickly, from one flight up. "I've been keeping my instrument here lately for jam sessions with Karel. It's in 508."

Nate stopped for a moment, lingering on a step, as if to consider what Santa had just told him, then hopped up the rest of the flight. He was feeling a tiny bit wary and didn't know why. It couldn't be the weather, not anymore anyway; they had just surmounted it. It couldn't be Santa, could it? There seemed no reason to be suspicious of him; from the first he'd been nothing but jolly, and he had, after all, talked to his dad on the phone and gotten permission for this fun gig. And they were in a setting he knew very well and felt totally at home in—the university campus, his dad's workplace. Even the castle was a familiar place and not at all off-putting to him; his dad had taken him along on several visits to Professor Jirak's office, and he had entertained himself with the drums in this or that practice cubbyhole on several of those visits. Thus the logic of a nine-year-old boy: It was sound enough as far as it went. It just didn't go far enough.

The boy brushed aside his qualms and caught up to Santa as they reached the top of the last staircase, turned left and walked the twenty-five or so paces to studio 508, which was unlit and the door to which was closed. Unease gripped Santa as he reached for the door handle. *Please be unlocked!* The accessibility of a chosen room on grab day was one of those uncontrollable variables that plagued many a "mission." And in this case there could be no plan B that didn't involve another faked call, this time to Karel, and at this point he didn't want to risk heightening the boy's suspicion, which he felt was still at a manageable level, but just barely.

He twisted the doorknob and felt great relief as the door gave way. Quickly flipping on the light switch to give the room some warmth, he extended an arm into the lit room invitingly. In contrast to the castle's grand and stately corridors, the studio could not have been plainer. Three long rows of florescent tubes, looking like so many trays of ice cubes, hung suspended from the ceiling, giving the room a harshly bright lighting; the ceiling and walls, a colorless gray and white, were otherwise quite bare; and the floor, of drab white vinyl tile with gray streaks, was cluttered with chairs and music stands which the students, after finishing rehearsal, had not bothered to move to the side. The grand piano placed in front of the great ceiling-high window with its rounded arch looking out onto the belfry gave the room its only touch of charm.

Nate stepped in tentatively as Santa unzipped his Santana red jacket, fitting it over the back of a chair. The boy immediately remarked on the obvious: "Karel's not here."

"Don't worry. I'm sure he's been delayed by driving conditions, coming in from Skaneateles. He'll be here. If he had to bail, he would've called me."

This made sense to Nate, and yet he could not dismiss the fact of Karel's absence from his mind. In fact, he realized he had been hoping that Karel would already be there when they arrived, and for reasons that had nothing to do with the jam session. Now his wariness was approaching the red zone and he found himself lingering near the door as Santa busied himself moving some music stands and other clutter out of the way. With mounting alarm it dawned on the boy that he was reluctant to move deeply inside the room for fear of giving Santa the chance to block a quick exit, should it come to that. Suddenly his flight instinct was screaming at him.

"Hey, take your coat off, Nate. Relax. Stay a while," Santa cajoled. "How about giving me a hand here clearing some space for the Driscoll trio?" He wanted to get the boy away from the door.

A single panicked thought filled Nate's mind: "Do I dare!" Feeling under a pressure of conflicting emotions he had never known, he wrestled with the question in a paralysis of anguish. At length, against his better judgment, and perhaps also because he couldn't quite get past his utter incredulity over the whole situation—*This can't really be happening!*—he moved gingerly towards a chair and slowly dragged it over to the wall, where he picked it up and inserted it on top of some others in the stacking pattern.

Meanwhile, Santa felt reassured just enough by this to step over to the instructor's desk, open the bottom drawer and pull out a small CD-player, which was his own and which he then placed on top of the piano. Pressing the play button, he turned and beamed at Nate as those insouciant opening chords of the bass and piano ignited the music that was his sexual elixir. "So what! ... so what!" he chanted, clapped and swayed, as Miles and the boys repeated the narcotizing phrase over and over. Soon he was like a whirling dervish slowly whipping himself into a trance state in the expectation of reaching some mystical No Man's Land beyond time and space, yet not beyond the body. A No Man's Land in which he would be *only* body and *nothing more than* body. With every whirl his eyes landed again on this vision of boyish beauty before him that was to be his deliverance, however briefly, fleetingly, from a world in which he could never feel at home, never feel whole.

But if Santa had any idea of his rising ecstasy's being contagious, he was quickly disabused of it. For Nate recognized the music at once as the standard of cool jazz it was, having listened to it countless times as it streamed out from his father's expensive Bose speakers. Much more critical, however, was his simultaneous mental linking of the familiar piece to some recent table talk to which he had been privy ... Dinner at the Jiraks. Santa holding forth to his enrapt listeners on the unshackling power of "So What." *When I hear it, I feel emancipated. I feel that nothing is beyond me. Nothing forbidden ...*

409

This flash memory was the trigger for Nate, propelling him from the viscous paralysis of doubt into an adrenalin rush of explosive action. He made a beeline for the door, a path momentarily left open to him when Santa's rhythmic gyrations had carried him over to a corner closet to check whether the two sleeping bags he had left on the shelf therein two days earlier were still there. The boy managed to twist the handle and get the door open to perhaps the width of his own body, but before he could slip out, a hand that felt like iron viciously pulled him back in, tearing his pullover sweater along the shoulder seam. Nate glanced down at the tear, then at the hand responsible for it that was still holding tight to the fabric and bit down on the knuckles of the hand's index and middle fingers as hard as he could, causing their owner to grimace in pain and fling him with tremendous force across the floor and against the stack of folding chairs near the wall, collapsing them with a deafening clatter.

Nate jumped to his feet and started screaming, "Help! Help me! Save me!", at the top of his lungs. Santa merely stood in front of the door, smiling wryly as he listened and rubbed his bloodied knuckles with the soft, soothing strokes of his fingertips. "Go ahead. Scream all you want," he said with mock encouragement as the boy stopped to catch his breath. "The rooms are sound-proofed for music rehearsal. And even if they weren't, there's no one here to hear you. Everybody's gone home for Christmas … But you know, Nate, I'm really sorry you and I have gotten off on the wrong foot here. I didn't mean for it to unfold this way, all this resistance and ill feeling between us. Maybe we could try to start over with a different attitude—you know, an attitude of Christmas cheer and mutual affection …" he said unctuously, knowing full well that there was no reeling this boy back in even on a line of his best bull. But he continued coaxing and wheedling anyway, using his syrupy southern tongue more to lull the boy into a momentary condition of animal-like dormancy than anything else as he moved towards him slowly, step by step.

"Yeah, right!" the boy barked back at him in defiance, pulling a nearby chair over to himself as a shield. "I know your kind of 'affection.'" Santa feigned a look of wide-eyed innocence, as if to say, "Who, me?", then gave a cynical grin as he moved closer still. Diabolical lust had taken complete possession of him: Once again, that depraved craving for total control over a boy's resistance had expunged all interest in the vision, however beatific, of his sweet surrender. Sexual mutuality held no allure.

Then something very strange happened. Just as Santa was about to bend over and wrest the chair from Nate's desperately clutching fingers, the lighting in the room seemed suddenly to go dim, as if someone were rotating a dimmer switch. Santa stopped at once, stood up and scanned the room for a silent intruder, then for a wall switch he assumed he hadn't noticed. He found neither. The quality of light seemed to settle at the low level appropriate to an intimate dinner or a seductive bedroom, a light meant as much to conceal as to reveal. And it had a kind of lambent greenish tint to it, almost as if the room were suddenly under water. Santa's next thought was that the storm was causing the power to fail, and he looked out the high-arched window to see nothing but specks of white beyond number pelting the glass panels.

His puzzlement at this weird and annoying occurrence caused a flutter in his solar plexus; after all, *it's always the little things, the details, that bite you in the ass.* But beneath the flutter was the nascent suspicion, horrifying beyond endurance and to be quashed at all costs, that this event, so innocuous in itself—*I mean, for Chrissake, it's only a power outage*—was more, so much more, than a mere detail. For this "special effect" was the commencement, at long last, of retribution. It was payback time. Did he know this? Was it clear to him? No, certainly not to his mind, but his body was another matter. It drove him to a frenzy of checking behavior—closet, tables, chairs, desk, anything that could serve as a hiding place, however improbable. Finally, he loped over to the door, opened it, and looked out to the left and right. No one, nothing. Quickly he ran over to the bannister and scanned the stairwell down to the basement. Again, nothing.

He came back into the room, slowly closing the door behind him, his gaze appearing now to be turned as much inward as outward in its mixture of fear and paranoia. He had lost interest in the boy, for the moment at least, bent as he was on getting to the bottom of these "disturbances." He squeezed his eyes shut several times in the hope of thereby normalizing the light, but it only clarified the flickering green with its eerie intimation of a sylvan aura. Nor did the surface under his feet give him any orientation since he could not see it clearly nor feel it keenly enough to tell whether it was floor or ground.

Then it was as if the green light began to emit clusters of strange, primitive sounds, brutish grunts and hacks and snorts, and the sharp rustle of something moving through thick brush. Santa shook his head as if to empty it of cranial malware, then looked fiercely at Nate in hopes of determining whether the boy was in fact experiencing the same reality as he. He couldn't tell, able only to see the boy's eyes peering at him from behind the overturned chair seat. But *was* it still a chair seat, still a chair, at all? The shadowy green atmosphere blanketed it with the ambiguity of a fallen tree, or a mound of vegetation, or a boulder. Was he still even "indoors" in any meaningful sense? The green aura had by now blocked out the window, obliterating all evidence of a blizzard, of winter, of a castle in the north country, leaving him in a sort of quasi tropical zone of consciousness that was neither inside nor out. It was its own singular space.

What happened next drained Santa of all confidence in his own sanity. There sounded from the grand piano, which stood some twenty feet away from him—whether in a music studio or in a jungle clearing he could not have said—a sequence of notes, eight of them, which Santa recognized as familiar but could not identify. They struck fear into his heart, for they were in fact those terrible notes of old proclaiming the "Dies Irae," the day of judgment of transgressions. The four couplets of deep, resonant notes were like four petrifying cannonades in awesome response to the airy arrogance of "So What." So what, indeed! Santa's fear, however, escalated swiftly to icy terror when, focusing hard with his 20/10 vision, he realized that he could not see anyone sitting at the piano.

He refused to accept the evidence, or lack thereof, of his senses and practically lunged half the length of the room over to the Steinway grand; he was seized with the need to lay eyes on the miscreant who must, so he thought, be hiding behind the keyboard and toying with his mind. But when he got there, he was thrown into an awful confusion of both reason and emotion, as he just barely caught a glimpse of what looked like a dark, pygmyish figure as it jumped from the keyboard noiselessly down onto the upholstered piano bench. Or was it a mountain ledge from which it had jumped down onto a lower ledge? The shimmering ambiguity of the green aura had so dislodged him from his sense of place and perspective that he could no longer trust his depth perception, nor, consequently, his reading of the size of things. Was it a small creature close up or a large one relatively far off? Either way, the figure stood up and turned towards him, all shiny black fur and menacing slits for eyes. Obviously a monkey or some sort of ape—but it had no tale, he reasoned, and so couldn't be a monkey. He was still trying to apply the logic of taxonomy, of classification into categories, in a manic and desperate effort to avoid taking in the experience as it was in all its horrific absurdity.

Then, gazing mesmerized at the dark, ape-like creature as it remained standing and swaying ever so slightly, he decided that it was indeed small and close by, not far away. And finally, he saw something that broke the back of his categorical logic: While the creature was definitely an ape, it was a *toy* ape! No question about it, he could tell its arms and torso were stuffed, its nose was a patch of brown leather and it had feet, cute feet, but no legs. Thus it was an impossibility on, not one, but two counts: It was a miniature gorilla that managed to be both artificial and real at the same time—it was a living toy.

The figure jumped down onto the floor—or ground—and began to hop-skip around Santa cautiously on its knuckles and feet, both made of nappy brown cloth, while he, spellbound, instinctively turned with it, making sure to keep his back away from it. He observed its movement intensely and involuntarily as he swiveled, the way one passively gazes at an impending accident one knows one cannot avoid. Nate watched the unfolding drama from behind his chair seat—or was it a tree stump—no less mystified by it all than his predator.

Then finally Santa, in another instinctive gesture of psychological self-defense, pushed every aspect of the astonishing creature out of his awareness except its diminutive size. He was determined to focus only on what made the thing ridiculous: its littleness. He was already impervious to the absurd fact of the creature's sheer impossibility. Impossible or not, it was somehow here, but it was, thankfully, small. His first move was to kick at it, but this quickly proved ineffective, since the thing had no trouble at all jumping out of the way. Indeed, the way it moved fascinated Santa, even in the midst of crisis, for it had a strangely filmic quality about it, the quality of a film running a tad slowly, thus giving the creature's movements a slightly herky-jerky or stop-action style, somewhat reminiscent of King Kong atop the Empire State Building as he swats away the buzzing planes. Was this, too, an effect of the greenish atmosphere that seemed to defamiliarize anything that lay within its aura?

But as slow as the creature's movements seemed, Santa could move no faster, which, in effect, rendered the whole issue of speed or quickness irrelevant. So, if he couldn't out-quick it, surely he must have the advantage in strength. *It's a puny thing, no more than a rat on two feet. Enough of this craziness—it's time for an asswhuppin'!* But of course he would have to catch it first, so he lunged down at it trying to anticipate its direction of flight. He lunged left, and of course it moved right. Santa bounced up immediately and grabbed a pointer from a nearby blackboard ledge, raising it threateningly as he stalked the furry creature, which, however, did not seem especially intimidated. Assuming an ape-like crouch himself, Santa slammed the stick down several times with all his might on the spot he thought the creature would be in but never was, evading each blow as it did with that weird, quasi mechanical way it had of moving, like an autonomous wind-up toy. Finally the pointer broke into two pieces, one landing at the creature's right foot.

It picked the fragment of stick up, which was now pointed at both ends, and angled over to Santa, who stood there stunned and could only watch incredulously. First looking up at his attacker, then down at his feet, the creature raised the pointed fragment up above its head and plunged it down with all the strength of an adult gorilla into the tongue section of Santa's left loafer. As if it were the pointed end of a railroad spike, the tip of the stick went through his foot and well beyond it into the surface beneath.

Santa howled in pain and crumpled, breaking the stick off beneath the soul of his shoe as he went down onto all fours. But as great as the pain was, it was muted by his sudden fury, a fury bringing with it near super-human strength as he shifted himself into a sitting posi-tion and proceeded to pull the stick out of his foot as easily as pulling a birthday candle out of its cake. Then, brandishing the bloodied fragment of stick, he turned over and lunged again at the creature, the latter standing this time at eye-level with him, and once again missed, which enraged him even more. The creature, a study in contrast, had easily stepped aside, and now just stood there impassively, staring at him, apparently immune to his antagonist's deftest moves, as though he were some avatar from a higher order that had nothing to fear from mere mortals, even those with the imposing physical agility of a Santa.

Now Santa rose up quickly on all fours in an attempt to stand, but the creature was even quicker to hop to a position directly behind him and grab onto his injured foot, squeezing the site of his wound to produce a pain so exquisite that it caused Santa to squeal in equal parts rage and submission, then rage heightened by the impulse to submit. The creature, totally unimpressed by all the histrionics, then began to twist Santa's injured foot, forcing him over onto his back on which he then lay stretched out. It then shuffled its cuddly, furry feet slowly, almost casually, perhaps even thoughtfully, as though savoring the moment, between Santa's jeans-clad legs the few steps up to his crotch, looked down at the cause of decades of horrific violence, all the suffering, all the misery of so many families, the loss of so many beautiful little boys, and swung its nappy hand up from the floor in a powerful arc straight through Santa's crotch and high into the air. There was no enraged howl, no livid scream from Santa this time, just a muted, quivering sort of cry, a whimper acknowledging defeat and imploring mercy.

And defeated he was, utterly, for the upraised furry little hand of the toy gorilla held within it its intended trophy, the guarantee that Samuel "Santa" Clause would prey no more; it held the bloody pound of flesh that had been Santa's genitalia. Santa lay there on the floor/ground, motionless and on his side, his trembling hands covering the gaping wound but unable to stanch the flow of blood into the small red pool forming around them. Still tucked behind his overturned chair seat, Nate had hidden his eyes at the climactic moment but was now again witness to the grotesque theater. After a while the creature let its trophy drop gently from its hand

and came around to Santa's face, where it stood looking sternly, but not without a hint of sorrow, into his eyes, Santa's head lying flat facing away from Nate.

Santa was now breathing heavily as he lay there completely still, only his eyes in movement as they followed the creature that now stood before him. He was no longer in pain; on the contrary, he was feeling quite comfortable and wished for nothing more than to continue lying there. This oddly agreeable condition was enhanced in no small measure by a feeling of profound relief, for he was emancipated at last from those bodily organs that had made his life a living hell, incarnating as they had, and as he could now clearly see, a drive that was nothing less than demonic. He thought back on his mother, on his friend Skeeter from the early days, on his old bass teacher at college, and even managed a warm, vaguely conciliatory memory of his father. Finally, gazing softly at the toy gorilla standing before him, he said, in a barely audible voice, "Thank you," closed his eyes and breathed his last.

The little ape now turned to Nate, those dark slits that had passed for eyes now opening up and, for all their artificiality, taking on a charcoal softness that penetrated the boy to his very marrow. He only half stood up from behind his chair, for he was still terrified, not by the unreality of the moment—he was still enough of a child to be open to the fantastic—but by its violence.

But he was also sensing something else, something most peculiar, something he couldn't comprehend and wasn't sure he could trust. It was fascination, utterly compelling in the way deep longing is compelling. Then, as the creature's gaze lingered on him and, in lingering, quickly deepened into something akin to compassion, the boy cried out involuntarily, "Mom?", almost without realizing what he was saying. The creature extended its still gaze, as if to make the image it beheld indelible, then nodded ever so slightly. Was it an acknowledgment?

After an exquisite moment, a timeless moment, both lowered their heads and turned, reluctantly it seemed, away from each other. The brief mutual spell was broken. Nate darted over to the chair over which Santa's jacket lay draped, and retrieved the phone from the pocket. He tapped in his father's number and got an immediate response:

"Hello?"

"Dad!"

"Nate! Oh, thank God! Where are you?"

"I'm on campus—"

"—My God! What are you doing over there? How did you get there?"

"I got a lift. I'll explain later. Dad, I need you to come and get me, okay?"

"Of course, I'll be right over. I'm at W.H. Smythe; I've been looking for you. We were worried when you didn't get off the bus."

"I'm fine, Dad, I'm okay. But something bad has happened. I'm in the music school, on the top floor, room 508."

"My God, Nate! What is it? What are you doing there? What's happened?"

"Well, there's a dead man lying on the floor here … At least I think he's dead—"

"—What? A *dead* man? How is that possible? Was there an accident?"

"It's … complicated, Dad. Could you just get over here right away?

"I'm on my way! You just stay put, do you hear? … You're not in any danger, are you?"

"No, I don't think so."

"*You don't think so?*" Oh, Christ! … Listen, are you alone in the room?"

"Yeah, … except for the dead guy."

"Okay, listen to me now. You just stay put right there in 508, okay? Now, if the dead guy moves, if he comes to, you get your ass out of there and run to the first person you can find, you hear me? And make sure you hold onto that phone so we stay in contact. By the way, where'd you get it—the phone, I mean?"

"It was in the dead guy's pocket."

"Oh, thank you, God! Anyway, hang on. I'll be there in a flash."

By this time Mark had already reached his car, parked in front of the school, and was pulling out onto the same street Santa had taken earlier with Nate. He made two quick phone calls as he drove, one to Hattie to relieve her anxiety and to learn that there was no change in Julie's somnolent condition, and one to 911 to report Nate's sketchy information. He was told the police were on their way.

33

The uniformed policeman standing sentry outside studio 508 gave a quick knock and, without waiting for a response, opened the door to announce the arrival of "Professor Mark Driscoll, the boy's father." Mark stepped in and saw the two plainclothes detectives sitting with his son. Nate ran to him and hugged him around the waist as the men introduced themselves. One, Detective Frank Hanrahan, was red-haired, ruddy and overweight; the other, Detective Asim Asghar, was a tall and slender black man with a pencil-thin moustache who looked as if he jogged ten miles a day.

"Nate, are you all right?" Mark asked urgently as he held Nate out in front of him and scanned his body.

"Yeah, I'm okay, Dad ... But *he's* not," Nate said, pointing to the body lying in the middle of the floor under a tarp."

Mark looked down at the vague form of the victim, then up at the two men as if to question.

They wasted no time. "Professor Driscoll," said Hanrahan, taking the lead, "I don't know how much your son told you on the phone about what happened here but he's told us one hell of a story. He claims the victim here was about to commit what sounds like a sexual assault on him when that toy gorilla over there on the piano suddenly showed up and attacked and killed the man ... by castration no less. He also claims you both know the victim."

"Oh my God! Nate, did he touch you? Who the hell is it?"

"Nathaniel calls him Santa," Hanrahan answered, raising the tarp to give Mark a good look. "The boy says he wasn't violated."

"Thank God! ...Yes, that's Santa all right. His actual name is Samuel Clause, I think. We only know him slightly, through a mutual acquaintance ... I can't believe this. It's—"

"—Dad, I ran into him at school. He said Mr. Jirak would be here and we'd have a jam session. He called you for permission ..."

"That's all right, Nate. He didn't call—he just pretended to. It's not your fault, not your fault at all," Mark said to the boy, anxious to console him and head off any self-blame he might be tempted to engage in. Then the improbable phrase "toy gorilla" kicked in and

Mark asked, stupefied, "Detective, did I hear you say 'toy gorilla'?"

"Yeah, Dad! Duncan did it! He saved me!" Nate blurted out.

"That's what the boy says," Hanrahan answered in an incredulous tone, motioning Mark to the piano where he pointed to an inert Duncan perched on the keyboard. Mark instinctively went to grab the familiar doll but Hanrahan stayed his hand, explaining, "Sorry Professor, nothing gets touched or moved in here till the fingerprinters and photographers have finished."

But Mark hardly heard the man, mesmerized as he was by the sight of his son's—and no less his wife's— beloved sidekick sitting there on the keys, slightly atilt. He was drawn by the sight of what looked like a dark stain covering the doll's frizzy black fingers and running up the inside of its right arm.

"Oh, I'm sure it's blood," Hanrahan said, following Mark's eyes. "The offender's offending anatomy is already on ice. But none of that really helps to explain what happened here, does it?"

"No, it doesn't," Mark replied. Then, after a brief but thoughtful pause, he said firmly, "Detective Hanrahan, my son has obviously been severely traumatized, and, for all I know, he's concocted this fantastic story about the gorilla to protect himself psychologically from whatever brutal events he *did* witness here. Which means I need to get him home to his mom and to some professional help ASAP. Do I have your permission to do that?"

"Yes, yes, of course, Professor," the man agreed, almost apologetically. "Normally we'd like him to give a statement sooner rather than later—you know, the freshness of the memories and so on—but in this case, I think you're right. It would probably be best to wait a day or two."

Detective Asghar nodded agreement and smiled at Nate, "Now you hang in there, li'l bro. You're gonna be just fine." Mark helped Nate on with his jacket as Asghar opened the door for them. "Safe home now."

As they left the building, Mark unconsciously kept hold of his son's gloved hand, as if he were five or six instead of nine. Nate, who was probably feeling five or six, allowed it without protest. They both noticed it had stopped snowing and that the cloud cover was breaking up, allowing streaks of blue sky to poke through. That was Syracuse: *If you don't like the weather, just wait five minutes.*

The ride home was mostly silent. Both father and son were shell-shocked, much more than they realized, and Mark needed what little focus he could muster just to drive safely. At one point Nate began what sounded like an apology: "Dad, I didn't mean to, I …" But Mark stopped him cold, intent on preventing his son from registering the horrific event in his psyche as in any sense his responsibility. It was bad enough that he would have to carry the sheer violence of it forever, without piling on guilt: "Nate, you're a nine-year-old boy. All the responsibility lies with him. Never think otherwise, do you hear me?" Nate nodded, reassured. Interestingly, not a single thought about Duncan, his magical appearance—"live"—or his fabulous deed occurred to either of them in the car, so wrapped up were they in concern for each other's wellbeing. At the moment, head-scratching over an imponderable mystery was a low priority.

When they got home and came in through the garage, Hattie dropped her cell phone down on the kitchen table and came running. She squealed with delight and gave Nate a deliriously happy bear hug in the mudroom that almost squeezed the air out of him: "Oh, you sweet boy! Thank God you're safe and sound … You are … safe and sound, aren't you?" Nate hugged his overjoyed second mother back and they all went into Julie's room to share the good news, in their euphoria understandably forgetting that such a moment of communion was in no way guaranteed.

And it was, in fact, a heartbreaking awakening, a merciless end to a short-lived euphoria. A cruel parody of life itself. They were startled to find Julie sitting with her head slumped over to one side, her chair still facing the glass doors as it had before lunch. Mark carefully turned her chair around to face inward, crouched down and took her left hand by the wrist, whether to feel for her pulse or just to connect with her is hard to say. Her mouth was slightly open, her neck bereft of all muscle tone.

After a long silence, he looked up, her hand still in his, and said softly, "I think she's gone."

"Oh, Mark, I got distracted," Hattie sobbed. "I was in the kitchen calling everybody I could think of about Nate—I was so scared—I forgot about—I mean, when I went to the kitchen, she had her head up in that calm state she was in when you left."

Mark held his hand up, not to rebuff but to console the distraught woman, slowly shaking his head as if to say, "Don't upset yourself, Hattie. It's all right. There is no blame to be cast here."

Nate gave Hattie another hug, which was his way of affirming his father's absolution of all three of them. There was just too much love in the room for it to be a moment of self-recrimination. She bent down and put her arms around the boy's neck, in that way the body has of expressing a myriad of complex emotions in utter simplicity.

But Nate had something else to offer as well. He looked up at his father and said, "Dad, she was there! I don't know how, but she was there. I mean, it was Duncan, sure, but it was also Mom. I could see it in the eyes—they were *her* eyes." Hearing this, Hattie bent down and removed the clip-on tray from Julie's chair, expecting to find Duncan nestled there in her lap, his usual spot. The lap she found, but no Duncan. "I *know* he was here, right where he always is," she said, confounded. "I remember having to push his little head down a tad when I put the tray in place for Julie's lunch … Oh my!"

"My guess is that, by now, Duncan is in a police evidence bag," Mark mused.

"There, you see? That's just mad weird!" Nate said emphatically, bringing his point home. Hattie and Mark just stood there looking at each other, mouths agape. Gone was any inclination on their part to disenchant the boy, not out of consideration for his feelings, which of course they had in abundance, but because they had caught his spirit of the fantastic. The spirit embodied by Duncan.